HARDPRESS.NET

ISBN: 978129033146

Published by:
HardPress Publishing
8345 NW 66TH ST #2561
MIAMI FL 33166-2626

Email: info@hardpress.net
Web: http://www.hardpress.net

THE CONVERT

THE MACMILLAN COMPANY
NEW YORK · BOSTON · CHICAGO
ATLANTA · SAN FRANCISCO

MACMILLAN & CO., LIMITED
LONDON · BOMBAY · CALCUTTA
MELBOURNE

THE MACMILLAN CO. OF CANADA, LTD.
TORONTO

THE CONVERT

BY

ELIZABETH ROBINS

AUTHOR OF "A DARK LANTERN,"
"THE MAGNETIC NORTH," ETC.

New York
THE MACMILLAN COMPANY
1913

Set up and electrotyped. Published October, 1907. Reprinted March, 1910; March, 1912; August, 1913.

Norwood Press
J. S. Cushing Co. — Berwick & Smith Co.
Norwood, Mass., U.S.A.

THE CONVERT

THE CONVERT

CHAPTER I

THE tall young lady who arrived fifteen minutes before the Freddy Tunbridges' dinner-hour, was not taken into the great empty drawing-room, but, as though she were not to be of the party expected that night, straight upstairs she went behind the footman, and then up more stairs behind a maid. The smart, white-capped domestic paused, and her floating muslin streamers cut short their aërial gyrations subsiding against her straight black back as she knocked at the night-nursery door. It was opened by a middle-aged head nurse of impressive demeanour. She stood there an instant eyeing the intruder with the kind of overbearing hauteur that in these days does duty as the peculiar hall-mark of the upper servant, being seldom encountered in England among even the older generation of the so-called governing class.

'It's too late to see the baby, miss. He's asleep.'

'Yes, I know; but the others are expecting me, aren't they?'

Question hardly necessary, perhaps, with the air full of cries from beyond the screen: 'Yes, yes.' 'We're waiting!' 'Mummy promised'—cut short by the nurse saying sharply, 'Not so much noise, Miss Sara.' But the presiding genius of the Tunbridge nursery opened the door a little wider and stood aside. Handsome compensation for her studied coldness was offered in the shrill shrieks of joy with which a little girl and a very small boy celebrated the lady's entrance. She, for her part, joined the austere nurse in saying, 'Sh! sh!' and in simulating consternation at the spectacle behind the screen, Miss Sara jumping up and down in the middle of her bed with wild brown hair swirling madly about a laughing but mutinous face. The visitor, hurrying forward, received the impetuous little girl in her arms, while the nurse described her own sentiments of horror and detestation of such performances, and hinted vaguely at Retribution that might with safety be looked for no later than the morrow. Nobody listened. Miss Levering nodded smiling across Sara's nightgowned figure to the little boy hanging over the side of the neighbouring cot. But he kept remonstrating, 'You always go to her first.'

The lady drew a flat, shiny wooden box out of the inside pocket of her cloak. The little girl seized it rapturously.

'Oh, did you only bring Sara's bock?' wailed the smaller Tunbridge. 'I told you expecially we wanted *two* bocks.'

'I've got two pockets and I've got two bocks. Let me give him his, Sara darling.'

But 'Sara darling' dropped her own 'bock' the better to cling round the neck of the giver.

Naturally Master Cecil sounded the horn of indignation.

'Hush!' commanded his sister. 'Don't you know his little lordship never did that?' And to emphasize this satirical appeal to a higher standard of manners, Sara loosened her tight-locked arms an instant; but still holding to the visitor with one hand, she picked up the pillow and deftly hurled it at the neighbouring cot, extinguishing the little boy. Through the general recriminations that ensued, the culprit cried with shrill rapture, 'Lady Gladys never pillow-fought! Lady Gladys was a little lady and never did *any*thing!' The merry eyes shamelessly invited Miss Levering to mock at Dampney's former charges. But the visitor detached herself from Miss Sara, and wishing apparently to ingratiate herself with the offended majesty of the nurse, Miss Levering said gravely over her shoulder, 'Now, lie down, Sara, and be a good girl.' Sara's reply to that was to (what she called) 'diddle up and down' on her knees and emit shrill squeals of some pleasurable emotion not defined. This, too, in spite of the fact that Dampney had picked up the pillow and was advancing upon Miss Sara with an expression calculated to shake the stoutest heart. It obviously shook the visitor's. 'Listen, Sara! If you don't be quiet and let nurse cover you up, she won't want me to stay.' Miss Levering actually got up off the little boy's bed, and stood as though ready to carry the obnoxious suggestion into instant effect.

Sara darted under the bedclothes like a rabbit into its burrow. The rigid woman, without words, restored the tousled pillow to the head of the bed, extracted Miss Sara from her hiding-place with one hand, smoothed out the rebellious legs with the other, covered the child firmly over, and tucked the bedclothes in.

'What's the use of all that? Mother always does it over again.'

'You know very well she's been and done it once already.'

'She's coming again if father doesn't need her.'

'There's a whole big dinner-party needing her, so you needn't think she can come twice to say good-night to a Jumping-Jack like you.'

'You ought to say a Jumping-Jill,' amended Sara.

During this interchange Master Cecil was complaining to the visitor —

'I can't see you with that thing all round your head.'

'Yes, take it off!' his sister agreed; and when the lady had unwound her lace scarf — 'Now the coat! And you have to sit on my bed this time. It's my turn.'

As the visitor divested herself of the long ermine-lined garment, 'Oh, you *are* pretty to-night!' observed the gallant young gentleman over the way, seeming not to have heard that these effects don't appeal to little boys.

Sara silently craned her neck. Even the high and mighty Mrs. Dampney, in the surreptitious way of the superior servant, without seeming to look, was covertly taking in the vision that the cloak had hitherto obscured. The little girl followed with critical eyes the movement of the tall figure, the graceful fall of the clinging black lace gown embroidered in yellow irises, the easy bend of the small waist in its jewelled belt of yellow. The growing approval in the little face culminated in an ecstatic 'Oh-h-h! let me see what's on your neck! That's new, isn't it?'

'No — very old.'

'I didn't know there were yellow diamonds,' said Sara.

'There are; but these are sapphires.'

'And the little stones round?'

'Yes, they're diamonds.'

'The hanging-down thing is *such* a pretty shape!'

'Yes, the fleur-de-lys is a pretty shape. It's the flower of France, you know — just as the thistle is the ——'

'There, now!' A penetrating whisper came from the other bed. 'She's *gone.*'

'It's you who've been keeping her here, you know.' Miss Levering bent her neat, dark head over the little girl, and the gleaming jewels swung forward.

'Yes,' said Cecil, in a tone of grandfatherly disgust; 'yelling like a wild Indian.'

'Well, you *cried*,' said his sister—'just because a feather pillow hit you.' Her eye never once left the glittering gaud.

'You see, Cecil is younger than you,' Miss Levering reminded her.

'Yes,' said Sara, with conscious superiority—'a whole year and eight months. But even when I was young *I* had sense.'

Miss Levering laughed. 'You're a horrid little Pharisee—and as wild as a young colt.' Contrary to received canons, the visitor seemed to find something reassuring in the latter reflection, for she kissed the small, self-righteous face.

'You just ought to have seen Sara this morning!' Cecil chuckled, with a generous admiration in family achievements. 'We waked up early, and Sara said, "Let's go mountaineering." So we did. All over the rocks and presserpittses.' He waved his hand comprehensively at the rugged scenery of the night-nursery.

'Of course we had to pile up the chairs and things,' his sister explained.

'And the coal scuttle.'

'And we made snow mountains out of the pillows. When the chairs wobbled, the coal and the pillows kept falling about; it was quite a real avalanche,' Sara said conversationally.

'I should think so,' agreed the guest.

'Yes; and it was glorious when Sara excaped to the top of the wardrobe.'

'To the w——' Miss Levering gasped.

'Yes. We were having the most perfectly fascinating time——' Sara took up the tale.

But Cecil suddenly sat bolt upright, his little face quite pink with excitement at recollection of these Alpine exploits.

'Yes, Sara had come down off the wardrobe—she'd been sitting on the carved piece—she says that's the Schreckhorn!—but she'd come down off it, and we was just jumping about all those mountains like two shamrocks——'

'Like what?'

'— when *she* came in.'

'Yes,' agreed Sara. 'Just when we're happiest *she* always comes interfiddling.'

'Oh, Sara mine, I rather like you!' said Miss Levering, laying her laughing face against the tousled hair.

'Now! Now!' cried Cecil, suddenly beating with his two fists on the counterpane as though he'd seen as much valuable time wasted as he felt it incumbent upon him to tolerate. 'Go on where you left off.'

'No, it's *my* visit this time.' Sara held fast to her friend. 'It's for me to say what we're going to talk about.'

'It's got to be alligators!' said Cecil, waving his arms.

'It *shan't* be alligators! I want to know more about Doris.'

'Doris!' Cecil's tone implied that the human intelligence could no lower sink.

'Yes. I expect you like her better than you do us.'

'Don't you think I ought to like my niece best?'

'No' — from Cecil.

'You said we belonged to you, too,' observed Miss Sara.

'Of course.'

'And all aunts,' she pursued, 'don't like their nieces so *dreadfully*.'

'Don't they?' inquired Miss Levering, with an elaborate air of innocence.

'You didn't say how-do-you-do to me,' said Cecil, with the air of one who makes a useful discovery.

'*What?*'

'Why, she went to you the minute I threw the pillow.'

'That was just to save me from being dead. It isn't a proper how-do-you-do when she doesn't hug you.'

'I'll hug you when I go.'

But a better plan than that occurred to Cecil. He flung down the covers with the decision of one called to set about some urgent business.

'Cecil! I simply won't have you catching cold!'

Before the words were out of Miss Levering's mouth he had tumbled out of bed and leapt into her lap. He clasped his arms round her neck with an air of rapturous devotion, but what he said was —

'Go on 'bout the alligator.'

'No, no. Go 'way!' protested Sara, pushing him with hands and feet.

'Sh! You really will have nurse back!'

That horrid thought coerced the prudent Sara to endurance of the interloping brother. And now of his own accord Cecil had taken his arms from round his friend's neck.

'That's horrid!' he said. 'I don't like that hard thing. Take it off.'

'Let me.' Sara sat up with alacrity. 'Let me.'

But Miss Levering undid the sapphire necklace herself. 'If you'll be very careful, Sara, I'll let you hold it.' It was as if she well knew the deft little hands she had delivered the ornament to, and knew equally well that in her present mood, absorption in the beauty of it would keep the woman-child still.

'There, that's better!' Cecil replaced his arms firmly where the necklace had been.

Miss Levering pulled up her long cloak from the bottom of the bed and wrapped the little boy in the warm lining. The comfort of the arrangement was so great, and it implied so little necessity for 'hanging on,' that Cecil loosed his arms and lay curled up against his friend.

She held him close, adapting her lithe slimness to the easy supporting and enfolding of the childish figure. The little girl was absorbed in the necklace after her strenuous hour; the boy, content for a moment, having gained his point, just to lie at his ease; the woman rested her cheek on his ruffled hair and looked straight before her.

As she sat there holding him, something came into her face, guiltless though it was of any traceable change, without the verifiable movement of a muscle, something none the less that would have minded the beholder uneasily to search the eyes for tears, and, finding no tears there, to feel no greater sense of reassurance.

So motionless she sat that presently the child turned up his rosy face, and seeing the brooding look, it was plain he had the sense of being somehow left behind. He put up his hand to her cheek, and rubbed it softly with his own.

'I don't like you like that. Tell me about ——'

'Like what?' said the lady.

'Like — I don't know.' Then, with a sudden inspiration, 'Uncle Ronald says you're like the Sphinx. Who are they?'

'Who are who?'

'Why, the Sfinks. Have they got a boy? Is the little Sfink as old as me? Oh, you only laugh, just like Uncle Ronald. He asked us why we liked you, and we told him.'

'You've never told me.'

'Oh, didn't we? Well, it's because you aren't beady.'

'Beady?'

'Yes. We hate all beady ladies, don't we, Sara?'

'Yes; but it's my turn.' However, she said it half-heartedly as she stopped drawing the shining jewels lightly through her slim fingers, and began gently to swing the fleur-de-lys back and forth like a pendulum that glanced bewitchingly in the light.

Miss Levering knew that the next phase would be to try it on, but for the moment Sara had still half an ear for general conversation.

'We hate them to have hard things on their shoulders!' Cecil explained.

'On their shoulders?' Miss Levering asked.

'Here, just in the way of our heads.'

'Yes, bead-trimming on their dresses,' explained the little girl.

'Hard stuff that scratches when they hold you tight.' Cecil cuddled his impudent round face luxuriously on the soft lace-covered shoulder of the visitor, and laughed up in her face.

'Aunts are very beady,' said Sara, absent-mindedly, as she tried the effect of the glitter against her night-gown.

'Grandmothers are worse,' amended Cecil. 'They're beady and bu-gly, too.'

'What's bewgly?'

'Well, it's what my grandmother called them when I pulled some of them off. Not proper bugles, you know, what you "too! too! too!" make music with when you're fighting the enemy. My grandmother thinks bugles are little shiny black things only about that long' — he measured less than an inch on his minute fore-finger — 'with long holes through so they can sew them on their clothes.'

'On their caps, too,' said Sara; 'only they're usurally white when they're on caps.'

'Here's your mother coming! Now, what will she say to you, Cecil?'

They turned their eyes to the door, strangely unwelcoming for Laura Tunbridge's children, and their young faces betrayed no surprise when the very different figure of Nurse Dampney emerged from behind the tall chintz screen that protected the cots from any draught through the opening door. Cecil, with an action of settled despair, turned from the spectacle, and buried his face for one last moment of comfort in Vida Levering's shoulder; while Sara, with a baleful glance, muttered —

'I knew it was that old interfiddler.'

'Now, Master Cecil ——'

'Yes, nurse.' Miss Levering carried him back to his cot.

'Mrs. Tunbridge has sent up, miss, to know if you've come. They're waiting dinner.'

'Not really! Is it a quarter past already?'

'More like twenty minutes, miss.'

The lady caught up her necklace, cut short her good-byes, and fled downstairs, clasping the shining thing round her neck as she went — a swaying figure in soft flying draperies and gleaming, upraised arms.

She entered the drawing-room with a quiet deliberation greater even than common. It was the effect that haste and contrition frequently wrought in her — one of the things that made folk call her 'too self-contained,' even 'a trifle supercilious.'

But when other young women, recognizing some not easily definable charm in this new-comer into London life, tried to copy the effect alluded to, it was found to be less imitable than it looked.

CHAPTER II

THERE were already a dozen or so persons in the gold-and-white drawing-room, yet the moment Vida Levering entered, she knew from the questing glance Mrs. Freddy sent past her children's visitor, that even now the party was not complete.

Other eyes turned that way as the servant announced 'Miss Levering.' It is seldom that in this particular stratum of London life anything so uncontrolled and uncontrollable as a 'sensation' is permitted to chequer the even distribution of subdued good humour that reigns so modestly in the drawing-rooms of the Tunbridge world. If any one is so ill-advised as to bring to these gatherings anything resembling a sensation, even if it is of the less challengeable sort of striking personal beauty, the general aim of the company is to pretend either that they see nothing unusual in the conjunction, or that they, for their part, are impervious to such impacts. Vida Levering's beauty was not strictly of the *éclatant* type. If it did — as could not be denied — arrest the eye, its refusal to let attenion go was mitigated by something in the quietness, the disarming softness, with which the hold was maintained. Men making her acquaintance frequently went through four distinct phases in their feeling about her. The first was the common natural one, the instant stirring of the pulses that beauty of any sort produces in persons having the eye that sees. The second stage was a rousing of the instinct to be 'on guard,' which feminine beauty not infrequently breeds in the breasts of men. Not on guard so much against the thing itself, or even against ready submission to it, but against allowing onlookers to be witness of such submission. Even the very young man knows either by experience or hearsay, that women have concentrated upon their faculty for turning this particular weapon to account, all the skill they would have divided among other resources had there been others. Yet the charm is something too delicious even to desire to escape from — the impulse centres in a determination to *seem* untouched, immune.

The third stage in this declension from pleasure through caution to reassurance is induced by something so gentle, so unemphatic in the Vida Levering aspect, so much what the man thinks 'feminine,' that even the wariest male is reassured. He comes to be almost as easy before this particular type of allurement as he would be with the frankly plain 'good sort'; only there is all about him the exquisite aroma of a subtle charm which he may almost persuade himself that he alone perceives, since this softly gracious creature seems so little to insist upon it — seems, indeed, to be herself unaware of its presence. Whereupon the man conceives a new idea of his own perspicacity in detecting a thing at once so agreeable and so little advertised. He may, with a woman of this kind, go long upon the third 'tack' — may, indeed, never know it was she who gently 'shunted' him, still unenlightened, and left him side-tracked, but cherishing to the end of time the soothing conviction that he 'might an' if he would.' To the more robust order of man will come a day of awakening, when he rubs his eyes and retreats hurriedly with a sense of good faith injured — nay, of hopes positively betrayed. If she were '*that* sort,' why not hang out some signal? It wasn't playing fair.

And so without anything so crude as a sensation, but with a retinue of covert looks following in her train, she made her way to the young hostess, and was there joined by two men and a middle-aged woman, who plainly had been a beauty, and though 'gone to fat,' as the vulgar say, had yet kept her complexion. With an air of genial authority, the pink-cheeked Lady John Ulland proceeded to appropriate the new-comer in the midst of a general hum of conversation, whose key to the sensitive ear had become a little heightened since the last arrival. The women grew more insistently vivacious in proportion as the men's minds seemed to wander from matters they had discussed contentedly enough before.

Mrs. Freddy Tunbridge was a very popular person. It was agreed that nobody willingly missed one of her parties. There were those who said this was not so much because of her and Mr. Freddy, though they were eminently likeable people; not merely because you met 'everybody' there, and not even because of the excellence of their dinners. Notoriously this last fact fails to appeal very powerfully to the majority of women, and it is they, not men, who make the social reputation of the hostess. There was in this particular case a theory, held even by those who did not care especially about Mrs. Freddy, that hers was an 'amusing,' above all, perhaps, a 'becoming,' house. People had a pleasant consciousness of looking uncommon well in her pretty drawing-room. Others said it wasn't the room, it was the lighting, which certainly was most discerningly done — not dim, and yet so far from glaring that quite plain people enjoyed there a brief unwonted hour of good looks. Only a limited amount of electricity was used, and that little was carefully masked and modulated, while the two great chandeliers each of them held aloft a very forest of wax candles. It was known, too, that the spell was in no danger of being rudely broken. The same tender but festive radiance would bathe the hospitable board of the great oak dining-room below.

And why were they not processing thither?

'Is it my sister who is late?' Miss Levering asked, turning her slim neck in that deliberate way of hers to look about the room.

'No; your sister is over there, talking to —— Oh — a ——' Mrs. Freddy, having looked round to refresh her memory, was fain to slur over the fact that Mrs. Fox-Moore was in the corner by the pierced screen, not talking to any one, but, on the contrary, staring dark-visaged, gloomy, sibylline, at a leaflet advertising a charity concert, a document conspicuously left by Mrs. Freddy on a little table. On her way to rescue Mrs. Fox-Moore from her desert island of utter loneliness, Mrs. Freddy saw Sir William Haycroft, the newly-made Cabinet Minister, rather pointedly making his escape from a tall, keen-looking, handsome woman wearing eye-glasses and iron-grey hair dressed commandingly.

Without a qualm Mrs. Freddy abandoned Mrs. Fox-Moore to prolonged exile, in order to soothe the ruffled minister.

'I think,' she said, pausing in front of the great man and delicately offering him an opportunity to make any predilection known — 'I think you know every one here.'

Haycroft muttered in his beard — but his eyes had lit upon the new face.

'Who's that?' he said; but his tone added, 'Not that it matters.'

'You don't know her? Well, that's a proof of how you've neglected your friends since the new Government came in. But you really mean it — that nobody has introduced you to Miss Levering yet? What *is* Freddy thinking about!'

'Dinner!' replied a voice at her elbow with characteristic laconism, and Freddy Tunbridge pulled out his watch.

'Oh, give them five minutes more,' said his wife, indulgently.

'That's not a daughter of old Sir Hervey?' pursued the other man, his eyes still on the young woman talking to Lady John and the foreign ambassador.

'Yes; go on,' said Mrs. Freddy, with as cloudless a brow as though she had no need to manufacture conversation while the dinner was being kept waiting. 'Go on! They *all* do it.'

'Do what?' demanded the great man, suspiciously.

'"Why haven't they seen her before" comes next. Then the next time you and I meet in the country or find ourselves alone in a crush, you'll be saying, "What's her story? Why hasn't a woman like that married?" They all do! You don't believe me? Just wait! Freddy shall take you over, and——' Was Mrs. Freddy beaming at the prospective success of her new friend, or was her vanity flattered by reflecting upon her own perspicacity? Unavoidable as it was in a way that Mrs. Graham Townley should be taken down to dinner by the new minister — nevertheless the antidote had been cleverly provided for. 'Freddy dear — why, I thought he was—— Oh, there he is!' Seeing her hungry husband safely anchored in front of the iris gown, instantly she abandoned the idea of disturbing him. 'After all,' she said, turning again to Haycroft, who had stood the image of stolid unimpressionableness — 'after all, Freddy's right. Since she's going to sit beside you at dinner, it's a good reason for not making you known to each other before. Or perhaps you never experience that awful feeling of being talked out by the time you go down, and not having a single thing left——' She saw that the great man was not going to vouchsafe any contribution to her small attempt to keep the ball rolling; so without giving him the chance to mark her failure by a silence, however brief, she chattered on. 'Though with Vida you're not likely to find yourself in that predicament. Is he, Ronald?' With the instinct of the well-trained female to draw into her circle any odd man hovering about on the periphery, Mrs. Freddy appealed to her brother-in-law. Lord Borrodaile turned in her direction his long sallow face — a face that would have been saturnine but for its touch of whimsicality and a singularly charming smile. 'My brother-in-law will bear me out,' Mrs. Freddy went on, quite as though breaking off a heated argument.

Lord Borrodaile sauntered up and offered a long thin hand to Haycroft ('the fella who's bringing the country to the dogs,' as Mrs. Freddy knew right well was his conviction).

Steering wide of politics, 'I gather,' he said, with his air of amiable boredom, 'that you were discussing what used in the days of my youth to be called a lady's "conversational powers."'

'I forbid you to apply such deadly phrases to my friend,' Mrs. Freddy denounced him. '*Your* friend, too!'

'I'll prove my title to the distinction by proclaiming that she has the subtlest art a woman can possess.'

'Ah, *that's* more like it!' said Mrs. Freddy, gaily. 'What is the subtlest art?'

'The art of being silent without being dull.'

If there was any sting in this for the lady nearest him, she gave no sign of making the personal application.

'Now I expressly forbid your encouraging Vida in silence! Most men like to be amused. You know perfectly well *you* do!'

'Ah, yes,' he said languidly, catching Haycroft's eye and almost making terms with him upon a common ground of masculine understanding. 'Yes, yes. It is well known what children we are. Pleased with a rattle!' Then, as if fearing he might be going too far, he smiled that disarming smile of his, and said good-humouredly, 'I know now why you are called a good hostess.'

'Why?' asked the lady a little anxiously, for his compliments were not always soothing.

A motion towards the watch-pocket. 'No one, to look at you, would suppose that your spirit was racked between the clock and the door.'

'Oh,' she said, relieved, 'if they come in five minutes or so, you'll see! The dinner won't be a penny the worse. Jules is such a wizard. All I mind is seeing Freddy fussed.' She turned with an engaging smile to her minister again. 'Freddy has the most angelic temper except when he's hungry — bless him! Now that he's talking to Vida Levering, Freddy'll forget whether it's before dinner or after.'

'What! what!' said a brisk old gentleman, with a face like a peculiarly wicked monkey. He abandoned Mrs. Townley with enthusiasm in order to say to his hostess, 'Show me the witch who can work that spell!'

'Oh, dear, I'm afraid,' said Mrs. Freddy, prettily, 'I'm dreadfully afraid that means you're starving! Does it make you morose as it does Freddy?' she asked, with an air of comic terror. 'Then we won't wait.' She tossed out one arm with a funny little movement that sent her thin draperies floating as though towards the bell.

'My dear lady!' the old gentleman arrested her. 'I hunger, it is true, but only for knowledge.' In a silent but rather horrible laugh he wrinkled up his aged nose, which was quite enough wrinkled and sufficiently 'up' already. 'Who *is* the witch?'

'Why, we were talking about a member of your family.' She turned again to the new minister. 'Mr. Fox-Moore — Sir — oh! how absurd! I was going to introduce two pillars of the State to one another. I *must* be anxious about those late people, after all.'

'As a matter of fact you and I never have met,' said Haycroft, cordially taking old Mr. Fox-Moore's hand. 'Beside you permanent officials we ephemeræ, the sport of parties ——'

'Ah, *that's* all right!' Mrs. Freddy's head, poised an instant on one side, seemed to say.

'Who is it? Who is late?' demanded Mrs. Graham Townley, whose entrance into the conversation produced the effect of the sudden opening of window and door on a windy day. People shrink a little in the draught, and all light, frivolous things are blown out of the way. English people stand this sort of thing very much as they stand the actual draughts in their cold houses. They feel it to be good for them on the whole. Mrs. Graham Townley was acknowledged to be a person of much character. Though her interest in public affairs was bounded only by the limits of the Empire, she had found time to reform the administration of a great London hospital. Also she was related to a great many people. In the ultra smart set she of course had no *raison d'être*, but in the older society it was held meet that these things be. So that when she put her question, not only was she not ignored, but each one felt it a serious thing for anybody to be so late that Mrs. Graham Townley instead of button-holing some one with, 'What, now, should you say is the extent of the Pan-

Islamic influence in Egypt?' should be reduced to asking, 'Who are we waiting for?'

'It's certain to be a man,' said Lady John Ulland, as calmly convinced as one who states a natural law.

'Why?' asked her niece, the charming girl in rose colour.

'No woman would dare to come in so late as this. She'd have turned back and telephoned that the horses had run away with her or something of the sort.'

'Dick Farnborough won't turn back.'

'Oh, Mr. Farnborough's the culprit!' said a smartly dressed woman, with a nervous, rather angry air, though the ropes of fine pearls she wore might, some would think, have soothed the most savage breast.

'Yes, Dick and Captain Beeching!' said Mrs. Freddy; 'and I shall give them just two minutes more!'

'Aunt Ellen *said* it couldn't be a woman,' remarked the girl in pink, as one struck with such perspicacity.

'Well, I wouldn't ask them again to *my* house,' said the discontented person with the pearls.

'Yes, she would,' Lady John said aside to Borrodaile. 'She has a daughter, and so have most of the London hostesses, and the young villains know it.'

'Oh, yes; sometimes they never turn up at all,' said the pink niece.

'After accepting!' ejaculated Lady Whyteleafe of the pearls.

'Oh, yes; sometimes they don't even answer.'

'I never heard of such impudence.'

'I have, twice this year,' said Mrs. Graham Townley, with that effect of breaking by main force into a conversation instead of being drawn into it. 'Twice in this last year I've sat with an empty place on one side of me at a dinner-party. On each occasion it was a young member of parliament who never turned up and never sent an apology.'

'The same man both times?' asked Lord Borrodaile.

'Yes; different houses, but the same man.'

'He *knew!*' whispered Borrodaile in Lady John's ear.

'Dick Farnborough has been complaining that since he smashed his motor all existence has become disorganized. I always feel'—the hostess addressed herself to the minister and the pearls—

'don't you, that one ought to stretch a point for people who have to go about in cabs?'

As Haycroft began a disquisition on the changes in social life initiated by the use of the motor-car, Mrs. Freddy floated away.

Borrodaile, looking after her, remarked, 'It's humane of my sister-in-law to think of making allowances. Most of us gratify the dormant cruelty in human nature by keeping an eagle eye on the wretched late ones when at last they *do* slink in. Don't you know' — he turned to Lady John — 'that look of half-resentful interest?'

'Perfectly. Every one wants to see whether these particular culprits wear their rue with a difference.'

'Or whether,' Borrodaile went on, 'whether, like the majority, they merely look abject and flustered, and whisper agitated lies. Personally I have known it to be the most interesting moment of the evening.'

What brought Mrs. Fox-Moore's plight forcibly home to Mrs. Freddy was seeing Vida leave her own animated group to join her sister. Mrs. Freddy made her way across the room, stopping a moment to say to Freddy as she passed —

'*Do* go and make conversation to Lady Whyteleafe.'

'Which is Lady Whyteleafe?' drawled Freddy.

'Oh, you *always* forget her! What *am* I to do with you? She's the woman with the pearls.'

'Not that cross-looking ——'

'Sh! Yes, darling, that's the one. She's only looking like that because you aren't talking to her;' and Mrs. Freddy overtook Vida just as she reached the Desert Island where Mrs. Fox-Moore stood, looking seaward for a sail.

A few moments later, after ringing for dinner, Mrs. Freddy paused an instant, taking in the fact that Lady Whyteleafe hadn't been made as happy by Mr. Tunbridge's attentions as his wife had prophesied. No, the angry woman with the pearls, so far from being intent upon Freddy's remarks, was levelling at Mrs. Freddy the critical eye that says, 'Now I shall see if I can determine just how miserably conscious you are that dinner's unpardonably late, everybody starving, and since you've only just rung, that you have at least eight minutes still to fill up before you'll hear that you are "served."' Lady Whyteleafe leaned against the back of the little periwinkle damask sofa, and waited to see Mrs. Freddy carry off these last minutes of suspense by an affectation of great good spirits.

But the lady under the social microscope knew a trick worth two of that. She could turn more than one mishap to account.

'Oh, Freddy! Oh, Lady Whyteleafe! I've just gone and said the most awful, dreadful, appalling thing! Oh, I should like to creep under the sofa and die!'

'What's up?' demanded Mr. Freddy, with an air of relief at being reinforced.

'I've been talking to Vida Levering and that funereal sister of hers.'

'Oh, Mrs. Fox-Moore!' said Lady Whyteleafe, obviously disappointed. 'She's a step-sister, isn't she?'

'Yes, yes. Oh, I wish she'd never stepped over my threshold!'

'Why?' said Mr. Freddy, sticking in his eye-glass.

'Don't, Freddy. Don't look at her. Oh, I wish I were dead!'

'What *have* you been doing? She looks as if she wished *she* were dead.'

'That's nothing. She always looks like that,' Lady Whyteleafe assured the pair.

'Yes, and she makes it a great favour to come. "I seldom go into society," she writes in her stiff little notes; and you're reminded that way, without her actually setting it down, that she devotes herself to good works.'

'Perhaps she doesn't know what else to do with all that money,' said the lady of the pearls.

'*She* hasn't got a penny piece.'

'Oh, is it all his? I thought the Leverings were rather well off.'

'Yes, but the money came through the second wife, Vida's mother. Oh, I hate that Fox-Moore woman!' Mrs. Freddy laughed ruefully. 'And I'm sure her husband is a great deal too good for her. But how *could* I have done it!'

'You haven't told us yet.'

'They asked me who was late, and I said Dick Farnborough, and that I hoped he hadn't forgotten, for I had Hermione Heriot here on purpose to meet him. And I told Vida about the Heriots trying to marry Hermione to that old Colonel Redding.'

'Oh, can't they bring it off?' said Lady Whyteleafe.

'I've been afraid they would. "It's so dreadful," I said, "to see a fresh young girl tied to a worn-out old man."'

'*Oh!*' remarked Lady Whyteleafe, genuinely shocked. 'And you said that to ——'

Mrs. Freddy nodded with melancholy significance. 'Even when Vida said, "It seems to do well enough sometimes," *still* I never never remembered the Fox-Moore story! And I went on about it being a miracle when it turned out even tolerably — and, oh, Heaven forgive me! I grew eloquent!'

'It's your passion for making speeches,' said Mr. Freddy.

At which, accountably to Lady Whyteleafe, Mrs. Freddy blushed and stumbled in this particular 'speech.'

'I know, I know,' she said, carrying it off with an air of comic contrition. 'I even said, "There's a modesty in nature that it isn't wise to overstep" (I'd forgotten some people think speech-making comes under that head). "It's been realized," I said — yes, rushing on my doom! — "it's been realized up to now only in the usual one-sided way — discouraging boys from marrying women old enough to be their mothers. But dear, blundering, fatuous man"' — she smiled into her husband's pleasantly mocking face — '"*he* thinks," I said, "at *any* age he's a fit mate for a fresh young creature in her teens. If they only knew — the dreadful old ogres!" Yes, I said that. I piled it on — oh, I stuck at nothing! "The men think an ugly old woman monopolizes all the opportunities humanity offers for repulsiveness. But there's nothing on the face of the earth as hideous," I said, "as an ugly old man. Doesn't it stand to reason? He's bound to go greater lengths than any woman can aspire to. There's more of him to *be* ugly, isn't there? I appealed to them — everything about him is bigger, coarser — he's much less human," says I, "and *much* more like a dreadful old monkey." I raised my wretched eyes, and there, not three feet away, was the aged husband of the Fox-Moore woman ogling Hermione Heriot! Oh, let me die!' Mrs. Freddy leaned against the blue-grey sofa for a moment and half closed her pretty eyes. The next instant she was running gaily across the room to welcome Richard Farnborough and Captain Beeching.

* * * * * * *

'I always know,' said Lord Borrodaile, glancing over the banisters as he and Vida went down — 'I always know the kind of party it's going to be when I see — certain people. Don't you?'

'I know who you mean,' Vida whispered back, her eyes on Mrs. Graham Townley's aggressively high-piled hair towering over the bald pate of the minister, as, side by side, they disappeared through the dining-room door. 'Why *does* Laura have her?'

'Well, she's immensely intelligent, they *say*,' he sighed.

'That's why I wonder,' laughed Vida. '*We* are rather frivolous, I'm afraid.'

'To tell the truth, I wondered, too. I even sounded my sister-in-law.'

'Well?'

'She said it was her Day of Reckoning. "I never ask the woman," she said, "except to a scratch party like this."'

'"Scratch party" — with you and me here!'

'Ah, we are the leaven. We make the compound possible.'

'Still, I don't think she ought to call it "scratch" when she's got an Ambassador and a Cabinet Minister ——'

'Just the party to ask a scratch Cabinet Minister to,' he insisted, stopping between the two cards inscribed respectively with their names. 'As for the Ambassador, he's an old friend of ours — knows his London well — knows we are the most tolerant society on the face of the earth.'

In spite of her companion's affectation of a smiling quarrelsomeness, Vida unfolded her table-napkin with the air of one looking forward to her *tête-à-tête* with the man who had brought her down. But Lord Borrodaile was a person most women liked talking to, and hardly had she begun to relish that combination in the man of careless pleasantry and pungent criticism, when Vida caught an agonized glance from her hostess, which said plainly, 'Rescue the man on your right,' — and lo! Miss Levering became aware that already, before the poor jaded politician had swallowed his soup, Mrs. Townley had fallen to catechising him about the new Bill — a theme talked threadbare by newspaperdom and all political England. But Mrs. Townley, albeit not exactly old, was one of those old-fashioned women who take what used to be called 'an intelligent interest in politics.' You may pick her out in any drawing-room from the fact that politicians shun her like the plague. Rich, childless, lonely, with more wits than occupation, practically shelved at a time when her intellectual life is most alert — the Mrs. Townleys of the world do, it must be admitted, labour under the delusion that men fighting the battle of public life, go out to dine for the express purpose of telling the intelligent female 'all about it.' She is a staunch believer not so much in women's influence as in woman's. And there is no doubt in her mind which woman's. If among her smart relations who ask her to their houses and go to hers (from that sentiment of the solidarity of the family so powerful in English life), if amongst these she succeeds from time to time in inducing two or three public officials, or even private members, to prove how good a cook she keeps, she thinks she is exercising an influence on the politics of her time. Her form of conversation consists in plying her victim with questions. Not here one there one, to keep the ball rolling, but a steady and pitiless fire of 'Do you think?' and '*Why* do you?'

Obedient to her hostess's wireless telegram, Miss Levering bent her head, and said to Mrs. Townley's neighbour —

'I know I ought not to talk to you till after the *entrée*.'

'Pray do!' said Sir William, with a sudden glint in his little eyes; and then with a burnt-child air of caution, 'Unless ——' he began.

'Oh, you make conditions!' said Miss Levering, laughing.

'Only one. Promise not' — he lowered his voice — 'promise not to say "Bill."'

'I won't even go so far as to say "William."'

He laughed as obligingly as though the jest had been a good one. A little ashamed, its maker hastened to leave it behind.

'There's nothing I should quite so much hate talking about as politics — saving your presence.'

'Ah!'

'I was thinking of something *much* more important.'

Even her rallying tone did not wholly reassure the poor man.

'More important?' he repeated.

'Yes; I long to know (and I long to be forgiven for asking), what Order that is you are wearing, and what you did to get it.'

Haycroft breathed freely. He talked for the next ten minutes about the bauble, making a humorous translation of its Latin 'posy,' and describing in the same vein the service to a foreign state that had won him the recognition. He wouldn't have worn the thing to-night except out of compliment to the ambassador from the Power in question. They were going on together to the reception at the Foreign Office. As to the Order, Haycroft seemed to feel he owed it to himself to smile at all such toys, but he did not disdain to amuse the pretty lady with the one in question, any more than being humane (and even genial sitting before Mrs. Freddy's menu), he would have refused to show the whirring wheels of his watch to a nice child. The two got on so well that the anxious look quite faded out of Mrs. Freddy's face, and she devoted herself gaily to the distinguished foreigner at her side. But Haycroft at a party was, like so many Englishmen, as the lilies of the field. They toil not, neither do they spin. The man Vida had rescued from Mrs. Graham Townley was, when in the society of women, so accustomed to seeing them take on themselves the onus of entertainment, was himself so unused to being at the smallest trouble, that when the 'Order' was exhausted, had Vida not invented another topic, there would have been an absolute cessation of all converse till Mrs. Graham Townley had again caught him up like a big reluctant fish on the hook of interrogation. At a reproachful aside from Lord Borrodaile, Miss Levering broke off in the middle of her second subject to substitute, 'But I am monopolizing you disgracefully,' and she half turned away from the eminent politician into whose slightly flushed face and humid eyes had come something like animation.

'Not at all. Not at all. Go on.'

'No, I've gone far enough. Do you realize that we left "Orders" and "Honours" half an hour ago, and ever since we've been talking scandal?'

'Criticizing life,' he amended — 'a pursuit worthy of two philosophers.'

'I did it —' said the lady, with an air of half-amused discontent with herself; 'you know why I did it.'

He met her eye, and the faint motion that indicated the woman on his other side. 'Terrible person,' he whispered. 'She goes out to dine as a soldier goes into action.'

For the next few minutes they made common cause in heaping ridicule on 'the political woman.'

'But, after all' — Vida pulled herself up — 'it may be only a case of sour grapes on my part. I'm afraid *my* conversation is inclined to be frivolous.'

He turned and gave her her reward — the feeling smile that says, '*Thank God!*' But, strangely, it did not reflect itself in the woman's face. Something quite different there, lurking under the soft gaiety. Was it consciousness of this being the second time during the evening that she had employed the too common vaunt of the woman of that particular world? Did some ironic echo reach her of that same boast (often as mirthless and as pitiful as the painted smile on the cruder face), the 'I'm afraid I'm rather frivolous' of the well-to-do woman, whose frivolity — invaluable asset! — is beginning to show wear?

'Well, to return to our mutton,' he said; and, as his companion seemed suddenly to be overtaken by some unaccountable qualm, 'What a desert life would be,' he added encouragingly, 'if we couldn't talk to the discreet about the indiscreet.'

'I wonder if there wouldn't be still more oases in the desert,' she said idly, 'if there were a new law made ——'

He glanced at her with veiled apprehension in the pause.

'You being so Liberal,' she went on with faint mockery, 'you're the very one to introduce the measure' (he shrank visibly, and seemed about to remind her of her pledge). 'It shall ordain,' she went on, 'that those who have found satisfactory husbands or wives are to rest content with their good fortune, and not be so greedy as to insist on having the children, too.'

'Oh!' His gravity relaxed.

'But, on the other hand, all the lonely women, the widows and spinsters, who haven't got anything else, *they* shall have the children.'

'I won't go so far as that,' he laughed, boundlessly relieved that the conversation was not taking the strenuous turn he for a moment feared. 'But I'll tell you what I'll do. I'll support a measure that shall make an allowance of *one* child to every single woman the proper and accepted arrangement. No questions asked, and no disgrace.'

'Disgrace!' she echoed, smiling. 'On the contrary, it should be the woman's title to honour! She should be given a beautiful Order like yours for service to the State.'

'Ah, yes! But, what then would we talk about?'

She had turned away definitely this time.

'Well,' said Borrodaile, a little mocking, 'what is it?'

'I don't know,' she answered. 'I don't know *what* it is that seizes hold of me after I've been chattering like this for an hour or more.'

Borrodaile bent his head, and glanced past Vida to the abandoned minister.

'Console me by saying a slight weariness.'

'More like loathing.'

'Not of *both* your neighbours, I hope.'

He lost the low 'Of myself.' 'But there's one person,' she said, with something like enthusiasm — 'one person that I respect and admire.'

'Oh!' He glanced about the board with an air of lazy interest. 'Which one?'

'I don't know her name. I mean the woman who dares to sit quite silent and eat her dinner without looking like a lost soul.'

'I've been saying you could do that.'

She shook her head. 'No, I've been engaged for the last hour in proving I haven't the courage. It's just come over me,' she said, her eyes in their turn making a tour of the table, and coming back to Borrodaile with the look of having caught up a bran-new topic on the way — 'it's just come over me, what we're all doing.'

'Are we all doing the same thing?'

'All the men are doing one thing. And all the women another.'

His idly curious look travelled up and down, and returned to her unenlightened.

'All the women,' she said, 'are trying with might and main to amuse the men, and all the men are more or less permitting the women to succeed.'

'I'm sorry,' he said, laughing, 'to hear of your being so overworked.'

'Oh, *you* make it easy. And yet' — she caught the gratitude away from her voice — 'I suppose I should have said something like that, even if I'd been talking to my other neighbour.'

Borrodaile's look went again from one couple to another, for, as usual in England, the talk was all *tête-à-tête*. The result of his inspection seemed not to lend itself to her mood.

'I can't speak for others, but for myself, I'm always conscious of wanting to be agreeable when I'm with you. I'm sorry' — he was speaking in the usual half-genial, half-jeering tone — 'very sorry, if I succeed so ill.'

'I've already admitted that with *me* you succeed to admiration. But you only try because it's easy.'

'Oh!' he laughed.

'You rather like talking to me, you know. Now, can you lay your hand on your heart ——'

'And deny it? Never!'

'Can you lay your hand on your heart, and say you've tried as hard to entertain your other neighbour as I have to keep mine going?'

'Ah, well, we men aren't as good at it. After all, it's rather the woman's "part," isn't it?'

'The art of pleasing? I suppose it is — but it's rather a Geisha view of life, don't you think?'

'Not at all; rightly viewed, it's a woman's privilege — her natural function.'

'Then the brutes are nobler than we.'

Wondering, he glanced at her. The face was wholly reassuring, but he said, with a faint uneasiness —

'If it weren't you, I'd say that sounds a little bitter.'

'Oh, no,' she laughed. 'I was only thinking about the lion's mane and the male bird's crest, and what the natural history bores say they're for.'

CHAPTER III

THE darkness and the quiet of Vida Levering's bedroom were rudely dispelled at a punctual eight each morning by the entrance of a gaunt middle-aged female.

It was this person's unvarying custom to fling back the heavy curtains, as though it gratified some strong recurrent need in her, to hear brass rings run squealing along a bar; as if she counted that day lost which was not well begun — by shooting the blinds up with a clatter and a bang!

The harsh ceremonial served as a sort of setting of the pace, or a metaphorical shaking of a bony fist in the face of the day, as much as to say, 'If I admit you here you'll have to toe the mark!'

It might be taken as proof of sound nerves that the lady in the bed offered no remonstrance at being jarred awake in this ungentle fashion.

Fourteen years before, when Vida Levering was only eighteen, she had tried to make something like a conventional maid out of the faithful Northumbrian. Rachel Wark had entered Lady Levering's service just before Vida's birth, and had helped to nurse her mistress through a mortal illness ten years later. After Sir Hervey Levering lost his wife, Wark became in time housekeeper and general factotum to the family. This arrangement held without a break until, as before hinted, Miss Vida, full of the hopeful idealism of early youth, had tried and ignominiously failed in her attempt to teach the woman gentler manners.

For Wark's characteristic retort had been to pack her box and go to spend sixteen months among her kinsfolk, where energy was accounted a virtue, and smooth ways held in suspicion. At the end of that time, seeming to judge the lesson she wished to impart had been sufficiently digested, Wark wrote to Miss Vida proposing to come back. For some months she waited for the answer. It came at last from Biarritz, where it appeared the young lady was spending the winter with her father. After an exchange of letters

Wark joined them there. In the twelve years since her return to the family, she had by degrees adapted herself to the task of looking after her young lady. The adaptation was not all on one side. Many of Vida's friends wondered that she could put up with a lady's maid who could do so few of the things commonly expected of that accomplished class.

'I don't want dressmaking going on in the house,' contentedly Vida told off her maid's negative qualifications, 'and I hate having anybody do my hair for me. Wark packs quite beautifully, and then I *do* like some one about me — that I like.'

In the early days what she had 'liked' most about the woman was that Wark had known and been attached to Lady Levering. There was no one else with whom Vida could talk about her mother.

By the time death overtook Sir Hervey two winters ago in Rome, Wark had become so essential a part of Vida's little entourage, that one of the excuses offered by that lady for not going to live with her half-sister in London had been — 'Wark doesn't always get on with other servants.' For several years Miss Levering's friends had been speaking of her as one fallen a victim to that passion for Italy that makes it an abiding place dearer than home to so many English-born. But the half-sister, Mrs. Fox-Moore, had not been misled either by that theory or by the difficulty as to pleasing Wark with the Queen Anne's Gate servants. 'It's not that Vida loves Italy so much as that, for some reason, she doesn't love England at all.' Nevertheless, Mrs. Fox-Moore after some months had persuaded her to 'bring Wark and try us.'

The experiment, now over a year old, seemed to have turned out well. If Vida really did not love her native land, she seemed to enjoy well enough what she called smiling 'the St. Martin's Summer' of her success in London society.

She turned over in her bed on this particular May morning, stretching out her long figure, and then letting it sink luxuriously back into relaxed quiescence with a conscious joy in prolonging those last ten minutes when sleep is slowly, softly, one after another, withdrawing her thousand veils.

Vaguely, as she lay there with face half buried in her pillow, vaguely she was aware that Wark was making even more noise than common.

When the woman had bustled in and bustled out several times, and deposited the shoes with a 'dump,' she reappeared with the delicate porcelain tray that bore the early tea. On the little table close to where the dark head lay half hidden, Wark set the fragile burden down — did it with an emphasis that made cup and saucer shiver and run for support towards the round-bellied pot.

Vida opened her heavy-lidded eyes. 'Really, Wark, you know, nobody on earth would let you wake them in the morning except me.' She sat up and pulled the pillow higher. 'Give me the tray here,' she said sleepily.

Wark obeyed. She had said nothing to Vida's reproof. She stood now by the bedside without a trace of either contrition or resentment in the wooden face that seemed, in recompense for never having been young, to be able successfully to defy the 'antique pencil.' Time had made but one or two faint ineffectual scratches there, as one who tries, and then abandons, an unpromising surface. The lack of record in the face lent it something almost cryptic. If there were no laughter-wrought lines about the eyes, neither was there mark of grief or self-repression near the mouth. She would, you felt, defy Time as successfully as she defied lesser foes. Even the lank, straw-coloured hair hardly showed the streaks of yellow-white that offered their unemphatic clue to Wark's age.

The sensitive face of the woman in the bed — even now with something of the peace of sleep still shadowing its brilliancy — gave by contrast an impression of vividness and eager sympathies. The mistress, too, looked younger than her years. She did not seem to wonder at the dull presence that seemed to be held there, prisoner-like, behind the brass bars at the foot of the bed. Wark sometimes gave herself this five minutes' *tête-à-tête* with her mistress before the business of the day began and all their intercourse was swamped in clothes.

'I meant to pin a paper on the door to say I wasn't to be called till ten,' said the lady, as though keeping up the little pretence of not being pleased.

'Didn't you sleep well, 'm?' The maid managed wholly to denude the question of its usual grace of solicitude.

'Yes; but it was so late when I began. We didn't get back till nearly three.'

'I didn't get much sleep, either.' It was an unheard-of admission from Wark.

'Oh!' said Vida, lazily sipping her tea. 'Bad conscience?'

'No,' she said slowly, 'no.'

As the woman raised her light eyes, Miss Levering saw, to her astonishment, that the lids were red. Wark, too, seemed uncomfortably aware of something unusual in her face, for she turned it away, and busied herself in smoothing down the near corner of the bath blanket.

'What kept *you* awake?' Miss Levering asked.

'Well, I suppose I'd better tell you while the other people aren't round. I want a day or two to go into the country.'

'Into the country?' No such request had been heard for a round dozen of years.

'I've got some business to see to.'

'At home? In Northumberland?'

'No.'

The tone seemed so little to promise anything in the nature of a confidence that Miss Levering merely said —

'Oh, very well. When do you want to go?'

'I could go to-morrow if ——' She stopped, and looked down at the hem of her long white apron.

Something unwonted in the wooden face prompted Miss Levering to say —

'What do you want to do in the country?'

'To see about a place that's been offered me.'

'A *place*, Wark!'

'Yes; post of housekeeper. That's what I really am, you know.'

Miss Levering looked at her, and set down the half-finished cup without opening her lips. If the speech had come from any other than Wark, it would have been easy to believe it merely the prelude to complaint of a fellow-servant or plea for a rise in wages. But if Wark objected to a fellow-servant, her own view of the matter had always been that the other one should go. Her mistress knew quite well that in the mouth of the woman standing there with red eyes at the foot of the bed, such an announcement as had just been made, meant more. And the consciousness seemed to bring with it a sense of acute discomfort not unmixed with anger. For there was a threat of something worse than an infliction of mere inconvenience. It was a species of desertion. It was almost treachery. They had lived together all the younger woman's life, except for those two years that followed on the girl's attempt to make a conventional servant out of a creature who couldn't be that, but who had it in her to be more.

They had been too long together for Wark not to divine something — through all the lady's self-possession — of her sense of being abandoned.

'It's having to tell you that that kept me awake.'

The wave of dull colour that mounted up to the bushy, straw-coloured eyebrows seemed on the way to have overflowed into her eyes. They grew redder than before, and slowly they filled.

'You don't like living here in this house.' Vida caught at the old complication.

'I've got used to it,' the woman said baldly. Then, after a little pause, during which she made a barely audible rasping to clear her throat, 'I don't like leaving you, miss. I always remember how, that time before — the only time I was ever away from you since you was a baby — how different I found you when I came back.'

'Different, Wark?'

'Yes, miss. It seemed like you'd turned into somebody else.'

'Most people change — develope — in those years just before twenty.'

'Not like you did, miss. You gave me a deal of trouble when you was little, but it nearly broke my heart to come back and find you so quieted down and wise-like.'

A flash of tears glimmered in the mistress's eyes, though her lips were smiling.

'Of course,' the maid went on, 'though you never told me about it, I know you had things to bear while I was away, or else you wouldn't have gone away from your home that time — a mere child — and tried to teach for a living.'

'It *was* absurd of me! But whosever fault it was, it wasn't yours.'

'Yes, miss, in a way it was. I owed it to your mother not to have left you. I've never told you how I blamed myself when I heard — and I didn't wonder at you. It *was* hard when your mother was hardly cold to see your father ——'

'Yes; now that's enough, Wark. You know we never speak of that.'

'No, we've never spoken about it. And, of course, you won't need me any more like you did then. But it's looking back and remembering — it's that that's making it so hard to leave you now. But ——'

'Well?'

'My friends have been talking to me.'

'About ——'

'Yes, this post.' Then, almost angrily, 'I didn't try for it. It's come after me. My cousin knows the man.'

'The man who wants you to go to him as housekeeper?' Vida wrinkled her brows. Wark hadn't said 'gentleman,' who alone in her employer's experience had any need of a housekeeper. 'You mean you don't know him yourself?'

'Not yet, 'm. I know he's a market gardener, and he wants his house looked after.'

'What if he does? A market gardener won't be able to pay the wages I ——'

'The wages aren't much to begin with — but he's getting along — except for the housekeeping. That's in a bad way.'

'What if it is? I never heard such nonsense. You don't want to leave me, Wark, for a market gardener you've never so much as seen;' and Miss Levering covered her discomfort by a little smiling.

'My cousin's seen him many a time. She likes him.'

'Let your cousin go, then, and keep his house for him.'

'My cousin has her own house to keep, and she's got a young baby.'

'Oh, the woman who brought her child here once?'

'Yes, 'm, the child you gave the coral beads to. My cousin has written and talked about it ever since.'

'About the beads?'

'About the market gardener. And the way his house is — Ever since we came back to England she's been going on at me about it. I told her all along I couldn't leave you, but she's always said (since that day you walked about with the baby and gave him the beads to play with, and wouldn't let her make him cry by taking them away) — ever since then my cousin has said you'd understand.'

'What would I understand?'

Wark laid her hand on the nearest of the shining bars of brass, and slowly she polished it with her open palm. She obviously found it difficult to go on with her defence.

'I wanted my cousin to come and explain to you.'

Here was Wark in a new light indeed! If she really wanted any creature on the earth to speak for her. As she stood there in stolid embarrassment polishing the shiny bar, Miss Levering clutched the tray to steady it, and with the other hand she pulled the pillow higher. One had to sit bolt upright, it seemed, and give this matter one's entire attention.

'I don't want to talk to your cousin about your affairs. We are old friends, Wark. Tell me yourself.'

She forced her eyes to meet her mistress's. 'He told my cousin: "Just you find me a good housekeeper," he said, "and if I like her," he said, "she won't be my housekeeper long."'

'Wark! *You!* You aren't thinking of marrying?'

'If he's what my cousin says ——'

'A man you've never seen? Oh, my *dear* Wark! Well, I shall hope and pray he won't think your housekeeping good enough.'

'He will! From what my cousin says, he's had a run of worthless huzzies. I don't expect he'll find much fault with *my* housekeeping after what he's been through.'

Vida looked wondering at the triumphant face of the woman.

'And so you're ready to leave me after all these years?'

'No, miss, I'm not to say "ready," but I think I'll have to go.'

'My poor old Wark' — the lady leaned over the tray — 'I could almost think you are in love with this man you've only heard about!'

'No, miss, I'm not to say in love.'

'I believe you are! For what other reason would you have for leaving me?'

The woman looked as if she could show cause had she a mind. But she said nothing.

'You know,' Vida pursued — 'you know quite well you don't need to marry for a home.'

'No, 'm; I'm quite comfortable, of course, with you. But time goes on. I don't get younger.'

'None of us do that, Wark.'

'That's just the trouble, miss. It ain't only *me*.'

Vida looked at her, more perplexed than ever by the curious regard in the hard-featured countenance. For there was something very like dumb reproach in Wark's face.

'Still,' said Miss Levering, 'you know, even if none of us do get younger, we are not any of us (to judge by appearances) on the brink of the grave. Even if I should be smashed up in a motor accident — I know you're always expecting that — even if I were killed to-morrow, still you'd find I hadn't forgotten you, Wark.'

'It isn't that, miss. It isn't death I'm afraid of.'

There was a pause — the longest that yet had come.

'What *are* you afraid of?' Miss Levering asked.

'It's — you see, I've been looking these twelve years to see you married.'

'Me? What's that got to do with ——'

'Yes, miss. You see, I've counted a good while on looking after children again some day. But if you won't get married ——'

Vida flung her hair back with a burst of not very merry laughter. 'If I won't, you must! But *why* in the world? I'd no idea you were so romantic. Why must there be a wedding in the family, Wark?'

'So there can be children, miss,' said the woman, stolidly.

'Well, there is a child. There's Doris.'

'Poor Miss Doris!' The woman shook her head. 'But she's got a good nurse. I say it, though she calls advice interfering. And Miss Doris has got a mother' (plain that Wark was again in the market garden). 'Yes, *she's* got a mother! and a sort of a father, and she's got a governess, and a servant to carry her about. I sometimes think what Miss Doris needs most is a little letting alone. Leastways, she don't need *me*. No, nor *you*, miss.'

'And you've given me up?' the mistress probed.

Wark raised her red eyes. 'Of course, miss, if I'm wrong ——' Her knuckly hand slid down from the brass bar, and she came round to the side of the bed with an unmistakable eagerness in her face. 'If you're going to get married, I don't see as I *could* leave ye.'

The lady's lips twitched with an instant's silent laughter, but there was something else than laughter in her eyes.

'Oh, I *can* buy you off, can I? If I give you my word — if to save you from need to try the great experiment, I'll sacrifice *my*self ——'

'I wouldn't like to see you make a sacrifice, miss,' Wark said, with perfect gravity. 'But' — as though reconsidering — 'you wouldn't feel it so much, I dare say, after the child was there.'

They looked at one another.

'If it's children you yearn for, my poor Wark, you've waited too long, I'm afraid.'

'Oh, no, miss.' She spoke with a fatuous confidence.

'Why, you must be fifty.'

'Fifty-three, miss. But' — she met her mistress's eye unflinching — 'Bunting — he's the market gardener — he's been married before. He's got three girls and two boys.'

'Heavens!' Vida fell back against the pillow. 'What a handful!'

'Oh, no, 'm. My cousin says they're nice children.' It would have been funny if it hadn't somehow been pathetic to see how instantly she was on the defensive. '"Healthy and hearty," my cousin says, all but the little one. She hardly thinks they'll raise *him*.'

'Well, I wish your market gardener had confined himself to raising onions and cabbages. If he hadn't those children I don't believe you'd dream of ——'

'Well, of course not, miss. But it seems like those children need some one to look after them more than — more than ——'

'Than I do? That ought to be true.'

'One of 'em is little more than a baby.' The wooden woman offered it as an apology.

'Take the tray,' said Vida.

From the look on her face you would say she knew she had lost the faithfullest of servants, and that five little children somewhere in a market garden had won, if not a mother, at least a doughty champion.

CHAPTER IV

No matter how late either Vida Levering or her half-sister had gone to bed the night before, they breakfasted, as they did so many other things, at the hour held to be most advantageous for Doris. Mr. Fox-Moore was sometimes there and often not. On those mornings when his health or his exertions the night previous did not prevent his appearance, there was little conversation at the Fox-Moore breakfast table, except such as was initiated by the only child of the marriage, a fragile girl of ten. Little Doris, owing to some obscure threat of hip-disease, made much of her progress about the house in a footman's arms. But hardly, so borne, would she reach the threshold of the breakfast room before her thin little voice might be heard calling out, '*Fa*-ther! *Fa*-ther!'

Those who held they had every ground for disliking the old man would have been surprised to watch him during the half hour that ensued, ministering to the rather querulous little creature, adapting his tone and view to her comprehension, with an art that plainly took its inspiration from affection. If Doris were not well enough to come down, Mr. Fox-Moore read his letters and glanced at 'the' paper, directing his few remarks to his sister-in-law, whom he sometimes treated in such a way as would have given a stranger the impression, in spite of the lady's lack of response, that there was some secret understanding between the two.

A great many years before, Donald Fox-Moore had tumbled into a Government office, the affairs of which he had ultimately got into such excellent running order, that, with a few hours' supervision from the chief each week, his clerks were easily able to maintain the high reputation of that particular department of the public service. What Mr. Fox-Moore did with the rest of his time was little known. A good deal of it was spent with a much younger bachelor brother near Brighton. At least, this was the family legend. In spite of his undoubted affection for his child, little of his leisure was wasted at home. When people looked at the sallow, smileless face of his wife they didn't blame him.

Sometimes, when a general sense of tension and anxiety betrayed his presence somewhere in the great dreary house, and the master yet forbore to descend for the early meal, he would rejoice the heart of his little daughter by having her brought to his room to make tea and share his breakfast.

On these occasions a sense of such unexpected surcease from care prevailed in the dining-room as called for some celebration of the holiday spirit. It found expression in the inclination of the two women to linger over their coffee, embracing the only sure opportunity the day offered for confidential exchange.

One of these occasions was the morning of Wark's warning, which, however, Vida determined to say nothing about till she was obliged. She had just handed up her cup for replenishing when the door opened, and, to the surprise of the ladies, the master of the house appeared on the threshold.

'Is — is anything the matter?' faltered his wife, half rising.

'Matter? Must something be the matter that I venture into my own breakfast-room of a morning?'

'No, no. Only I thought, as Doris didn't come, you were breakfasting upstairs, too.' No notice being taken of this, she at once set about heating water, for no one expected Mr. Fox-Moore to drink tea made in the kitchen.

'I thought,' said he, twitching an open newspaper off the table and folding it up — 'I thought I asked to be allowed the privilege of opening my paper for myself.'

'Your *Times* hasn't been touched,' said his wife, anxiously occupied with the spirit-lamp.

He stopped in the act of thrusting the paper in his pocket and shook it.

'What do you call this?'

'That is my *Times*,' she said.

'*Your Times?*'

'I ordered an extra copy, because you dislike so to have yours looked at till you've finished with it.'

'Dreadful hardship *that* is!' he said, glancing round, and seeing his own particular paper neatly folded and lying still on the side table.

'It was no great hardship when you read it before night. When you don't, it's rather long to wait.'

'To wait for what?'

'For the news of the day.'

'Don't you get the news of the day in the *Morning Post?*'

'I don't get such full Parliamentary reports nor the foreign correspondence.'

'Good Lord! what next?'

'I think you must blame me,' said Vida, speaking for the first time. 'I'm afraid you'll find it's only since I've been here that Janet has broken loose and taken in an extra copy.'

'Oh, it's on your account, is it?' he grumbled, but the edge had gone out of his ill-humour. 'I suppose you *have* to keep up with politics or you couldn't keep the ball rolling as you did last night?'

'Yes,' said Vida, with an innocent air. 'It is well known what superhuman efforts we have to make before we can qualify ourselves to talk to men.'

'Hm!' grumbled Fox-Moore. 'I never saw *you* at a loss.'

'You did last night.'

'No, I didn't. I saw you getting on like a house afire with Haycroft and the beguiling Borrodaile. It's a pity all the decent men are married.'

Mrs. Fox-Moore allowed her own coffee to get cold while she hovered over the sacred rite of scientific tea-making. Mr. Fox-Moore, talking to Vida about the Foreign Office reception, to which they had all gone on after the Tunbridges' dinner, kept watching with a kind of half-absentminded scorn his wife's fussily punctilious pains to prepare the brew 'his way.' When all was ready and the tea steaming on its way to him in the hands of its harassed maker, he curtly declined it, got up, and left the room. A moment after, the shutting of the front door announced the beginning of yet another of the master's absences.

'How can you stand it?' said Vida, under her breath.

'Oh, I don't mind his going away,' said the other, dully.

'No; but his coming back!'

'One of the things I'm grateful to Donald for' — she spoke as if there were plenty more — 'he is very good to you, Vida.' And in her tone there was criticism of the beneficiary.

'You mean, he's not as rude to me as he is to you?'

'He is even forbearing. And you — you rather frighten me sometimes.'

'I see that.'

'It would be very terrible for *me* if he took it into his head not to like you.'

'If he took it into his head to forbid your having me here, you mean.'

'But even when you aren't polite he just laughs. Still, he's not a patient man.'

'Do you think you have to tell me that?'

'No, dear, only to remind you not to try him too far. For my sake, Vida, don't ever do that.'

She put out her yellow, parchment-like hand, and her sister closed hers over it an instant.

'Here's the hot milk,' said Vida. 'Now we'll have some more coffee.'

'Are you coming with me to-day?' Mrs. Fox-Moore asked quite cheerfully for her as the servant shut the door.

'Oh, is this Friday? N — no.' The younger woman looked at the chill grey world through the window, and followed up the hesitating negative with a quite definite, 'I couldn't stand slums to-day.' The two exchanged the look that means, 'Here we are again up against this recurring difference.' But there was no ill-humour in either face as their eyes met.

Between these two daughters of one father existed that sort of haunting family resemblance often seen between two closely related persons, despite one being attractive and the other in some way repellent. The observer traces the same lines in each face, the same intensification of 'the family look' in the smile, and yet knows that the slight disparity in age fails to account for a difference wide as the poles.

And not alone difference of taste, of environment and experience, not these alone make up the sum of their unlikeness. You had only to look from the fresh simplicity of white muslin blouse and olive-coloured cloth in the one case, to the ungainly expensiveness of the black silk gown of the married woman, in order to get from the first a sense of dainty morning freshness, and from Mrs. Fox-Moore not alone a lugubrious *memento mori* sort of impression, but that more disquieting reminder of the ugly and over-elaborate thing life is to many an estimable soul. Janet Fox-Moore had the art of rubbing this dark fact in till, so to speak, the black came off.

She seemed to achieve it partly by dint of wearing (instead of any relief of lace or even of linen at her throat) a hard band of that passementerie secretly so despised of the little Tunbridges. This device did not so much 'finish off' the neck of Mrs. Fox-Moore's gowns, as allow the funereal dulness of them to overflow on to her brown neck. It even cast an added shadow on her sallow cheek. The figure of the older woman, gaunt and thin enough, announced the further constriction of the corset. By way of revenge the sharp shoulder-blades poked the corset out till it defined a ridge in the black silk back. In front, too, the slab-like figure declined co-operation with the corset, and withdrew, leaving a hiatus that the silk bodice clothed though it did not conceal. You could not have told whether the other woman wore that ancient invention for a figure insufficient or over-exuberant. As you followed her movements, easy with the ease of a child, while she walked or stooped or caught up the fragile Doris, or raised her arm to take a book from the shelf, you got an impression of a physique in perfect because unconscious harmony with its environment. If, on the contrary, you watched but so much as the nervous, uncertain hand of the other woman, you would know here was one who had spent her years in alternately grasping the nettle and letting it go — reaping only stings in life's fair fields. Easy for any one seeing her in these days (though she wasn't thirty-six) to share Mrs. Freddy's incredulous astonishment at hearing from Haycroft the night before that Janet Levering had been 'the beauty of her family.' Mrs. Freddy's answer had been, 'Oh, don't make fun of her!' and Haycroft had had to assure her of his seriousness, while the little hostess still stared uncertain.

'The *lines* of her face are rather good,' she admitted. 'Oh, but those yellow and pink eyes, and her general muddiness!'

'Yes, yes,' Sir William had agreed. 'She's changed so that I would never have known her, but her colouring used to be her strong point. I assure you she was magnificent — oh, much more striking than the younger sister!'

The bloodless-looking woman who sat uneasily at her own board clutching at a thin fragment of cold dry toast that hung cheerlessly awry in the silver rack, like the last brown leaf to a frosty tree, while she crunched the toast, spoke dryly of the poor; of how 'interesting many of them are;' how when you take the trouble to understand them, you no longer lump them all together in a featureless misery, you realize how significant and varied are their lives.

'Not half as significant and varied as their smells,' said her unchastened sister.

'Oh, you sometimes talk as if you had no heart!'

'The trouble is, I have no stomach. When you've lured me into one of those dingy alleys and that all-pervading greasy smell of poverty comes flooding into my face — well, simply all my most uncharitable feelings rise up in revolt. I want to hold my nose and hide my eyes, and call for the motor-car. Running away isn't fast enough,' she said, with energy and a sudden spark in her golden-brown eye.

Mrs. Fox-Moore poised the fat silver jug over her own belated cup, and waited for the thick cream to come out in a slow and grudging gobbet with a heavy plump into the coffee. As she waited, she gently rebuked that fastidiousness in her companion that shrank from contact with the unsavoury and the unfortunate.

'It isn't only my fastidiousness, as you call it, that is offended,' Vida retorted. 'I am penetrated by the hopelessness of what we're doing. It salves my conscience, or *yours* ——' Hurriedly she added, '—— that's not what you mean to do it for, I *know*, dear — and you're an angel and I'm a mere cumberer of the earth. But when I'm only just "cumbering," I feel less a fraud than when I'm pretending to do good.'

'You needn't pretend.'

'I can't do anything else. To go among your poor makes me feel in my heart that I'm simply flaunting my better fortune.'

'I never saw you flaunting it.'

'Well, I assure you it's when you've got me to go with you on one of your Whitechapel raids that I feel most strongly how outrageous it is that, in addition to all my other advantages, I should buy self-approval by doing some tuppenny-ha'penny service to a toiling, starving fellow-creature.'

Mrs. Fox-Moore set down her coffee-cup. 'You mustn't suppose ——' she began.

'No, no,' Vida cut her short. 'I don't doubt *your* motives. I know too well how ready you are to sacrifice yourself. But it does fill me with a kind of rage to see some of those smug Settlement workers, the people that plume themselves on leaving luxurious homes. They don't say how hideously bored they were in them. They are perfectly enchanted at the excitement and importance they get out of going to live among the poor, who don't want them ——'

'Oh, my dear Vida!'

'Not a little bit! Well, the *wily* paupers do, perhaps, for what they can get out of our sort.'

Mrs. Fox-Moore cast down her eyes as though convicted by the recollection of some concrete example.

'We're only scratching at the surface,' Vida said — 'such an ugly surface, too! And the more we scratch, the uglier things come to light.'

'You make too much of that disappointment at Christmas.'

'I wasn't even thinking of the hundredth time you've been disillusioned.' Vida threw down her table napkin, and stood up. 'I was thinking of people like our young parson cousin.'

'George ——'

Vida made a shrug of half-impatient, half-humorous assent. 'Leaves the Bishop's Palace and comes to London. He, too, wants "to live for the poor." Never for an instant one of them. Always the patron — the person something may be got out of — or, at all events, hoped from.'

She seemed to be about to leave the room, but as her sister answered with some feeling, 'No, no, they love and respect him!' Vida paused, and brought up by the fire that the sudden cold made comforting.

'George is a different man since he's found his vocation,' Mrs. Fox-Moore insisted. 'You read it in his face.'

'Oh, if all you mean is that *he's* happier, why not? He's able to look on himself as a benefactor. He's tasting the intoxication of the King among Beggars.'

'You are grossly unfair, Vida.'

'So he thinks when I challenge him: "What good, what earthly good, is all this unless an anodyne — for you — is good?"'

'It seems to me a very real good that George Nuneaton and his kind should go into the dark places and brighten hopeless lives with a little Christian kindness — sometimes with a little timely counsel.'

'Yes, yes,' said the voice by the fire; 'and a little good music — don't forget the good music.'

'An object-lesson in practical religion, isn't that something?'

'Practical! Good Heaven! A handful of complacent, expensively educated young people playing at reform. The poor wanting work, wanting decent housing — wanting *bread* — and offered a little cultivated companionship.'

'Vida, what have you been reading?'

'Reading? I've been visiting George at his Settlement. I've been intruding myself on the privacy of the poor once a week with you — and I'm done with it! Personally I don't get enough out of it to reconcile me to their getting so little.'

'You're burning,' observed the toneless voice from the head of the table.

'Yes, I believe I was a little hot,' Vida laughed as she drew her smoking skirt away from the fire. But she still stood close to the cheerful blaze, one foot on the fender, the green cloth skirt drawn up, leaving the more delicate fabric of her silk petticoat to meet the fiery ordeal. 'If it annoys you to hear me say that's my view of charity, why, don't make me talk about it;' but the face she turned for an instant over her shoulder was far gentler than her words. 'And don't in future' — she was again looking down into the fire, and she spoke slowly as one who delivers a reluctant ultimatum — 'don't ask me to help, except with money. *That* doesn't cost so much.'

'I am disappointed.' Nothing further, but the sound of a chair moved back, eloquent somehow of a discouragement deeper than words conveyed.

Vida turned swiftly, and, coming back to her sister, laid an arm about her shoulder.

'I'm a perfect monster! But you know, my dear, you rather goaded me into saying all this by looking such a martyr when I've tried to get out of going ——'

'Very well, I won't ask you again.' But the toneless rejoinder was innocent of rancour. Janet Fox-Moore gave the impression of being too chilled, too drained of the generous life-forces, even for anger.

'Besides,' said Vida, hurriedly, 'I'd nearly forgotten; there's the final practising at eleven.'

'*I'd* forgotten your charity concert was so near!' As Mrs. Fox-Moore gathered up her letters, she gave way for the first time to a wintry little smile.

'The concert's mine, I admit, but the charity's the bishop's. What absurd things we women fill up the holes in our lives with!' Vida said, as she followed her sister into the hall. 'Do you know the real reason I'm getting up this foolish concert?'

'Because you like singing, and do it so well that — yes, without your looks and the indescribable "rest," you'd be a success. I told you that, when I begged you to come and try London.'

'The reason I'm slaving over the concert — it isn't all musical enthusiasm. It amuses me to organize it. All the ticklish, difficult, "bothering" part of getting up a monster thing of this sort, reconciling malcontents, enlisting the great operatic stars and not losing the great social lights — it all interests me like a game. I'm afraid the truth is I like managing things.'

'Perhaps Mrs. Freddy's not so far wrong.'

'Does Mrs. Freddy accuse me of being a "managing woman," horrid thought?'

'She was talking about you in her enthusiastic way when she was here the other day. "Vida could administer a state," she said. Yes, *I* laughed, too, but Mrs. Freddy shook her head quite seriously, and said, "To think of a being like Vida — not even a citizen."'

'I'm not a citizen?' exclaimed the lady, laughing down at her sister over the banisters. 'Does she think because I've lived abroad I've forfeited my rights of ——'

'No, all she means is —— Oh, you know the bee she's got in her bonnet. She means, as she'll tell you, that "you have no more voice in the affairs of England than if you were a Hottentot."'

'I can't say I've ever minded that. But it has an odd sound, hasn't it — to hear one isn't a citizen.'

'Mrs. Freddy forgets ——'

'I know! I know what you're going to say,' said the other, light-heartedly. 'Mrs. Freddy forgets our unique ennobling influence;' and the tall young woman laughed as she ran up the last half of the long flight of stairs. At the top she halted a moment, and called down to Mrs. Fox-Moore, who was examining the cards left the day before, 'Speaking of our powerful influence over our men-folk — Mr. Freddy wasn't present, was he, when she aired her views?'

'No.'

'I thought not. Her influence over Mr. Freddy is maintained by the strictest silence on matters he isn't keen about.'

CHAPTER V

SEEING Ulland House for the first time on a fine afternoon in early May against the jubilant green of its woodland hillside, the beholder, a little dazzled in that first instant by the warmth of colour burning in the ancient brick, might adapt the old dean's line and call the coral-tinted structure rambling down the hillside, 'A rose-red dwelling half as old as Time.'

Its original architecture had been modified by the generations as they passed. One lord of Ulland had expressed his fancy on the eastern façade in gable and sculptured gargoyle; another his fear or his defiance in the squat and sturdy tower with its cautious slits in lieu of windows. Yet another Ulland had brought home from eighteenth-century Italy a love of colonnades and terraced gardens; and one still later had cut down to the level of the sward the high ground-floor windows, so that where before had been two doors or three, were now a dozen giving egress to the gardens.

The legend so often encountered in the history of old English houses was not neglected here — that it had been a Crusader of this family who had himself brought home from the Holy Land the Lebanon cedar that spread wide its level branches on the west, cutting the sunset into even bars. Tradition also said it was a counsellor of Elizabeth who had set the dial on the lawn. Even the latest lord had found a way to leave his impress upon the time. He introduced 'Clock golf' at Ulland. From the upper windows on the south and west the roving eye was caught by the great staring face of this new timepiece on the turf — its Roman numerals showing keen and white upon the vivid green. On the other side of the cedar, that incorrigible Hedonist, the crumbling dial, told you in Latin that he only marked the shining hours. But the brand new clock on the lawn bore neither watchword nor device — seemed even to have dropped its hands as though in modesty withheld from pointing to hours so little worthy of record.

Two or three men, on this fine Saturday, had come down from London for the week-end to disport themselves on the Ulland links, half a mile beyond the park. After a couple of raw days, the afternoon had turned out quite unseasonably warm, and though the golfers had come back earlier than usual, not because of the heat but because one of their number had a train to catch, they agreed it was distinctly reviving to find tea served out of doors.

Already Lady John was in her place on the pillared colonnade, behind the urn. Already, too, one of her pair of pretty nieces was at hand to play the skilful lieutenant. Hermione Heriot, tactful, charming, twenty-five, was equally ready to hand bread and butter, or, sitting quietly, to perform the greater service — that of presenting the fresh-coloured, discreetly-smiling vision called 'the typical English girl.' Miss Heriot fulfilled to a nicety the requirements of those who are sensibly reassured by the spectacle of careful conventionality allied to feminine charm — a pleasant conversability that may be trusted to soothe and counted on never to startle. Hermione would almost as soon have stood on her head in Piccadilly as have said anything original, though to her private consternation such perilous stuff had been known to harbour an uneasy instant in her bosom. She carried such inconvenient cargo as carefully hidden as a conspirator would a bomb under his cloak. It had grown to be as necessary to her to agree with the views and fashions of the majority as it was disquieting to her to see these contravened, or even for a single hour ignored. From the crown of her carefully dressed head to the tips of her pointed toes she was engaged in testifying her assent to the prevailing note. Despite all this to recommend her, she was not Lady John's favourite niece. No doubt about Jean Dunbarton holding that honour; and, to Hermione's credit, her own love for her cousin enabled her to accept the situation with a creditable equability. Jean Dunbarton was due now at any moment, she having already sent over her luggage with her maid the short two miles from the Bishop's Palace, where the girl had dined and slept the night before.

The rest of the Ulland House party were arriving by the next train. As Miss Levering was understood to be one of those expected it will be seen that a justified faith in the excellence of the Ulland links had not made Lady John unmindful of the wisdom of including among 'the week-enders' a nice assortment of pretty women for the amusement of her golfers in the off hours.

Of this other young lady swinging her golf club as she came

across the lawn with the men — sole petticoat among them — it could not be pretended that any hostess, let alone one so worldly-wise as Lady John Ulland, would look to have the above-hinted high and delicate office performed by so upright and downright — not to say so bony — a young woman, with face so like a horse, and the stride of a grenadier. Under her short leather-bound skirt the great brown-booted feet seemed shamelessly to court attention — as it were out of malice to catch your eye, while deliberately they trampled on the tenderest traditions clinging still about the Weaker Sex.

Lady John held in her hand the top of the jade and silver tea-caddy. Hermione, as well as her aunt, knew that this top held four teaspoonsful of tea. Lady John filled it once, filled it twice, and turned the contents out each time into the gaping pot. Then, absent-mindedly, she paused, eyeing the approaching party,— that genial silver-haired despot, her husband, walking with Lord Borrodaile, the gawky girl between them, except when she paused to practise a drive. The fourth person, a short, compactly knit man, was lounging along several paces behind, but every now and then energetically shouting out his share in the conversation. The ground of Lady John's interest in the group seemed to consist in a half-mechanical counting of noses. Her eyes came back to the tea-table and she made a third addition to the jade and silver measure.

'We shall be only six for the first brew,' prompted the girl at her side.

'Paul Filey is mooning somewhere about the garden.'

'Oh!'

'Why do you say it like that?'

Hermione's eyes rested a moment on the golfer who was bringing up the rear. He was younger than his rather set figure had at a distance proclaimed him.

'I was only thinking Dick Farnborough can't abide Paul,' said the girl.

'A typical product of the public school is hardly likely to appreciate an undisciplined creature with a streak of genius in him like Paul Filey.'

'Oh, I rather love him myself,' said the girl, lightly, 'only as Sophia says he does talk rather rot at times.'

With her hand on the tea-urn, releasing a stream of boiling water into the pot, Lady John glanced over the small thickset angel that poised himself on one podgy foot upon the lid of the urn.

'Sophia's too free with her tongue. It's a mistake. It frightens people off.'

'Men, you mean?'

'Especially men.'

'I often think,' said the young woman, 'that men — all except Paul — would be more shocked at Sophia — if — she wasn't who she is.'

'No doubt,' agreed her aunt. 'Still I sympathize with her parents. I don't see how they'll ever marry her. She might just as well be Miss Jones — that girl — for all she makes of herself.'

'Yes; I've often thought so, too,' agreed Hermione, apparently conscious that the very most was made of *her*.

'She hasn't even been taught to walk.' Lady John was still watching the girl's approach.

'Yet she looks best out of doors,' said Hermione, firmly.

'Oh, yes! She comes into the drawing-room as if she were crossing a ploughed field!'

'All the same,' said Hermione, under her breath, 'when she *is* indoors I'd rather see her walking than sitting.'

'You mean the way she crosses her legs?'

'Yes.'

'But that, too — it seems like so many other things, a question only of degree. Nobody objects to seeing a pair of neat ankles crossed — it looks rather nice and early Victorian. Nowadays lots of girls cross their knees — and nobody says anything. But Sophia crosses her — well, her *thighs*.'

And the two women laughed understandingly.

A stranger might imagine that the reason for Lady Sophia's presence in the party was that she, by common consent, played a capital game of golf — 'for a woman.' That fact, however, was rather against her. For people who can play the beguiling game, *want* to play it — and want to play it not merely now and then out of public spirit to make up a foursome, but constantly and for pure selfish love of it. Woman may, if she likes, take it as a compliment to her sex that this proclivity — held to be wholly natural in a man — is called 'rather unfeminine' in a woman. But it was a defect like the rest, forgiven the Lady Sophia for her father's sake. Lord Borrodaile, held to be one of the most delightful of men, was much in request for parties of this description. One reason for his daughter's being there was that it glossed the fact that Lady Borrodaile was not — was, indeed, seldom present, and one may say never missed, in the houses frequented by her husband.

But as he and his friends not only did not belong to, but looked down upon, the ultra smart set, where the larger freedoms are practised in lieu of the lesser decencies, Lord Borrodaile lived his life as far removed from any touch of scandal and irregularity as the most puritanic of the bourgeoisie. Part and parcel of his fastidiousness, some said — others, that from his Eton days he had always been a lazy beggar. As though to show that he did not shrink from reasonable responsibility towards his female impedimenta, any inquiry as to the absence of Lady Borrodaile was met by reference to Sophia. In short, where other attractive husbands brought a boring wife, Lord Borrodaile brought an undecorative daughter. While to the onlooker nearly every aspect of this particular young woman would seem destined to offend a beauty-loving, critical taste like that of Borrodaile, he was probably served, as other mortals are, by that philosophy of the senses which brings in time a deafness and a blindness to the unloveliness that we needs must live beside. Lord Borrodaile was far too intelligent not to see, too, that when people had got over Lady Sophia's uncompromising exterior, they found things in her to admire as well as to stand a little in awe of. Unlike one another as the Borrodailes were, in one respect they presented to the world an undivided front. From their point of view, just as laws existed to keep other people in order, so was 'fashion' an affair for the middle classes. The Borrodailes might dress as dowdily as they pleased, might speak as uncompromisingly as they felt inclined. Were they not Borrodailes of Borrodaile? Though open expression of this spirit grows less common, they would not have denied that it is still the prevailing temper of the older aristocracy. And so it has hitherto been true that among its women you find that sort of freedom which is the prerogative of those called the highest and of those called the lowest. It is the women of all the grades between these two extremes who have dared not to be themselves, who ape the manners, echo the catchwords, and garb themselves in the elaborate ugliness, devised for the blind meek millions.

As the Lady Sophia, now a little in advance of her companions, came stalking towards the steps, out from a little path that wound among the thick-growing laurels issued Paul Filey. He raised his eyes, and hurriedly thrust a small book into his pocket. The young lady paused, but only apparently to pat, or rather to administer an approving cuff to, the Bedlington terrier lying near the lower step.

'Well,' she said over her shoulder to Filey, 'our side gave a good account of itself that last round.'

'I was sure it would as soon as my malign influence was removed.'

'Yes; from the moment I took on Dick Farnborough, the situation assumed a new aspect. You'll *never* play a good game, you know, if you go quoting Baudelaire on the links.'

'Poor Paul!' his hostess murmured to her niece, 'I always tremble when I see him exposed to Sophia's ruthless handling.'

'Yes,' whispered Hermione. 'She says she's sure he thinks of himself as a prose Shelley; and for some reason that infuriates Sophia.'

With a somewhat forced air of amusement, Mr. Filey was following his critic up the steps, she still mocking at his 'drives' and the way he negotiated his bunkers.

Arrived at the top of the little terrace, whose close-shorn turf was level with the flagged floor of the colonnade, Mr. Filey sought refuge near Hermione, as the storm-tossed barque, fleeing before the wind, hies swift to the nearest haven.

Bending over the Bedlington, the Amazon remained on the top step, her long, rather good figure garbed in stuff which Filey had said was fit only for horse-blankets, but which was Harris tweed slackly belted by a broad canvas girdle drawn through a buckle of steel.

'*Will* you tell me,' he moaned in Hermione's ear, 'why the daughter of a hundred earls has the manners of a groom, and dresses herself in odds and ends of the harness room?'

'Sh! Somebody told her once you'd said something of that sort.'

'No!' he said. 'Who?'

'It wasn't I.'

'Of course not. But did she mind? What did she say, eh?'

'She only said, "He got that out of a novel of Miss Broughton's."'

Filey looked a little dashed. 'No! Has Miss Broughton said it, too? Then there are more of them!' He glanced again at the Amazon. 'Horrible thought!'

'Don't be so unreasonable. She couldn't play golf in a long skirt and high heels!'

'Who *wants* a woman to play golf?'

Hermione gave him his tea with a smile. She knew with an absolute precision just how perfectly at that moment she herself was presenting the average man's picture of the ideal type of reposeful womanhood.

As Lord John and the two other men, his companions, came up the steps in the midst of a discussion —

'If you stop to argue, Mr. Farnborough,' said Lady John, holding out a cup, 'you won't have time for tea before you catch that train.'

'Oh, thank you!' He hastened to relieve her, while Hermione murmured regrets that he wasn't staying. 'Lady John didn't ask me,' he confided. As he saw in Hermione's face a project to intercede for him, he added, 'And now I've promised my mother — we've got a lot of people coming, and two men short!'

'Two men short! how horrible for her!' She said it half laughing, but her view of the reality of the dilemma was apparent in her letting the subject drop.

Farnborough, standing there tea-cup in hand, joined again in the discussion that was going on about some unnamed politician of the day, with whose character and destiny the future of England might quite conceivably be involved.

Before a great while this unnamed person would be succeeding his ailing and childless brother. There were lamentations in prospect of his too early translation to the Upper House.

The older men had been speaking of his family, in which the tradition of public service, generations old, had been revived in the person of this younger son.

'I have never understood,' Lord John was saying, 'how a man with such opportunities hasn't done more.'

'A man as able, too,' said Borrodaile, lazily. 'Think of the tribute he wrung out of Gladstone at the very beginning of his career. Whatever we may think of the old fox, Gladstone had an eye for men.'

'Be *quiet*, will you!' Lady Sophia administered a little whack to the Bedlington. 'Sh! Joey! don't you hear they're talking about our cousin?'

'Who?' said Filey, bending over the lady with a peace-offering of cake.

'Why, Geoffrey Stonor,' answered Sophia.

'*Is* it Stonor they mean?'

'Well, of course.'

'How do you know?' demanded Filey, in the pause.

'Oh, wherever there are two or three gathered together talking politics and "the coming man" — who has such a frightful lot in him that very little ever comes out — it's sure to be Geoffrey Stonor they mean, isn't it, Joey?'

'Perhaps,' said her father, dryly, 'you'll just mention that to him at dinner to-night.'

'*What!*' said Farnborough, with a keen look in his eyes. 'You don't mean he's coming here!'

Sophia, too, had looked round at her host with frank interest.

'Comin' to play golf?'

'Well, he mayn't get here in time for a round to-night, but we're rather expecting him by this four-thirty.'

'What fun!' Lady Sophia's long face had brightened.

'May I stay over till the next train?' Farnborough was whispering to Lady John as he went round to her on the pretext of more cream. 'Thank you — then I won't go till the six forty-two.'

'I didn't know,' Lady Sophia was observing in her somewhat crude way, 'that you knew Geoffrey as well as all that.'

'We don't,' said Lord John. 'He's been saying for years he wanted to come down and try our links, but it's by a fluke that he's coming, after all.'

'He never comes to see *us*. He's far too busy, ain't he, Joey, even if we can't see that he accomplishes much?'

'Give him time and you'll see!' said Farnborough, with a wag of his head.

'Yes,' said Lord John, 'he's still a young man. Barely forty.'

'Barely forty! *They* believe in prolonging their youth, don't they?' said Lady Sophia to no one in particular, and with her mouth rather more full of cake than custom prescribes. 'Good thing it isn't us, ain't it, Joey?'

'For a politician forty *is* young,' said Farnborough.

'Oh, don't I know it!' she retorted. 'I was reading the life of Randolph Churchill the other day, and I came across a paragraph of filial admiration about the hold Lord Randolph had contrived to get so early in life over the House of Commons. It occurred to me to wonder just how much of a boy Lord Randolph was at the time. I was going to count up when I was saved the trouble by coming to a sentence that said he was then "an unproved stripling of thirty-two." You shouldn't laugh. It wasn't meant sarcastic.'

'Unless you're leader of the Opposition, I suppose it's not very easy to do much while your party's out of power,' hazarded Lady John, 'is it?'

'One of the most interesting things about our coming back will be to watch Stonor,' said Farnborough.

'After all, they said he did very well with his Under Secretaryship under the last Government, didn't they?' Again Lady John appealed to the two elder men.

'Oh, yes,' said Borrodaile. 'Oh, yes.'

'And the way'—Farnborough made up for any lack of enthusiasm—'the way he handled that Balkan question!'

'All that was pure routine,' Lord John waved it aside. 'But if Stonor had ever looked upon politics as more than a game, he'd have been a power long before this.'

'Ah,' said Borrodaile, slowly, 'you go as far as that? I doubt myself if he has enough of the demagogue in him.'

'But that's just why. The English people are not like the Americans or the French. The English have a natural distrust of the demagogue. I tell you if Stonor once believed in anything with might and main, he'd be a leader of men.'

'Here he is now.'

Farnborough was the first to distinguish the sound of carriage wheels behind the shrubberies. The others looked up and listened. Yes, the crunch of gravel. The wall of laurel was too thick to give any glimpse from this side of the drive that wound round to the main entrance. But some animating vision nevertheless seemed miraculously to have penetrated the dense green wall, to the obvious enlivenment of the company.

'It's rather exciting seeing him at close quarters,' Hermione said to Filey.

'Yes! He's the only politician I can get up any real enthusiasm for. He's so many-sided. I saw him yesterday at a Bond Street show looking at caricatures of himself and all his dearest friends.'

'Really. How did he take the sacrilege?'

'Oh, he was immensely amused at the fellow's impudence. You see, Stonor could understand the art of the thing as well as the fun — the fierce economy of line —— '

Nobody listened. There were other attempts at conversation, mere decent pretence at not being absorbed in watching for the appearance of Geoffrey Stonor.

CHAPTER VI

THERE was the faint sound of a distant door's opening, and there was a glimpse of the old butler. But before he could reach the French window with his announcement, his own colourless presence was masked, wiped out — not as the company had expected by the apparition of a man, but by a tall, lightly-moving young woman with golden-brown eyes, and wearing a golden-brown gown that had touches of wallflower red and gold on the short jacket. There were only wallflowers in the small leaf-green toque, and except for the sable boa in her hand (which so suddenly it was too warm to wear) no single thing about her could at all adequately account for the air of what, for lack of a better term, may be called accessory elegance that pervaded the golden-brown vision, taking the low sunlight on her face and smiling as she stepped through the window.

It was no small tribute to the lady had she but known it, that her coming was not received nor even felt as an anti-climax.

As she came forward, all about her rose a significant Babel: 'Here's Miss Levering!' 'It's Vida!' 'Oh, how do you *do!*' — the frou-frou of swishing skirts, the scrape of chairs pushed back over stone flags, and the greeting of the host and hostess, cordial to the point of affection — the various handshakings, the discreet winding through the groups of a footman with a fresh teapot, the Bedlington's first attack of barking merged in tail-wagging upon pleased recognition of a friend; and a final settling down again about the tea-table with the air full of scraps of talk and unfinished questions.

'You didn't see anything of my brother and his wife?' asked Lord Borrodaile.

'Oh, yes,' his host suddenly remembered. 'I thought the Freddys were coming by that four-thirty as well as ——'

'No — nobody but me.' She threw her many-tailed boa on the back of the chair that Paul Filey had drawn up for her between the hostess and the place where Borrodaile had been sitting.

'There are two more good trains before dinner ——' began Lord John.

'Oh, didn't I tell you,' said his wife, as she gave the cup just filled for the new-comer into the nearest of the outstretched hands — 'didn't I tell you I had a note from Mrs. Freddy by the afternoon post? They aren't coming.'

Out of a little chorus of regret, came Borrodaile's slightly mocking, 'Anything wrong with the precious children?'

'She didn't mention the children — nor much of anything else — just a hurried line.'

'The children were as merry as grigs yesterday,' said Vida, looking at their uncle across the table. 'I went on to the Freddys' after the Royal Academy. No!' she put her cup down suddenly. 'Nobody is to ask me how I like my own picture! The Tunbridge children ——'

'That thing Hoyle has done of you,' said Lord Borrodaile, deliberately, 'is a very brilliant and a very misleading performance.'

'Thank you.'

Filey and Lord John, in spite of her interdiction, were pursuing the subject of the much-discussed portrait.

'It certainly is one aspect of you ——'

'Don't you think his Velasquez-like use of black and white ——'

'The tiny Tunbridges, as I was saying,' she went on imperturbably, 'were having a teafight when I got there. I say "fight" advisedly.'

'Then I'll warrant,' said their uncle, 'that Sara was the aggressor.'

'She was.'

'You saw Mrs. Freddy?' asked Lady John, with an interest half amused, half cynical, in her eyes.

'For a moment.'

'She doesn't confess it, I suppose,' the hostess went on, 'but I imagine she is rather perturbed;' and Lady John glanced at Borrodaile with her good-humoured, worldly-wise smile.

'Poor Mrs. Freddy!' said Vida. 'You see, she's taken it all quite seriously — this Suffrage nonsense.'

'Yes;' Mrs. Freddy's brother-in-law had met Lady John's look with the same significant smile as that lady's own — 'Yes, she's naturally feeling rather crestfallen — perhaps she'll *see* now!'

'Mrs. Freddy crestfallen, what about?' said Farnborough. But he was much preoccupied at that moment in supplying Lady Sophia with bits of toast the exact size for balancing on the Bedlington's nose. For the benefit of his end of the table Paul Filey had begun to describe the new one-man show of caricatures of famous people just opened in Bond Street. The 'mordant genius,' as he called it, of this new man — an American Jew — offered an irresistible opportunity for phrase-making. And still on the other side of the tea urn the Ullands were discussing with Borrodaile and Miss Levering the absent lady whose 'case' was obviously a matter of concern to her friends.

'Well, let us hope,' Lord John was saying as sternly as his urbanity permitted — 'let us hope this exhibition in the House will be a lesson to her.'

'*She* wasn't concerned in it!' Vida quickly defended her.

'Nevertheless we are all hoping,' said Lady John, 'that it has come just in time to prevent her from going over the edge.'

'Over the edge!' Farnborough pricked up his ears at last in good earnest, feeling that the conversation on the other side had grown too interesting for him to be out of it any longer. 'Over what edge?'

'The edge of the Woman Suffrage precipice,' said Lady John.

'You call it a precipice?' Vida Levering raised her dark brows in a little smile.

'Don't you?' demanded her hostess.

'I should say mud-puddle.'

'From the point of view of the artist' — Paul Filey had begun laying down some new law, but turning an abrupt corner, he followed the wandering attention of his audience — 'from the point of view of the artist,' he repeated, 'it would be interesting to know what the phenomenon is, that Lady John took for a precipice and that Miss Levering says is a mud-puddle.'

'Oh,' said Lord John, thinking it well to generalize and spare Mrs. Freddy further rending, 'we've been talking about this public demonstration of the unfitness of women for public affairs.'

'Give me some more toast dice!' Sophia said to Farnborough. 'You haven't seen Joey's new accomplishment. They're only discussing that idiotic scene the women made the other night.'

'Oh, in the gallery of the House of Commons?'

'Yes, wasn't it disgustin'?' said Paul Filey, facing about suddenly with an air of cheerful surprise at having at last hit on something that he and Lady Sophia could heartily agree about.

'Perfectly revolting!' said Hermione Heriot, not to be out of it. For it is well known that, next to a great enthusiasm shared, nothing so draws human creatures together as a good bout of cursing in common. So with emphasis Miss Heriot repeated, 'Perfectly revolting!'

Her reward was to see Paul turn away from Sophia and say, in a tone whose fervour might be called marked —

'I'm glad to hear you say so!'

She consolidated her position by asking sweetly, 'Does it need saying?'

'Not by people like you. But it *does* need saying when it comes to people we know ——'

'Like Mrs. Freddy. Yes.'

That unfortunate little lady seemed to be 'getting it' on all sides. Even her brother-in-law, who was known to be in reality a great ally of hers — even Lord Borrodaile was chuckling as though at some reflection distinctly diverting.

'Poor Laura! She was being unmercifully chaffed about it last night.'

'I don't myself consider it any longer a subject for chaff,' said Lord John.

'No,' agreed his wife; '*I* felt that before this last outbreak. At the time of the first disturbance — where was it? — in some town in the North several weeks ago ——'

'Yes,' said Vida Levering; 'I almost think that was even worse!'

'Conceive the sublime impertinence,' said Lady John, 'of an ignorant little factory girl presuming to stand up in public and interrupt a speech by a minister of the Crown!'

'I don't know what we're coming to, I'm sure!' said Borrodaile, with a detached air.

'Oh, *that* girl — beyond a doubt,' said his host, with conviction — 'that girl was touched.'

'Oh, beyond a doubt!' echoed Mr. Farnborough.

'There's something about this particular form of feminine folly ——' began Lord John.

But he wasn't listened to — for several people were talking at once.

After receiving a few preliminary kicks, the subject had fallen, as a football might, plump into the very midst of a group of schoolboys. Its sudden presence there stirred even the sluggish to unwonted feats. Every one must have his kick at this Suffrage Ball, and manners were for the nonce in abeyance.

In the midst of an obscuring dust of discussion, floated fragments of condemnation: 'Sexless creatures!' 'The Shrieking Sisterhood!' etc., in which the kindest phrase was Lord John's repeated, 'Touched, you know,' as he tapped his forehead — 'not really responsible, poor wretches. Touched.'

'Still, everybody doesn't know that. It must give men a quite horrid idea of women,' said Hermione, delicately.

'No' — Lord Borrodaile spoke with a wise forbearance — 'we don't confound a handful of half-insane females with the whole sex.'

Dick Farnborough was in the middle of a spirited account of that earlier outbreak in the North —

'She was yelling like a Red Indian, and the policeman carried her out scratching and spitting ——'

'Ugh!' Hermione exchanged looks of horror with Paul Filey.

'Oh, yes,' said Lady John, with disgust, 'we saw all that in the papers.'

Miss Levering, too, had turned her face away — not as Hermione did, to summon a witness to her detestation, but rather as one avoiding the eyes of the men.

'You see,' said Farnborough, with gusto, 'there's something about women's clothes — *especially* their hats, you know — they — well, they ain't built for battle.'

'They ought to wear deer-stalkers,' was Lady Sophia's contribution to the New Movement.

'It is quite true,' Lady John agreed, 'that a woman in a scrimmage can never be a heroic figure.'

'No, that's just it,' said Farnborough. 'She's just funny, don't you know!'

'I don't agree with you about the fun,' Borrodaile objected. 'That's why I'm glad they've had their lesson. I should say there was almost nothing more degrading than this public spectacle of ——' Borrodaile lifted his high shoulders higher still, with an effect of intense discomfort. 'It never but once came my way that I remember, but I'm free to own,' he said, 'there's nothing that shakes my nerves like seeing a woman struggling and kicking in a policeman's arms.'

But Farnborough was not to be dissuaded from seeing humour in the situation.

'They say they swept up a peck of hairpins after the battle!'

As though she had had as much of the subject as she could very well stand, Miss Levering leaned sideways, put an arm behind her, and took possession of her boa.

'They're just ending the first act of *Siegfried*. How glad I am to be in your garden instead of Covent Garden!'

Ordinarily there would have been a movement to take the appreciative guest for a stroll.

Perhaps it was only chance, or the enervating heat, that kept the company in their chairs listening to Farnborough —

'The cattiest one of the two, there she stood like this, her clothes half torn off, her hair down her back, her face the colour of a lobster and the crowd jeering at her ——'

'I don't see how you could stand and look on at such a hideous scene,' said Miss Levering.

'Oh — I — I didn't! I'm only telling you how Wilkinson described it. He said ——'

'How did Major Wilkinson happen to be there?' asked Lady John.

'He'd motored over from Headquarters to move a vote of thanks to the chairman. He said he'd seen some revolting things in his time, but the scrimmage of the stewards and the police with those women ——!' Farnborough ended with an expressive gesture.

'If it was as horrible as that for Major Wilkinson to look on at — what must it have been for those girls?' It was Miss Levering speaking. She seemed to have abandoned the hope of being taken for a stroll, and was leaning forward, chin in hand, looking at the fringe of the teacloth.

Richard Farnborough glanced at her as if he resented the note of wondering pity in the low tone.

'It's never so bad for the lunatic,' he said, 'as for the sane people looking on.'

'Oh, I don't suppose *they* mind,' said Hermione — 'women like *that*.'

'It's flattery to call them women. They're sexless monstrosities,' said Paul Filey.

'You know some of them?' Vida raised her head.

'*I?*' Filey's face was nothing less than aghast at the mere suggestion.

'But you've seen them ——?'

'Heaven forbid!'

'But I suppose you've gone and listened to them haranguing the crowds.'

'Now *do* I look like a person who ——'

'Well, you see we're all so certain they're such abominations,' said Vida, 'I thought maybe some of us knew something about them.'

Dick Farnborough was heard saying to Lord John in a tone of cheerful vigour —

'Locking up is too good for 'em. I'd give 'em a good thrashin'.'

'Spirited fellow!' said Miss Levering, promptly, with an accent that brought down a laugh on the young gentleman's head.

He joined in it, but with a *naïf* uneasiness. What's the matter with the woman? — his vaguely bewildered face seemed to inquire. After all, I'm only agreeing with her.

'Few of us have time, I imagine,' said Filey, 'to go and listen to their ravings.'

As Filey was quite the idlest of men, without the preoccupation of being a tolerable sportsman or even a player of games, Miss Levering's little laugh was echoed by others beside Lady Sophia.

'At all events,' said Vida to Lord Borrodaile, as she stood up, and he drew her chair out of her way, 'even if we don't know much about these women, we've spent a happy hour denouncing them.'

'Who's going to have a short round before sundown?' said Lady Sophia, getting up briskly. '*You*, of course, Mr. Filey. Or are you too "busy"?'

'Say too thirsty. May I?' He carried his cup round to Lady John, not seeming to see Hermione's hospitable hand held out for it.

In the general shuffle Farnborough found himself carried off by Sophia and Lord John.

'Who is our fourth?' said Lady Sophia, suddenly.

'Oh, Borrodaile!' Lord John stopped halfway across the lawn and called back, 'aren't you coming?'

'It's not a bit of use,' said Sophia. 'You'll see. He's safe to sit there and talk to Miss Levering till the dressing-bell rings.'

'Isn't she a *nice* creature!' said Lord John. 'I can't think how a woman like that hasn't got some nice fella to marry her!'

* * * * * * *

'Would you like to see my yellow garden, Vida?' Lady John asked. 'It's rather glorious at this moment.'

Obvious from the quick lifting of the eyes that the guest was on the point of welcoming the proposal, had Filey not swallowed his belated cup of tea with surprising quickness after saying, 'What's a yellow garden?' in the unmistakable tone of one bent upon enlarging his experience. Lady John, with all her antennæ out, lost no time in saying to Vida —

'Perhaps you're a little tired. Hermione, you show Mr. Filey the garden. And maybe, Lord Borrodaile would like to see it, too.'

Although the last-named failed to share the enthusiasm expected in a gardener, he pulled his long, slackly-put-together figure out of the chair and joined the young people.

When they were out of earshot, 'What's the matter?' asked Lady John.

'Matter?'

'Yes, what did poor Paul say to make you fall upon him like that?'

'I didn't "fall upon" him, did I?'

'Well, yes, I rather thought you did.'

'Oh, I suppose I — perhaps it did jar on me, just a little, to hear a cocksure boy ——'

'He's not a boy. Paul is over thirty.'

'I was thinking of Dick Farnborough, too — talking about women like that, before women.'

'Oh, all they meant was ——'

'Yes, I know. Of course we *all* know they aren't accustomed to treating our sex in general with overmuch respect when there are only men present — but — do you think it's quite decent that they should be so free with their contempt of women before us?'

'But, my dear Vida! *That* sort of woman! Haven't they deserved it?'

'That's just what nobody seems to know. I've sat and listened to conversations like the one at tea for a week now, and I've said as much against those women as anybody. Only to-day, somehow, when I heard that boy — yes, I was conscious I didn't like it.'

'You're behaving exactly as Dr. Johnson did about Garrick. You won't allow any one to abuse those women but yourself.'

Lady John cleared the whole trivial business away with a laugh.

'Now, be nice to Paul. He's dying to talk to you about his book. Let us go and join them in the garden. See if you can stand before my yellow blaze and not feel melted.'

The elder woman and the younger went down the terrace through a little copse to her ladyship's own area of experimentation. A gate of old Florentine scrolled iron opened suddenly upon a blaze of yellow in all the shades from the orange velvet of the wallflower through the shaded saffron of azalias and a dozen tints of tulip to the palest primrose and jonquil.

The others were walking round the enclosing grass paths that served as broad green border, and Filey, who had been in all sorts of queer places, said the yellow garden made him think of a Mexican serapé — 'one of those silk scarves, you know — native weaving made out of the pineapple fibre.'

But Vida only said, 'Yes. It's a good scheme of colour.'

She sat on the rustic seat while Lady John explained to Lord Borrodaile, whose gardens were renowned, how she and Simonson treated this and that plant to get so fine a result. Filey had lost no time in finding a place for himself by Miss Levering, while Hermione trailed dutifully round the garden with the others. Occasionally she looked over her shoulder at the two on the seat by the sunken wall — Vida leaning back in the corner motionless, absolutely inexpressive; Filey's eager face bent forward. He was moving his hands in a way he had learned abroad.

'You were rather annoyed with me,' he was saying. 'I saw that.'

The lady did not deny the imputation.

'But you oughtn't to be. Because you see it's only because my ideal of woman is' — again that motion of the hands — '*what* it is, that when I see her stepping down from her pedestal I ——' the hands indicated consternation, followed hard by cataclysmic ruin. 'Of course, lots of men don't care. I *do*. I care enormously, and so you must forgive me. Won't you?' He bent nearer.

'Oh, *I've* nothing to forgive.'

'I know without your telling me, I feel instinctively, *you* more than most people — you'd simply loathe the sort of thing we were talking about at tea — women yelling and fighting men ——'

'Yes — yes, don't go all over that.'

'No, of course I won't,' he said soothingly. 'I can feel it to my very spine, how you shrink from such horrors.'

Miss Levering, raising her eyes suddenly, caught the look Hermione cast backward as Lady John halted her party a moment near the pansy-strip in the gorgeous yellow carpet spread out before them.

'Don't you want to sit down?' Vida called out to the girl, drawing aside her gown.

'What?' said Hermione, though she had heard quite well. Slowly she retraced her steps down the grass path as if to have the words repeated.

But if Miss Levering's idea had been to change the conversation, she was disappointed. There was nothing Paul Filey liked better than an audience, and he had already the impression that Miss Heriot was what he would have scorned to call anything but 'simpatica.'

'I'm sure you've shown the new garden to dozens already,' Miss Levering said to the niece of the house. 'Sit down and confess you've had enough of it!'

'Oh, I don't think,' began Hermione, suavely, 'that one ever gets too much of a thing like that!'

'There! I'm glad to hear you say so. How can we have too much beauty!' exclaimed Filey, receiving the new occupant of the seat as a soul worthy of high fellowship. Then he leaned across Miss Heriot and said to the lady in the corner, 'I'm making that the theme of my book.'

'Oh, I heard you were writing something.'

'Yes, a sort of plea for the æsthetic basis of society! It's the only cure for the horrors of modern civilization — for the very thing we were talking about at tea! What is it but a loss of the sense of beauty that's to blame?' Elbows on knees, he leaned so far forward that he could see both faces, and yet his own betrayed the eye turned inward — the face of the one who quotes. The ladies knew that he was obliging them with a memorized extract from 'A Plea for the Æsthetic Basis.' 'Nothing worse can happen to the world than loss of its sense of Beauty. Men, high and low alike, cling to it still as incarnated in women.' (Hermione crossed her pointed toes and lowered her long eyelashes.) 'We have made Woman the object of our deepest adoration! We have set her high on a throne of gold. We have searched through the world for jewels to crown her. We have built millions of temples to our ideal of womanhood and called them homes. We have fought and wrought and sung for her — and all we ask in return is that she should tend the sacred fire, so that the light of Beauty might not die out of the world.' He was not ill-pleased with his period. 'But women' — he leaned back, and illustrated with the pliant white hands that were ornamented with outlandish rings — 'women are not content with their high and holy office.'

'*Some* women,' amended Hermione, softly.

'There are more and more every day who are not content,' he said sternly; then, for an instant unbending and craning a little forward, 'Of course I don't mean you — *you* are exceptions — but of women in the mass! Look at them! They force their way into men's work, they crowd into the universities — yes, yes' (in vain Hermione tried to reassure him by 'exceptions') — 'Beauty is nothing to them! They fling aside their delicate, provocative draperies, they cast off their scented sandals. They pull on brown boots and bicycling skirts! They put man's yoke of hard linen round their ivory throats, and they scramble off their jewelled thrones to mount the rostrum and the omnibus!'

'Why? *Why* do they?' Vida demanded, laughing. 'Nobody ever tells me why. I can't believe they're as unselfish as *you* make out.'

'I!'

'You ought to admire them if they voluntarily give up all those beautiful things — knowing beforehand they'll only win men's scorn. For you've always warned them!'

He didn't even hear. 'Ah, Ladies, Ladies!' half laughing, but really very much in earnest, he apostrophized the peccant sex, 'I should like to ask, are we men to look upon our homes as dusty din-filled camps on the field of battle, or as holy temples of Peace? Ah!' He leaned back in his corner, stretched out his long legs, and thrust his restless hands in his pockets. 'If they knew!'

'Women?' asked Hermione, with the air of one painstakingly brushing up crumbs of wisdom.

Paul Filey nodded.

'Knew ——?'

'They would see that in the ugly scramble they had let fall their crowns! If they only knew,' he repeated, 'they would go back to their thrones, and, with the sceptre of beauty in one hand and the orb of purity in the other, they would teach men to worship them again.'

'And then?' said Miss Levering.

'Then? Why, men will fall on their knees before them.' As Miss Levering made no rejoinder, 'What greater victory do women want?' he demanded.

For the first time Miss Levering bent her head forward slightly as though to see how far he was conscious of the fatuity of his climax. But his flushed face showed a childlike good faith.

'Eh? Will any one tell me what they *want?*'

'Since you need to ask,' said the gently smiling woman in the corner, 'perhaps there's more need to show than I'd quite realized.'

'I don't think you quite followed,' he began, with an air of forbearance. 'What I mean is ——'

Miss Levering jumped up. 'Lord Borrodaile!' He was standing at the little iron gate waiting for his hostess, who had stopped to speak to one of the gardeners. 'Wait a moment!' Vida called, and went swiftly down the grass path. He had turned and was advancing to meet her. 'No, come away,' she said under her breath, 'come away quickly' — (safe on the other side of the gate) — 'and talk to me! Tell me about old, half-forgotten pictures or about young rose trees.'

'Is something the matter?'

'I'm ruffled.'

'Who has ruffled you?' His tone was as serene as it was sympathetic.

'Several people.'

'Why, I thought you were never ruffled.'

'I'm not, often.'

They turned down into a little green aisle between two dense thickets of rhododendrons.

'It's lucky you are here,' she said irrelevantly.

He glanced at her face.

'It's not luck. It's foresight.'

'Oh, you arranged it? Well, I'm glad.'

'So am I,' he answered quietly. 'We get on rather well together,' he added, after a moment.

She nodded half absently. 'I feel as if I'd known you for years instead of for months,' she said.

'Yes, I have rather that feeling, too. Except that I'm always a little nervous when I meet you again after an interval.'

'Nervous,' she frowned. 'Why nervous?'

'I'm always afraid you'll have some news for me.'

'What news?'

'Oh, the usual thing. That a pleasant friendship is going to be interrupted if not broken by some one's carrying you off. It would be a pity, you know.'

'Then you don't agree with Lord John.'

'Oh, I suppose you *ought* to marry,' he said, with smiling impatience, 'and I'm very sure you will! But I shan't like it' — he wound up with an odd little laugh —'and neither will you.'

'It's an experiment I shall never try.'

He smiled, but as he glanced at her he grew grave. 'I've heard more than one young woman say that, but you look as if it might really be so.'

'It is so.'

He waited, and then, switching at the wild hyacinths with his stick —

'Of course,' he said, 'I have no right to suppose you are going to give me your reasons.'

'No. That's why I shall never even consider marrying — so that I shall not have to set out my reasons.'

He had never seen that look in her face before. He made an effort to put aside the trouble of it, saying almost lightly —

'I often wonder why people can't be happy as they are!'

'They think of the future, I suppose.'

'There's no such thing as the future.'

'You can't say there's no such thing as growth. If it's only a garden, it's natural to like to see life unfolding — that's the future.'

'Yes, in spite of resolutions, you'll be trying the great experiment.' He said it wearily.

'Why should you mind so?' she asked curiously; 'you are not in love with me.'

'How do you know?'

'Because you give me such a sense of rest.'

'Thank you.' He caught himself up. 'Or perhaps I should thank my grey hair.'

'Grey hair doesn't bring the thing I mean. I've sometimes wished it did. But our friendship is an uncommonly peaceful one, don't you think?'

'Yes; I think it is,' he said. 'All the same, you know there's a touch of magic in it.' But, as though to condone the confession, 'You haven't told me why you were ruffled.'

'It's nothing. I dare say I was a little tired.'

They had come out into the park. 'I hurried so to catch the train. My sister's new coachman is stupid about finding short cuts in London, and we got blocked by a procession — a horrible sort of demonstration, you know.'

'Oh, the unemployed.'

'Yes. And I got so tired of leaning out of the window and shouting directions that I left the maid and the luggage to come later. I got out of the brougham and ran through a slum, or I'd have lost my train. I nearly lost it anyway, because I saw a queer picture that made me stop.' She stopped again at the mere memory of it.

'In a second-hand shop?'

He turned his pointed face to her, and the grey-green eyes wore a gleam of interest that few things could arouse in their cool depths.

'No, not in a shop.' She stopped and leaned against a tree. 'In the street. It was a middle-aged workman. When I caught sight of his back and saw his worn clothes — the coat went up in the middle, and had that despairing sag on both sides — it crossed my mind, here's another of those miserable, unemployed wastrels obstructing my way! Then he looked round and I saw — solid content in his face!' She stopped a moment.

'So he *wasn't* one of the ——'

'Well, I wondered. I couldn't see at first what it was he had looked round at. Then I noticed he had a rope in his hand, and was dragging something. As the people who had been between us hurried on I saw — I saw a child, two or three years old, in a flapping, pink sun-bonnet. He was sitting astride a toy horse. The horse was clumsily made, and had lost its tail. But it had its head still, and the board it was mounted on had fat, wooden rollers. The horse was only about that long, and so near the ground that, for all his advantage in the matter of rollers, still the little rider's feet touched the pavement. They even trailed and lurched, as the horse went on, in that funny, spasmodic gait. The child had to half walk, or, rather, make the motions — you know, without actually bearing any of even his own weight. The slack-shouldered man did it all. I crossed to the other side of the street, and stood and watched them till, as I say, I nearly lost my train. The dingy workman, smoking imperturbably, dragging the grotesque, almost hidden, horse — the delighted child in the flapping sun-bonnet — the crisis when they came to the crossing! The man turned and called out something. The child declined to budge. I wondered what would happen. So did the man. He waited a moment, and puffed smoke and considered. The baby dug his heels in the pavement and shouted. Then I saw the man carefully tilt the toy horse up by the rope. I stood and watched the successful surmounting of the obstacle, and the triumphant progress as before — sun-bonnet flapping, smoke curling. Of course the man was content! He had lost the battle. You saw that in his lined face. What did it matter? *He held the future by a string.*'

Lord Borrodaile lifted his eyes and looked at her. Without a word the two walked on.

The first to speak after the silence was the man. He pointed out a curious effect of the light, and reminded her who had painted it best —

'Corot could do these things!' — and he flung a stone in passing at the New Impressionists.

At the Lodge Gate they found Lady John with Filey and Hermione.

'We thought if we walked this way we might meet Jean and her bodyguard. But I mustn't go any further.' Lady John consulted her watch. 'The rest of you can take your time, but I have to go and receive my other guest.'

Filey and Hermione were still at the gate. The girl had caught sight of Farnborough being driven by the park road to the station.

'Oh, I do believe it's the new mare they're trying in the dogcart,' said Hermione. 'Let's wait and see her go by.'

Borrodaile and his companion kept at Lady John's side.

'I'm glad,' said Vida, 'that I shall at last make acquaintance with your Jean.'

'Yes; it's odd your never having met, especially as she knows your cousins at Bishopsmead so well.'

'I've been so little in England ——'

'Yes, I know. A great business it is,' Lady John explained to Lord Borrodaile, 'each time to get that crusty old Covenanter, Jean's grandfather, to allow her to stay at Bishopsmead. So it's the sadder for them to have her visit cut short.'

'Why is it cut short?' he asked.

'Because the hostess took to her bed yesterday with a chill, and her temperature was a hundred and one this afternoon.'

'Really?' said Miss Levering. 'I hadn't heard ——'

'She is rather bad, I'm afraid. We are taking over another of her guests. Of course you know him — Geoffrey Stonor.'

'Taking him over?' Miss Levering repeated.

'Yes; he was originally going to Bishopsmead this week-end, but as he's been promising for ages to come here, it's been arranged that we should take him off their hands. Of course we're delighted.'

Miss Levering walked on, between her two companions, looking straight in front of her. As Lady John, with a glance at her watch, quickened the pace —

'I'm rather unhappy at what you tell me about my cousin,' said Vida. 'She's a delicate creature.' Then, as though acting on a sudden impulse, Vida paused. 'You mustn't mind, Lady John, but I shall have to go to her. Can I have a trap of some sort to take me over?'

She put aside the objections with a gentle but unmistakable decision that made Lady John say —

'I'm sure I've alarmed you more than there was the least need for. But the carriage shall wait and bring you back just as soon as you've satisfied yourself.'

'I can't tell, of course, till I've seen Mary. But may my maid be told not to unpack ——'

'Not unpack!'

'In case I have to send for my things.'

'My *dear!*' Lady John stopped short for very vexation. '*Don't* desert us! I've been so congratulating myself on having you, since I knew Geoffrey Stonor was coming.' Again she glanced nervously at her watch. 'He is due in ten minutes! John won't like it if I'm not there.'

As she was about to hurry on, the other slackened pace. She seemed to be revolving some further plan.

'Why shouldn't' — she turned suddenly — 'why shouldn't the dogcart take me on after dropping Mr. Farnborough at the station? Yes, that will be simplest. Mr. Farnborough!' she waved to him as the cart came in sight, 'Wait! Good-bye! Forgive my rushing off, won't you?' she called back over her shoulder, and then with that swift, light step of hers, she covered by a short cut the little distance that lay between her and the lodge gate.

'I wish I'd held my tongue,' said Lady John almost angrily as she hastened in the opposite direction. Already some sense seemed to reach her of the hopelessness of expecting Vida's return. 'I didn't *dream* she cared so much for that dull cousin of hers!'

'Do you think she really does?' said Borrodaile, dryly.

CHAPTER VII

About Vida's little enterprise on a certain Sunday a few weeks later was an air of elaborate mystery. Yet the expedition was no further than to Trafalgar Square. It was there that those women, the so-called 'Suffragettes,' in the intervals of making worse public disturbances, were rumoured to be holding open-air meetings — a circumstance distinctly fortunate for any one who wanted to 'see what they were like,' and who was yet unwilling to commit herself by doing anything so eccentric as publicly to seek admission under any roof known to show hospitality to 'such goings on.' In those days, only a year ago, and yet already such ancient history that the earlier pages are forgotten and scarce credible if recalled, it took courage to walk past the knots of facetious loafers, and the unblushing Suffragette poster, into the hall where the meetings were held. Deliberately to sit down among odd, misguided persons in rows, to listen to, and by so much to lend public countenance to 'women of that sort' — the sort that not only wanted to vote (quaint creatures!), but were not content with merely wanting to — for the average conventional woman to venture upon a step so compromising, to risk seeming for a moment to take these crazy brawlers seriously, was to lay herself open to 'the comic laugh' — most dreaded of all the weapons in the social armoury. But it was something wholly different to set out for a Sunday Afternoon Concert, or upon some normal and recognized philanthropic errand, and on the way find one's self arrested for a few minutes by seeing a crowd gathered in a public square. Yet it had not been easy to screw Mrs. Fox-Moore up to thinking even this non-committal measure a possible one to pursue. 'What would anybody think,' she had asked Vida, 'to see them lending even the casual support of a presence (however ironic) to so reprehensible a spectacle!' Had it not been for very faith in the eccentricity of the proceeding — one wildly unlikely to be adopted, Mrs. Fox-Moore felt, by any one else of 'their kind' — she would never have consented to be drawn into Vida's absurd project.

Of course it was absolutely essential to disguise the object of the outing from Mr. Fox-Moore. Not merely because with the full weight of his authority he would most assuredly have forbidden it, but because of a nervous prefiguring on his wife's part of the particular things he would say, and the particular way he would look in setting his extinguisher on the enterprise.

Vida, from the first, had never explained or excused herself to him, so that when he asked at luncheon what she was going to do with this fine Sunday afternoon, she had simply smiled, and said, 'Oh, I have a tryst to keep.'

It was her sister who added anxiously, 'Is Wood leading now at the Queen's Hall Concerts?' And so, without actually committing herself to a lie, gave the impression that music was to be their quest.

An hour later, while the old man was nursing his gout by the library window, he saw the ladies getting into a hansom. In spite of the inconvenience to his afflicted member he got up and opened the window.

'Don't tell me you're doing anything so rational — you two — as going to a concert.'

'Why do you say that? You know I never like to take the horses out on Sunday ——'

'Rubbish! You think a dashing, irresponsible hansom is more in keeping with the Factory Girls' Club or some giddy Whitechapel frivolity!'

Mrs. Fox-Moore gave her sister a look of miserable apprehension; but the younger woman laughed and waved a hand. She knew that, even more than the hansom, their 'get up' had given them away. It must be confessed she had felt quite as strongly as her sister that it wouldn't do to be recognized at a Suffragette meeting. Even as a nameless 'fine lady' standing out from a mob of the dowdy and the dirty, to be stared at by eyes however undiscerning, under circumstances so questionable, would be distinctly distasteful.

So, reversing the order of Nature, the butterfly had retired into a 'grubby' state. In other words, Vida had put on the plainest of her discarded mourning-gowns. From a small Tuscan straw travelling-toque, the new maid, greatly wondering at such instructions, had extracted an old paste buckle and some violets, leaving it 'not fit to be seen.' In spite of having herself taken these precautions, Vida had broken into uncontrollable smiles at the apparition of Mrs. Fox-Moore, asking with pride —

'Will I do? I look quite like a Woman of the People, don't I?'

The unconscious humour of the manifestation filled Miss Levering with an uneasy merriment every time she turned her eyes that way.

Little as Mr. Fox-Moore thought of his wife's taste, either in clothes or in amusements, he would have been more mystified than ever he had been in his life had he seen her hansom, ten minutes later, stop on the north side of Trafalgar Square, opposite the National Gallery.

'Look out and see,' she said, retiring guiltily into the corner of the conveyance. 'Are they there?' And it was plain that nothing could more have relieved Mrs. Fox-Moore at that moment than to hear 'they' were not.

But Vida, glancing discreetly out of the side window, had said —

'There? I should think they are — and a crowd round them already. Look at their banners!' and she laughed as she leaned out and read the legend, 'We demand VOTES FOR WOMEN' inscribed in black letters on the white ground of two pieces of sheeting stretched each between a pair of upright poles, standing one on either side of the plinth of Nelson's column. In the very middle, and similarly supported, was a banner of blood red. Upon this one, in great white letters, appeared the legend —

'EFFINGHAM, THE ENEMY
OF
WOMEN AND THE WORKERS.'

As Vida read it out —

'*What!*' ejaculated her sister. 'They haven't really got that on a banner!' And so intrigued was she that, like some shy creature dwelling in a shell, cautiously she protruded her head out of the shiny, black sheath of the hansom.

But as she did so she met the innocent eye of a passer-by, tired of craning his neck to look back at the meeting. With precipitation Mrs. Fox-Moore withdrew into the innermost recesses of the black shell.

'Come, Janet,' said Vida, who had meanwhile jumped out and settled the fare.

'Did that man know us?' asked the other, lifting up the flap from the back window of the hansom and peering out.

'No, I don't think so.'

'He stared, Vida. He certainly stared very hard.'

Still she hesitated, clinging to the friendly shelter of the hansom.

'Oh, come on! He only stared because —— He took you for a Suffragette!' But the indiscretion lit so angry a light in the lady's eye, that Vida was fain to add, 'No, no, do come — and I'll tell you what he was really looking at.'

'What?' said Mrs. Fox-Moore, putting out her head again.

'He was struck,' said Vida, biting her lip to repress smiles, 'by the hat of the Woman of the People.'

But the lady was too entirely satisfied with her hat to mind Vida's poking fun at it.

'"Effingham, the Enemy!"' Mrs. Fox-Moore read for herself as they approached the flaunting red banner. 'How perfectly outrageous!'

'How perfectly *silly!*' amended the other, 'when one thinks of that kind and charming Pillar of Excellence!'

'I told you they were mad as well as bad.'

'I know; and now we're going to watch them prove it. Come on.'

'Why, they've stopped the fountains!' Mrs. Fox-Moore spoke as though detecting an additional proof of turpitude. 'Those two policemen,' she went on, in a whisper, 'why are they looking at *us* like that?'

Vida glanced at the men. Their eyes were certainly fixed on the two ladies in a curious, direct fashion, not exactly impudent, but still in a way no policeman had ever looked at either of them before. A coolly watchful, slightly contemptuous stare, interrupted by one man turning to say something to the other, at which both grinned. Vida was conscious of wishing that she had come in her usual clothes — above all, that Janet had not raked out that 'jumble sale' object she had perched on her head.

The wearer of the incriminatory hat, acting upon some quite unanalyzed instinct to range herself unmistakably on the side of law and order, paused as they were passing the two policemen and addressed them with dignity.

'Is it safe to stop and listen for a few minutes to these people?'

The men looked at Mrs. Fox-Moore with obvious suspicion.

'I cawn't say,' said the one nearest.

'Do you expect any trouble?' she demanded.

There was a silence, and then the other policeman said with a decidedly snubby air —

'It ain't our business to go *lookin'* fur trouble;' and he turned his eyes away.

'Of course not,' said Vida, pleasantly, coming to her sister's rescue. 'All this lady wants to be assured of is that there are enough of you present to make it safe ——'

'If ladies wants to be safe,' said number one, 'they'd better stop in their 'omes.'

'That's the first rude policeman I ever ——' began Mrs. Fox-Moore, as they went on.

'Well, you know he's only echoing what we all say.'

Vida was looking over the crowd to where on the plinth of the historic column the little group of women and a solitary man stood out against the background of the banners. Here they were — these new Furies that pursued the agreeable men one sat by at dinner — men who, it was well known, devoted their lives — when they weren't dining — to the welfare of England. But were these frail, rather depressed-looking women — were they indeed the ones, outrageously daring, who broke up meetings and bashed in policemen's helmets? Nothing very daring in their aspect to-day — a little weary and preoccupied they looked, as they stood up there in twos and threes, talking to one another in that exposed position of theirs, while from time to time about their ears like spent bullets flew the spasmodic laughter and rude comment of the crowd — strangely unconscious, those 'blatant sensation-mongers,' of the thousand eyes and the sea of upturned faces!

'Not *quite* what I expected!' said Mrs. Fox-Moore, with an unmistakable accent of disappointment. It was plainly her meaning that to a general reprehensibleness, dulness was now superadded.

'Perhaps these are not the ones,' said Vida, catching at hope.

Mrs. Fox-Moore took heart. 'Suppose we find out,' she suggested.

They had penetrated the fringe of a gathering composed largely of weedy youths and wastrel old men. A few there were who looked like decent artizans, but more who bore the unmistakable aspect of the beery out-of-work. Among the strangely few women, were two or three girls of the domestic servant or Strand Restaurant cashier class — wearers of the cheap lace blouse and the wax bead necklace.

Mrs. Fox-Moore, forgetting some of her reluctance now that she was on the spot, valiantly followed Vida as the younger woman threaded her way among the constantly increasing crowd. Just in front of where the two came to a final standstill was a quiet-looking old man with a lot of unsold Sunday papers under one arm and wearing like an apron the bill of the *Sunday Times*. Many of the boys and young men were smoking cigarettes. Some of the older men had pipes. Mrs. Fox-Moore commented on the inferior taste in tobacco as shown by the lower orders. But she, too, kept her eyes glued to the figures up there on the plinth.

'They've had to get men to hold up their banners for them,' laughed Vida, as though she saw a symbolism in the fact, further convicting these women of folly.

'But there's a well-dressed man — that one who isn't holding up anything that I can see — what on earth is *he* doing there?'

'Perhaps he'll be upholding something later.'

'Going to speak, you mean?'

'It may be a debate. Perhaps he's going to present the other side.'

'Well, if he does, I hope he'll tell them plainly what he thinks of them.'

She said it quite distinctly for the benefit of the people round her. Both ladies were still obviously self-conscious, occupied with the need to look completely detached, to advertise: '*I'm* not one of them! Never think it!' But it was gradually being borne in upon them that they need take no further trouble in this connection. Nobody in the crowd noticed any one except 'those ordinary looking persons,' as Mrs. Fox-Moore complainingly called them, up there on the plinth — 'quite like what one sees on the tops of omnibuses!' Certainly it was an exercise in incongruity to compare these quiet, rather depressed looking people with the vision conjured up by Lord John's 'raving lunatics,' 'worthy of the straight jacket,' or Paul Filey's 'sexless monstrosities.'

'It's rather like a jest that promised very well at the beginning, only the teller has forgotten the point. Or else,' Vida added, looking at the face of one of the women up there — 'or else the mistake was in thinking it a jest at all!' She turned away impatiently and devoted her attention to such scraps of comment as she could overhear in the crowd — or such, rather, as she could understand.

'That one — that's just come — yes, in the blue tam-o'-shanter, that's the one I was tellin' you about,' said a red-haired man, with a cheerful and rubicund face.

'*Looks* like she'd be 'andy with her fists, don't she?' contributed a friend alongside. The boys in front and behind laughed appreciatively.

But the ruddy man said, 'Fists? No. *She's* the one wot carries the dog-whip;' and they all craned forward with redoubled interest. It is sad to be obliged to admit that the two ladies did precisely the same.

While the boys were, in addition, cat-calling and inquiring about the dog-whip —

'That must be the woman the papers have been full of,' Mrs. Fox-Moore whispered, staring at the new-comer with horrified eyes.

'Yes, no doubt.' Vida, too, scrutinized her more narrowly.

The wearer of the 'Tam' was certainly more robust-looking than the others, but even she had the pallor of the worker in the town. She carried her fine head and shoulders badly, like one who has stooped over tasks at an age when she should have been running about the fields. She drew her thick brows together every now and then with an effect of determination that gave her well-chiselled features so dark and forbidding an aspect it was a surprise to see the grace that swept into her face when, at something one of her comrades said, she broke into a smile. Two shabby men on Vida's left were working themselves into a fine state of moral indignation over the laxity of the police in allowing these women to air their vanity in public.

'Comin' here with tam-o'-shanters to tell us 'ow to do our business.'

'It's part o' wot I mean w'en I s'y old England's on the down gryde.'

'W'ich is the one in black — this end?' his companion asked, indicating a refined-looking woman of forty or so. 'Is that Miss ——?'

'Miss,' chipped in a young man of respectable appearance just behind. '*Miss?* Why, that's the mother o' the Gracchi,' and there was a little ripple of laughter.

'Hasn't she got any of her jewels along with her to-day?' said another voice.

'What do they mean?' demanded Mrs. Fox-Moore.

Vida shook her head. She herself was looking about for some one to ask.

'Isn't it queer that you and I have lived all this time in the world and have never yet been in a mixed crowd before in all our lives? — never *as a part of it.*'

'I think myself it's less strange we haven't done it before than that we're doing it now. There's the woman selling things. Let us ask her ——'

They had noticed before a faded-looking personage who had been going about on the fringe of the crowd with a file of propagandist literature on her arm. Vida beckoned to her. She made her way with some difficulty through the chaffing, jostling horde, saying steadily and with a kind of cheerful doggedness —

'Leaflets! Citizenship of Women, by Lothian Scott! Labour Record! Prison Experiences of Miss ——'

'How much?' asked Miss Levering.

'What you like,' she answered.

Miss Levering took her change out in information. 'Can you tell me who the speakers are?'

'Oh, yes.' The haggard face brightened before the task. 'That one is the famous Miss Claxton.'

'With her face screwed up?'

'That's because the sun is in her eyes.'

'She isn't so bad-looking,' admitted Mrs. Fox-Moore.

'No; but just wait till she speaks!' The faded countenance of the woman with the heavy pile of printed propaganda on her arm was so lit with enthusiasm, that it, too, was almost good-looking, in the same way as the younger, more regular face up there, frowning at the people, or the sun, or the memory of wrongs.

'Is Miss Claxton some relation of yours?' asked Mrs. Fox-Moore.

'No, oh, no, I don't even know her. She hasn't been out of prison long. The man in grey — he's Mr. Henry.'

'Out of prison! And Henry's the chairman, I suppose.'

'No; the chairman is the lady in black.' The pamphlet-seller turned away to make change for a new customer.

'Do you mean the mother of the Gracchi?' said Vida, at a venture, and saw how if she herself hadn't understood the joke the lady with the literature did. She laughed good-humouredly.

'Yes; that's Mrs. Chisholm.'

'What!' said a decent-looking but dismal sort of shopman just behind, 'is that the mother of those dreadful young women?'

Neither of the two ladies were sufficiently posted in the nefarious goings on of the 'dreadful' progeny quite to appreciate the by-stander's surprise, but they gazed with renewed interest at the delicate face.

'What can the man mean! She doesn't *look* ——' Mrs. Fox-Moore hesitated.

'No,' Vida helped her out with a laughing whisper; 'I agree she doesn't *look* big enough or bad enough or old enough or bold enough to be the mother of young women renowned for their dreadfulness. But as soon as she opens her mouth no doubt we'll smell the brim-stone. I wish she'd begin her raging. Why are they waiting?'

'It's only five minutes past,' said the lady with the literature. 'I think they're waiting for Mr. Lothian Scott. He's ill. But he'll come!' As though the example of his fidelity to the cause nerved her to more earnest prosecution of her own modest duty, she called out, 'Leaflets! Citizenship of Women, by Lothian Scott!'

'Wot do they give ye,' inquired a half-tipsy tramp, 'fur 'awkin' that rot about?'

She turned away quite unruffled. 'Citizenship of Women, one penny.'

'I hope you *do* get paid for so disagreeable a job — forgive my saying so,' said Vida.

'Paid? Oh, no!' she said cheerfully. 'I'm too hard at work all week to help much. And I can't speak, so I do this. Leaflets! Citizenship ——'

'Is that pinched-looking creature at the end,' — Mrs. Fox-Moore detained the pamphlet-seller to point out a painfully thin, eager little figure sitting on the ledge of the plinth and looking down with anxious eyes at the crowd — 'is that one of them?'

'Oh, yes. I thought everybody knew *her*. That's Miss Mary O'Brian.'

She spoke the name with an accent of such protecting tenderness that Vida asked —

'And who is Miss Mary O'Brian?' But the pamphlet-seller had descried a possible customer, and was gone.

'Mary O'Brian,' said a blear-eyed old man, 'is the one that's just come out o' quod.'

'Oh, thank you.' Then to her sister Vida whispered, 'What is quod?'

But Mrs. Fox-Moore could only shake her head. Even when they heard the words these strange fellow-citizens used, meaning often failed to accompany sound.

'Oh, is *that* Mary?' A rollicking young rough, with his hat on the extreme back of his head, began to sing, 'Molly Darling.'

''Ow'd yer like the skilly?' another shouted up at the girl.

'Skilly?' whispered Mrs. Fox-Moore.

Vida in turn shook her head. It wasn't in the dictionary of any language she knew. But it seemed in some way to involve dishonour, for the chairman, who had been consulting with the man in grey, turned suddenly and faced the crowd. Her eyes were shining with the light of battle, but what she said in a peculiarly pleasant voice was —

'Miss O'Brian has come here for the express purpose of telling you how she liked it.'

'Oh, she's going to tell us all about it. 'Ow *nice!*' But they let the thin little slip of a girl alone after that.

It was a new-comer, a few moments later who called out from the fringe of the crowd —

'I say, Mary, w'en yer get yer rights will y' be a perliceman?' Even the tall, grave guardians of the peace ranged about the monument, even they smiled at the suggested image.

After all, it might not be so uninteresting to listen to these people for a few minutes. It wasn't often that life presented such an opportunity. It probably would never occur again. These women on the plinth must be not alone of a different world, but of a different clay, since they not only did not shrink from disgracing themselves

—women had been capable of that before—but these didn't even mind ridicule. Which was new.

Just then the mother of the Gracchi came to the edge of the plinth to open the meeting.

'Friends!' she began. The crowd hooted that proposition to start with. But the pale woman with the candid eyes went on as calmly as though she had been received with polite applause, telling the jeering crowd several things they certainly had not known before, that, among other matters, they were met there to pass a censure on the Government——

'Haw! haw!'

''Ear, 'ear!' said the deaf old newsvendor, with his free hand up to his ear.

'And to express our sympathy with the brave women——'

The staccato cries throughout the audience dissolved into one general hoot; but above it sounded the old newsvendor's ''Ear, 'ear!'

''E can't 'ear without 'e shouts about it.'

'Try and keep *yerself* quiet,' said he, with dignity. 'We ain't 'ere to 'ear *you*.'

'——sympathy with the brave women,' the steady voice went on, 'who are still in prison.'

'Serve 'em jolly well right!'

'Give the speaker a chaunce, caun't ye?' said the newsvendor, with a withering look.

It was plain this old gentleman was an unblushing adherent to the cause (undismayed by being apparently the only one in that vicinity), ready to cheer the chairman at every juncture, and equally ready to administer caustic reproof to her opponents.

'Our friends who are in prison, are there simply for trying to bring before a member of the Government——'

'Good old Effingham. Three cheers for Effingham!'

'Oh, yes,' said the newsvendor, 'go on! 'E needs a little cheerin', awfter the mess 'e's made o' things!'

'For trying to put before a member of the Government a statement of the injustice——'

'*That* ain't why they're in gaol. It's fur ringin' wot's-'is-name's door-bell.'

'Kickin' up rows in the street——'

'Oh, you shut up,' says the old champion, out of patience. 'You've 'ad 'arf a pint too much.'

Everybody in the vicinity was obliged to turn and look at the youth to see what proportion of the charge was humour and how much was fact. The youth resented so deeply the turn the conversation had taken that he fell back for a moment on bitter silence.

'When you go to call on some one,' the chairman was continuing, with the patient air of one instructing a class in a kindergarten, 'it is the custom to ring the bell. What do you suppose a door-bell is for? Do you think our deputation should have tried to get in without ringing at the door?'

'They 'adn't no business goin' to 'is private 'ouse.'

'Oh, look 'ere, just take that extry 'arf pint outside the meetin' and cool off, will yer?'

It was the last time that particular opponent aired his views. The old man's judicious harping on the ''arf pint' induced the ardent youth to moderate his political transports. They were not rightly valued, it appeared. After a few more mutterings he took his 'extry 'alf pint' into some more congenial society. But there were several others in the crowd who had come similarly fortified, and they were everywhere the most audible opponents. But above argument, denial, abuse, steadily in that upper air the clear voice kept on —

'Do you think they *wanted* to go to his house? Haven't you heard that they didn't do that until they had exhausted every other means to get a hearing?'

To the shower of denial and objurgation that greeted this, she said with uplifted hand —

'Stop! Let me tell you about it.'

The action had in it so much of authority that (as it seemed, to their own surprise) the interrupters, with mouths still open, suspended operations for a moment.

'Why, this is a woman of education! What on earth is a person like that doing in this *galère?*' Vida asked, as if Mrs. Fox-Moore might be able to enlighten her. 'Can't she see — even if there were anything in the "Cause," as she calls it — what an imbecile waste of time it is talking to these louts?'

'There's a good many voters here,' said a tall, gloomy-looking individual, wearing a muffler in lieu of a collar. 'She's politician enough to know that.'

Mrs. Fox-Moore looked through the man. 'The only reassuring thing I see in the situation,' she said to her sister, 'is that they don't find many women to come and listen to their nonsense.'

'Well, they've got you and me! Awful thought! Suppose they converted us!'

Mrs. Fox-Moore didn't even trouble to reply to such levity. What was interesting was the discovery that this 'chairman,' before an audience so unpromising, not only held her own when she was interrupted and harassed by the crowd — even more surprising she bore with the most recalcitrant members of it — tried to win them over, and yet when they were rude, did not withhold reproof, and at times looked down upon them with so fine a scorn that it seemed as if even those ruffianly young men felt the edge of it. Certainly a curious sight — this well-bred woman standing there in front of the soaring column, talking with grave passion to those loafers about the 'Great Woman Question,' and they treating it as a Sunday afternoon street entertainment.

The next speaker was a working woman, the significance of whose appearance in that place and in that company was so little apprehended by the two ladies in the crowd that they agreed in laughingly commiserating the chairman for not having more of her own kind to back her up in her absurd contention. Though the second speaker merely bored the two who, having no key either to her pathos or her power, saw nothing but 'low cockney effrontery' in her effort, she nevertheless had a distinct success with the crowd. Here was somebody speaking their own language — they paid her the tribute of their loudest hoots mixed with applause. She never lost her hold on them until the appearance on the plinth of a grave, rugged, middle-aged man in a soft hat.

'That's 'im!'

'Yes. Lothian Scott!'

Small need for the chairwoman to introduce the grey man with the northern burr in his speech, and the northern turn for the uncompromising in opinion. Every soul there save the two 'educated' ladies knew this was the man who had done more to make the Labour Party a political force to be reckoned with than any other creature in the three kingdoms. Whether he was conscious of having friends in a gathering largely Tory (as lower-class crowds still are), certainly he did not spare his enemies.

During the first few minutes of a speech full of Socialism, Mrs. Fox-Moore (stirred to unheard-of expressiveness) kept up a low, running comment —

'Oh, of *course!* He says that to curry favour with the mob — a rank demagogue, this man! Such pandering to the populace!' Then, turning sharply to her companion, '*He wants votes!*' she said, as though detecting in him a taste unknown among the men in her purer circle. 'Oh, no doubt he makes a very good thing out of it! Going about filling the people's heads with revolutionary ideas! Monstrous wickedness, *I* call it, stirring up class against class! I begin to wonder what the police are thinking about.' She looked round uneasily.

The excitement had certainly increased as the little grey politician denounced the witlessness of the working-class, and when they howled at him, went on to expound a trenchant doctrine of universal Responsibility, which preceded the universal Suffrage that was to come. Much of what he said was drowned in uproar. It had become clear that his opinions revolted the majority of his hearers even more than they did the two ladies. So outraged were the sensibilities of the hooligan and the half-drunk that they drowned as much of the speech as they were able in cat-calls and jeers. But enough still penetrated to ears polite not only to horrify, but to astonish them — such force has the spoken word above even its exaggeration in cold print.

The ladies had read — sparingly, it is true — that these things were said, but to *hear* them!

'He doesn't, after all, seem to be saying what the mob wants to hear,' said the younger woman.

'No; mercifully the heart of the country is still sound!'

But for one of these two out of the orderlier world, the opposition that the 'rank demagogue' roused in the mob was to light a lamp whereby she read wondering the signs of an unsuspected bond between Janet Fox-Moore and the reeking throng.

When, contrary to the old-established custom of the demagogue, the little politician in homespun had confided to the men in front of him what he thought of them, he told them that the Woman's Movement which they held themselves so clever for ridiculing, was in much the same position to-day as the Extension of Suffrage for men was in '67. Had it not been for demonstrations (beside which the action that had lodged the women in gaol was innocent child's play), neither he, the speaker, nor any of the men in front of him would have the right to vote to-day.

'You ridicule and denounce these women for trying peacefully — yes, I say *peacefully* — to get their rights as citizens. Do you know what our fathers did to get ours? They broke down Hyde Park railings, they burnt the Bristol Municipal Buildings, they led riots, and they shed blood. These women have hurt nobody.'

'What about the policeman?'

He went on steadily, comparing the moderation of the women with the red-hot violence of their Chartist forbears — till one half-drunken listener, having lost the thread, hiccuped out —

'Can't do nothin' — them women. Even after we've showed 'em *'ow!*'

'Has he got his history right?' Vida asked through her smiling at the last sally. 'Not that it applies, of course,' she was in haste to add.

'Oh, what does it matter?' Her sister waved it aside. 'An unscrupulous politician hasn't come here to bother about little things like facts.'

'I don't think I altogether agree with you *there*. That man may be a fanatic, but he's honest, I should say. Those Scotch peasants, you know ——'

'Oh, because he's rude, and talks with a burr, you think he's a sort of political Thomas Carlyle?'

Though Vida smiled at the charge, something in her alert air as she followed the brief recapitulation of the Chartist story showed how an appeal to justice, or even to pity, may fail, where the rousing of some dim sense of historical significance (which is more than two-thirds fear), may arrest and even stir to unsuspected deeps. The grave Scotsman's striking that chord even in a mind as innocent as Vida's, of accurate or ordered knowledge of the past, even here the chord could vibrate to a strange new sense of possible significance in this scene '—— after all.' It would be queer, it would be horrible, it was fortunately incredible, but what if, 'after all,' she were ignorantly assisting at a scene that was to play its part in the greatest revolution the world had seen? Some such mental playing with possibilities seemed to lurk behind the intent reflective face.

'There are far too many voters already,' her sister had flung out.

'Yes — yes, a much uglier world they want to make!'

But in the power to make history — if these people indeed had that, then indeed might they be worth watching — even if it were only after one good look to hide the eyes in dismay. That possibility of historic signifi nce had suddenly lifted the sordid exhibition to a different plane.

As the man, amid howls, ended his almost indistinguishable peroration, the unmoved chairman stepped forward again to try to win back for the next speaker that modicum of quiet attention which he, at all events, had the art of gaining and of keeping. As she came forward this time one of her auditors looked at the Woman Leader in the Crusade with new eyes — not with sympathy, rather with a vague alarm. Vida Levering's air of almost strained attention was an unconscious public confession: 'I haven't understood these strange women; I haven't understood the spirit of the mob that hoots the man we know vaguely for their champion; I haven't understood the allusions nor the argot that they talk; I can't check the history that peasant has appealed to. In the midst of so much that is obscure, it is meet to reserve judgment.' Something of that might have been read in the look lifted once or twice as though in wonderment, above the haggard group up there between the guardian lions, beyond even the last reach of the tall monument, to the cloudless sky of June. Was the great shaft itself playing a part in the impression? Was it there not at all for memory of some battle long ago, but just to mark on the fair bright page of afternoon a huge surprise? What lesser accent than just this Titanic exclamation point could fitly punctuate the record of so strange a portent! — women confronting the populace of the mightiest city in the world — pleading in her most public place their right to a voice in her affairs.

In the face of this unexpected mood of receptivity, however unwilling, came a sharp corrective in the person of the next speaker.

'Oh, it's not going to be one that's been to prison!'

'Oh, dear! It's the one with the wild black hair and the awful "picture hat"!' But they stared for a few moments as if, in despite of themselves, fascinated by this lady be-feathered, be-crimped, and be-ringed, wearing her huge hat cocked over one ear with a defiant coquetry above a would-be conquering smile. The unerring wits in the crowd had already picked her out for special attention, but her active 'public form' was even more torturing to the fastidious feminine sense than her 'stylish' appearance. For her language, flowery and grandiloquent, was excruciatingly genteel, one moment conveyed by minced words through a pursed mouth, and the next carried away on a turgid tide of rhetoric — the swimmer in this sea of sentiment flinging out braceleted arms, and bawling appeals to the '*Wim—men—nof—Vinglund!*' The crowd howled with derisive joy.

All the same, when they saw she had staying power, and a kind of Transpontine sense of drama in her, the populace mocked less and applauded more. Why not? She was very much like an overblown Adelphi heroine, and they could see her act for nothing. But every time she apostrophized the '*Wim—men—nof—Vinglund!*' two of those same gave way to overcharged feelings.

'Oh, my dear, I can't stand this! I'm going home!'

'Yes, yes. Let's get away from this terrible female. I suppose they keep back the best speakers for the last.'

The two ladies turned, and began to edge their way out of the tightly packed mass of humanity.

'It's rather a pity, too,' said Mrs. Fox-Moore, looking back, 'for this is the only chance we'll ever have. I did want to hear what the skilly was.'

'Yes, and about the dog-whip.'

'Skilly! Sounds as if it might be what she hit the policeman with.' Mrs. Fox-Moore was again pausing to look back. 'That gyrating female is more what I expected them *all* to be.'

'Yes; but just listen to that.'

'To what?'

'Why, the way they're applauding her.'

'Yes, they positively revel in the creature!'

It was a long, tiresome business this worming their way out. They paused again and again two or three times, looking back at the scene with a recurrent curiosity, and each time repelled by the platform graces of the lady who was so obviously enjoying herself to the top of her bent. Yet even after the fleeing twain arrived on the fringe of the greatly augmented crowd, something even then prevented their instantly making the most of their escape. They stood criticizing and denouncing.

Again Mrs. Fox-Moore said it was a pity, since they were there, that they should have to go without hearing one of those who had been in prison, 'For we'll never have another chance.'

'Perhaps,' said her sister, looking back at the gesticulating figure — 'perhaps we're being a little unreasonable. We were annoyed at first because they weren't what we expected, and when we get what we came to see, we run away.'

While still they lingered, with a final fling of arms and toss of plumes, the champion of the women of England sat down in the midst of applause.

'You hear? It's all very well. Most of them simply loved it.'

And now the chairman, in a strikingly different style, was preparing the way for the next speaker, at mention of whom the crowd seemed to feel they'd been neglecting their prerogative of hissing.

'What name did she say? Why do they make that noise?'

The two ladies began to worm their way back; but this was a different matter from coming out.

'Wot yer doin'?' some one inquired sternly of Mrs. Fox-Moore.

Another turned sharply, 'Look out! Oo yer pushin', old girl?'

The horrid low creatures seemed to have no sense of deference. And the stuff they smoked!

'Pah!' observed Mrs. Fox-Moore, getting the full benefit of a noxious puff. '*Pah!*'

'*Wot!*' said the smoker, turning angrily. 'Pah to you, miss!' He eyed Mrs. Fox-Moore from head to foot with a withering scorn. 'Comin' 'ere awskin' us fur votes' (Vida nearly fainted), 'and ain't able to stand a little tobacco.'

'Stand in front, Janet,' said Miss Levering, hastily recovering herself. '*I* don't mind smoke,' she said mendaciously, trying to appease the defiler of the air with a little smile. Indeed, the idea of Mrs. Fox-Moore having come to 'awsk' this person for a vote was sufficiently quaint.

'This is the sort of thing they mean, I suppose,' said that lady, 'when they talk about cockney humour. It doesn't appeal to me.'

Vida bit her lip. Her own taste was less pure. 'We needn't try to get any nearer,' she said hastily. 'This chairman-person can make herself heard without screeching.'

But having lost the key during the passage over the pipe, they could only make out that she was justifying some one to the mob, some one who apparently was coming in for too much sharp criticism for the chairman to fling her to the wolves without first diverting them a little. The battle of words that ensued was almost entirely unintelligible to the two ladies, but they gathered, through means more expressive than speech, that the chairman was dealing with some sort of crisis in the temper of the meeting, brought about by the mention of a name.

The only thing clear was that she was neither going to give in, nor going to turn over the meeting in a state of ferment to some less practised hand.

'Yes, she did! She had a perfect right,' the chairman maintained against a storm of noes — 'more than a right, *a duty*, to perform in going with that deputation on public business to the house of a public servant, since, unlike the late Prime Minister, he had refused to women all opportunity to treat with him through the usual channels always open to citizens having a political grievance.'

'Citizens? Suffragettes!'

'Very well.' She set her mouth. 'Suffragettes if you like. To get an abuse listened to is the first thing; to get it understood is the next. Rather than not have our cause stand out clear and unmistakable before a preoccupied, careless world, we accept the clumsy label; we wear it proudly. And it won't be the first time in history that a name given in derision has become a badge of honour!'

Why, the woman's eyes were suffused! — a flush had mounted up to her hair!

How she cared!

'Yer ain't told us the reason ye *want* the vote.'

'Reason? Why, she's a woman!'

'Haw! haw!'

The speaker had never paused an instant, but it began to be clear that she heard any interruption it suited her to hear.

'Some one asking, at this time of day, why women want the vote? Why, for exactly the same reason that you men do. Because, not having any voice in public affairs, our interests are neglected; and since woman's interests are man's, all humanity suffers. We want the vote, because taxation without representation is tyranny; because the laws as they stand bear hardly on women; and because those unfair, man-made laws will never be altered till women have a share in electing the men who control legislation.'

'Yer ought ter leave politics to us ——'

'We can't leave politics to the men, because politics have come into the home, and if the higher interests of the home are to be served, women must come into politics.'

'That's a bad argument!'

'Wot I always say is ——'

'Can't change nature. Nature says ——'

'Let 'er st'y at 'ome and mind 'er business!'

The interjections seemed to come all at once. The woman bent over the crowd. Nothing misty in her eyes now — rather a keener light than before.

'Don't you see,' she appealed to them as equals — 'don't you see that in your improvement of the world you men have taken women's business out of her home? In the old days there was work and responsibility enough for woman without going outside her own gate. The women were the bakers and brewers, the soap and candle-makers, the loom-workers of the world. You men,' she said, delicately flattering them, '*you* have changed all that. You have built great factories and warehouses and mills. But how do you keep them going? By calling women to come in their thousands and help you. But women love their homes. You couldn't have got these women out of their homes without the goad of poverty. You men can't always earn enough to keep the poor little home going, so the women work in the shops, they swarm at the mill gates, and the factories are full.'

'True! True, every blessed word!' said the old newsvendor.

'Hush!' she said. 'Don't interrupt. In taking women's business out of the home you haven't freed her from the need to see after the business. The need is greater than ever it was. Why, eighty-two per cent of the women of this country are wage-earning women! Yet, you go on foolishly echoing: Woman's place is at home.'

'True! True!' said the aged champion, unabashed.

'Then there are those men, philanthropists, statesmen, who believe they are safeguarding the interests of women by making laws restricting their work, and so restricting their resources without ever consulting these women. If they consulted these women, they would hear truths that would open their blind eyes. But no, the woman isn't worthy of being consulted. She is worthy to do the highest work given to humanity, to bear and to bring up children; she is worthy to teach and to train them; she is worthy to pay the taxes that she has no voice in levying. If she breaks the law that she has no share in making, she is worth hanging, but she is not worth consulting about her own affairs — affairs of supremest importance to her very existence — affairs that no man, however great and good, can understand so well as she. She will never get justice until she gets the vote. Even the well-to-do middle-class woman ——'

'Wot are *you?*'

'And even the woman of what are called the upper classes — even she must wince at the times when men throw off the mask and let her see how in their hearts they despise her. A few weeks ago Mr. Lothian Scott ——'

'Boo! Boo!'

'Hooray!'

''ray for Lothian Scott!'

In the midst of isolated cheers and a volume of booing, she went on —

'When he brought a resolution before the House of Commons to remove the sex disqualification, what happened?'

'Y' kicked up a row!'

'Lot o' yer got jugged!'

'The same thing happened that has been happening for half a century every time the question comes up in that English Parliament that Englishmen are supposed to think of with such respect as a place of dignity. What *happened?*' She leaned forward and her eyes shone. 'What happened in that sacred place, that Ark where they safeguard the honour of England? What happened to *our* honour, that these men dare tell us is so safe in their hands? Our cause was dragged through filth. The very name "woman" was used as a signal for jests and ribald laughter, and for such an exhibition of sex rancour and mistrust that it passed imagination to think what the mothers and wives of the members must think of the public confession of the deep disrespect their menfolk feel for them. Some one here spoke of "a row."' She threw back her head, and faced the issue as though she knew that by bringing it forward herself, she could turn the taunt against the next speaker into a title of respect. 'You blame us for making a scene in that holy place! You would have us imitate those other women — the well-behaved — the women who think more of manners than of morals. There they were — for an example to us — that night of the debate, that night of the "row" — there they sat as they have always done, like meek mute slaves up there in their little gilded pen, ready to listen to any insult, ready to smile on the men afterward. In only one way, but it was an important exception, in just one way that debate on Woman Suffrage differed from any other that had ever taken place in the House of Commons.'

A voice in the crowd was raised, but before the jeer was out Mrs. Chisholm had flung down her last ringing sentences.

'There were *others* up there in the little pen that night! — women, too — but women with enough decency to be revolted, and with enough character to resent such treatment as the members down there on the floor of the House were giving to our measure. Though the women who ought to have felt it most sat there cowed and silent, I am proud to think there were other women who cried out, "*Shame!*" Yes, yes,' she interrupted the interrupters, 'those women were dragged away to prison, and all the world was aghast. But I tell you that cry was the beginning of a new chapter in human history. It began with "Shame!" but it will end with "Honour."'

The old newsvendor led the applause.

'Janet! That woman never spat in a policeman's face.'

'Pull down your veil,' was the lady's sharp response. 'Quick ——'

'My ——'

'Yes, pull it down, and don't turn round.'

A little dazed by the red-hot torrent the woman on the plinth was still pouring down on the people, Vida's mind at the word 'veil,' so peremptorily uttered, reverted by some trick of association to the Oriental significance of that mark in dress distinctively the woman's.

'Why should I pull down my veil?' she answered abstractedly.

'They're looking this way. Don't turn round. Come, come.'

With a surprising alacrity and skill Mrs. Fox-Moore made her way out of the throng. Vida, following, yet looking back, heard —

'Now, I want you men to give a fair hearing to a woman who ——'

'Vida, *don't* look! Mercifully, they're too much amused to notice us.'

Disobeying the mandate, the younger woman's eyes fell at last upon the figures of two young men hovering on the outer circle. The sun caught their tall, glossy hats, played upon the single flower in the frock coat, struck on the eyeglass, and gleamed mockingly on the white teeth of the one who smiled the broadest as they both stood, craning their necks, whispering and laughing, on the fringe of the crowd.

'Why, it's Dick Farnborough — and that friend of his from the Austrian Embassy.'

Vida pulled down her veil.

CHAPTER VIII

DEVOUTLY thankful at having escaped from her compromising position unrecognized, Mrs. Fox-Moore firmly declined to go 'awskin' fur the vote' again! When Vida gave up her laughing remonstrance, Mrs. Fox-Moore thought her sister had also given up the idea. But as Vida afterwards confessed, she told herself that she would go 'just once more.' It could not be but what she was under some illusion about that queer spectacle. From one impression each admitted it was difficult to shake herself free. Whatever those women were or were not, they weren't fools. What did the leaders (in prison and out), what did they think they were accomplishing, besides making themselves hideously uncomfortable? The English Parliament, having flung them out, had gone on with its routine, precisely as though nothing had happened. *Had* anything happened? That was the question. The papers couldn't answer. They were given over to lies. The bare idea of women pretending to concern themselves with public affairs — from the point of view of the Press, it was enough to make the soberest sides shake with Homeric laughter.

So, then, one last time to see for one's self. And on this occasion no pettiness of disguise, Miss Levering's aspect seemed to say — no recurrence of any undignified flight. She had been frightened away from her first meeting, but she would not be frightened from the second, which was also to be the last.

An instinct unanalyzed, but significant of what was to follow, kept her from seeking companionship outside. Had Wark not gone over to the market-gardener, her former mistress would have had no misgiving about taking the woman into her confidence. But Wark, with lightning rapidity, had become Mrs. Anderson Slynes, and was beyond recall. So the new maid was told the following Sunday, that she might walk with her mistress across Hyde Park (where the papers said the meetings in future were to be), carrying some music which had to be returned to the Tunbridges.

Pursuing this programme, what more natural than that those two chance pedestrians should be arrested by an apparition on their way, of a flaming banner bearing, along with a demand for the vote, an outrageous charge against a distinguished public servant — 'a pity the misguided creatures didn't know him, just a little!'

Yes. There it was! a rectangle of red screaming across the vivid green of the park not a hundred yards from the Marble Arch, the denunciatory banner stretched above the side of an uncovered van. A little crowd of perhaps a hundred collected on one side of the cart — the loafers on the outermost fringe, lying on the grass. Never a sign of a Suffragette, and nearly three o'clock! Impossible for any passer-by to carry out the programme of pausing to ask idly, 'What are those women screeching about?'

Seeming to search in vain for some excuse to linger, Miss Levering's wandering eye fell upon a young mother wheeling a perambulator. She had glanced with mild curiosity at the flaunting ensign, and then turned from it to lean forward and straighten her baby's cap.

'I wonder what *she* thinks of the Woman Question,' Miss Levering observed, in a careless aside to her maid.

Before Gorringe could reply: 'Doddy's a bootiful angel, isn't Doddy?' said the young mother, with subdued rapture.

'Ah, she's found the solution,' said the lady, looking back.

Other pedestrians glanced at the little crowd about the cart, read demand and denunciation on the banner, laughed, and they, too, for the most part, went on.

An Eton boy, who looked as if he might be her grandson, came by with a white-haired lady of distinguished aspect, who held up her voluminous silken skirts and stared silently at the legend.

'Do you see what it says?' the Eton boy laughed as he looked back. '"*We demand the vote.*" Fancy! They "demand" it. What awful cheek!' and he laughed again at the fatuity of the female creature.

Vida glanced at the dignified old dame as though with an uneasy new sense of the incongruity in the attitude of those two quite commonplace, everyday members of a world that was her world, and that yet could for a moment look quite strange.

She turned and glanced back at the ridiculous cart as if summoning the invisible presence of Mrs. Chisholm to moderate the insolence of the budding male. Still there was no sign either of Mrs. Chisholm or any of her fellow-conspirators against the old order of the world. Miss Levering stood a moment hesitating.

'I believe I'm a little tired,' she said to the discreet maid. 'We'll rest here a moment,' and she sat down with her back to the crowd.

A woman, apparently of the small shopkeeping class, was already established at one end of the only bench anywhere near the cart. Her child who was playing about, was neatly dressed, and to Vida's surprise wore sandals on her stockingless feet. This fashion for children, which had been growing for years among the upper classes, had found little imitation among tradesmen or working people. They presumably were still too near the difficulty of keeping their children in shoes and stockings, to be able to see anything but a confession of failure in going without. In the same way, the 'Simple Life,' when led by the rich, wears to the poverty-struck an aspect of masked meanness — a matter far less tolerable in the eyes of the pauper than the traditional splendour of extravagance in the upper class, an extravagance that feeds more than the famished stomach with the crumbs that it lets fall.

As Miss Levering sat watching the child, and wondering a little at the sandals, the woman caught her eye.

'Could you please tell me the time?' she asked.

Miss Levering took out her watch, and then spoke of the wisdom of that plan of sandals.

The woman answered with such self-possession and good sense, that the lady sent a half-amused glance over her shoulder as if relishing in advance the sturdy disapproval of this highly respectable young mother when she should come to realize how near she and the precious daughter were to the rostrum of the Shrieking Sisterhood. It might be worth prolonging the discussion upon health and education for the amusement there would be in seeing what form condemnation of the Suffragettes took among people of this kind. By turning her head to one side, out of the tail of her eye the lady could see that an excitement of some sort was agitating the crowd. The voices rose more shrill. People craned and pushed. A derisive cheer went up as a woman appeared on the cart. The wearer of the tam-o'-shanter! Three others followed — all women. Miss Levering saw without seeming to look, still listening while the practical-minded mother talked on about her child, and what 'was good for it.' All life had resolved itself into pursuit of that.

An air of semi-abstraction came over the lady. It was as if in the presence of this excellent bourgeoise she felt an absurd constraint in showing an interest in the proceedings of these unsexed creatures behind them.

To her obvious astonishment the mother of the child was the first to jump up.

'Now they're going to begin!' she said briskly.

'Who?' asked Miss Levering.

'Why, the Suffrage people.'

'Oh! Are *you* going to listen to them?'

'Yes; that's what I've come all this way for.' And she and her bare-legged offspring melted into the growing crowd.

Vida turned to the maid and met her superior smile. 'That woman says she has come a long way to hear these people advocating Woman's Suffrage,' and slowly with an air of complete detachment she approached the edge of the crowd, followed by the supercilious maid. They were quickly hemmed in by people who seemed to spring up out of the ground. It was curious to look back over the vivid green expanse and see the dotted humanity running like ants from all directions to listen to this handful of dowdy women in a cart!

In finding her way through the crowd it would appear that the lady was not much sustained by the presence of a servant, however well-meaning. Much out of place in such a gathering as Mrs. Fox-Moore or any ultra-oldfashioned woman was, still more incongruous showed there the relation of mistress and maid. The punctilious Gorringe was plainly horrified at the proximity to her mistress of these canaille, and the mistress was not so absorbed it would seem but what she felt the affront to seemliness in a servant's seeing her pushed and shoved aside — treated with slight regard or none. Necessary either to leave the scene with lofty disapproval, or else make light of the discomfort.

'It doesn't matter!' she assured the girl, who was trying to protect her mistress's dainty wrap from contact with a grimy tramp. And, again, when half a dozen boys forced their way past, 'It's all right!' she nodded to the maid, 'it's no worse than the crowd at Charing Cross coming over from Paris.'

But it was much worse, and Gorringe knew it. 'The old man is standing on your gown, miss.'

'Oh, would you mind ——' Miss Levering politely suggested another place for his feet.

But the old man had no mind left for a mere bystander — it was all absorbed in Suffragettes.

''is feet are filthy muddy, 'm,' whispered Gorringe.

It may have been in part the maid's genteel horror of such proximities that steeled Miss Levering to endure them. Under circumstances like these the observant are reminded that no section of the modern community is so scornfully aristocratic as our servants. Their horror of the meanly-apparelled and the humble is beyond the scorn of kings. The fine lady shares her shrinking with those inveterate enemies of democracy, the lackey who shuts the door in the shabby stranger's face, and the dog who barks a beggar from the gate.

And so while the maid drew her own skirts aside and held her nose high in the air, the gentlewoman stood faintly smiling at the queer scene.

Alas! no Mrs. Chisholm. It looked as if they must have been hard up for speakers to-day, for two of them were younger even than Miss Claxton of the tam-o'-shanter. One of them couldn't be more than nineteen.

'How dreadful to put such very young girls up there to be stared at by all these louts!'

'Oh, yes, 'm, quite 'orrid,' agreed the maid, but with the air of 'What can you expect of persons so low?'

'However, the young girls seem to have as much self-possession as the older ones!' pursued Miss Levering, as she looked in vain for any sign of flinching from the sallies of cockney impudence directed at the occupants of the cart.

They exhibited, too, what was perhaps even stranger — an utter absence of any flaunting of courage or the smallest show of defiance. What was this armour that looked like mere indifference? It couldn't be that those quiet-looking young girls *were* indifferent to the ordeal of standing up there before a crowd of jeering rowdies whose less objectionable utterances were: 'Where did you get that 'at?' 'The one in green is my girl!' 'Got yer dog-whip, miss?' and such-like utterances.

The person thus pointedly alluded to left her companions ranged along the side of the cart against the background of banner, while she, the famous Miss Claxton, took the meeting in charge. She wasted no time, this lady. Her opening remarks, which, in the face of a fire of interruption, took the form of an attack upon the Government, showed her an alert, competent, cut-and-thrust, imperturbably self-possessed politician, who knew every aspect of the history of the movement, as able to answer any intelligent question off-hand as to snub an impudent irrelevance, able to take up a point and drive it well in — to shrug and smile or frown and point her finger, all with most telling effect, and keep the majority of her audience with her every minute of the time.

As a mere exhibition of nerve it was a thing to make you open your eyes. Only a moment was she arrested by either booing or applause. When a knot of young men, who had pushed their way near the front, kept on shouting argument and abuse, she interrupted her harangue an instant. Pointing out the ring-leader —

'Now you be quiet, if you please,' she said. 'These people are here to listen to *me*.'

'No, they ain't. They come to see wot you look like.'

'That can't be so,' she said calmly, 'because after they've seen us they stay.' Then, as the interrupter began again, 'No, it's no use, my man' — she shook her head gently as if almost sorry for him — 'you can't talk *me* down!'

'Now, ain't that just *like* a woman!' he complained to the crowd.

Just in front of where Miss Levering and her satellite first came to a standstill, was a cheerful, big, sandy man with long flowing moustachios, a polo cap, and a very dirty collar. At intervals he inquired of the men around him, in a great jovial voice, 'Are we down-'earted?' as though the meeting had been called, not for the purpose of rousing interest in the question of woman's share in the work of the world, but as though its object were to humiliate and disfranchise the men. But his exclamation, repeated at intervals, came in as a sort of refrain to the rest of the proceedings.

'The Conservatives,' said the speaker, 'had never pretended they favoured broadening the basis of the franchise. But here were these Liberals, for thirty years they'd been saying that the demand on the part of women for political recognition commanded their respect, and would have their support, and yet there were four hundred and odd members who had got into the House of Commons very largely through the efforts of women — oh, yes, we know all about that! We've been helping the men at elections for years.'

'What party?'

Adroitly she replied, 'We have members of every party in our ranks.'

'Are you a Conservative?'

'No, I myself am not a Conservative ——'

'You work for the Labour men — I know!'

'It's child's play belonging to any party till we get the vote,' she dismissed it. 'In future we are neither for Liberal nor Conservative nor Labour. We are for Women. When we get the sex bar removed, it will be time for us to sort ourselves into parties. At present we are united against any Government that continues to ignore its duty to the women of the country. In the past we were so confiding that when a candidate said he was in favour of Woman's Suffrage (he was usually a Liberal), we worked like slaves to get that man elected, so that a voice might be raised for women's interests in the next Parliament. Again and again the man we worked for got in. But the voice that was to speak for us — that voice was mute. We had served his purpose in helping him to win his seat, and we found ourselves invariably forgotten or ignored. The Conservatives have never shown the abysmal hypocrisy of the Liberals. We can get on with our open enemies; it's these *cowards*' ('Boo!' and groans) — 'these cowards, I say — who, in order to sneak into a place in the House, pretend to sympathize with this reform — who use us, and then betray us; it's these who are women's enemies!'

'Why are you always worrying the Liberals? Why don't you ask the Conservatives to give you the vote?'

'You don't go to a person for something he hasn't got unless you're a fool. The Liberals are in power; the Liberals were readiest with fair promises; and so we go to the Liberals. And we shall continue to go to them. We shall never leave off' (boos and groans) 'till they leave office. Then we'll begin on the Conservatives.' She ended in a chorus of laughter and cheers, 'I will now call upon Miss Cynthia Chisholm to propose the resolution.'

Wherewith the chairman gave way to the younger of the two girls. This one of the Gracchi — a gentle-seeming creature, carelessly dressed, grave and simple — faced the mob with evident trepidation, a few notes, to which she never referred, in her shaking hand. What brought a girl like that here? — was the question on the few thoughtful faces in the crowd confronting her. She answered the query by introducing the resolution in an earnest little speech which, if it didn't show that much of the failure and suffering that darken the face of the world is due to women's false position, showed, at all events, that this young creature held a burning conviction that the subjection of her sex was the world's Root-Evil. With no apparent apprehension of the colossal audacity of her position, the girl moved gravely that 'this meeting demands, of the Government the insertion of an enfranchisement clause in the Plural Voting Bill, and demands that it shall become law during the present session.' Her ignorance of Parliamentary procedure was freely pointed out to her.

'No,' she said, 'it is you who are ignorant — of how pressing the need is. You say it is "out of order." If treating the women of the country fairly is out of order, it is only because men have made a poor sort of order. It is the *order* that should be changed.'

Of course that dictum received its due amount of hooting.

'The vote is the reward for defending the country,' said a voice.

'No,' said the girl promptly, 'for soldiers and sailors don't vote.'

'It implies fitness for military service,' somebody amended.

'It *shouldn't,*' said Nineteen, calmly; 'it ought to imply merely *a stake* in the country. No one denies we have that.'

The crowd kept on about soldiering, till the speaker was goaded into saying —

'I don't say women like fighting, but women *can* fight! In these days warfare isn't any more a matter of great physical strength, and a woman can pull a trigger as well as a man. The Boer women found that out — and so has the Russian. I don't like thinking about it myself — for I seem to realize too clearly what horrors those women endured before they could carry bombs or shoulder rifles.'

'Rifles? Why a woman can't never hit *nothing.*'

'It is quite true we can't most of us even throw a stone straight — the great mass of women never in all their lives wanted to hit anybody or anything. And that' — she came nearer, and leaned over the side of the cart with scared face — 'it's that that makes it so dreadful to realize how at last when women's eyes are opened — when they see their homes and the holiest things in life threatened and despised, how quickly after all *they can learn the art of war.*'

'With hatpins!' some one called out.

'Yes, scratching and spitting,' another added.

That sort of interruption did not so much embarrass her, but once or twice she was nearly thrown off her beam-ends by men and boys shouting, 'Wot's the matter with yer anyway? Can't yer get a husband?' and such-like brilliant relevancies. Although she flushed at some of these sallies, she stuck to her guns with a pluck that won her friends. In one of the pauses a choleric old man gesticulated with his umbrella.

'If what the world needed was Woman's Suffrage, it wouldn't have been left for a minx like you to discover it.' At which volleys of approval.

'That gentleman seems to think it's a new madness that we've recently invented.' The child seemed in her loneliness to reach out for companioning. She spoke of 'our friend John Stuart Mill.'

'Oo's Mill?'

'That great Liberal wrote in 1867 ——' But Mill and she were drowned together. She waited a moment for the flood of derision to subside.

''E wouldn't 'ad nothin' to do with yer if 'e'd thought you'd go on like you done.'

'Benjamin Disraeli was on our side. Mazzini — Charles Kingsley. As long ago as 1870, a Woman's Suffrage Bill that was drafted by Dr. Pankhurst and Mr. Jacob Bright passed a second reading."

'The best sort of women *never* wanted it.'

'The kind of women in the past who cared to be associated with this reform — they were women like Florence Nightingale, and Harriet Martineau, and Josephine Butler, and the two thousand other women of influence who memorialized Mr. Gladstone.'

Something was called out that Vida could not hear, but that brought the painful scarlet into the young face.

'Shame! shame!' Some of the men were denouncing the interjection.

After a little pause the girl found her voice. 'You make it difficult for me to tell you what I think you ought to know. I don't believe I could go on if I didn't see over there the Reformer's Tree. It makes me think of how much had to be borne before other changes could be brought about.' She reminded the people of what had been said and suffered on that very spot in the past, before the men standing before her had got the liberties they enjoyed to-day.

'They were *men!*'

'Yes, and so perhaps it wasn't so hard for them. I don't know, and I'm sure it was hard enough. When we women remember what *they suffered* — though you think meanly of us because we can't be soldiers, you may as well know we are ready to do whatever has to be done — we are ready to bear whatever has to be borne. There seem to be things harder to face than bullets, but it doesn't matter, they'll be faced.'

The lady standing with her maid in the incongruous crowd, looked round once or twice with eyes that seemed to say, 'How much stranger life is than we are half the time aware, and how much stranger it bids fair to be!' The rude platform with the scarlet backing flaming in the face of the glorious summer afternoon, near the very spot upon which the great battles for Reform had been fought out in the past, and in place of England's sturdy freeman making his historic appeal for justice, and admission to the Commons — a girl pouring out this stream of vigorous English, upholding the cause her family had stood for. Her voice failed her a little towards the close, or rather it did not so much fail as betray to any sensitive listener the degree of strain she put upon it to make it carry above laughter and interjection. As she raised the note she bent over the crowd, leaning forward, with her neck outstretched, the cords in it swelling, and the heat of the sun bringing a flush and a moisture to her face, steadying her voice as the thought of the struggle to come, shook and clouded it, and calling on the people to judge of this matter without prejudice. It was a thing to live in the memory — the vision of that earnest child trying to fire the London louts with the great names of the past, and failing to see her bite her lip to keep back tears, and, bending over the rabble, find a choked voice to say —

'If your forefathers and foremothers who suffered for the freedom you young men enjoy — if they could come out of their graves to-day and see how their descendants use the great privileges they won — I believe they would go back into their graves and pull the shrouds over their eyes to hide them from your shame!'

'Hear! Hear!' 'Right you are.'

But she was done. She turned away, and found friendly hands stretched out to draw her to a seat.

The next speaker was an alert little woman with a provincial accent and the briskness of a cock-sparrow, whose prettiness, combined with pertness, rather demoralized the mob.

'Men and women,' she began, pitching her rather thin voice several notes too high.

'Men and women!' some one piped in mimicry; and the crowd dissolved in laughter.

It was curious to note again how that occasional exaggerated shrillness of the feminine voice when raised in the open air — how it amused the mob. They imitated the falsetto with squeals of delight. Each time she began afresh she was met by the shrill echo of her own voice. The contest went on for several minutes. The spectacle of the agitated little figure, bobbing and gesticulating and nothing heard but shrill squeaks, raised a very pandemonium of merriment. It didn't mend matters for her to say when she did get a hearing —

'I've come all the way from ——' (place indistinguishable in the confusion) 'to talk to you this afternoon ——'

''ow kind!'

'Do you reely think they could spare you?'

'And I'm going to convert every man within reach of my voice.'

Groans, and 'Hear! Hear!'

'Let's see you try!'

She talked on quite inaudibly for the most part. A phrase here and there came out, and the rest lost. So much hilarity in the crowd attracted to it a bibulous gentleman, who kept calling out, 'Oh, the pretty dear!' to the rapture of the bystanders. He became so elevated that the police were obliged to remove him.

When the excitement attending this passage had calmed down, the reformer was perceived to be still piping away.

''ow long are you goin' on like this?'

'Ain't you *never* goin' to stop?'

'Oh, not for a long time,' she shrilled cheerfully. 'I've got the accumulations of *centuries* on me, and I'm only just beginning to unload! Although we haven't got the vote — *not yet* — never mind, we've got our tongues!'

'Lord, don't we know it!' said a sad-faced gentleman, in a rusty topper.

'This one's too intolerable,' said a man to his companion.

'Yes; she ought to be smacked.'

They melted out of the crowd.

'We've got our tongues, and I've been going round among all the women I know getting them to promise to *use* their tongues ——'

'You stand up there and tell us they needed *urgin'?*'

'To use their tongues to such purpose that it won't be women, but *men*, who get up the next monster petition to Parliament asking for Woman's Suffrage."

She went down under a flood of jeers, and rose to the surface again to say —

'A man's petition, praying Parliament for goodness' sake give those women the vote! Yes, you'd better be seeing about that petition, my friends, for I tell you there isn't going to be any peace till we get the franchise.'

'Aw now, they'd give *you* anything!'

When the jeering had died a little, and she came to the top once more, she was discovered to be shouting —

'You men 'ad just better keep an eye on us ——'

'Can't take our eyes off yer!'

'We Suffragettes *never* have a Day of Rest! Every day in the week, while you men are at work or sitting in the public-house, we are visiting the women in their homes, explaining and stirring them up to a sense of their wrongs.'

'This I should call an example of what *not* to say!' remarked a shrewd-looking man with a grin.

The crowd were ragging the speaker again, while she shouted —

'We are going to effect such a revolution as the world has never seen!'

'I'd like to bash her head for her!'

'We let them know that so long as women have no citizenship they are outside the pale of the law. If we are outside the law, we can't *break* the law. It is not our fault that we're outlaws. It is you men's fault.'

'Don't say that,' said a voice in mock agony. 'I love you so.'

'I know you can't help it,' she retorted.

'If we gave you the vote, what would you do with it? Put it in a pie?'

'Well, I wouldn't make the *hash* of it you men do!' and she turned the laugh. 'Look at you! *Look* at you!' she said, when quiet was restored.

The young revellers gave a rather blank snigger, as though they had all along supposed looking at them to be an exhilarating occupation for any young woman.

'What do you do with your power? You throw it away. You submit to being taxed and to *our* being taxed to the tune of a hundred and twenty-seven millions, that a war may be carried on in South Africa — a war that most of you know nothing about and care nothing about — a war that some of us knew only too much about, and wanted only to see abandoned. We see constantly how you men either misuse the power you have or you don't use it at all. Don't appreciate it. Don't know what to do with it. Haven't a notion you ought to be turning it into good for the world. Hundreds of men don't care anything about political influence, except that women shouldn't have it.'

She was getting on better till some one called out, 'You ought to get married.'

'I'm going to. If you don't be good you won't be asked to the wedding.'

Before the temptation of a retort she had dropped her argument and encouraged personalities. In vain she tried to recover that thread of attention which, not her interrupter, but herself had snapped. She retired in the midst of uproar.

The chairman came forward and berated the crowd for its un-English behaviour in not giving a speaker a fair hearing.

A man held up a walking-stick. 'Will you just tell me one thing, miss ——'

'Not now. When the last speaker has finished there will be ten minutes for questions. And I may say that it is a great and rare pleasure to have any that are intelligent. Don't waste anything so precious. Just save it up till you're asked for it. I want you now to give a fair hearing to Mrs. Bewley.'

This was a wizened creature of about fifty, in rusty black, widow of a stonemason and mother of four children — 'four *livin'*,' she said with some significance. She added her mite of testimony to that of the 96,000 organized women of the mills, that the workers in her way of life realized how their condition and that of the children would be improved 'if the women 'ad some say in things.'

'It's quite certain,' she assured the people, 'there ought to be women relief-officers and matrons in the prisons. And it's very 'ard on women that there isn't the same cheap lodgin'-'ouse accommodation fur single women as there is fur single men. It's very 'ard on poor girls. It's worse than 'ard. But men won't never change that. We women 'as got to do it.'

'Go 'ome and get your 'usban's tea!' said a new-comer, squeezing her way into the tight-packed throng, a queer little woman about the same age as the speaker, but dressed in purple silk and velvet, and wearing a wonderful purple plush hat on a wig of sandy curls. She might have been a prosperous milliner from the Commercial Road, and she had a meek man along who wore the husband's air of depressed responsibility. She was spared the humiliating knowledge, but she was taken at first for a sympathizer with the Cause. In manners she was precisely like what the Suffragette was at that time expected to be, pushing her way through the crowd, and vociferating 'Shyme!' to all and sundry. The men who had been pleasantly occupied in boo-ing the speaker turned and glared at her. The hang-dog husband had an air of not observing. Some of the boys pushed and harried her, but, to their obvious surprise, they heard her advising the rusty widow: 'Go 'ome and get your 'usban's tea!' She varied that advice by repeating her favourite 'Shyme!' varied by 'Wot beayviour! — old enough to know better. Every good wife oughter stay at 'ome and darn 'er 'usban's socks and make 'im comftubble.'

After delivering which womanly sentiment she would nod her

purple plumes and smile at the men. It was the sorriest travesty of similar scenes in a politer world. To the credit of the loafers about her, they did not greatly encourage her. She was perhaps overmature for her *rôle*. But they ceased to jostle her. They even allowed her to get in front of them. The tall, rusty woman in the cart was meanwhile telling a story of personal experience of the operation of some law which shut out from any share in the benefits of the new Act which regulates the feeding of school children, the very people most in need of it. For it appeared that orphans and the children of widows were excluded. The Bill provided only for children living under their father's roof. If the roof was kept over them by the shackled hands of the mother, according to the speaker, they might go hungry.

'No, no,' Miss Levering shook her head, explaining to her maid. 'I don't doubt the poor soul has had some difficulty, some hard experience, but she can't be quoting the law correctly.'

Nevertheless, in the halting words of the woman who had suffered, if only from misapprehension upon so grave a point, there was a rude eloquence that overbore the lady's incredulity. The crowd hissed such gross unfairness.

'If women 'ad 'ave made the laws, do you think we'd 'ave 'ad one like that disgracin' the statue-book? No! And in all sorts o' ways it looks like the law seems to think a child's got only one parent. I'd like to tell them gentlemen that makes the laws that (it may be different in their world, I only speak for my little corner of it) — but in 'Ackney it looks like when a child's got only one parent, that one is the mother.'

'Sy, let up, old gal! there's some o' them young ones ain't 'ad a show yet.'

'About time you had a rest, mother!'

'If the mother dies,' she was saying, 'wot 'appens?'

'Let's 'ope she goes to heaven.'

'Wot 'appens to the pore little 'ome w'en the mother dies? Why, the pore little home is sold up, and the children's scattered among relations, or sent out so young to work it makes yer 'art ache. But if a man dies — you see it on every side, *in 'Ackney* — the widow takes in sewin', or goes out charin', or does other people's washin' as well as 'er own, or she mykes boxes — *something* er ruther, any'ow, that makes it possible fur 'er to keep 'er 'ome together. You don't see the mother scatterin' the little family w'en the only parent the law seems to reconize is dead and gone. I say ——'

'You've a been sayin' it for a good while. You must be needin' a cup o' tea yerself.'

'In India I'm told they burn the widows. In England they do worse than that. They keep them *half* alive.'

The crowd rose to that, with the pinched proof before their eyes.

'Just enough alive to suffer through their children. And so the workin' women round about where I live — that's 'Ackney — they say if we ain't 'eathins in this country let's give up 'eathin ways. Let the mothers o' this country 'ave their 'ands untied. We're willin' to work for our children, but it breaks our 'earts to work without tools. The tool we're needin' is the tool that mends the laws. I 'ave pleasure in secondin' the resolution.'

With nervously twitching lips the woman sat down. They cheered her lustily — a little out of sympathy, a good deal from relief that she had finished, and a very different sort of person was being introduced by the chairman.

CHAPTER IX

'I WILL now call upon the last speaker. Yes, I will answer any general questions *after* Miss Ernestine Blunt has spoken.'

'Oh, I sy!'

''Ere's Miss Blunt.'

'Not that little one?'

'Yes. This is the one I was tellin' you about.'

People pushed and craned their necks, the crowd swayed as the other one of the two youngest 'Suffragettes' came forward. She had been sitting very quietly in her corner of the cart, looking the least concerned person in Hyde Park. Almost dull the round rather pouting face with the vivid scarlet lips; almost spleepy the heavy-lidded eyes. But when she had taken the speaker's post above the crowd, the onlooker wondered why he had not noticed her before.

It seemed probable that all save those quite new to the scene had been keeping an eye on this person, who, despite her childish look, was plainly no new recruit. Her self-possession demonstrated that as abundantly as the reception she got — the vigorous hoots and hoorays in the midst of clapping and cries —

'Does your mother know you're out?'

'Go 'ome and darn your stockens.'

'Hurrah!'

'You're a disgryce!'

'I bet on little Blunt!'

'Boo!'

Even in that portion of the crowd that did not relieve its feelings by either talking or shouting, there was observable the indefinable something that says, 'Now the real fun's going to begin.' You see the same sort of manifestation in the playhouse when the favourite comedian makes his entrance. He may have come on quite soberly only to say, 'Tea is ready,' but the grin on the face of the public is as ready as the tea. The people sit forward on the edge of their seats, and the whole atmosphere of the theatre undergoes some subtle change. So it was here.

And yet in this young woman was the most complete lack of any dependence upon 'wiles' that platform ever saw. Her little off-hand manner seemed to say, 'Don't expect me to encourage you in any nonsense, and, above all, don't dare to presume upon my youth.'

She began by calling on the Government to save the need of further demonstration by giving the women of the country some speedy measure of justice. 'They'll have to give it to us in the end. They might just as well do it gracefully and at once as do it grudgingly and after more "scenes."' Whereupon loud booing testified to the audience's horror of anything approaching unruly behaviour. 'Oh, yes, you are scandalized at the trouble we make. But — I'll tell you a secret' — she paused and collected every eye and ear — '*we've only just begun!* You'd be simply *staggered* if you knew what the Government still has to expect from us, if they don't give us what we're asking for.'

'Oh, ain't she just *awful!*' sniggered a girl with dyed hair and gorgeous jewelry.

The men laughed and shook their heads. She just was! They crowded nearer.

'You'd better take care! There's a policeman with 'is eye on you.'

'It's on you, my friends, he's got his eye. You saw a little while ago how they had to take away somebody for disturbing our meeting. It wasn't a woman.'

'Hear, hear!'

'The police are our friends, when the Government allows them to be. The other day when there was that scene in the House, one of the policemen who was sent up to clear the gallery said he wished the members would come and do their own dirty work. They hate molesting us. We don't blame the police. We put the blame where it belongs — on the Liberal Government.'

'Pore old Gov'mint — gettin' it 'ot!'

'Hooray fur the Gov'mint!'

'We see at last — it's taken us a long time, but we see at last — women get nothing even from their professed political friends, they've nothing whatever to expect by waiting and being what's called "ladylike."'

'Shame!'

'We don't want to depreciate the work of preparation the older, the "ladylike," Suffrage women did, but we came at last to see that all that was possible to accomplish that way had been done. The Cause hadn't moved an inch for years. It was even doing the other thing. Yes, it was going backward. Even the miserable little pettifogging share women had had in Urban and Borough Councils — even that they were deprived of. And they were tamely submitting! Women who had been splendid workers ten years ago, women with the best capacities for public service, had fallen into a kind of apathy. They were utterly disheartened. Many had given up the struggle. That was the state of affairs with regard to Woman's Suffrage only a few short months ago. We looked at the Suffragists who had grown grey in petitioning Parliament and being constitutional and "ladylike," and we said, "*That's no good.*"'

Through roars of laughter and indistinguishable denunciation certain fragments rose clear —

'So you tried being a public nuisance!'

'A laughing-stock!'

'When we got to the place where we were a public laughing-stock we knew we were getting on.' The audience screamed. '*We began to feel encouraged!*' A very hurricane swept the crowd. Perhaps it was chiefly at the gleam of eye and funny little wag of the head with the big floppity hat that made the people roar with delight. 'Yes; when things got to that point even the worst old fogey in the Cabinet ——'

'Name! Name!'

'No, we are merciful. We withhold the name!' She smiled significantly, while the crowd yelled. 'Even the very fogeyest of them all you'd think might have rubbed his eyes and said, "Everybody's laughing at them — why, there must be something serious at the bottom of this!" But no; the members of the present Government *never* rub their eyes.'

'If you mean the Prime Minister ——'

'Hooray for the ——'

Through the cheering you heard Ernestine saying, 'No, I *didn't* mean the Prime Minister. The Prime Minister, between you and me, is as good a Suffragist as any of us. Only he —— well, he likes his comfort, does the Prime Minister!'

When Ernestine looked like that the crowd roared with laughter. Yet it was impossible not to feel that when she herself smiled it was because she couldn't help it, and not, singularly enough, because of any dependence she placed upon the value of dimples as an asset of persuasion. What she seemed to be after was to stir these people up. It could not be denied that she knew how to do it, any more than it could be doubted that she was ignorant of how large a part in her success was played by a peculiarly amusing and provocative personality. Always she was the first to be grave again.

'Now if you noisy young men can manage to keep quiet for a minute, I'll tell you a little about our tactics,' she said obligingly.

'We know! Breakin' up meetings!'

'*Rotten* tactics!'

'That only shows you don't understand them yet. Now I'll explain to you.'

A little wind had sprung up and ruffled her hair. It blew open her long plain coat. It even threatened to carry away her foolish flapping hat. She held it on at critical moments, and tilted her delicate little Greuze-like face at a bewitching angle, and all the while that she was looking so fetching, she was briskly trouncing by turns the Liberal party and the delighted crowd. The man of the long moustachios, who had been swept to the other side of the monument, returned to his old inquiry with mounting cheer —

'Are we down'earted? *Oh*, no!'

'Pore man! 'Ave a little pity on us, miss!'

There were others who edged nearer, narrowing their eyes and squaring their shoulders as much as to say, 'Now we'll just trip her up at the first opportunity.'

'That's a very black cloud, miss,' Gorringe had whispered several minutes before a big raindrop had fallen on the lady's upturned face.

As Gorringe seemed to be the only one who had observed the overclouding of the sky, so she seemed to be the only one to think it mattered much. But one by one, like some species of enormous black 'four-o-clocks,' umbrellas blossomed above the undergrowth at the foot of the monument. The lady of the purple plumes had long vanished. A few others moved off, head turned over shoulder, as if doubtful of the policy of leaving while Ernestine was explaining things. The great majority turned up their coat collars and stood their ground. The maid hurriedly produced an umbrella and held it over the lady.

''Igher up, please, miss! Caun't see,' said a youth behind.

Nothing cloudy about Ernestine's policy: Independence of all parties, and organized opposition to whatever Government was in power, until something was done to prove it that friend to women it pretended to be.

'We are tired of being lied to and cheated. There isn't a man in the world whose promise at election time I would trust!'

It struck some common chord in the gathering. They roared with appreciation, partly to hear that baby saying it.

'No, not one!' she repeated stoutly, taking the raindrops in her face, while the risen wind tugged at her wide hat. 'They'll promise us heaven, and earth, and the moon, and the stars, just to get our help. Oh, we are old hands at it now, and we can see through the game!'

'Old 'and *she* is! Ha! ha! Old 'and!'

'Do they let you sit up for supper?'

'We are going to every contested election from this on.'

'Lord, yes! Rain or shine *they* don't mind!'

'They'll find they'll always have us to reckon with. And we aren't *the least bit* impressed any more, when a candidate tells us he's in favour of Woman's Suffrage. We say, "Oh, we've got four hundred and twenty of your kind already!"'

'Oh! oh!'

'Haw! haw!'

'Oo did you say that to?'

By name she held up to scorn the candidates who had given every reason for the general belief that they were indifferent, if not opposed, to Woman's Suffrage till the moment came for contesting a seat.

'Then when they find us there (we hear it keeps them awake at night, thinking we always *will* be there in future!) — when they find us there, they hold up their little white flags. Yes. And they say, "Oh, but I'm in favour of Votes for Women!" We just smile.'

The damp gathering in front of her hallooed.

'Yes. And when they protest what splendid friends of the Suffrage they are, we say, "You don't care twopence about it. You are like the humbugs who are there in the House of Commons already."'

'Humbugs!'

'Calls 'em 'umbugs to their fyces! Haw! haw!'

Roars and booing filled the air.

'We know, for many of us helped to put them there. But that was before we knew any better. *Never again!*'

Once more that wise little wag of the head, while the people shrieked with laughter. It was highly refreshing to think those Government blokes couldn't take in Ernestine.

'It's only the very young or the very foolish who will ever be caught that way again,' she assured them.

''Ow old are you?'

'Much too old to ——'

'Just the right age to think about gettin' married,' shouted a pasty-faced youth.

'Haw! haw!'

Then a very penetrating voice screamed, 'Will you be mine?' and that started off several others. Though the interruptions did not anger nor in the least discompose this surprising young person in the cart — so far at least as could be seen — the audience looked in vain for her to give the notice to these that she had to other interruptions. It began to be plain that, ready as she was to take 'a straight ball' from anybody in the crowd, she discouraged impertinence by dint of an invincible deafness. If you wanted to get a rise out of Ernestine you had to talk about her 'bloomin' policy.' No hint in her of the cheap smartness that had wrecked the other speaker. In that highly original place for such manifestation, Ernestine offered all unconsciously a new lesson of the moral value that may lie in good-breeding. She won the loutish crowd to listen to her on her own terms.

'Both parties,' she was saying, 'have been glad enough to use women's help to get candidates elected. We've been quite intelligent enough to canvass for them; we were intelligent enough to explain to the ignorant men ——' She acknowledged the groans by saying, 'Of course there are none of that sort here, but elsewhere there are such things as ignorant men, and women by dozens and by scores are sent about to explain to them why they should vote this way or that. But as the chairman told you, any woman who does that kind of thing in the future is a very poor creature. She deserves no sympathy when her candidate forgets his pledge and sneers at Womanhood in the House. If we put ourselves under men's feet we must *expect* to be trodden on. We've come to think it's time women should give up the door-mat attitude. That's why we've determined on a policy of independence. We see how well independence has worked for the Irish party — we see what a power in the House even the little Labour party is, with only thirty members. Some say those thirty Labour members lead the great Liberal majority by the nose ——'

'Hear! hear!'

'Rot!'

They began to cheer Lothian Scott. Some one tossed Mr. Chamberlain's name into the air. Like a paper balloon it was kept afloat by vigorous puffings of the human breath. ''Ray fur Joe!' 'Three cheers for Joe!' — and it looked as if Ernestine had lost them.

'Listen!' She held out her hands for silence, but the tumult only grew. 'Just a moment. I want to tell you men — here's a friend of yours — he's a new-comer, but he looks just your kind! Give him a hearing.' She strained her voice to overtop the din. 'He's a *Liberal*.'

'Hooray!'

'Yes, I thought you'd listen to a Liberal. He's asking that old question, Why did we wait till the Liberals came in? Why didn't we worry the Conservatives when they were in power? The answer to that is that the Woman's Suffrage cause was then still in the stage of mild constitutional propaganda. Women were still occupied in being ladylike and trying to get justice by deserving it. Now wait a moment.' She stemmed another torrent. 'Be quiet, while I tell you something. You men have taught us that women can get a great deal by coaxing, often far more than we deserve! But justice isn't one of the things that's ever got that way. Justice has to be fought for. Justice has to be won.'

Howls and uproar.

'You men ——' (it began to be apparent that whenever the

roaring got so loud that it threatened to drown her, she said, 'You men —' very loud, and then gave her voice a rest while the din died down that they might hear what else the irrepressible Ernestine had to say upon that absorbing topic). 'You men discovered years ago that you weren't going to get justice just by deserving it, or even by being men, so when you got tired of asking politely for the franchise, you took to smashing windows and burning down Custom Houses, and overturning Bishops' carriages; while *we*, why, we haven't so much as upset a curate off a bicycle!'

Others might laugh, not Ernestine.

'You men,' she went on, 'got up riots in the streets — *real* riots where people lost their lives. It may have to come to that with us. But the Government may as well know that if women's political freedom has to be bought with blood, we can pay that price, too.'

Above a volley of boos and groans she went on, 'But we are opposed to violence, and it will be our last resort. We are leaving none of the more civilized ways untried. We publish a great amount of literature — I hope you are all buying some of it — you can't understand our movement unless you do! We organize branch unions and we hire halls — we've got the Somerset Hall tonight, and we hope you'll all come and bring your friends. We have very interesting debates, and *we* answer questions, politely!' she made her point to laughter. 'We don't leave any stone unturned. Because there are people who don't buy our literature, and who don't realize how interesting the Somerset Hall debates are, we go into the public places where the idle and the foolish, *like that man just over there!* — where they may point and laugh and make their poor little jokes. But let me tell you we never hold a meeting where we don't win friends to our cause. A lot of you who are jeering and interrupting now are going to be among our best friends. *All* the intelligent ones are going to be on our side.'

Above the laughter, a rich groggy voice was heard, 'Them that's against yer are all drunk, miss' (hiccup). 'D—don't mind 'em!'

Ernestine just gave them time to appreciate that, and then went on —

'Men and women were never meant to fight except side by side. You've been told by one of the other speakers how the men suffer by the women more and more underselling them in the Labour market ——'

'Don't need no tellin'.'

'Bloody black-legs!'

'Do you know how that has come about? I'll tell you. It's come about through your keeping the women out of your Unions. You never would have done that if they'd had votes. You saw the important people ignored them. You thought it was safe for you to do the same. But I tell you it *isn't ever* safe to ignore the women!'

High over the groans and laughter the voice went on, 'You men have got to realize that if our battle against the common enemy is to be won, you've got to bring the women into line.'

'What's to become of chivalry?'

'What *has* become of chivalry?' she retorted; and no one seemed to have an answer ready, but the crowd fell silent, like people determined to puzzle out a conundrum.

'Don't you know that there are girls and women in this very city who are working early and late for rich men, and who are expected by those same employers to live on six shillings a week? Perhaps I'm wrong in saying the men expect the women to live on that. It may be they *know* that no girl can — it may be the men know how that struggle ends. But do they care? Do *they* bother about chivalry? Yet they and all of you are dreadfully exercised for fear having a vote would unsex women. We are too delicate — women are such fragile flowers.' The little face was ablaze with scorn. 'I saw some of those fragile flowers last week — and I'll tell you where. Not a very good place for gardening. It was a back street in Liverpool. The "flowers"' (oh, the contempt with which she loaded the innocent word!) — 'the flowers looked pretty dusty — but they weren't quite dead. I stood and looked at them! hundreds of worn women coming down steep stairs and pouring out into the street. What had they all been doing there in that — garden, I was going to say! — that big grimy building? They had been making cigars! — spending the best years of their lives, spending all their youth in that grim dirty street making cigars for men. Whose chivalry prevents that? Why were they coming out at that hour of the day? Because their poor little wages were going to be lowered, and with the courage of despair they were going on strike. No chivalry prevents men from getting women at the very lowest possible wage — (I want you to notice the low wage is the main consideration in all this) — men get these women, that they say are so tender and delicate, to undertake the almost intolerable toil of the rope-walk. They get women to make bricks. Girls are driven — when they are not driven to worse — they are driven to being lodging-house slaveys or over-worked scullions. *That's* all right! Women are graciously permitted to sweat over other people's washing, when they should be caring for their own babies. In Birmingham' — she raised the clear voice and bent her flushed face over the crowd — 'in Birmingham those same "fragile flowers" make bicycles to keep alive! At Cradley Heath we make chains. At the pit brows we sort coal. But a vote would soil our hands! You may wear out women's lives in factories, you may sweat them in the slums, you may drive them to the streets. You *do*. But a vote would unsex them.'

Her full throat choked. She pressed her clenched fist against her chest and seemed to admonish herself that emotion wasn't her line.

'If you are intelligent you know as well as I do that women are exploited the length and the breadth of the land. And yet you come talking about chivalry! Now, I'll just tell you men something for your future guidance.' She leaned far out over the crowd and won a watchful silence. '*That talk about chivalry makes women sick.*' In the midst of the roar, she cried, 'Yes, they mayn't always show it, for women have had to learn to conceal their deepest feelings, but depend on it that's how they feel.'

Then, apparently thinking she'd been serious enough, 'There might be some sense in talking to us about chivalry if you paid our taxes for us,' she said; while the people recovered their spirits in roaring with delight at the coolness of that suggestion.

'If you forgave us our crimes because we are women! If you gave annuities to the eighty-two women out of every hundred in this country who are slaving to earn their bread — many of them having to provide for their children; some of them having to feed sick husbands or old parents. But chivalry doesn't carry you men as far as that! No! No further than the door! You'll hold that open for a lady and then expect her to grovel before such an exhibition of *chivalry!* We don't need it, thank you! We can open doors for ourselves.'

She had quite recovered her self-possession, and it looked, as she faced the wind and the raindrops, as if she were going to wind up in first-class fighting form. The umbrellas went down before a gleam of returning sun. An aged woman in rusty black, who late in the proceedings had timidly adventured a little way into the crowd, stood there lost and wondering. She had peered about during the last part of Miss Blunt's speech with faded incredulous eyes, listened to a sentence or two, and then, turning with a pathetic little nervous laugh of apology, consulted the faces of the Lords of Creation. When the speaker was warned that a policeman had his eye on her, the little old woman's instant solicitude showed that the dauntless Suffragist had both touched and frightened her. She craned forward with a fluttering anxiety till she could see for herself. Yes! A stern-looking policeman coming slow and majestic through the crowd. Was he going to hale the girl off to Holloway? No; he came to a standstill near some rowdy boys, and he stared straight before him — herculean, impassive, the very image of conscious authority. Whenever Ernestine said anything particularly dreadful, the old lady craned her neck to see how the policeman was taking it. When Ernestine fell to drubbing the Government, the old lady, in her agitation greatly daring, squeezed up a little nearer as if half of a mind to try to placate that august image of the Power that was being flouted. But it ended only in trembling and furtive watching, till Ernestine's reckless scorn at the idea of chivalry moved the ancient dame faintly to admonish the girl, as a nurse might speak to a wilful child. 'Dear! *Dear!*' — and then furtively trying to soothe the great policeman she twittered at his elbow, 'No! No! she don't mean it!'

When Ernestine declared that women could open doors for themselves, some one called out —

'When do you expect to be a K.C.?'

'Oh, quite soon,' she answered cheerfully, with her wind-blown hat rakishly over one ear, while the boys jeered.

'Well,' said the policeman, 'she's pawsed 'er law examination!' As some of the rowdiest boys, naturally surprised at this interjection, looked round, he rubbed it in. 'Did better than the men,' he assured them.

Was it possible that this dread myrmidon of the law was vaunting the prowess of the small rebel?

Miss Levering moved nearer. 'Is that so? Did I understand you ——'

With a surly face he glanced round at her. Not for this lady's benefit had the admission been made.

'So they say!' he observed, with an assumption of indifference, quite other than the tone in which he had betrayed where his sympathies, in spite of himself, really were. Well, well, there were all kinds, even of people who looked so much alike as policemen.

Now the crowd, with him and Miss Levering as sole exceptions, were dissolved again in laughter. What had that girl been saying?

'Yes, we're spectres at the Liberal feast; and we're becoming inconveniently numerous. We've got friends everywhere. Up and down the country we go organizing ——'

''Ow do you go — in a pram?' At which the crowd rocked with delight.

The only person who hadn't heard the sally, you would say, was the orator. On she went —

'Organizing branches and carrying forward the work of propaganda. You people in London stroll about with your hands in your pockets and your hats on the back of your heads, and with never a *notion* of what's going on in the world that thinks and works. That's the world that's making the future. Some of you understand it so little you think all that we tell you is a joke — just as the governing class used to laugh at the idea of a Labour Party in conservative England. While those people were laughing, the Labour men were at work. They talked and wrote; they lectured, and printed, and distributed, and organized, and one fine day there was a General Election! To everybody's astonishment, thirty Labour men were returned to Parliament! Just that same sort of thing is going on now among women. We have our people at work everywhere. And let me tell you, the most wonderful part of it all is to discover how little teaching we have to do. How *ready* the women are, all over the three kingdoms.'

'Rot!'

'The women are against it.'

'Read the letters in the papers.'

'Why don't more women come to hear you if they're so in favour?'

'The converted don't need to come. It's you who need to

come!' Above roars of derision: 'You felt that or, of course, you wouldn't be here. Men are so reasonable! As to the women who write letters to the papers to say they're against the Suffrage, they are very ignorant, those ladies, or else it may be they write their foolish letters to please their menfolk. Some of them, I know, think the end and aim of woman is to please. I don't blame them; it's the penalty of belonging to the parasite class. But those women are a poor little handful. They write letters to prove that they "don't count," and they *prove it.*' She waved them away with one slim hand. 'That's one reason we don't bother much with holding drawing-room meetings. The older Suffragists have been holding drawing-room meetings *for forty years!*' She brought it out to shouts. 'But we go to the mill gates! That's where we hold our meetings! We hold them at the pit-brow; we hold them everywhere that men and women are working and suffering and hoping for a better time.'

With that Miss Ernestine sat down. They applauded her lustily; they revelled in laughing praise, yielding to a glow that they imagined to be pure magnanimity.

'Are there any questions?' Miss Claxton, with her eyes still screwed up to meet the returning sun and the volley of interrogatory, appeared at the side of the cart. 'Now, one at a time, please. What? I can't hear when you all talk together. Write it down and hand it to me. Now, you people who are nearer — what? Very well! Here's a man who wants to know whether if women had the vote wouldn't it make dissension in the house, when husband and wife held different views?' She had smiled and nodded, as though in this question she welcomed an old friend, but instead of answering it she turned to the opposite side and looked out over the clamourers on the left. They were engaged for the most part in inquiring about her matrimonial prospects, and why she had carried that dog-whip. Something in her face made them fall silent, for it was both good-humoured and expectant, even intent. 'I'm waiting,' she said, after a little pause. 'At every meeting we hold there's usually another question put at the same time as that first one about the quarrels that will come of husbands and wives holding different opinions. As though the quarrelsome ones had been waiting for women's suffrage before they fell out! When the man on my right asks, "Wouldn't they quarrel?" there's almost always another man on my left who says, "If women were enfranchised we wouldn't be an inch forrader, because the wife would vote as her husband told her to. The man's vote would simply be duplicated, and things would be exactly as they were." Neither objector seems to see that the one scruple cancels the other. But to the question put this afternoon, I'll just say this.' She bent forward, and she held up her hand. 'To the end of time there'll be people who won't rest till they've found something to quarrel about. And to the end of time there'll be wives who follow blindly where their husbands lead. And to the end of time there'll be husbands who are influenced by their wives. What's more, all this has gone on ever since there were husbands, and it will go on as long as there are any left, and it's got no more to do with women's voting than it has with their making cream tarts. No, not half as much!' she laughed. 'Now, where's that question that you were going to write?'

Some one handed up a wisp of white paper. Miss Claxton opened it, and upon the subject presented she embarked with the promising beginning, 'Your economics are pretty wobbly, my friend,' and proceeded to clear the matter up and incidentally to flatten out the man. One wondered that under such auspices 'Question Time' was as popular as it obviously was. There is no doubt a fearful joy in adventuring yourself in certain danger before the public eye. Besides the excitement of taking a personal share in the game, there is always the hope that it may have been reserved to you to stump the speaker and to shine before the multitude.

A gentleman who had vainly been trying to get her to hear him, again asked something in a hesitating way, stumbling and going back to recast the form of his question.

He was evidently quite in earnest, but either unaccustomed to the sound of his own voice or unnerved to find himself bandying words in Hyde Park with a Suffragette. So when he stuck fast in the act of fashioning his phrases, Miss Claxton bent in the direction whence the voice issued, and said, briskly obliging —

'You needn't go on. I know the rest. What this gentleman is trying to ask is ——'

And although no denial on his part reached the public ear, it was not hard to imagine him seething with indignation, down there helpless in his crowded corner, while the facile speaker propounded as well as demolished his objection to her and all her works.

'Yes; one last question. Let us have it.'

'How can you pretend that women want the vote? Why, there are hardly any here.'

'More women would join us openly but for fear of their fellow-cowards. Thousands upon thousands of women feel a sympathy with this movement they dare not show.'

'Lots of women don't want the vote.'

'What women don't want it? Are you worrying about a handful who think because they have been trained to like subservience everybody else ought to like subservience, too? The very existence of a movement like this is a thorn in their sleek sides. We are a reproach and a menace to such women. But this isn't a movement to compel anybody to vote. It is to give the right to those who *do* want it — to those signatories of the second largest petition ever laid on the table of the House of Commons — to the 96,000 textile workers — to the women who went last month in deputation to the Prime Minister, and who represented over half a million belonging to Trades Unions and organized societies. To — perhaps more than all, to the unorganized women, those whose voices are never heard in public. *They*, as Mrs. Bewley told you — they are beginning to want it. The women who are made to work over hours — *they* want the vote. To compel them to work over hours is illegal. But who troubles to see that laws are fairly interpreted for the unrepresented? I know a factory where a notice went up yesterday to say that the women employed there will be required to work twelve hours a day for the next few weeks. Instead of starting at eight, they must begin at six, and work till seven. The hours in this particular case are illegal — as the employer will find out!' she threw in with a flash, and one saw by that illumination the avenue through which his enlightenment would come. 'But in many shops where women work, twelve hours a day is legal. Much of women's employment is absolutely unrestricted, except that they may not be worked on Sunday. And while all that is going on, comfortable gentlemen sit in armchairs and write alarmist articles about the falling birth-rate and the horrible amount of infant mortality. A Government calling itself Liberal goes pettifogging on about side issues, while women are debased and babies die. Here and there we find a man who realizes that the main concern of the State should be its children, and that you can't get worthy citizens where the mothers are sickly and enslaved. The question of statecraft, rightly considered, always reaches back to the mother. That State is most prosperous that most considers her. No State that forgets her can survive. The future is rooted in the well-being of women. If you rob the women, your children and your children's children pay. Men haven't realized it — your boasted logic has never yet reached so far. Of all the community, the women who give the next generation birth, and who form its character during the most impressionable years of its life — of all the community, these mothers now or mothers to be ought to be set free from the monstrous burden that lies on the shoulders of millions of women. Those of you who want to see women free, hold up your hands."

A strange, orchid-like growth sprang up in the air. Hands gloved and ungloved, hands of many shades and sizes, hands grimy and hands ringed.

Something curious to the unaccustomed eye, these curling, clutching, digitated members raised above their usual range and common avocations, suddenly endowed with speech, and holding forth there in the silent upper air for the whole human economy.

'Now, down.' The pallid growth vanished. 'Those against the freedom of women.' Again hands, hands. Far too many to suit the promoters of the meeting. But Miss Claxton announced, 'The ayes are in the majority. The meeting is with us.'

'She can't even count!' The air was full of the taunting phrase — 'Can't count!'

'Yes,' said Miss Claxton, wheeling round again upon the people, as some of her companions began to get down out of the cart. 'Yes, she can count, and she can see when men don't play fair. Each one in that group held up *two* hands when the last vote was taken.' She made a great deal of this incident, and elevated it into a principle. 'It is entirely characteristic of the means men will stoop to use in opposing the Women's Cause.'

To hoots and groans and laughter the tam-o'-shanter disappeared.

'Rank Socialists every one of 'em!' was one of the verdicts that flew about.

'They ought *all* to be locked up.'

'A danger to the public peace.'

A man circulating about on the edge of the crowd was calling out, ''Andsome souvenir. Scented paper 'andkerchief! With full programme of Great Suffragette Meeting in 'Yde Park!'

As the crowd thinned, some of the roughs pressing forward were trying to 'rush' the speakers. The police hastened to the rescue. It looked as if there would be trouble. Vida and her maid escaped towards the Marble Arch.

''Andsome scented 'andkerchief! Suffragette Programme!' The raucous voice followed them, and not the voice alone. Through the air was wafted the cheap and stifling scent of patchouli.

CHAPTER X

JEAN DUNBARTON received Mr. Geoffrey Stonor upon his entrance into Mrs. Freddy's drawing-room with a charming little air of fluttered responsibility.

'Mrs. Freddy and I have been lunching with the Whyteleafes. She had to go afterwards to say good-bye to some people who are leaving for abroad. So Mrs. Freddy asked me to turn over my Girls' Club to your cousin Sophia ——'

'Are you given to good works, too?' he interrupted. 'What a terribly philanthropic age it is!'

Jean smiled as she went on with her explanation. 'Although it wasn't her Sunday, Sophia, like an angel, has gone to the club. And I'm here to explain. Mrs. Freddy said if she wasn't back on the stroke ——'

'Oh, I dare say I'm a trifle early.'

It was a theory that presented fewer difficulties than that he should be kept waiting.

'I was to beg you to give her a few minutes' grace in any case.'

Instead of finding a seat, he stood looking down at the charming face. His indifference to Mrs Freddy's precise programme lent his eyes a misleading look of absent-mindedness, which dashed the girl's obvious excitement over the encounter.

'I see,' he had said slowly. What he saw was a graceful creature of medium height, with a clear colour and grey-blue eyes fixed on him with an interest as eager as it was frank. What the grey-blue eyes saw was probably some glorified version of Stonor's straight, firm features, a little blunt, which lacked that semblance of animation given by colour, and seemed to scorn to make up for it by any mobility of expression. The grey eyes, set somewhat too prominently, were heavy when not interested, and the claim to good looks which nobody had dreamed of denying seemed to rest mainly upon the lower part of his face. The lips, over-full, perhaps, were firmly moulded, but the best lines were those curves from the ear to the quite beautiful chin. The gloss on the straight light-brown hair may have stood to the barber's credit, but only health could keep so much grace still in the carriage of a figure heavier than should be in a man of forty — one who, without a struggle, had declined from polo unto golf. There was no denying that the old expression of incipient sullenness, fleeting or suppressed, was deepening into the main characteristic of his face, though it was held that he, as little as any man, had cause to present that aspect to a world content to be his oyster. Yet, as no doubt he had long ago learned, it was that very expression which was the cause of much of the general concern people seemed to feel to placate, to amuse, to dispel the menace of that cloud. The girl saw it, and her heart failed her.

'Mrs. Freddy said if I told you the children were in the garden expecting you, you wouldn't have the heart to go away directly.'

'She is right. I *haven't* the heart.' And in that lifting of his cloud, the girl's own face shone an instant.

'I should have felt it a terrible responsibility if you were to go.' She spoke as if the gladness that was not to be repressed called for some explanation. 'Mrs. Freddy says that she and Mr. Freddy see so little of you nowadays. That was why she made such a point of my coming and trying to — to ——'

'You needed a great deal of urging then?' He betrayed the half-amused, half-ironic surprise of the man accustomed to find people ready enough, as a rule, to clutch at excuse for a *tête-à-tête*. Although she had flushed with mingled embarrassment and excitement, he proceeded to increase her perturbation by suggesting, 'Mrs. Freddy had to overcome your dislike for the mission.'

'Dislike? Oh, no!'

'What then?'

'My — well ——' She lifted her eyes, and dared to look him full in the face as she said, 'I suppose you know you are rather alarming.'

'Am I?' he smiled.

People less interested in him than Jean were grateful to Geoffrey Stonor when he smiled. They felt relieved from some intangible responsibility for the order of the universe.

The girl brightened wonderfully. 'Oh, yes, very alarming indeed,' she assured him cheerfully.

'How do you make that out?'

'I don't need to "make it out." It's so very plain.' Then a little hastily, as if afraid of having said something that sounded like impious fault-finding, 'Anybody's alarming who is so — so much talked about, and so — well, like you, you understand.'

'I don't understand,' he objected mendaciously — 'not a little bit.'

'I think you must,' she said, with her candid air. 'Though I had made up my mind that I wouldn't be afraid of you any more since our week-end at Ulland.'

'Ah, that's better!'

There was nothing in the words, but in the gentleness with which he brought them out, so much that the girl turned her eyes away and played with the handle of her parasol.

'Have you been reading any more poetry?' he said.

'No.'

'No? Why not?'

She shook her head. 'It doesn't sound the same.'

'What! I spoilt it for you?'

She laughed, and again she shook her head, but with something shy, half-frightened in her look. Nervously she dashed at a diversion.

'I'm afraid I was a little misleading about the children. They aren't in the garden yet. Shall we go up and see them having tea?'

'Oh, no, it would be bad for their little digestions to hurry them.'

He sat down. Her face gave him as much credit as though he had done some fine self-abnegating deed.

They spoke of that Sunday walk in the valley below the Ulland links, and the crossing of a swollen little stream on a rotting and rickety log.

'I *had* to go,' she explained apologetically. 'Hermione had gone on and forgotten the puppy hadn't learnt to follow. I was afraid he'd lose himself.'

'It *was* a dangerous place to go across,' he said, as if to justify some past opinion.

Her eyes were a little mischievous. 'I never thought *you'd* come.'

'Why?' he demanded.

'Oh, because I thought you'd be too ——' His slow look quickened as if to surprise in her some reflection upon his too solid flesh — or might it even be upon the weight of years? But the uncritical admiration in her face must have reassured him before the words, 'I thought you'd be too grand. It was delightful to find you weren't.'

He kept his eyes on her. 'Are you always so happy?'

'Oh, I hope not. That would be rather too inhuman, wouldn't it?'

'Too celestial, perhaps!' He laughed — but he was looking into the blue of her eyes as if through them he too had caught a glimpse of Paradise. 'I remember thinking at Ulland,' he said more slowly again, 'I had never seen any one quite so happy.'

'I was happy at Ulland. But I'm not happy now.'

'Then your looks belie you.'

'No, I am very sad. I have to go away from this delightful London to Scotland. I shall be away for weeks. It's too dismal.'

'Why do you go?'

'My grandfather makes me. He hates London. And his dreary old house on a horrible windy hill — he simply loves that!'

'And you don't love it at all. I see.' He seemed to be thinking out something.

Compunction visited the face before him. 'I didn't mean to say I didn't love it *at all.* It's like those people you care to be with for a little while, but if you must go being with them for ever you come to hate them — almost.'

They sat silent for a moment, then with slow reflectiveness, like one who thinks aloud, he said —

'I have to go to Scotland next week.'

'Do you! What part?'

'I go to Inverness-shire.'

'Why, that's where we are! Near ——'

'Why shouldn't I drop down upon you some day?'

'Oh, *will* you? That would be ——' She seemed to save herself from some gulf of betrayal. 'There are walks about my grandfather's more beautiful than anything you ever saw — or perhaps I ought to say more beautiful than anything *I* ever saw.'

'Nicer walks than at Ulland?'

'Oh, no comparison! One is a bridle-path all along a wonderful brown trout stream that goes racing down our hill. There's a moor on one side, and a wood on the other, and a peat bog at the bottom.'

'We might perhaps stop short of the bog.'

'Yes, we'd stop at old McTaggart's. He's the head-keeper and a real friend. McTaggart "has the Gaelic." But he hasn't much else, so perhaps you'd prefer his wife.'

'Why should I prefer his wife?'

Jean's face was full of laughter. Stonor's plan of going to Scotland had singularly altered the character of that country. Its very inhabitants were now perceived to be enlivening even to talk about; to *know* — the gamekeeper's wife alone — would repay the journey thither.

'I assure you Mrs. McTaggart is a travelled, experienced person.'

He shook his head while he humoured her. 'I'm not sure travel or experience is what we chiefly prize — in ladies.'

'Oh, isn't it? I didn't know, you see. I didn't know how dreadfully you might miss the terribly clever people you're accustomed to in London.'

'It's because of the terribly clever people we are glad to go away.'

He waxed so eloquent in his admiration of the womanly woman (who seemed by implication to have steered clear of Mrs. McTaggart's pitfalls), that Jean asked with dancing eyes —

'Are you consoling me for not being clever?'

'Are you sure you aren't?'

'Oh, dear, yes. No possible shadow of doubt about it.'

'Then,' he laughed, 'I'm coming to Inverness-shire! I'll even go so far as to call on the McTaggarts if you'll undertake that she won't instruct me about foreign lands.'

'No such irrelevance! She'd tell you about London. She was here for six whole months. And she got something out of it I don't believe even you have. A Certificate of Merit.'

'No. London certainly never gave me one.'

'You see! Mrs. McTaggart lived the life of the Metropolis with such success that she passed an examination before she left. The subject was: "Incidents in the Life of Abraham." It says so on the certificate. She has it framed and hung in the parlour.'

He smiled. 'I admit few can point to such fruits of Metropolitan Ausbildung. But I think I shall prefer the burnside — or even the bog.'

'No; the moors. They're best of all.' She sat looking straight before her, with her heart's deep well overflowing at her eyes. As if she felt vaguely that some sober reason must be found for seeing those same moors in this glorified light all of a sudden, she went on, 'I'll show you a special place where white heather grows, and the rabbits tumble about as tame as kittens. It's miles away from the sea, but the gulls come sunning themselves and walking about like pigeons. I used to hide up there when I was little and naughty. Nobody ever found the place out except an old gaberlunzie, and I gave him tuppence not to tell.'

'Yes, show me that place.' His face was wonderfully attractive so!

'And we'll take The Earthly — William Morris — along, won't we?'

'I thought you'd given up reading poetry.'

'Yes — to myself. I used to think I knew about poetry, yes, better than anybody but the poets. There are people as arrogant as that.'

'Why, it's worse than Mrs. McTaggart!'

The girl was grave, even tremulous. 'But, no! I never had a notion of what poetry really was till down at Ulland you took my book away from me, and read aloud ——'

* * * * * * *

Mr. Freddy let himself and Lord Borrodaile in at the front door so closely on the heels of Mrs. Freddy that the servant who had closed the door behind her had not yet vanished into the lower regions. At a word from that functionary, Mr. Freddy left his brother depositing hat and stick with the usual deliberation, and himself ran upstairs two steps at a time. He caught up with his wife just outside the drawing-room door, as she paused to take off her veil in front of that mirror which Mrs. Freddy said should be placed between the front door and the drawing-room in every house in the land for the reassurance of the timid feminine creature. She was known to add privately that it was not ignored by men — and that those who came often, contracted a habit of hurrying upstairs close at the servant's heels, in order to have two seconds to spare for furtive consultation, while he went on to open the drawing-room door. She had observed this pantomime more than once, leaning over the banisters, herself on the way downstairs.

'They tell me Stonor's been here half an hour,' said Mr. Freddy, breathlessly. 'You're dreadfully late!'

'No, darling ——'

He held out his watch to confound her. 'You tell me you aren't late?'

'Sh — no. I do so sympathize with a girl who has no mother,' with which enigmatic rejoinder she pushed open the door, and went briskly through the double drawing-room to where Mr. Geoffrey Stonor and Jean Dunbarton were sitting by a window that overlooked the square.

Stonor waved away Mrs. Freddy's shower of excuses, saying —

'You've come just in time to save us from falling out. I've been telling Miss Dunbarton that in another age she would have been a sort of Dinah Morris, or more likely another St. Ursula with a train of seven thousand virgins.'

'And all because I've told him about my Girls' Club! and ——'

'Yes,' he said, '"and" ——' He turned away and shook hands with his two kinsmen. He sat talking to them with his back to the girl.

It was a study in those delicate weights and measures that go to estimating the least tangible things in personality, to note how his action seemed not only to dim her vividness but actually to efface the girl. In the first moments she herself accepted it at that. Her looks said: He is not aware of me any more — ergo, I don't exist.

During the slight distraction incident to the bringing in of tea, and Mr. Freddy's pushing up some of the big chairs, Mr. Stonor had a moment's remembrance of her. He spoke of his Scottish plans and fell to considering dates. Then all of a sudden she saw that again and yet more woundingly his attention had wandered. The moment came while Lord Borrodaile was busy Russianizing a cup of tea, and Mr. Freddy, balancing himself on very wide-apart legs in front of his wife's tea-table, had interrogated her —

'What do you think, shall I ring and say we aren't at home?'

'Perhaps it would be ——' Mrs. Freddy's eye flying back from Stonor caught her brother-in-law's. 'Freddy' — she arrested her husband as he was making for the bell — 'say, "except to Miss Levering."'

'All right. Except to Miss Levering.' And it was at that point that Jean saw she wasn't being listened to.

Even Mrs. Freddy, looking up, was conscious of something in Stonor's face that made her say —

'Old Sir Hervey's youngest daughter. You knew *him*, I suppose, even if you haven't met her. Jean, you aren't giving Mr. Stonor anything to eat.'

'No, no, thanks. I don't know why I took this.' He set down his tea-cup. 'I never have tea.'

'You're like everybody else,' said the girl, in a half-petulant aside.

'Does nobody have tea?'

She lowered her voice while the others discussed who had already been sent away, and who might still be expected to invade.

'Nobody remembers anybody else when that Miss Levering of theirs is to the fore. You began to say when — to talk about Scotland.'

He had taken out his watch. 'I was wondering if the children were down yet. Shall we go and see?'

Jean jumped up with alacrity.

'Sh!' Mrs. Freddy held up a finger and silenced her little circle. 'They must have thought I was ringing for toast — somebody's being let in!'

'Let's hope it's Miss Levering,' said Mr. Freddy.

'I must see those young barbarians of yours before I go,' said Stonor, rising with decision.

The sound of voices on the stair was quite distinct now. By the time the servant had opened the door and announced: 'Mrs. Heriot, Miss Heriot, Captain Beeching,' Mr. Freddy, the usually gracious host, was leading the way through the back drawing-room, unblushingly abetting Mr. Stonor's escape under the very eyes of persons who would have gone miles on the chance of meeting him.

Small wonder that Jean was consoled for knowing herself too shy to follow, if she remembered that he had actually asked her to do so! She showed no surprise at the tacit assumption on the part of his relations that Geoffrey Stonor could never be expected to sit there as common mortals might, making himself more or less agreeable to whoever might chance to drop in. Unless they were 'very special' of course he couldn't be expected to put up with them.

But what on earth was happening! No wonder Mrs. Freddy looked aghast. For Mrs. Heriot had had the temerity to execute a short cut and waylay the escaping lion. 'Oh, how do you do?' — she thrust out a hand. And he went out as if she had been thin air! It was the kind of insolence that used to be more common, because safer, than it is likely to be in future — a form of condoned brutality that used to inspire more awe than disgust. People were guilty even of a slavish admiration of those who had the nerve to administer this wholly disproportionate reproof to the merely maladroit. It could be done only by one whom all the world had conspired to befog and befool about his importance in the scheme of things.

Small wonder the girl, too, was bewildered. For no one seemed to dream of resenting what had occurred. The lesson conveyed appeared to be that the proper attitude to certain of your fellow-creatures was very much the traditional one towards royalty. You were not to speak unless you were spoken to. And yet this man who with impunity snubbed persons of consideration, was the same one who was coming to call on Sally McTaggart — he was going to walk the bridle-path along the burnside to the white heather haven.

With the dazed look in her eyes, and cheeks scarlet with sympathy and confusion, the girl had run forward to greet her aunt, and to do her little share toward dissipating the awkward chill that had fallen on the company.

After producing a stammered, 'Oh — a — I thought it was ——' the immediate effect on Mrs. Heriot was to make her both furious and cowed. Though a nervous stream of talk trickled on, Mrs. Freddy's face did not lose its flustered look nor did the company regain its ease, until a further diversion was created by the appearance of Miss Levering with an alert, humorous-looking man of middle-age in her train.

'Mr. Greatorex was passing just in time to help me out of my hansom,' was her greeting to Mrs. Freddy.

'And I,' said the gentleman, 'insisted on being further rewarded by being brought in.'

'*That* is Miss Levering?' whispered Jean, partly to distract her aunt.

'Yes; why not?' said Lord Borrodaile, overhearing.

'Oh, I somehow imagined her different.'

'She *is* different,' said Aunt Lydia, with bitter gloom. 'You would never know in the least what she was like from the look of her.'

Lord Borrodaile's eyes twinkled. 'Is that so?' he said, indulgent to a mood which hardly perhaps made for dispassionate appraisement.

'You don't believe it!' said Mrs. Heriot. 'Of course not!'

'I was only thinking what a fillip it gave acquaintance to be in doubt whether a person was a sinner or a saint.'

'It wouldn't for me,' said Jean.

'Oh, you see, you're so Scotch.'

He was incorrigible!

'I didn't hear, who is the man?' Jean asked, as those not knowing usually did.

Although far from distinguished in appearance, Mr. Greatorex would have stood in no danger of being overlooked, even if he had not those twinkling jewel-like eyes, and two strands of coal-black hair trained across his large bumpy cranium, from the left ear to the right, and securely pasted there.

'It's that wretched radical, St. John Greatorex.' Mrs. Heriot turned from her niece to Lord Borrodaile. 'What foundation is there,' she demanded, 'for the rumour that he tells such good stories at dinner? *I* never heard any.'

'Ah, I believe he keeps them till the ladies have left the room.'

'You don't like him, either,' said Mrs. Heriot, reaching out for the balm of alliance with Lord Borrodaile.

But he held aloof. 'Oh, they say he has his points — a good judge of wine, and knows more about Parliamentary procedure than most of us.'

'How you men stand up for one another! You know perfectly well you can't endure him.' Mrs. Heriot jerked her head away and faced the group round the tea-table. 'What is she saying? That she's been to a Suffrage meeting in Hyde Park!'

'How could she! Nothing would induce me to go and listen to such people!' said Miss Dunbarton.

Her eyes, as well as Mrs. Heriot's, were riveted on the tall figure, tea-cup in hand, moving away from the table now to make room for some new arrivals, and drawing after her a portion of the company, including Lady Whyteleafe and Richard Farnborough, who one after another had come in a few moments before. It was to the young man that Greatorex was saying, with a twinkle, 'I am sure Mr. Farnborough agrees with me.'

Slightly self-conscious, he replied, 'About Miss Levering being too — a ——'

'For that sort of thing altogether "too."'

'How do you know?' said the lady herself, with a teasing smile.

Greatorex started out of the chair in which he had just deposited himself at her side. 'God bless my soul!' he said.

'She's only saying that to get a rise out of you.' Farnborough seemed unable to bear the momentary shadow obscuring the lady's brightness.

'Ah, yes' — Greatorex leaned back again — 'your frocks aren't serious enough.'

'Haven't I been telling you it's an exploded notion that the Suffrage people are all dowdy and dull?'

'Pooh!' said Mr. Greatorex.

'You talk about some of them being pretty,' Farnborough said. '*I* didn't see a good-looking one among 'em.'

'Ah, you men are so unsophisticated; you missed the fine feathers.'

'Plenty o' feathers on the one I heard.'

'Yes, but not *fine* feathers. A man judges of the general effect. We can, at a pinch, see past unbecoming clothes, can't we, Lady Whyteleafe? We see what women could make of themselves if they took the trouble.'

'All the same,' said the lady appealed to, 'it's odd they don't see how much better policy it would be if they *did* take a little trouble about their looks. Now, if we got our maids to do those women's hair for them — if we lent them our French hats — ah, *then*' — Lady Whyteleafe nodded till the pear-shaped pearls in her ears swung out like milk-white bells ringing an alarum — 'they'd convert you creatures fast enough then.'

'Perhaps "convert" is hardly the word,' said Vida, with ironic mouth. As though on an impulse, she bent forward to say, with her lips near Lady Whyteleafe's pearl drop: 'What if it's the aim of the movement to get away from the need of just these little dodges?'

'Dodges?'

But without the exclamation, Miss Levering must have seen that she had been speaking in an unknown tongue. A world where beauty exists for beauty's sake — which is love's sake — and not for tricking money or power out of men, even the possibility of such a world is beyond the imagining of many.

Something was said about a deputation of women who had waited on Mr. Greatorex.

'Hm, yes, yes.' He fiddled with his watch chain.

As though she had just recalled the circumstances, 'Oh, yes,' Vida said, 'I remember I thought at the time, in my modest way, it was nothing short of heroic of them to go asking audience of their arch opponent.'

'It didn't come off!' He wagged his strange head.

'Oh,' she said innocently, 'I thought they insisted on bearding the lion in his den.'

'Of course I wasn't going to be bothered with a lot of ——'

'You don't mean you refused to go out and face them!'

He put on a comic look of terror. 'I wouldn't have done it for worlds! But a friend of mine went and had a look at 'em.'

'Well,' she laughed, 'did he get back alive?'

'Yes, but he advised me not to go. "You're quite right," he said. "Don't you think of bothering," he said. "I've looked over the lot," he said, "and there isn't a week-ender among 'em."'

Upon the general laugh that drew Hermione and Captain Beeching into the group, Jean precipitated herself gaily into the conversation. 'Have they told you about Mrs. Freddy's friend who came to tea here in the winter?' she asked Hermione. 'He was a member of Parliament, too — quite a little young one — he said women would never be respected till they had the vote!'

Mr. Greatorex snorted, the other men smiled, and all the women, except Aunt Lydia, did the same.

'I remember telling him,' Mrs. Heriot said, with marked severity, 'that he was too young to know what he was talking about.'

'Yes, I'm afraid you all sat on the poor gentleman,' said Lord Borrodaile.

'It was such fun. He was flat as a pancake when we'd done with him. Aunt Ellen was here. She told him with her most distinguished air she didn't want to be respected.'

'Dear Lady John!' murmured Miss Levering. 'I can hear her!'

'Quite right,' said Captain Beeching. 'Awful idea to think you're *respected.*'

'Simply revolting,' agreed Miss Heriot.

'Poor little man!' laughed Jean, 'and he thought he was being *so* agreeable!'

'Instead of which it was you.'

Miss Levering said the curious words quite pleasantly, but so low that only Jean heard them.

The girl looked up. 'Me?'

'You had the satisfaction of knowing you had made yourself immensely popular with all other men.'

The girl flushed. 'I hope you don't think I did it for that reason.'

The little passage was unnoticed by the rest of the company, who were listening to Lord Borrodaile's contented pronouncement: 'I'm afraid the new-fangled seed falls on barren ground in our old-fashioned gardens — *pace* my charming sister-in-law.'

Greatorex turned sharply. 'Mrs. Tunbridge! God bless my soul, you don't mean ——'

'There is one thing I will say for her' — Mrs. Freddy's brother-in-law lazily defended the honour of the house — 'she doesn't, as a rule, obtrude her opinions. There are people who have known her for years, and haven't a notion she's a light among the misguided.'

But Greatorex was not to be reassured. 'Mrs. Tunbridge! Lord, the perils that beset the feet of man!' He got up with a half-comic ill humour.

'You're not going!' The hostess flitted over to remonstrate. 'I haven't had a word with you.'

'Yes, yes; I'm going.'

Mrs. Freddy looked bewildered at the general laugh.

'He's heard aspersions cast upon your character,' said Lord Borrodaile. 'His moral sense is shocked.'

'Honestly, Mrs. Tunbridge' — Farnborough was for giving her

a chance to clear herself — 'what do you think of your friends' recent exploits?'

'My friends?'

'Yes; the disorderly women.'

'They are not my friends,' said Mrs. Freddy, with dignity, 'but I don't think you must call them ——'

'Why not?' said Lord Borrodaile. '*I* can forgive them for worrying the Liberals' — he threw a laughing glance at Greatorex — 'but they *are* disorderly.'

'Isn't the phrase consecrated to a different class?' said Miss Levering, quietly.

'You're perfectly right.' Greatorex, for once, was at one with Lord Borrodaile. 'They've become nothing less than a public nuisance. Going about with dog-whips and spitting in policemen's faces.'

'I wonder,' said Mrs. Freddy, with a harassed air — 'I wonder if they did spit!'

'Of course they did!' Greatorex exulted.

'You're no authority on what they do,' said Mrs. Freddy. 'You run away.'

'Run away?' He turned the laugh by precipitately backing away from her in a couple of agitated steps. 'Yes, and if ever I muster up courage to come back, it will be to vote for better manners in public life, not worse than we have already.'

'So should I,' observed Mrs. Freddy, meekly. 'Don't think I defended the Suffragettes.'

'But still,' said Miss Levering, with a faint accent of impatience, 'you *are* an advocate for the Suffrage, aren't you?'

'I don't beat the air.'

'Only policemen,' Greatorex mocked.

'If you cared to know the attitude of the real workers in the Reform,' Mrs. Freddy said plaintively, 'you might have seen in any paper that we lost no time in dissociating ourselves from the two or three hysterical ——' She caught her brother-in-law's critical eye, and instantly checked her flow of words.

There was a general movement as Greatorex made his good-byes. Mrs. Heriot signalled her daughter.

In the absence of the master, Lord Borrodaile made ready to do the honours of the house to a lady who had had so little profit of her visit. Beeching carried off the reluctant Farnborough. Mrs. Freddy kept up her spirits until after the exodus; then, with a sigh, she sat down beside Vida. 'It's true what that old cynic says,' she admitted sorrowfully. 'The scene has put back the Reform a generation.'

'It must have been awfully exciting. I wish I'd been there,' said Jean.

'I *was* there.'

'Oh, was it as bad as the papers said?'

'Worse. I've never been so moved in public — no tragedy, no great opera ever gripped an audience as the situation in the House did that night. There we all sat breathless — with everything more favourable to us than it had been within the memory of woman. Another five minutes and the resolution would have passed. Then — all in a moment' — Mrs. Freddy clasped her hands excitedly — 'all in a moment a horrible, dingy little flag was poked through the grille of the Woman's Gallery — cries — insults — scuffling — the police — the ignominious turning out of the women — *us* as well as the —— Oh, I can't *think* of it without ——' She jumped up and walked to and fro. 'Then the next morning!' She paused. 'The people gloating. Our friends antagonized — people who were wavering — nearly won over — all thrown back! Heart-breaking! Even my husband! Freddy's been an angel about letting me take my share when I felt I must — but, of course, I've always known he doesn't like it. It makes him shy. I'm sure it gives him a horrid twist inside when he sees even the discreetest little paragraph to say that I am "one of the speakers." But he's always been an angel about it before this. After the disgraceful scene, he said, "It just shows how unfit women are for any sort of coherent thinking or concerted action."'

'To think,' said Jean, more sympathetically, 'that it should be women who've given their own scheme the worst blow it ever had!'

'The work of forty years destroyed in five minutes!'

'They must have felt pretty sick,' said the girl, 'when they waked up the next morning — those Suffragettes.'

'I don't waste any sympathy on *them*. I'm thinking of the penalty *all* women have to pay because two or three hysterical ——'

'Still, I think I'm sorry for them,' the girl persisted. 'It must be dreadful to find you've done such a lot of harm to the thing you care most about in the world.'

'Do you picture the Suffragettes sitting in sack-cloth?' said Vida, speaking at last.

'Well, they can't help realizing *now* what they've done.'

'Isn't it just possible they realize they've waked up interest in the Woman Question so that it's advertised in every paper, and discussed under every roof, from Land's End to John-o'-Groats? Don't you think *they* know there's been more said and written about it in these days since the scene than in the ten years before it!'

'You aren't saying you think it was a good way to get what they wanted!' exclaimed Mrs. Freddy.

'I'm only pointing out that it seems not such a bad way to get it known they *do* want something, and—"want it bad,"' Vida added, smiling.

Jean drew her low chair almost in front of the lady who had so wounded her sensibilities a little while before with that charge of popularity-hunting.

'Mrs. Tunbridge says before that horrid scene everything was favourable at last,' the girl hazarded.

'Yes,' said Mrs. Freddy, 'we never had so many friends in the House before ——'

'"Friends,"' echoed the other woman, with a faint smile.

'Why do you say it like that?'

'Because I was thinking of a funny story—(he *said* it was funny)—a Liberal Whip told me the other day. A Radical member went out of the House after his speech in favour of the Women's Bill, and as he came back half an hour later he heard some members talking in the lobby about the astonishing number who were going to vote for the measure. And the Friend of Woman dropped his jaw and clutched the man next him. "My God!" he said, "you don't mean they're going to *give* it to them!"'

'Sh! Here is Ronald.' Mrs. Freddy's tact brought her smiling to her feet as the figure of her brother-in-law appeared in the doorway. But she turned her back on him and affected absorption in the tableau presented by Jean leaning forward, elbow on knee, chin in hand, gazing steadily in Vida Levering's face.

'I don't want to interrupt you two,' said the hostess, 'but I think you must look at the pictures.'

'Oh, yes, I brought them specially' — Lord Borrodaile deflected his course in order to take up from the table two squares of cardboard tied face to face with tape.

'Bless the man!' Mrs. Freddy contemplated him with smiling affectation of scorn. 'I mean the new photographs of the children. He's thinking of some reproductions Herbert Tunbridge got while he was abroad — pictures of things somebody's unearthed in Sicily or Cyprus.'

'Crete, my dear.' He turned his back on the fond mother and Jean who was already oh-ing with appreciation at the first of a pile of little Saras and Cecils. When he came back to his corner of the sofa he made no motion to undo his packet, but 'Now then!' he said, as he often did on sitting down beside Vida Levering — as though they had been interrupted on the verge of coming to an agreement about something.

She, with an instinct of returning the ball, usually tossed at him some scrap of news or a jest, or some small social judgment. This time when he uttered his 'Now then,' with that anticipatory air, she answered instantly — 'Yes; something rather odd has been happening. I've been seeing beyond my usual range.'

'Really!' He smiled at her with a mixture of patronage and affection. 'And did you find there was "something new under the sun" after all?'

'Well, perhaps not so new, though it seemed new to me. But something differently looked at. Why do we pretend that all conversion is to some religious dogma — why not to a view of life?'

'Bless my soul! I begin to feel nervous.'

'Do you remember once telling me that I had a thing that was rare in my sex — a sense of humour?'

'I remember often thinking it,' he said handsomely.

'It wasn't the first time I'd heard that. And it was one of the compliments I liked best.'

'We all do. It means we have a sense of proportion — the mental suppleness that is capable of the ironic view; an eye that can look right as well as left.'

She nodded. 'When you wrote to me once, "My dear Ironist," I — yes — I felt rather superior. I'm conscious now that it's been a piece of hidden, intellectual pride with me that I could smile at most things.'

'Well, do you mean to forswear pride? For you can't live without smiling.'

'I've seen something to-day that I don't feel I want to smile at. And yet to you it's the most ludicrous spectacle in London.'

'This is all very mysterious.' He turned his long, whimsical face on one side as he settled himself more comfortably against the cushion.

'You heard why I was late?' she said.

'I took the liberty of doubting the reason you gave!'

'You mustn't. It wasn't even my first offence.'

'You must find time hang very heavy on your hands.'

'On the contrary. I've never known the time to go so fast. Oh, heaps of people would do what I have, if they only knew how queer and interesting it is, and how already the outer aspect of the thing is changing. At the first meetings very few women of any class. Now there are dozens — scores. Soon there'll be hundreds. There were three thousand people in the park this afternoon, so a policeman told me, but hardly any of the class that what Dick Farnborough calls "runs England."'

'I suppose not.'

'You don't even know yet you'll have to deal with all that passionate feeling, all that fixed determination to bring about a vast, far-reaching change! — a change so great ——'

'That it would knock civilized society into a cocked hat.'

'I wonder.'

'You *wonder?*'

'I wonder if you oughtn't to be reassured by the — bigness of the thing. It isn't only these women in Hyde Park. They have a Feministe Movement in France. They say there's a Frauenbewegung in Germany. From Finland to Italy ——'

'Oh, yes, strikes and uprisings. It's an uneasy Age.'

'People in India wanting a greater share in the government ——'

'Mad as the Persians ——' he smiled — 'fancy *Persians* clamouring for a representative chamber! It's a sort of epidemic.'

'The Egyptians, too, restless under "benefits." And now everywhere, as if by some great concerted movement — the Women!'

'Yes, yes; there's plenty of regrettable restlessness up and down the world, a sort of wave of revolt against the constituted authorities. If it goes too far — nothing for us but a military despotism!'

She shook her head with a look of such serene conviction that he persisted, 'I'd be sorry if we came to it — but if this spirit grows, this rebellion against all forms of control ——'

'No, no, against other people's control. Suppose it ends in people learning self-control.'

'That's the last thing the masses can do. There are few, even of the *élite*, who have ever done it, and they belong to the Moral Aristocracy — the smallest and most rigid in the world. This thing that you're just opening your eyes to, is the rage against restraint that goes with decadence. But the phlegmatic Englishman won't lead in that dégringolade.'

'You mean we won't be among the first of the great nations to give women the Suffrage?'

'*England?*' The slow head-shake and the smile airily relegated the Woman's Movement to the limbo of the infinitely distant.

'Just because the men won't have it?' and for the second time she said, 'I wonder. For myself, I rather think the women are going to win.'

'Not in my time. Not even in yours.'

'Why?'

'Oh, the men will never let it come to the point.'

'It's interesting to hear you say that. You justify the militant women, you know.'

'That is perhaps *not* to hit the bull's eye!' he said, a little grimly. Then dropping his unaccustomed air of chill disapproval, he appealed to his friend's better taste. A confession of sheer physical loathing crept into his face as he let fall two or three little sentences about these women's offence against public decorum. 'Why, it is as hideous as war!' he wound up, dismissing it.

'Perhaps it *is* war.' Her phrase drew the cloud of menace down again; it closed about them. It seemed to trouble her that he would not meet her gaze. 'Don't think ——' she prayed, and stumbling against the new hardness in his face, broke off, withdrew her eyes and changed the form of what she had meant to say. 'I think I like good manners, too, but I see it would be a mistake to put them first. What if we have to earn the right to be gentle and gracious without shame?'

'You seriously defend these people!'

'I'm not sure they haven't taken the only way.' She looked at her friend with a fresh appeal in her eyes. But his were wearing their new cold look. She seemed to nerve herself to meet some numbing danger of cowardice. 'The old rule used to be patience — with no matter what wrong. The new feeling is: shame on any one who weakly suffers wrong! Isn't it too cheap an idea of morals that women should take credit for the enduring that keeps the wrong alive? You won't say women have no stake in morals. Have we any right to let the world go wrong while we get compliments for our forbearance and for pretty manners?'

'You began,' said Borrodaile, 'by explaining other women's notions. You have ended by seeming to adopt them as your own. But you are a person of some intelligence. You will open your eyes before you go too far. You belong to the people who are responsible for handing on the world's treasure. As we've agreed, there never was a time when it was attacked from so many sides. Can't you see what's at stake?'

'I see that many of the pleasantest things may be in eclipse for a time.'

'My dear, they would die off the face of the earth.'

'No, they are too necessary.'

'To you and me. Not to the brawlers in Hyde Park. The life of civilized beings is a very complex thing. It isn't filled by good intentions nor even by the cardinal virtues. The function of the older societies is to hand on the best things the world has won, so that those who come after, instead of having to go back to barbarism, may start from where the best of their day left off. We do for manners and the arts in general what the Moors did for learning when the wild hordes came down. There were capital chaps among the barbarians,' he smiled, 'I haven't a doubt! But it was the men who held fast to civilization's clue, they were the people who mattered. *We* matter. We hold the clue.' He was recovering his spirits. 'Your friends want to open the gates still wider to the Huns. You want even the Moors overwhelmed.'

'Many women are as jealous to guard the old gains as the men are. Wait!' She leaned forward. 'I begin to see! They are more keen about it than the mass of men. The women! They are civilization's only ally against your brother, the Goth.'

He laughed. 'When you are as absurd as that, my dear, I

don't mind. No, not a little bit. And I really believe I'm too fond of you to quarrel on any ground.'

'You don't care enough about anything to quarrel about it,' she said, smiling, too. 'But it's just as well' — she rose and began to draw on her glove — 'just as well that each of us should know where to find the other. So tell me, what if it should be a question of going forward in the suffrage direction or going back?'

'You mean ——'

'—— on from latchkeys and University degrees to Parliament, or back.'

'Oh, back,' he said hastily. 'Back. Yes, back to the harem.'

When the words were out, Lord Borrodaile had laughed a little uneasily — like one who has surprised even himself by some too-illuminating avowal. 'See here,' he put out a hand. 'I'm not going to let you go for a minute or two. I've brought something to show you. This foolish discussion put it out of my head.' But the revealing word he had flung out — it seemed to have struck wide some window that had been shuttered close before. The woman stood there in the glare. She did not refuse to be drawn back to her place on the sofa, but she looked round first to see if the others had heard and how they took it. A glimpse of Mrs. Freddy's gown showed her out of earshot on the balcony.

'I've got something here really rather wonderful,' Lord Borrodaile went on, with that infrequent kindling of enthusiasm. He had taken one of the unmounted photographs from between its two bits of cardboard and was holding it up before his eyeglass. 'Yes, he's an extraordinary beggar!' — which remark in the ears of those who knew his lordship, advertized his admiration of either some man of genius or 'Uebermensch' of sorts. Before he shared the picture with his companion he told her of what was not then so widely known—details of that most thrilling moment perhaps in all the romance of archæology—where the excavators of Knossos came upon the first authentic picture of a man belonging to that mysterious and forgotten race that had raised up a civilization in some things rivalling the Greek—a race that had watched Minoan power wane and die, and all but the dimmest legend of it vanish, before the builders of Argos and Mycenæ began laying their foundation stones. Borrodaile, with an accent that for him was almost emotion, emphasized the strangeness to the scholar of having to abandon the old idea of the Greek being the sole flower of Mediterranean civilization. For here was this wonderful island folk — a people standing between and bridging East and West — these Cretan men and women who, though they show us their faces, their delicate art and their stupendous palaces, have held no parley with the sons of men, some say for three and thirty centuries. 'But wait! They'll tell us tales before those fellows have done! I wouldn't mind hearing what this beggar has to say for himself!' At last he shared the picture. They agreed that he was a beggar to be reckoned with — this proud athlete coming back to the world of men after his long sleep, not blinded by the new day, not primitive, apologetic, but meeting us with a high imperial mien, daring and beautiful.

'What do you suppose he is carrying in that vase?' Vida asked; 'or is that some trophy?'

'No, no, it's the long drinking cup — to the expert eye that is added evidence of his high degree of civilization. But *think*, you know, a man like that walking the earth so long before the Greeks! And here. This courtly train looking on at the games. What do you say to the women!'

'Why, they had got as far as flouncing their gowns and puffing their sleeves! Their hair!' — 'Dear me, they must have had a M. Raoul to ondulé and dress it.' 'Amazing! — was there ever anything so modern dug out of the earth before?' 'No, nothing like it!' he said, holding the pictures up again between the glass and his kindling eye. 'Ce sont vraiment des Parisiennes!'

Over his shoulder the modern woman looked long at that strange company. 'It is nothing less than uncanny,' she said at last. 'It makes one vaguely wretched.'

'What does?'

'To realize that so long ago the world had got so far. Why couldn't people like these go further still? Why didn't their sons hold fast what so great a race had won?'

'These things go in cycles.'

'Isn't that a phrase?' — the woman mused — 'to cover our ignorance of how things go — and why? Why should we be so content to go the old way to destruction? If I were "the English" of this splendid specimen of a Cretan, I would at least find a new way to perdition.'

'Perhaps we shall!'

They sat trying from the accounts of Lord Borrodaile's archæological friends to reconstruct something of that vanished world. It was a game they had played at before, with Etruscan vases and ivories from Ephesus — the man bringing to it his learning and his wit, the woman her supple imagination and a passion of interest in the great romance of the Pilgrimage of Man.

But to-day she bore a less light-hearted part — 'It all came to an end!' she repeated.

'Well, so shall we.'

'But — we — *you* will leave your like behind to "hold fast to the clue," as you said a little while ago.'

'Till the turn of the wheel carries the English down. Then somewhere else on our uneasy earth men will begin again ——'

'—— the fruitless round! But it's horrible — the waste of effort in the world! It's worse than horrible. It's insane.' She looked up suddenly into his face. 'You are wise. Tell me what you think the story of the world means, with its successive clutches at civilization — all those histories of slow and painful building — by Ganges and by Nile and in the Isles of Greece.'

'It's a part of the universal rhythm that all things move to — Nature's way,' he answered.

'Or was it because of some offence against one of her high laws that she wiped the old experiments out? What if the meaning of history is that an Empire maintained by brute force shall perish by brute force!'

'Ah,' he fixed her with those eyes of his. 'I see where you are going.'

'You can't either of you go anywhere,' said Mrs. Freddy, appearing through the balcony window, 'till you've seen the children's pictures.' Vida's eye had once more fallen on the reproduction of one of the Cretan frescoes with a sudden intensification of interest.

'What is it?' Borrodaile asked, looking over her shoulder.

Woman-like she offered the man the outermost fringe of her thought. 'Even Lady Whyteleafe,' she said, 'would be satisfied with the attention they paid to their hair.'

'Come, you two.' Mrs. Freddy was at last impatient. 'Jean's

got the *really* beautiful pictures, showing them to Geoffrey. Let us all go down to help him to decide which is the best.'

'Geoffrey?'

'Geoffrey Stonor — you know him, of course. But nobody knows the very nicest side of Geoffrey, do they?' she appealed to Borrodaile, — 'nobody who hasn't seen him with children?'

'I never saw him with children,' said Vida, buttoning the last button of her glove.

'Well, come down and watch him with Sara and Cecil. They perfectly adore him.'

'No, it's too late.'

But the fond mother drew her friend to the window. 'You can see them from here.'

Vida was not so hurried, apparently, but what she could stand there taking in the picture of Sara and Cecil climbing about their big, kind cousin, with Jean and Mr. Freddy looking on.

'Children!' Their mother waved a handkerchief. 'Here's another friend! Chil—— They're too absorbed to notice,' she said apologetically, turning to find Vida had left the window, and was saying good-bye to Borrodaile.

'Oh, yes,' he agreed, 'they won't care about anybody else while Geoffrey is there.' Lord Borrodaile stooped and picked up a piece of folded paper off the sofa. 'Did I drop that?' He opened it. '*Votes for*——' He read the two words out in an accent that seemed to brand them with foolishness, even with vulgarity. 'No, decidedly I did not drop it.'

He was conveying the sheet to the wastepaper basket as one who piously removes some unsavoury litter out of the way of those who walk delicately. Miss Levering arrested him with outstretched hand.

'Do you want it?' His look adjured her to say, 'No.'

'Yes, I want it.'

'What for?' he persisted.

'I want it for an address there is on it.'

CHAPTER XI

It was Friday, and Mrs. Fox-Moore was setting out to alleviate the lot of the poor in Whitechapel.

'Even if it were not Friday,' Vida said slyly as her sister was preparing to leave the house, 'you'd invent some errand to take you out of the contaminated air of Queen Anne's Gate this afternoon.'

'Well, as I told you,' said the other woman, nervously, 'you ask that person here on your own responsibility.'

Vida smiled. 'I'm obliged to ask people here if I want to see them quietly. You make such a fuss when I suggest having a house of my own!'

Mrs. Fox-Moore ignored the alternative. 'You'll see you're only making trouble for yourself. You'll have to pay handsomely for your curiosity.'

'Well, I've been rather economical of late. Maybe I'll be able "to pay."'

'Don't imagine you'll be able to settle an account of that kind with a single cheque. Give people like that an inch, and they'll expect a weekly ell.'

'Are you afraid she'll abstract the spoons?'

'I'm not only afraid, I *know* she won't be satisfied with one contribution, or one visit. She'll regard it as the thin end of the wedge — getting her nose into a house of this kind.' Irresistibly the words conjured up a vision of some sharp-visaged female marauder insinuating the tip of a very pointed nose between the great front door and the lintel. 'I only hope,' the elder woman went on, 'that I won't be here the first time Donald encounters your new friend on the doorstep. *That's* all!'

Wherewith she departed to succour women and children at long range in the good old way. Little Doris was ill in bed. Mr. Fox-Moore was understood to have joined his brother's coaching party. The time had been discreetly chosen — the coast was indubitably clear. But would it remain so?

To insure that it should, Miss Levering had a private conference with the butler.

'Some one is coming to see me on business.'

'Yes, miss.'

'At half-past five.'

'Yes, miss.'

'I specially don't want to be interrupted.'

'No, miss.'

'Not by *any*body, no matter whom.'

'Very well, miss.' A slight pause. 'Shall I show the gentleman into the drawing-room, miss?'

'It's not a gentleman, and I'll see her upstairs in my sitting-room.'

'Yes, miss. Very well, miss.'

'And don't forget — to *any* one else I'm not at home.'

'No, miss. What name, miss?'

Vida hesitated. The servants nowadays read everything. 'Oh, you can't make a mistake. She —— It will be a stranger — some one who has never been here before. Wait! I'll look out of the morning-room window. If it is the person I'm expecting, I'll ring the bell. You understand. If the morning-room bell has rung just as this person comes, it will be the one I'm expecting.'

'Yes, miss.' With a splendid impassivity in the face of precautions so unprecedented, the servant withdrew.

Vida smiled to herself as she leaned back among the cushions of her capacious sofa, cutting the pages of a book. A pleasant place this room of hers, wide and cool, where the creamy background of wall and chintz-cover was lattice-laced with roses. The open windows looked out upon one of those glimpses of greenery made vivid to the London eye, not alone by gratitude, but by contrast of the leafage against the ebonized bark of smoke-ingrained bole and twig.

The summer wind was making great, gentle fans of the plane branches; it was swaying the curtains that hung down in long, straight folds from the high cornices. No other sound in the room but the hard grate of the ivory paper-knife sawing its way through a book whose outside alone (a muddy-brown, pimpled cloth) proclaimed it utilitarian. Among the fair-covered Italian volumes, the vellum-bound poets, and those friends-for-a-lifetime wearing linen or morocco to suit a special taste; above all, among that greater company 'quite impudently French' that stood close ranked on shelves or lay about on tables — the brown book on its dusty modern theme wore the air of a frieze-coated yeoman sitting amongst broadcloth and silk. The reader glanced from time to time at the clock. When the small glittering hand on the porcelain face pointed to twenty minutes past five, the lady took her book and her paper-knife into a front room on the floor below. She sat down behind the lowered persienne, and every now and then lifted her eyes from the page and peered out between the tiny slits. As the time went on she looked out oftener. More than once she half rose and seemed about to abandon all hope of the mysterious visitor when a hansom dashed up to the door. One swift glance: 'They go in cabs!' — and Miss Levering ran to the bell.

A few moments after, she was again established in her sofa corner, and the door of her sitting-room opened. 'The lady, miss.' Into the wide, harmonious space was ushered a hot and harassed-looking woman, in a lank alpaca gown and a tam-o'-shanter. Miss Claxton's clothes, like herself, had borne the heat and burden of the day. She frowned as she gave her hand.

'I am late, but it was very difficult to get away at all.'

Miss Levering pushed towards her one of the welcoming great easy-chairs that stood holding out cool arms and a lap of roses. The tired visitor, with her dusty clothes and brusque manner, sat down without relaxing to the luxurious invitation. Her stiffly maintained attitude and direct look said as plain as print, Now what excuse have you to offer for asking me to come here? It may have been recollection of Mrs. Fox-Moore's fear of 'the thin end of the wedge' that made Miss Levering smile as she said —

'Yes, I've been expecting you for the last half hour, but it's very good of you to come at all.'

Miss Claxton looked as if she quite agreed.

'You'll have some tea?' Miss Levering was moving towards the bell.

'No, I've had my tea.'

The queer sound of 'my' tea connoting so much else! The hostess subsided on to the sofa.

'I heard you speak the other day as I told you in my note. But all the same I came away with several unanswered questions — questions that I wanted to put to you quietly. As I wrote you, I am not what *you* would call a convert. I've only got as far as the inquiry stage.'

Miss Claxton waited.

'Still, if I take up your time, I ought not to let you be out of pocket by it.'

The hostess glanced towards the little spindle-legged writing-table, where, on top of a heap of notes, lay the blue oblong of a cheque-book.

'We consider it part of every day's business to answer questions,' said Miss Claxton.

'I suppose I can make some little contribution without — without its committing me to anything?'

'Committing you ——'

'Yes; it wouldn't get into the papers,' she said, a little shame-faced, 'or — or anything like that.'

'It wouldn't get into the papers unless you put it in.'

The lady blinked. There was a little pause. She was not easy to talk to — this young woman. Nor was she the ideal collector of contributions.

'That was a remarkable meeting you had in Hyde Park last Sunday.'

'Remarkable? Oh, no, they're all pretty much alike.'

'Do they all end like that?'

'Oh, yes; people come to scoff, and by degrees we get hold of them — even the Hyde Park loafers.'

'I mean, do they often crowd up and try to hustle the speakers?'

'Oh, they are usually quite good-natured.'

'You handled them wonderfully.'

'We're used to dealing with crowds.'

Her look went round the room, as if to say, 'It's this kind of thing I'm not used to, and I don't take to it over-kindly.'

'In the crush at the end,' said Miss Levering, 'I overheard a scrap of conversation between two men. They were talking about you. "Very good for a woman," one said.'

Miss Claxton smiled a scornful little smile.

'And the other one said, "It would have been very good for

a man. And personally," he said, "I don't know many men who could have kept that crowd in hand for two hours." That's what two men thought of it.'

She made no answer.

'It doesn't seem to me possible that your speakers average as good as those I heard on Sunday.'

'We have a good many who speak well, but we look upon Ernestine Blunt as our genius.'

'Yes, she seems rather a wonderful little person, but I wrote to you because — partly because you are older. And you gave me the impression of being extremely level-headed.'

'Ernestine Blunt is level-headed too,' said Miss Claxton, warily.

She was looking into the lady's face, frowning a little in that way of hers, intent, even somewhat suspicious.

'Oh, I dare say, but she's such a child!'

'We sometimes think Ernesfine Blunt has the oldest head among us.'

'Really,' said Miss Levering. 'When a person is as young as that, you don't know how much is her own and how much borrowed.'

'She doesn't need to borrow.'

'But *you*. I said to myself, "That woman, who makes other things so clear, she can clear up one or two things for me."'

'Well, I don't know.' More wary than ever, she suspended judgment.

'I noticed none of you paid any attention when the crowd called out — things about ——'

Miss Claxton's frown deepened. It was plain she heard the echo of that insistent, never-answered query of the crowd, 'Got your dog-whip, miss?' She waited.

It looked as though Miss Levering lacked courage to repeat it in all its violent bareness.

'—— when they called out things — about the encounters with the police. It's those stories, as I suppose you know, that have set so many against the movement.'

No word out of Miss Claxton. She sat there, not leaning back, nor any longer stiffly upright, but hunched together like a creature ready to spring.

'I believed those stories too; but when I had watched you, and listened to you on Sunday,' Miss Levering hastened to add, a little shamefaced at the necessity, 'I said to myself, not' (suddenly she stopped and smiled with disarming frankness) — 'I didn't say, "That woman's too well-behaved, or too amiable;" I said, "She's too intelligent. That woman never spat at a policeman."'

'Spit? No,' she said grimly.

'"Nor bit, nor scratched, nor any of those things. And since the papers have lied about that," I said to myself, "I'll go to headquarters for information."'

'What papers do you read?'

'Oh, practically all. This house is like a club for papers and magazines. My brother-in-law has everything.'

'The *Clarion?*'

'No, I never saw the *Clarion.*'

'The *Labour Leader?*'

'No.'

'The *Labour Record?*'

'No.'

'It is the organ of our party.'

'I — I'm afraid I never heard of any of them.'

Miss Claxton smiled.

'I'll take them in myself in future,' said the lady on the sofa. 'Was it reading those papers that set you to thinking?'

'Reading papers? Oh, no. It was ——' She hesitated, and puckered up her brows again as she stared round the room.

'Yes, go on. That's one of the things I wanted to know, if you don't mind — how you came to be identified with the movement.'

A little wearily, without the smallest spark of enthusiasm at the prospect of imparting her biography, Miss Claxton told slowly, even dully, and wholly without passion, the story of a hard life met single-handed from even the tender childhood days — one of those recitals that change the relation between the one who tells and the one who listens — makes the last a sharer in the life to the extent that the two can never be strangers any more. Though they may not meet, nor write, nor have any tangible communication, there is understanding between them.

At the close Miss Levering stood up and gave the other her hand. Neither said anything. They looked at each other.

After the lady had resumed her seat, Miss Claxton, as under some compulsion born of the other's act of sympathy, went on —

'It is a newspaper lie — as you haven't needed to be told — about the spitting and scratching and biting — but the day I was arrested, the day of the deputation to Effingham, I saw a policeman knocking some of our poorer women about very roughly' (it had its significance, the tone in which she said 'our poorer women'). 'I called out that he was not to do that again. He had one of our women like this, and he was banging her against the railings. I called out if he didn't stop I would make him. He kept on' — a cold glitter came into the eyes — 'and I struck him. I struck the coward in the face.'

The air of the mild luxurious room grew hot and quivered. The lady on the sofa lowered her eyes.

'They must be taught,' the other said sternly, 'the police must be taught, they are not to treat our women like that. On the whole the police behave well. But their power is immense and almost entirely unchecked. It's a marvel they are as decent as they are. How should *they* be expected to know how to treat women? What example do they have? Don't they hear constantly in the courts how little it costs a man to be convicted of beating his own wife?' She fired the questions at the innocent person on the sofa, as if she held her directly responsible for the need to ask them. 'Stealing is far more dangerous; yes, even if a man's starving. That's because bread is often dear and women are always cheap.'

She waited a moment, waited for the other to contradict or at least resent the dictum. The motionless figure among the sofa cushions, whose very look and air seemed to proclaim 'some of us are expensive enough,' hardly opened her lips to say, as if to herself —

'Yes, women are cheap.'

Perhaps Miss Claxton thought the agreement lacked conviction, for she went on with a harsh hostility that seemed almost personal —

'We'd rather any day be handled by the police than by the self-constituted stewards of political meetings.'

Partly the words, even more the look in the darkening face, made Miss Levering say —

'That brings me to something else I wanted to be enlightened about. One reason I wrote to ask for a little talk with *you* specially, was because I couldn't imagine your doing anything so futile as to pit your physical strength — considerable as it may be — but to pit your muscle against men's is merely absurd. And I, when I saw how intelligent you were, I saw that you know all that quite as well as I. Why, then, carry a whip?'

The lowered eyelids of the face opposite quivered faintly.

'You couldn't think it would save you from arrest.'

'No, not from arrest.' The woman's mouth hardened.

'I know' — Miss Levering bridged the embarrassment of the pause — 'I know there must be some rational explanation.'

But if there were it was not forthcoming.

'So you see your most indefensible and even futile-appearing action gave the cue for my greatest interest,' said Vida, with a mixture of anxiety and bluntness. 'For just the woman you were, to do so brainless a thing — what was behind? That was what I kept asking myself.'

'It — isn't — only — *rough* treatment one or two of us have met' — she pulled out the words slowly — 'it's sometimes worse.' They both waited in a curious chill embarrassment. 'Not the police, but the stewards at political meetings, and the men who volunteer to "keep the women in order," they' — she raised her fierce eyes and the colour rose in her cheeks — 'as they're turning us out they punish us in ways the public don't know.' She saw the shrinking wonder in the woman opposite, and she did not spare her. 'They punish us by underhand maltreatment — of the kind most intolerable to a decent woman.'

'Oh, no, no!' The other face was a flame to match.

'Yes!' She flung it out like a poisoned arrow.

'How *dare* they!' said Vida in a whisper.

'They know we dare not complain.'

'Why not?'

A duller red overspread the face as the woman muttered, 'Nobody, no woman, wants to talk about it. And if we did they'd only say, "See! you're killing chivalry." *Chivalry!*' She laughed. It was not good to hear a laugh like that.

The figure on the sofa winced. 'I assure you people don't know,' said Vida.

'It's known well enough to those who've had to suffer it, and it's known to the brutes of men who ——'

'Ah, but you *must* realize' — Miss Levering jumped to her feet — 'you must admit that the great mass of men would be indignant if they knew.'

'You think so?' The question was insulting in its air of forbearance with a fairy-tale view of life.

'Think so? I *know* it. I should be sorry for my own powers of judgment if I believed the majority of men were like the worst specimens — like those you ——'

'Oh, well, we don't dwell on that side. It's enough to remember that women without our incentive have to bear worse. It's part of a whole system.'

'I shall never believe that!' exclaimed Vida, thinking what was meant was an organized conspiracy against the Suffragettes.

'Yes, it's all part of the system we are in the world to overturn. Why should we suppose we'd gain anything by complaining? Don't hundreds, thousands of meek creatures who have never defied anybody, don't they have to bear worse ignominies? Every man knows that's true. Who troubles himself? What is the use, we say, of crying about individual pains and penalties? No. The thing is to work day and night to root out the system that makes such things possible.'

'I still don't understand — why you thought it would be a protection to carry ——'

'A man's fear of ridicule will restrain him when nothing else will. If one of them is publicly whipped, *and by a woman,* it isn't likely to be forgotten. Even the fear of it — protects us from some things. After an experience some of the women had, the moment our committee decided on another demonstration, little Mary O'Brian went out, without consulting anybody, and bought me the whip. "If you will go," she said, "you shan't go unarmed. If we have that sort of cur to deal with, the only thing is to carry a dog-whip." '

Miss Claxton clenched her hands in their grey cotton gloves. There was silence in the room for several seconds.

'What we do in asking questions publicly — it's only what

men do constantly. The greatest statesman in the land stops to answer a man, even if he's a fool naturally, or half drunk. They treat those interrupters with respect, they answer their questions civilly. They are men. They have votes. But women: "Where's the chucker out?"'

'Are you never afraid that all you're going through may be in vain?'

'No. We are quite certain to succeed. We have found the right way at last.'

'You mean what are called your tactics?'

'I mean the spirit of the women. I mean: not to mind the price. When you've got people to feel like that, success is sure.'

'But it comes very hard on those few who pay with the person, as the French say, pay with prison — and with —— '

'Prison isn't the worst!'

A kind of shyness came over the woman on the sofa; she dropped her eyes from the other's face.

'Of course,' the ex-prisoner went on, 'if more women did a little it wouldn't be necessary for the few to do so much.'

'I suppose you are in need of funds to carry on the propaganda.'

'Money isn't what is most needed. One of our workers — a little mill girl — came up from the country with only two pounds in her pocket to rouse London. And she did it!' her comrade exulted. 'But there's a class we don't reach. If only' — she hesitated and glanced reflectively at the woman before her.

'Yes?' Miss Levering's eye flew to the cheque-book.

'If only we could get women of influence to understand what's at stake,' said Miss Claxton, a little wistfully.

'They don't?'

'Oh, some. A few. As much as can be expected.'

'Why do you say that?'

'Well, the upper-class women, I don't say all' (she spoke as one exercising an extreme moderation); 'but many of them are such sexless creatures.'

Miss Levering opened wide eyes — a glint of something like amazed laughter crossed her face, as she repeated —

'*They* are sexless, you think?'

'We find them so,' said the other, firmly.

'Why'—Miss Levering smiled outright—'that's what they say of you.'

'Well, it's nonsense, like the rest of what they say.'

The accusation of sexlessness brought against the curled darlings of society by these hard-working, hard-hitting sisters of theirs was not the least ironic thing in the situation.

'Why do you call them ——?'

'Because we see they have no sex-pride. If they had, they couldn't do the things they do.'

'What sort of things?'

'Oh, I can't go into that.' She stood up and tugged at her wrinkled cotton gloves. 'But it's easy for us to see they're sexless.' She seemed to resent the unbelief in the opposite face. 'Lady Caterham sent for me the other day. You may have heard of Lady Caterham.'

Miss Levering suppressed the fact of how much, by a vague-sounding—

'Y—yes.'

'Well, she sent for me to —— Oh, I suppose she was curious!'

'Like me,' said the other, smiling.

'*She's* a very great person in her county, and she *said* she sympathized with the movement—only she didn't approve of our tactics, she said. We are pretty well used by now to people who don't approve of our tactics, so I just sat and waited for the "dog-whip."'

It was obvious that the lady without influence in her county winced at that, almost as though she felt the whip on her own shoulders. She was indeed a hard-hitter, this woman.

'I don't go about talking of why I carry a whip. I *hate* talking about it,' she flung the words out resentfully. 'But I'd been sent to try to get that woman to help, and so I explained. I told her when she asked why it seemed necessary'—again the face flushed—'I told her!—more than I've told you. And will you believe it, she never turned a hair. Just sat there with a look of cool curiosity on her face. Oh, they have no sex-pride, those upper-class women!'

'Lady Caterham probably didn't understand.'

'Perfectly. She asked questions. No, it just didn't matter much to her that a woman should suffer that sort of thing. She didn't feel the indignity of it. Perhaps if it had come to her, *she* wouldn't have suffered,' said the critic, with a grim contempt.

'There may be another explanation,' said Miss Levering, a little curtly, but wisely she forbore to present it.

If the rough and ready reformer had chilled her new sympathizer by this bitterness against 'the parasite class,' she wiped out the memory of it by the enthusiasm with which she spoke of those other women, her fellow-workers.

'Our women are wonderful!' she lifted her tired head. 'I knew they'd never had a chance to show what they were, but there are some things —— No! I didn't think women had it in them.'

She had got up and was standing now by the door, her limp gown clinging round her, her weather-beaten Tam on one side. But in the confident look with which she spoke of 'our women,' the brow had cleared. You saw that it was beautiful. Miss Levering stood at the door with an anxious eye on the stair, as if fearful of the home-coming of 'her fellow-coward,' or, direr catastrophe — old Mr. Fox-Moore's discovering the damning fact of this outlaw's presence under his roof! Yet, even so, torn thus between dread and desire to pluck out the heart of the new mystery, 'the militant woman,' Miss Levering did not speed the parting guest. As though recognizing fully now that the prophesied use was not going to be made of the 'thin end of the wedge,' she detained her with —

'I wonder when I shall see you again.'

'I don't know,' said the other, absently.

'When is the next meeting?'

'Next Sunday. Every Sunday.'

'I shall be glad to hear you speak again; but—you'll come and see me — here.'

'I can't. I'm going away.'

'Oh! To rest, I hope.'

'Rest?' She laughed at an idea so comic. 'Oh, no. I'm going to work among the women in Wales. We have great hopes of those West-country women. They're splendid! They're learning the secret of co-operation, too. Oh, it's good stuff to work on — the relief of it after London!'

Miss Levering smiled. 'Then I won't be seeing you very soon.'

'No.' She seemed to be thinking. 'It's true what I say of the Welsh women, and yet we oughtn't to be ungrateful to our London women either.' She seemed to have some sense of injustice on her soul. 'We've been seeing just recently what they're made of, too!' She paused on the threshold and began to tell in a low voice of women 'new to the work,' who had been wavering, uncertain if they could risk imprisonment — poor women with husbands and children. 'When they heard *what it might mean* — this battle we're fighting — they were ashamed not to help us!'

'You mean ——' Vida began, shrinking.

'Yes!' said the other, fiercely. 'The older women saw they ought to save the younger ones from having to face that sort of thing. That was how we got some of the wives and mothers.'

She went on with a stern emotion that was oddly contagious, telling about a certain scene at the Headquarters of the Union. Against the grey and squalid background of a Poor Women's movement, stood out in those next seconds a picture that the true historian who is to come will not neglect. A call for recruits with this result — a huddled group, all new, unproved, ignorant of the ignorant. The two or three leaders, conscience-driven, feeling it necessary to explain to the untried women that if they shared in the agitation, they were not only facing imprisonment, but unholy handling.

'It was only fair to let them know the worst,' said the woman at the door, 'before they were allowed to join us.'

As the abrupt sentences fell, the grim little scene was reconstituted; the shrinking of the women who had offered their services ignorant of this aspect of the battle — their horror and their shame. At the memory of that hour the strongly-controlled voice shook.

'They cried, those women,' she said.

'But they came?' asked the other, trembling, as though for her, too, it was vital that these poor women should not quail.

'Yes,' answered their leader a little hoarsely, 'they came!'

CHAPTER XII

ONE of the oddest things about these neo-Suffragists was the simplicity with which they accepted aid — the absence in the responsible ones of conventional gratitude. This became matter for both surprise and instruction to the outsider. It no doubt had the effect of chilling and alienating the 'philanthropist on the make.' Even to the less ungenerous, not bargainers for approbation or for influence, even in their case the deep-rooted suspicion we have been taught to cultivate for one another, makes the gift of good faith so difficult that it can be given freely only to people like these, people who plainly and daily suffered for their creed, who stood to lose all the things most of us strive for, people who valued neither comfort, nor money, nor the world's good word. That they took help, and even sacrifice, as a matter of course, seemed in them mere modesty and sound good sense; tantamount to saying, 'I am not so silly or self-centred as to suppose you do this for *me*. You do it, of course, for the Cause. The Cause is yours — is all Women's. You serve humanity. Who am I that I should thank you?'

This attitude extended even to acts that were in truth prompted less by concern for the larger issue than by sheer personal interest.

Vida Levering's first experience of this 'new attitude' came one late afternoon while on her way to leave cards on some people in Grosvenor Road. Driving through Pimlico about half-past six, she lifted up her eyes at the sound of many voices and beheld a mob of men and boys in the act of pursuing a little group of women, who were fleeing up a side street away from the river. The natural shrinking and disgust of 'the sheltered woman' showed in the face of the occupant of the brougham as she leaned forward and said to the coachman —

'Not this way! Don't you see there's some disturbance? Turn back.'

The man obeyed. The little crowd had halted. It looked as

if the thief, or drunken woman, or what not, had been surrounded and overwhelmed. The end of the street abutted on Pimlico Pier. Two or three knots of people were still standing about, talking and looking up the street at the little crowd of shouting, gesticulating rowdies. A woman with a perambulator, making up her mind at just the wrong moment to cross the road, found herself almost under the feet of the Fox-Moore horses. The coachman pulled up sharply, and before he had driven on, the lady's eyes had fallen on an inscription in white chalk on the flagstone —

'VOTES FOR WOMEN.

'Meeting here to-night at a quarter to six.'

The occupant of the carriage turned her head sharply in the direction of the 'disturbance,' and then —

'After all, I must go up that street. Drive fast till you get near those people. Quick!'

'Up *there*, miss?'

'Yes, yes. Make haste!' For the crowd was moving on, and still no sign of a policeman.

By the time the brougham caught up with them, the little huddle of folk had nearly reached the top of the street. In the middle of the *mêlée* a familiar face. Ernestine Blunt!

'Oh, Henderson!' — Miss Levering put her head out of the window — 'that girl! the young one! She's being mobbed.'

'Yes, miss.'

'But something must be done! Hail a policeman.'

'Yes, miss.'

'Do you *see* a policeman?'

'No, miss.'

'Well, stop a moment,' for even at this slowest gait the brougham had passed the storm centre.

The lady hanging out of the window looked back and saw that Ernestine's face, very pink as to cheeks, very bright as to eyes, was turned quite unruffled on the rabble.

'Can't you see the meeting's over?' she called out. 'You boys go home now and think about what we've told you.'

The reply to that was a laugh and a concerted 'rush' that all but carried the girl and her companions off their feet. To Henderson's petrifaction, the door of the brougham was hastily opened and then slammed to, leaving Miss Levering in the road, saying to him over her shoulder —

'Wait just round the corner, unless I call.'

With which she hurried across the street, her eyes on the little face that, in spite of its fresh colouring, looked so pathetically tired. Making her way round the outer fringe of the crowd, Vida saw on the other side — near where Ernestine and her sore-beset companions stood with their backs to the wall — an opening in the dingy ranks. Fleet of foot, she gained it, thrust an arm between the huddled women, and, taking the foolhardy girl by the sleeve, said, *sotto voce* —

'Come! Come with me!'

Ernestine raised her eyes, fixed them for one calm instant on Vida Levering's face, and then, turning round, said —

'Where's Mrs. Brown?'

'Never mind Mrs. Brown!' whispered the strange lady, drawing off as the rowdy young men came surging round that side.

There was another rush and a yell, and Vida fled. When next she turned to look, it was to see two women making a sudden dash for liberty. They had escaped through the rowdy ranks, and they tore across the street, running for their lives and calling for help as they ran.

Vida, a shade or two paler, stood transfixed. What was going to happen? But there was the imperturbable Ernestine holding the forsaken position, still the centre of the pushing, shouting little mob who had jeered frantically as the other women fled.

It was too much. Not Ernestine's isolation alone, the something childish in the brilliant face would have enlisted a less sympathetic observer. A single moment's wavering and the lady made for the place where the besiegers massed less thick. She was near enough now to call out over the rowdies' heads —

'Come. Why do you stay there?'

Faces turned to look at her; while Ernestine shouted back the cryptic sentence —

'It wasn't my bus!'

Bus? Had danger robbed her of her reason? The boys were cheering now and looking past Miss Levering: she turned, bewildered, to see 'Mrs. Brown' and a sister reformer mounting the top of a sober London Road car. They had been running for that, then — and not for life! Miss Levering raised her hand and her voice as she looked back at Ernestine —

'I've got a trap. Come!'

'Where?'

Ernestine stepped out from the vociferating, jostling crowd and followed the new face as simply as though she had been waiting for just that summons. The awful moment was when, with a shout, the tail of rowdies followed after. Miss Levering had not bargained for that. Her agitated glance left the unsavoury horde at her heels and went nervously up and down the street. It was plainly not only, nor even chiefly, the hooligans she feared, but the amazéd eye of some acquaintance. Bad enough to meet Henderson's!

'Jump in!' she said hastily to the girl, and then, 'Go on!' she called out desperately, flying in after Ernestine and slamming the door. 'Drive *fast!*' She thrust her head through the window to add, '*Anywhere!*' And she sank back. 'How dreadful that was!'

'What was?' said the rescued one, glancing out of the carriage with an air of suddenly renewed interest.

'Why, the attack of those hooligans on a handful of defenceless women.'

'Oh, they weren't attacking us.'

'What were they doing?'

'Oh, just running after us and screaming a little.'

'But I *saw* them — pushing and jostling and ——'

'Oh, it was all quite good-natured.'

'You mean you weren't frightened?'

'There's nothing to be frightened at.' She was actually saying it in a soothing, 'motherly' sort of way, calculated to steady the lady's nerves — reassuring the rescuer.

Vida's eye fell on the festoon of braid falling from the dark cloth skirt.

'Well, the polite attentions of your friends seem to have rather damaged your gown.'

Over a big leather portfolio that she held clasped in her arms, Ernestine, too, looked down at the torn frock.

'That foolish trimming — it's always getting stepped on.'

Miss Levering's search had produced a pin.

'No; I'll just pull it off.'

Ernestine did so, and proceeded to drop a yard of it out of the window. Miss Levering began to laugh.

'Which way are we going?' says Miss Blunt, looking out. 'I have to be at Battersea at ——'

'What were you doing at Pimlico Pier?'

'Holding a meeting for the Government employees — the people who work for the Army and Navy Clothing Department.'

'Oh. And you live at Battersea?'

'No; but I have a meeting there to-night. We had a very good one at the Docks, too.' Her eyes sparkled.

'A Suffrage meeting?'

'Yes; one of the best we've had ——'

'When was that?'

'During the dinner hour. The men stood with their pails and ate while they listened. They were quite nice and understanding, those men.'

'What day was that?'

'This morning.'

'And the Battersea meeting?'

'That's not for another hour; but I have to be there first — to arrange.'

'When do you dine?'

'Oh, I'll get something either before the meeting or after — whenever there's time.'

'Isn't it a pity not to get your food regularly? Won't you last longer if you do?'

'Oh, I shall last.' She sat contentedly, hugging her big portfolio.

The lady glanced at the carriage clock. 'In the house where I live, dinner is a sort of sacred rite. If you are two seconds late you are disgraced, so I'm afraid I can't ——'

'There's the bus I was waiting for!' Ernestine thrust her head out. 'Stop, will you!' she commanded the astonished Henderson. 'Good-bye.' She nodded, jumped out, shut the door, steadied her hat, and was gone.

It was so an acquaintance began that was destined to make a

difference to more than one life. Those days of the summer that Miss Claxton spent indoctrinating the women of Wales, and that Mrs. Chisholm utilized in 'organizing Scotland,' were dedicated by Ernestine and her friends to stirring up London and the various dim and populous worlds of the suburbs.

Much oftener than even Mrs. Fox-Moore knew, her sister, instead of being in the houses where she was supposed to be, and doing the things she was expected to be doing, might have been seen in highly unexpected haunts prosecuting her acquaintance with cockney crowds, never learning Ernestine's fearlessness of them, and yet in some way fascinated almost as much as she was repelled. At first she would sit in a hansom at safe distance from the turmoil that was usually created by the expounders of what to the populace was a 'rum new doctrine' invented by Ernestine. Miss Levering would lean over the apron of the cab hearing only scraps, till the final, 'Now, all who are in favour of Justice, hold up their hands.' As the crowd broke and dissolved, the lady in the hansom would throw open the doors, and standing up in front of the dashboard, she would hail and carry off the arch-agitator, while the crowd surged round. Several times this programme had been carried out, when one afternoon, after seeing the girl and her big leather portfolio safe in the cab, and the cab safe out of the crowd, Vida heaved a sigh of relief.

'*There!* Now tell me, what did you do yesterday?' — meaning, How in the world did you manage without me to take care of you?

'Yesterday? We had a meeting down at the Woolwich Arsenal. And we distributed handbills for two hours. And we had a debate in the evening at the New Reform Club.'

'Oh, you didn't hold a meeting here in the afternoon?'

'Yes we did. I forgot that.' She seemed also to have forgotten that her new friend had been prevented from appearing to carry her off.

Miss Levering smiled down at her. 'What a funny little person you are. Do you know who I am?'

'No.'

'It hasn't ever occurred to you to ask?'

The face turned to her with a half roguish smile. 'Oh, I thought you looked all right.'

'I'm the person who had the interview with your friend, Miss

Claxton.' As no recollection showed in the face, 'At Queen Anne's Gate,' she added.

'I don't think I knew about that,' said Ernestine, absently. Then alert, disdainful, 'Fancy the member for Wrotton saying —— Yes, we went to see him this morning.'

'Oh, that is very exciting! What was he like?'

'Quite a feeble sort of person, I thought.'

'Really!' laughed Miss Levering.

'He talked such nonsense to us about that old Plural Voting Bill. His idea seemed to be to get us to promise to behave nicely while the overworked House of Commons considered the iniquity of some men having more than one vote — they hadn't a minute this session to consider the much greater iniquity of no women having any vote at all! Of course he said he *had* been a great friend to Woman Suffrage, until he got shocked with our tactics.' She smiled broadly. 'We asked him what he'd ever done to show his friendship.'

'Well?'

'He didn't seem to know the answer to that. What strikes me most about men is their being so illogical.'

* * * * * * *

Lady John Ulland had been openly surprised, even enthusiastically grateful, at discovering before this that Vida Levering was ready to help her with some of the unornamental duties that fall to the lot of the 'great ladies' of England.

'I don't know what that discontented creature, her sister, means by saying Vida is so unsympathetic about charity work.'

Neither could Lady John's neighbour, the Bishop, understand Mrs. Fox-Moore's reproach. Had not his young kinswoman's charity concerts helped to rebuild the chantry?

'Such a *nice creature!*' was Lord John's contribution. Then, showing the profundity of his friendly interest, 'Why doesn't she find some nice fella to marry her?'

'People don't marry so early nowadays,' his wife reassured him.

Lord Borrodaile, to whom Vida still talked freely, he alone had some understanding of the changed face life was coming to wear for her. When he found that laughing at her failed of the desired effect, he offered touching testimony to his affection for her by trying to understand. It was no small thing for a man like Borrodaile, who, for the rest, found it no easier than others of his class rightly to interpret the modern scene as looked down upon from the narrow lancet of the mediæval tower which was his mind.

When she got him to smile at her report of the humours of the populace, he did so against his will, shaking his long Van Dyke head, and saying —

'It spoils the fun for me to think of your being there. I have a quite unconquerable distrust of eccentricity.'

'There's nothing the least original about my mixing with "The People," as my sister would call them. The women of my world would often go slumming. The only difference between me and them may be that I, perhaps, shall go a little farther, that's all.'

'Well, I devoutly hope you won't!' he said, with unusual emphasis. 'Let the proletariat attend to the affairs of the proletariat. They don't need a woman like you.'

'They not only need — what's more, they are getting, all kinds! It's that, more than anything else, that shows their strength. The miracle it is, to see the way they all work together! Women, the poorest and most ignorant (except of hardship), working shoulder to shoulder with women of substance and position. Oh, yes, they are winning over that sort, teachers and university graduates — a whole group who would be called Intellectuals if they were men — all doing what men have said women could never do — pulling together. And, oh! that reminds me,' she said suddenly, smiling as one who has thought of a capital joke at her companion's expense: 'it's my duty to warn you. I went with your daughter to lunch at her Country Club, and they were all discussing the Suffrage! A good dozen! And Sophia — well, Sophia came out in a new light. I want you, please, to believe *I've* never talked to her.'

'Oh,' said Borrodaile, with an unconscious arrogance, 'Sophia doesn't wait to be talked to. She takes her own line. Politics are a tradition with our women. I found her reading the parliamentary debates when she was fourteen.'

'And your boys, are they equally ——?'

He sighed. 'The world has got very topsy-turvy. All my girls are boys — and all my boys are girls.'

'Well, Sophia can take care of the Country Club! I remember how we scoffed when she organized it.'

'It's had precisely the effect I expected. Takes her away from her own home, where she ought to be ——'

'Who wants her at home?'

Unblushingly he answered, '*I* do.'

'Why, you're never there yourself.' He blinked. 'When you aren't in your garden you're ——'

'Here?' he laughed.

'I don't myself,' she went on, '*I* don't belong to any clubs ——'

'I should hope not, indeed! Where should I go for tea and for news of the workings of the Zeitgeist?' he mocked.

'But I begin to see what women's clubs are for.'

'They're for the dowdy, unattached females to meet and gossip in, to hold feeble little debates in, to listen to pettifogging little lectures, and imagine they're *dans le mouvement*.'

'They are to accustom women to thinking and acting together. While you and I have been laughing at them, they've been building up a huge machinery of organization, ready to the hand of the chief engineer who is to come.'

'Horrible thought!'

'Well, horrible or not, I don't despise clubs any more. They're largely responsible for the new corporate spirit among women.'

He pulled himself out of the cavernous comfort of his chair, and stood glooming in front of the screen that hid the fireless grate.

'Clubs, societies, leagues, they're all devices for robbing people of their freedom. It's no use to talk to me. I'm one of the few individualists left in the world. I never wanted in my life to belong to any body.' Her pealing laughter made him explain, smiling, 'To any corporation, was what I meant.'

'No, no. You got it right the first time! The reason that, in spite of my late perversities, you don't cast me off is because I'm one of the few women who don't make claims.'

'It is the claim of the community that I resent. I want to keep clear of all complication. I want to be really free. I could never have pledged myself to any Church or any party.'

'Perhaps' — she smiled at him — 'perhaps that's why you are a beautiful and ineffectual angel.'

'The reason I never did is because I care about liberty — the thing itself. You are in danger, I see, of being enamoured of the name. In thought women are always half a century or so behind. What patriot's voice is heard in Europe or America to-day? Where is the modern Kossuth, Garibaldi? What poet goes out in these times to die at Missolonghi? Just as men are finding out the vanity of the old dreams, the women seem to be seizing on them. The mass of intelligent men have no longing for political power. If a sort of public prominence is thrust on men'—he shrugged as if his shoulders chafed under some burden—'*in their hearts* they curse their lot. I suppose it's all so new to the woman she is amused. She even—I'm *told*'—his lifted hand, with the closed fingers suddenly flung open, advertised the difficulty a sane person found in crediting the uncanny rumour—'I'm *told* that women even like public dinners.'

'Well, you do.'

'I?'

'You go—to all the most interesting ones.'

'Part of my burden! Unlike your new friends, there's nothing I hate so much, unless it is having to make a speech.'

'Well, now, shall I stop "playing at ma'ams" and just say that when I hear a man like you explaining in that superior way how immensely he *doesn't care*, I seem to see that that is precisely the worst indictment against your class. If special privilege breeds that——'

It merely amused him to see that she was forgetting herself. He sat down again. He stretched out his long legs and interlaced his fingers across his bulging shirt front. His air of delicate mockery supplied the whip.

'If,' Vida went on with shining eyes, 'if to be able to care and to work and to sacrifice, if to get those impulses out of life, you must carry your share of the world's burden, then no intelligent creature can be sorry the day is coming when all men will have to——' She took breath, a little frightened to see where she was going.

'Have to——?' he encouraged her, lazily smiling.

'Have to work, or else not eat.'

'Even under your hard rule I wouldn't have to work much. My appetite is mercifully small.'

'It would grow if you sweated for your bread.'

'Help! help!' he said, not above his usual tone, but slowly

he turned his fine head as the door opened. He fixed the amused grey-green eyes on old Mr. Fox-Moore: 'A small and inoffensive pillar of the Upper House is in the act of being abolished.'

'What, is she talking politics? She never favours me with her views,' said Fox-Moore, with his chimpanzee smile.

When Borrodaile had said good-bye, Vida followed him to the top of the stairs.

'It's rather on my mind that I — I've not been very nice to you.'

'"I would not hear thine enemy say so."'

'Yes, I've been rather horrid. I went and Trafalgar-Squared you, when I ought to have amused you.'

'But you have amused me!' His eyes shone mischievously.

'Oh, very well.' She took the gibe in good part, offering her hand again.

'Good-bye, my dear,' he said gently. 'It's great fun having you in the world!' He spoke as though he had personally arranged this provision against dulness for his latter end.

The next evening he came up to her at a party to ask why she had absented herself from a dinner the night before where he expected to find her.

'Oh, I telephoned in the morning they weren't to expect me.'

'What were you doing, I should like to know?'

'No, you wouldn't like to know. But you couldn't have helped laughing if you'd seen me.'

'Where?'

'Wandering about the purlieus of Battersea.'

'Bless me! Who with?'

'Why, with that notorious Suffragette, Miss Ernestine Blunt. Oh, you'd have stared even harder if you'd seen us, I promise you! She with a leather portfolio under one arm — a most business-like apparatus, and a dinner-bell in one hand.'

'A *dinner* bell!' He put his hand to his brow as one who feels reason reeling.

'Yes, holding fast to the clapper so that we shouldn't affright the isle out of season. I, if you please, carrying an armful of propagandist literature.'

'Good Lord! *Where* do you say these orgies take place?'

'Near the Fire Station on the far side of Battersea Park.'

'I think you are in great need of somebody to look after you,' he laughed, but no one who knew him could mistake his seriousness. 'Come over here.' He found a sofa a little apart from the crush. 'Who goes with you on these raids?'

'Why, Ernestine — or rather, I go with her.'

'But who takes care of you?'

'Ernestine.'

'Who knows you're doing this kind of thing?'

'Ernestine — and you. It's a secret.'

'Well, if I'm the only sane person who knows — it's something of a responsibility.'

'I won't tell you about it if it oppresses you.'

'On the contrary, I insist on your telling me.'

Vida smiled reflectively. 'The mode of procedure strikes one as highly original. It is simple beyond anything in the world. They select an open space at the convergence of several thoroughfares — if possible, near an omnibus centre. For these smaller meetings they don't go to the length of hiring a lorry. Do you know what a lorry is?'

'I regret to say my education in that direction leaves something to be desired.'

'Last week I was equally ignorant. To-day I can tell you all about it. A lorry is a cart or a big van with the top off. But such elegancies are for the parks. In Battersea, you go into some modest little restaurant, and you say, "Will you lend me a chair?" This is a surprise for the Battersea restaurateur.'

'Naturally — poor man!'

'Exactly. He refuses. But he also asks questions. He is amazed. He is against the franchise for women. "You'll *never* get the vote!" "Well, we must have something," says Ernestine. "I'm sure it isn't against your principles to lend a woman a chair." She lays hands on one. "I never said you could have one of my ——" "But you meant to, didn't you? Isn't a chair one of the things men have always been ready to offer us? Thank you. I'll take good care of it and bring it back quite safe." Out marches Ernestine with the enemy's property. She carries the chair into the road and plants it in front of the Fire Station. Usually there are two or three "helpers." Sometimes Ernestine, if you please, carries the meeting entirely on her own shoulders — those same shoulders being about so wide. Yes, she's quite a little thing. If there are helpers she sends them up and down the street sowing a fresh crop of handbills. When Ernestine is ready to begin she stands up on that chair, in the open street and, as if she were doing the most natural thing in the world, she begins ringing that dinner bell. Naturally people stop and stare and draw nearer. Ernestine tells me that Battersea has got so used now to the ding-dong and to associating it with "our meeting," that as far off as they hear it the inhabitants say, "It's the Suffragettes! Come along!" and from one street and another the people emerge laughing and running. Of course as soon as there is a little crowd that attracts more, and so the snowball grows. Sometimes the traffic is impeded. Oh, it's a much odder world than I had suspected!' For a moment laughter interrupted the narrative. '"The Salvation Army doesn't *quite* approve of us," Ernestine says, "and the Socialists don't love us either! We always take their audiences away from them—poor things," says Ernestine, with a sympathetic air. "*You* do!" I say, because'—Vida nodded at Lord Borrodaile—'you must know Ernestine is a beguiler.'

'Oh, a beguiler. I didn't suppose——'

'No, it's against the tradition, I know, but it's true. She herself, however, doesn't seem to realize her beguilingness. "It isn't any one in particular they come to hear," she says, "it's just that a woman making a speech is so much more interesting than a man making a speech." It surprises you? So it did me.'

'Nothing surprises me!' said Borrodaile, with a wave of his long hands.

'Last night she was wonderful, our Ernestine! Even I, who am used to her, I was stirred. I was even thrilled. She had that crowd in the hollow of her hand! When she wound up, "The motion is carried. The meeting is over!" and climbed down off her perch, the mob cheered and pressed round her so close that I had to give up trying to join her. I extricated myself and crossed the street. She is so little that, unless she's on a chair, she is swallowed up. For a long time I couldn't see her. I didn't know whether she was taking the names and addresses of the people who want to join the Union, or whether she had slipped away and gone home, till I saw practically the whole crowd moving off after her up the street. I followed for some distance on the off-side. She went calmly on her way, a tiny figure in a long grey coat between two helpers, the Lancashire cotton-spinner and the Cockney working woman, with that immense tail of boys and men (and a few women) all following after — quite quiet and well-behaved — just following, because it didn't occur to them to do anything else. In a way she was still exercising her hold over her meeting. I saw, presently, there was one person in front of her — a great big fellow — he looked like a carter — he was carrying home the chair!'

They both laughed.

'Well, she's found a thick-and-thin advocate in you apparently,' said Borrodaile.

'Ah! if only you could *see* her! trudging along, apparently quite oblivious of her quaint following, dinner bell in one hand, leather case piled high with "tracts" on the other arm, some of the leaflets sliding off, tumbling on to the pavement.' Vida laughed as she recalled the scene. 'Then dozens of hands darting out to help her to recover her precious property! After the chair had been returned the crowd thinned, and I crossed over to her.'

'You in that *mêlée!*' Borrodaile ejaculated. 'Well, Ernestine hadn't the quaintness all to herself.'

'No. Oh, no,' Vida agreed. 'I thought of you, and how you'd look if you had come on us suddenly. After the crowd had melted and the helpers had vanished into the night, we went on together — all the way, from the Battersea Fire Station to Sloane Square, did Ernestine and I walk, talking reform last night. You laugh? So do I; but not at Ernestine. She's a most wonderful person. I sometimes ask myself if the world will ever know half how wonderful. You, for instance, you haven't, after all I've said, you haven't *an idea!*'

'Oh, I don't doubt — I don't think I ever doubted that women have a facility in speech — no, no, I'm not gibing! I don't even doubt they can, as you say, sway and control crowds. But I maintain it is very bad for the women.'

'How is it bad?'

'How can it fail to be! All that horrible publicity. All that concentrating of crude popular interest on themselves! Believe me, nobody who watches a public career carefully but sees the demoralizing effect the limelight has even on men's characters.

N

And I suppose you'll admit that men are less delicately organized than women.'

'I can only say I've seen the sort of thing you mean in our world, where a good many women have only themselves to think about. I've looked in vain for those evil effects among the Suffrage women. It almost seems, on the contrary, as if there were something ennobling in working for a public cause.'

'Personally, I can't say I've observed it — not among the political women of my acquaintance!'

'But you only know the old kind. Yes, the kind whose idea of influence is to make men fall in love with them, whose idea of working is to put on a smart gown and smile their prettiest. No, I agree that *isn't* necessarily ennobling!'

'I see, it's the new taste in manners and the new arts of persuasion that make the ideal women and' — with an ironic little bow — 'the impassioned convert.'

'I'm bound to admit,' she said stoutly, 'that I think the Suffrage movement in England has the advantage of being engineered by a very remarkable set of women. Not in ability alone, but in dignity of character. People will never know, I sometimes think, how much the movement has owed to being taken in hand by just these particular women. I don't pretend they're the average. They're very far above the average. And what the world will owe to them I very much doubt if even the future will know. But I seem to be the only one who minds.' She laughed. 'I could take my oath *they* never give the matter a thought. One thing ——' She leaned forward and then checked herself. 'No, I've talked about them enough!'

She opened her fan and looked about the crowded room.

'Say what you were going to. I'm reconciled. I see what's coming.'

'What's coming?'

'Yes. Go on.'

She looked at him a little perplexed over the top of her fan.

'I was only going to say that what struck me particularly in that girl, for instance, is her inaccessibility to flattery. I've watched her with men.'

'Of course! She knew you were watching her. She no doubt thinks the eyes of the world are upon her.'

'On the contrary, it's her unselfconsciousness that's the most surprising thing about her. Or, no! It's something more interesting even than that. She *is* conscious, in a way, of the hold she has on the public. But it hasn't any of the deteriorating effect you were deprecating. I've been moved once or twice to congratulate her. She takes it as unmoved as a child. It's just as if you said to a little thing of three, "What a clever baby you are!" or, "You've got the most beautiful eyes in the world." The child would realize that you meant well, that you were being pleasant, but it wouldn't think about either its cleverness or its eyes. It's like that with Ernestine. When I said to her, "You made an astoundingly good speech to-night. The best I've heard even you make," she looked at me with a sort of half-absent-minded, half-wondering expression, without a glimmer of personal vanity. When I was so ill-advised as not to drop the subject, when I ventured to say something more about that great gift of hers, she interrupted me with a little laugh, "It's a sign of grace in you not to get tired of our speeches," she said. "I suppose we repeat ourselves a good deal. You see that's just what we've got to do. We've got to *hammer it in*." But the fact is that she doesn't repeat herself, that she's always fresh and stimulating, because — I suppose it's because she's always thinking of the Great Impersonal Object, and talking about it out of her own eager heart. Ernestine? She's as unhackneyed as a spring morning!'

'Oh, very well. I'll go.'

'Go? Where?' for he still sat there.

'Why, to hear your paragon. I've seen that was what you were leading up to.'

'N — no. I don't think I want you to go.'

'Oh, yes, you do. I knew you'd make me sooner or later.'

'No, don't be afraid.' She stood up.

'I'm not afraid. I'm eager,' he laughed.

She shook her head. 'No, I'll never take you.'

'Why not?'

'Because — it isn't all Ernestine and skittles. And because you'd make me keenly alive again to all sorts of things that I see now don't matter — things that have lost some of their power to trouble me, but that I should feel for you.'

'What sort of ——'

'Oh, oddities, uglinesses — things that abound, I'm told, at all men's meetings, and that yet, somehow, we'd like to eliminate from women's quite on the old angel theory. No, I won't take you!'

CHAPTER XIII

THE following afternoon, at half-past five, the carelessly dressed, rather slouching figure of Lord Borrodaile might have been seen walking along the Thames Embankment in the neighbourhood of Pimlico Pier. He passed without seeing the only other person visible at that quiet hour — one of the 'unemployed,' like himself, but save in that respect sufficiently unlike the Earl of Borrodaile was the grimy, unshaven tramp collapsed in one corner of the double-seated municipal bench. Lord Borrodaile's fellow-citizen leaned heavily on one of the stout scrolls of ironwork which, repeated at regular intervals on each side, divided the seat into six compartments. No call for any one to notice such a man — there are so many of them in these piping times of peace and prosperity. Then, too, they go crawling about our world protected from notice, as the creatures are who take their colouring from bark or leaf or arctic snows. So these other forms of life, weather-beaten, smoke-begrimed, subdued to the hues of the dusty roads they travel, and the unswept spaces where they sleep — over these the eye glides unseeing.

As little interested in the gentleman as the gentleman was in him, the wastrel contemplated the river with grimly speculative eye. But when suddenly Borrodaile's sauntering figure came to a standstill near the lower end of the bench, the tramp turned his head and watched dully the gloveless hands cross one over the other on the knob of the planted umbrella; the bent head; one hand raised now, groping about the waistcoat, lighting upon what it sought and raising a pince-nez, through which he read the legend scrawled in chalk upon the pavement. With a faint saturnine smile Lord Borrodaile dropped the glass, and took his bearings. He consulted his watch, and walked on.

Upon his return a quarter of an hour later, he viewed the same little-alluring prospect from the opposite side of the street. The tramp still stared at the river, but on his side of the bench, at the other end, sat a lady reading a book. Between the two motionless figures and the parapet, a group of dirty children were wrangling. Lord Borrodaile crossed the wide street and paused a moment just behind the lady. He leaned forward as if to speak to her across the middle division of the bench. But he reconsidered, and turning his back to her, sat down and drew an evening paper out of his pocket. He was so little like that glittering figment, the peer of popular imagination, that the careless sobriety of dress and air in the person of this third occupant of the capacious double bench struck an even less arresting note than the frank wretchedness of the other man.

Presently one of the children burst out crying, and continued to howl lustily till the lady looked up from her page and inquired what was the matter. The unwashed infant stared open-mouthed at this intruder upon her grief. Instead of answering, she regarded the lady with a bored astonishment, as who should say: What are you interrupting me for, just in the middle of a good yell? She then took up the strain as nearly as possible where she had left off. She was getting on very well with this second attempt at a demonstration until Miss Levering made some mention of a penny, whereupon the infant again suspended her more violent manifestations, though the tears kept rolling down.

After various attempts on the lady's part, the little girl was induced to come and occupy the middle place on the river side of the bench, between Vida and the tramp. While the lady held the penny in her hand, and cross-examined the still weeping child, Borrodaile sat quietly listening behind his paper. When the child couldn't answer those questions that were of a general nature, the tramp did, and the three were presently quite a pleasant family party. The only person 'out of it' was the petrified gentleman on the other side.

A few minutes before the arrival of the Suffragettes, two nondescript young men, in a larky mood, appeared with the announcement that they'd seen 'one of them' at the top of Ranelagh Street.

'That'll be the little 'un,' said the tramp to nobody. 'You don't ketch 'er bein' late!'

'Blunt! No — cheeky little devil,' remarked one of the young men, offering a new light upon the royal virtue of punctuality; but from the enthusiasm with which they availed themselves of the rest of Lord Borrodaile's side of the bench, it was obvious they had hurried to the spot with the intention of securing front seats at the show.

'Of course it ain't goin' to be as much fun as the 'Yde Park Sunday aufternoons. Jim Wrightson goes to them. Keeps things lively — 'e does.'

'Kicks up a reg'lar shindy, don't 'e?'

'Yes. We can't do nothin' 'ere — ain't enough' — whether of space or of spirited young men he did not specify.

As they lit their cigarettes the company received further additions — one obviously otherwise employed than with politics. Her progress — was it symbolic? — was necessarily slow, for a small child clung to her skirt, and she trundled a sickly boy in a go-cart. The still sniffling person in possession of the middle seat on the other side (her anxious and watery eye fixed on the penny) was told by Miss Levering to make room for the new-comers. The child's way of doing so was to crowd closer to the neighbourhood of the fascinating coin. But that mandate to 'make room' had proved a conversational opening through which poured — or trickled rather — the mother's sorry little history. Her husband was employed in the clothing department of the Army and Navy Stores — yes, nine years now. He was considered very lucky to keep his place when the staff was reduced. But the costliness of raising the children! It was well that three were dead. If she had it all to do over again — no! no!

The seeming heartlessness with which she envisaged the non-existence of her babies contrasted strangely with her patient tenderness to the querulous boy in the go-cart.

Meanwhile Miss Levering had not forgotten her earlier acquaintance. As the wan mother watched the end of the transaction which left the sniffler now quite consoled, in possession of the modest coin, she said naïvely —

'When anybody gives one of my children a penny, I always save half of it for them the next day.'

Vida Levering turned her head away, and in so doing met Lord Borrodaile's eyes over the back of the bench. She gave a faint start of surprise, and then —

'She saves half of it!' was all she said.

Borrodaile, glancing shrewdly over the further augmented gathering, asked the invariable question —

'How do you account for the fact that so few women are here to show their interest in a matter that's supposed to concern them so much?' Vida craned her head. 'Beside you, only one!' Borrodaile's mocking voice went on. 'Isn't this an instance of your sex's indifference to the whole thing? Isn't it equally an instance of man's keenness about public questions?' He couldn't forbear adding in a whisper, 'Even such a question, and such men?'

Vida still craned, searching in vain for refutation in female form. But she did not take her failure lying down.

'The men who are here,' she said, 'the great majority of men at all open-air meetings seem to be loafers. Woman — whatever else she may or may not be — isn't a loafer!' Through Borrodaile's laugh she persisted. 'A woman always seems to have something to do, even if it's of the silliest description. Yes, and if she's a decent person at all, she's not hanging about at street corners waiting for some diversion!'

'Not bad; not bad! I see you are catching the truly martial spirit.'

'That's them, ain't it?' One of the young men jumped up.

Vida turned her head in time to see the meeting between two girls and a woman arriving from opposite directions.

'Yes,' she whispered; 'that's Ernestine with the pile of handbills on her arm.'

The lady sent out smiles and signals of welcome with a lifted hand. The busy propagandist took no notice. She was talking to her two companions, one of whom, the younger with head on one side, kept shooting out glances half provocative, half appealing, towards Lord Borrodaile and the young men. She seemed as keenly alive to the fact of these male presences as the two other women seemed oblivious.

'Which is the one,' asked Lord Borrodaile, 'that you were telling me about?'

'Why, Ernestine Blunt — the pink-cheeked one in the long alpaca coat.'

'She doesn't look so very devilish,' he laughed. After an impatient moment's hope that devilishness might develop, he said, 'She hasn't seen you yet.'

'Oh, yes, she has.'

'Then she isn't as overjoyed as she ought to be.'

'She'd be surprised to know she was expected to be overjoyed.'

'Why? Aren't you very good to her?'

'No. She's been rather good to me, though she doesn't take very much stock in me.'

'Why doesn't she?'

'Oh, there are only two kinds of people that interest Ernestine. Those who'll be active in carrying on the propaganda, and those who have yet to be converted.'

'Well, I'm disappointed,' he teased, perceiving how keen his friend was that he should not be. 'The other one would be more likely to convert *me*.'

'Oh, you only say that because the other one's tall, and makes eyes!' Vida denounced him, to his evident diversion.

Whatever his reasons were, the young men seemed to share his preference. They were watching the languishing young woman, who in turn kept glancing at them. Ernestine, having finished what she was saying, made her way to where Miss Levering sat, not, it would appear, for any purpose so frivolous as saying good evening, but to deposit what were left of the handbills and the precious portfolio in the care of one well known by now to have a motherly oversight of such properties.

Lord Borrodaile's eyes narrowed with amusement as he watched the hurried pantomime.

Instead of 'Thank you,' as Vida meekly accepted the incongruous and by no means light burden: 'We are short of speakers,' said Ernestine. 'You'll help us out, won't you?' As though it were the simplest thing in the world.

Lord Borrodaile half rose in protest.

'No,' said Vida. 'I won't speak till I have something to say.'

'I should have thought there was plenty to *say!*' said the girl.

'Yes, for you. You know such a lot,' smiled her new friend. 'I must get some first-hand knowledge, too, before I try to stand up and speechify.'

'It's now we need help. By-and-by there'll be plenty. But I'm not going to worry you,' she caught herself up. Then, confidentially, 'We've got one new helper that we've great hopes of. She joined to-day.'

'Some one who can speak?'

'Oh, she'll speak, I dare say, by and by.'

'What does she do in the meantime — to ——' (to account for your enthusiasm, was implied) 'to show she's a helper? Subscribes?'

'I expect she'll subscribe, too. She takes such an interest. Plenty of courage, too.'

'How do you know?'

'Well' — the voice dropped — 'she's *all right*, but she belongs to rather stodgy people. Bothers about respectability, and that sort of thing. But she came along with me this afternoon distributing handbills all over the City for two hours! Not many women of her kind are ready to do *that* the first thing.'

'No, I dare say not,' said Vida, humbly.

'And one thing I thought a very good sign' — Ernestine bent lower in her enthusiasm — 'when we got to Finsbury Circus she said' — Ernestine paused as if struck afresh by the merits of the new recruit — 'she said, "*Give me a piece of chalk!*"'

'Chalk! What did she want with ——?'

Borrodaile, too, leaned nearer.

'She saw me beginning to write meeting notices on the stones. Of course, the people stopped and stared and laughed. But she, instead of getting shy, and pretending she hadn't anything to do with me, she took the chalk and wrote, "Votes for Women!" all over the pavement of Finsbury Circus.' Ernestine paused a moment that Miss Levering might applaud the new 'helper.' 'I thought that a very good sign in such a respectable person.'

'Oh, yes; a most encouraging sign. Is it the one in mauve who did that?'

'No, that's — I forget her name — oh, Mrs. Thomas. She's new, too. I'll have to let her speak if you won't,' she said, a trifle anxiously.

'Mrs. Thomas, by all means,' murmured Borrodaile, as Ernestine, seeing her plea was hopeless, turned away.

Vida caught her by the coat. 'Where are the others? The rest of your *good* speakers?'

'Scattered up and down. Getting ready for the General Election. That's why we have to break in new people. Oh, she sent me some notes, that girl did. I must give them back to her.'

Ernestine stooped and opened the portfolio on Miss Levering's lap. She rummaged through the bulging pockets.

'I thought,' said Miss Levering, with obvious misgiving, 'I thought I hadn't seen that affected-looking creature before.'

'Oh, she'll get over all that,' Ernestine whispered. 'You haven't much opinion of our crowds, but they can teach people a lot.'

'Teach them not to hold their heads like a broken lily?'

'Yes, knock all sorts of nonsense out and stiffen them up wonderfully.'

She found the scrap of paper, and shut the portfolio with a snap.

'Now!'

She stood up, took in the fact of the audience having increased and a policeman in the offing. She summoned her allies.

'It's nearly time for those Army and Navy workers to come out. The men will come first,' she said, 'and five minutes after, they let the women out. I'll begin, and then I think you'd better speak next,' she said, handing the die-away young woman her notes. 'These seem all right.'

'Oh, but, Miss Blunt,' she whispered, 'I'm so nervous. How am I ever to face all those men?'

'You'll find it quite easy when once you are started,' said Ernestine, in a quiet undertone.

'But I'm so afraid that, just out of pure nervousness, I'll say the wrong thing.'

'If you do, I'll be there,' returned the chairman, a little grimly.

'But it's the very first time in my life ——'

'Now, look here ——'

Ernestine reached out past this person who was luxuriating in her own emotions, and drew the ample mauve matron into the official group close to where Miss Levering sat nursing the hand-bills.

'It's easy enough talking to these little meetings. They're quite good and quiet — not a bit like Hyde Park.' (One of the young men poked the other. They exchanged looks.) 'But there are three things we all agree it's just as well to keep in mind: Not to talk about ourselves' — she measured off the tit-bits of wisdom with a slim forefinger — 'not to say anything against the press, and, if possible, remember to praise the police.'

'Praise the police!' ejaculated the mauve matron.

'Sh!' said Ernestine, softly. But not so easily was the tide of indignation stemmed.

'I saw with my own eyes ——' began the woman.

'Yes, yes, but ——' she lowered her voice, Borrodaile had to strain to catch what she said, 'you see it's no use beating our heads against a stone wall. A movement that means to be popular must have the police on its side. After all, they do very well — considering.'

'Considering they're men?' demanded the matron.

'Anyhow,' Ernestine went on, 'even if they behaved ten times worse, it's not a bit of good to antagonize the police or the press. If they aren't our friends, we've got to make them our friends. They're both *much* better than they were. They must be encouraged!' said the wise young Daniel, with a little nod. Then as she saw or felt that the big matron might elude her vigilance and break out into indiscretion, 'Why, we had a reporter in from the *Morning Magnifier* only to-day. He said, "The public seems to have got tired of reading that you spit and scratch and prod policemen with your hatpins. Now, do you mind saying what is it you really do?" I told him to come here this afternoon. Now, when I've opened the meeting, *you'll* tell him!'

'Oh, *dear!*' the young woman patted her fringe, 'do you suppose we'll be in the *Magnifier* to-morrow? How dreadful!'

During this little interchange a procession of men streaming homeward in their hundreds came walking down the Embankment in twos and threes or singly, shambling past the loosely gathered assemblage about the bench.

The child on the riverward side still clutching its penny was unceremoniously ousted. As soon as Ernestine had mounted the seat the slackly held gathering showed signs of cohesion. The waiting units drew closer. The dingy procession slowed — the workmen, looking up at the young face with the fluttering sycamore shadows printed on its pink and white, grinned or frowned, but many halted and listened. Through the early part of the speech Miss Levering kept looking out of the corner of her eye to see what effect it had on Borrodaile. But Borrodaile gave no sign. Ernestine was trying to make it clear what a gain it would be, especially to this class, if women had the vote. An uphill task to catch and hold the attention of those tired workmen. They hadn't stopped there to be made to think — if they weren't going to be amused, they'd go home. A certain number did go home, after pausing to ask the young Reformer, more or less good-humouredly, why she didn't get married. Lord Borrodaile had privately asked for enlightenment on the same score. Vida had only smiled. One man varied the monotony by demanding why, if it would be a good thing for the working class to have women voting, why didn't the Labour Party take up the question.

'Some of the Labour Party have,' Ernestine told them, 'but the others are afraid. They've been told that women are such slaves to convention — such timid creatures! They know their own women aren't, but they're doubtful about the rest. The Labour Party, you know' — she spoke with a condescending forbearance — 'the Labour Party is young yet, and knows what it's like to feel timid. Some of the Labour men have the wild notion that women would all vote Conservative.'

'So they would!'

But Ernestine shook her head. 'While we are trying to show the people who say that, that even if they were right, it would be no excuse whatever for denying our claim to vote whichever way we thought best. While we are going to the root of the principle of the thing, another lot of logical gentlemen are sure to say, "Oh, it would never do to have women voting. They'd be going in for all sorts of new-fangled reforms, and the whole place would be turned upside down!" So between the men who think we'd all turn Tory and the men who are sure we'd all be Socialists, we don't seem likely to get very far, unless we do something to show them we mean to have it for no better reason than just that we're human beings!'

'Isn't she delightfully — direct!' whispered Miss Levering, eager to cull some modest flower of praise.

'Oh, direct enough!' His tone so little satisfied the half-maternal pride of the other woman that she was almost prepared for the slighting accent in which he presently asked, 'Is this the sort of thing that's supposed to convert people to a great constitutional change?'

'It isn't our women would get the vote,' a workman called out. 'It's the rich women.'

'Is it only the rich men who have the vote?' demanded Ernestine 'You know it isn't. We are fighting to get the franchise on precisely the same terms aˢ men.'

For several moments the wrangle went on.

'Would wives have a vote?'

She showed how that could be made a matter of adjustment. She quoted the lodger franchise and the latch-key decision.

Vida kept glancing at Borrodaile. As still he made no sign, 'Of course,' the lady whispered across the back of the bench, 'of course, you think she's an abomination, but ——' she paused for a handsome disavowal. Borrodaile looked at the eager face — Vida's, for Miss Blunt's was calm as a May morning. As he did not instantly speak, 'But you can't deny she's got extremely good wits.'

He seemed to relent before such persuasiveness. 'She's got a delicious little face,' he admitted, thinking to say the most.

'Oh, her *face!* That's scarcely the point.'

'It's always the point.'

'It's the principle that's at stake,' Ernestine was saying. 'The most out-and-out Socialist among us would welcome the enfranchisement of six duchesses or all the women born with red hair; we don't care on what plea the entering wedge gets in. But let me tell you there aren't any people on earth so blind to their own interests as just you working men when you oppose or when you are indifferent to women's having votes. All women suffer — but it's the women of your class who suffer most. *Isn't* it? Don't you men know — why, it's notorious! — that the women of the working class are worse sweated even than the men?'

'So they are!'

'If you don't believe me, *ask* them. Here they come.'

It was well contrived — that point! It struck full in the face of the homeward-streaming women who had just been let out.

'We know, and you men know ——' the speaker nailed her advantage, 'that even the Government that's being forced to become a model employer where men are concerned, the very *Government* is responsible for sweating thousands of women in State employments! We know and you know that in those workrooms over yonder these very women have been sitting weighed down by the rumour of a reduction in their wages already so much below the men's. They've sat there wondering whether they can risk a strike. Women — it's notorious,' she flung it out on a wave of passion, 'women everywhere suffer most from the evils of our social system. Why not? They've had no hand in it! Our social system is the work of men! Yet we must work to uphold it! this system that crushes us. We must swell the budget, we must help to pay the bill! What *fools* we've all been! What fools we are if we don't do something!'

'Gettin' up rows and goin' to 'Olloway's no good.'

While she justified the course that led to Holloway —

'Rot! Piffle!' they interjected. One man called out: 'I'd have some respect for you if you'd carried a bomb into the House of Commons, but a miserable little scuffle with the police!'

'Here's a gentleman who is inciting us to carry bombs. Now, that shocks me.'

The crowd recovered its spirits at the notion of the champion-shocker shocked.

'We've been dreadfully browbeaten about our tactics, but that gentleman with his bad advice makes our tactics sound as innocent and reasonable as they actually are. When you talk in that wild way about bombs — you — I may be a hooligan' — she held up the delicate pink-and-white face with excellent effect — 'but you do shock me.'

It wore well this exquisitely humorous jest about shocking a Suffragette. The whole crowd was one grin.

'I'm specially shocked when I hear a *man* advocating such a thing! You men have other and more civilized ways of getting the Government to pay attention to abuses. Now listen to what I'm saying: for it's the justification of everything we are going to do in the future, *unless* we get what we're asking for! It's this. Our justification is that men, even poor men, have that powerful leverage of the vote. You men have no right to resort to violence; you have a better way. We have *no* way but agitation. A *Liberal* Government that refuses ——'

'Three cheers for the Liberals! Hip, hip ——'

'My friend, I see you are young,' says Ernestine.

'Lord, wot are you?' the young man hurled back.

'Before I got my political education, when *I* was young and innocent, like this gentleman, who still pins his faith to the Liberals, I, too, hoped great things from them. My friends, it's a frame of mind we outlive!' — and her friends shrieked with delight.

'Well, it's one way for a girl to amuse herself till she gets married,' said Borrodaile.

'Why, that's just what the hooligans all say!' laughed Vida. 'And, like you, they think that if a woman wants justice for other women she must have a grievance of her own. I've heard them ask Ernestine in Battersea — she has valiant friends there — "Oo's 'urt *your* feelin's?" they say. "Tell me, and I'll punch 'is 'ead." But you aren't here to listen to *me!*' Vida caught herself up. 'This is about the deputation of women that waited on the Prime Minister.'

'Didn't get nothin' out of him!' somebody shouted.

'Oh, yes, we did! We got the best speech in favour of Woman's Suffrage that any of us ever heard.'

'Haw! Haw! Clever ol' fox!'

''E just buttered 'em up! But 'e don't do nothin'.'

'Oh, yes, he did something!'

'What?'

'He gave us advice!' They all laughed together at that in the most friendly spirit in the world. 'Two nice pieces,' Ernestine held up each hand very much like a school child rejoicing over slices of cake. 'One we are taking' — she drew in a hand — 'the other we aren't' — she let it fall. 'He said we must win people to our way of thinking. We're doing it; at a rate that must astonish, if it doesn't even embarrass him. The other piece of distinguished advice he gave us was of a more doubtful character.' Her small hands took it up gingerly. Again she seemed to weigh it there in the face of the multitude. 'The Prime Minister said we "must have patience." She threw the worthless counsel into the air and tossed contempt after it. 'It is man's oldest advice to woman!'

'All our trouble fur nothin'!' groaned an impish boy.

'We see now that patience has been our bane. If it hadn't been for this same numbing slavish patience we wouldn't be standing before the world to-day, political outcasts — catalogued with felons and lunatics ——'

'And peers!' called a voice.

'We are *done* with patience!' said Ernestine, hotly; 'and for that reason there is at last some hope for the women's cause. Now Miss Scammell will speak to you.'

A strange thing happened when Miss Scammell got up. She seemed to leave her attractiveness, such as it was, behind when she climbed up on the bench. Standing mute, on a level with the rest, her head deprecatingly on one side, she had pleased. Up there on the bench, presuming to teach, she woke a latent cruelty in the mob. They saw she couldn't take care of herself, and so they 'went for her' — the very same young men who had got up and given her a choice of the seats they had been at the pains to come early to secure. To be sure, when, with a smile, she had sat down only a quarter of an hour before, in the vacated place of one of them, the other boy promptly withdrew with his pal. It would have been too compromising to remain alongside the charmer. But when Miss Scammell stood up on that same bench, she was assumed to have left the realm of smiles and meaning looks where she was mistress and at home. She had ventured out into the open, not only without the sword of pointed speech — that falls to few — but this young lady had not even the armour of absolute earnestness. When she found that smiling piteously wouldn't do, she proceeded, looking more and more like a scared white rabbit, to tell about the horrible cases of lead-poisoning among the girls in certain china and earthenware works. All that she had to say was true and significant enough. But it was no use. They jeered and howled her down for pure pleasure in her misery. She trembled and lost her thread. She very nearly cried. Vida wondered that the little chairwoman didn't fly to the rescue. But Ernestine sat quite unmoved looking in her lap.

'Lamentable exhibition!' said Borrodaile, moving about uneasily.

The odd thing was that Miss Scammell kept on with her prickly task.

'Why don't you make her sit down?' Vida whispered to Miss Blunt.

'Because I've got to see what she's made of.'

'But surely you see! She's awful!'

'Not half so bad as lots of men when they first try. If she weathers this, she'll be a speaker some day.'

At last, having told her story through the interruptions — told it badly, brokenly, but to the end — having given proofs that lead-poisoning among women was on the increase and read out from her poor crumpled, shaking notes, the statistics of infant and still-birth mortality, the unhappy new helper sat down.

Miss Blunt leaned over, and whispered, 'That's all right! I was wrong. This is nearly as bad as Hyde Park,' and with that jumped up to give the crowd a piece of her mind.

They sniggered, but they quieted down, all but one.

'Yes, you are the gentleman, you there with the polo cap, who doesn't believe in giving a fair hearing. I would like to ask that man who thinks himself so superior, *that* one in the grey cap, whether he is capable of standing up here on this bench and addressing the crowd.'

'Hear, hear.'

'Yes! Get on the bench. Up with him.'

A slight scrimmage, and an agitated man was observed to be seeking refuge on the outskirts.

'Bad as Miss Scammell was, she made me rather ashamed of myself,' Vida confided to Borrodaile.

'Yes,' he said sympathetically, 'it always makes one rather ashamed — even if it's a man making public failure.'

'Oh, that wasn't what I meant. *She* at least tried. But I — I feel I'm a type of all the idle women the world over. Leaving it to the poor and the ill-equipped to ——'

'To keep the world from slipping into chaos?' he inquired genially.

She hadn't heard. Her eyes were fastened on the chairwoman.

'After all, they've got Ernestine,' Vida exulted under her breath.

Borrodaile fell to studying this aspect of the face whose every change he had thought he knew so well. What was the new thing in it? Not admiration merely, not affection alone — something almost fierce behind the half-protecting tenderness with which she watched the chairman's duel with the mob. Borrodaile lifted a hand — people were far too engrossed, he knew, to notice — and he laid it on Vida's, which had tightened on the back of the bench.

'My dear!' he said wondering and low as one would to wake a sleepwalker.

She answered without looking at him, 'What is it?'

He seemed not to know quite how to frame his protest.

'She can carry *you* along at least!' he grumbled. 'You forget everybody else!'

Vida smiled. It was so plain whom he meant by 'everybody.' Lord Borrodaile gave a faint laugh. He probably knew that would 'bring her round.' It did. It brought her quick eyes to his face; it brought low words.

'*Please!* Don't let her see you — laughing, I mean.'

'You can explain to her afterwards that it was you I was laughing at.' As that failed of specific effect, 'You really are a little ridiculous,' he said again, with the edge in his voice, 'hanging on the lips of that Backfisch as if she were Demosthenes.'

'We don't think she's a Demosthenes. We know she is something much more significant — for *us*.'

'What?'

'She's Ernestine Blunt.'

Clean out of patience, he turned his back.

'Am I alone?' she whispered over his shoulder, as if in apology. 'Look at all the other women. Some of them are very intelligent. Our interest in our fellow-woman seems queer and unnatural to you because you don't realize Mrs. Brown has always been interested in Mrs. Jones.'

'Oh, has she?'

'Yes. She hasn't said much to Mr. Brown about it,' Vida admitted, smiling, because a man's interest in woman is so limited.'

Borrodaile laughed. 'I didn't know that was his failing!'

'I mean his interest is of one sort. It's confined to the woman he finds interesting in *that* way at *that* minute. Other women bore him. But other women have always been mightily interesting to us! Now, sh! let's listen.'

'I can understand those callow youths,' unwarily he persisted; 'she's pink and pert and all the rest, but *you* ——'

'Oh, will you *never* understand? Don't you know women are more civilized than men?'

'Woman! she'll be the last animal domesticated.' It seemed as if he preferred to have her angry rather than oblivious of him.

But not for nothing did she belong to a world which dares to say whatever it wants to say.

'We are civilized enough, at all events' — there was an ominous sparkle in her eye — 'to listen to men speakers clever or dull — we listen quietly enough. But men! — a person must be of your own sex for you to be able to regard him without distraction. If the woman is beautiful enough, you are intoxicated. If she's plain enough, you are impatient. All you see in any woman is her sex. You can't *listen*.'

'Whew!' remarked Borrodaile.

'But *I* must listen — I haven't got over being ashamed to find how much this girl can teach me.'

'I'm sorry for you that any of Miss Scammell's interesting speech was lost,' the chairman was saying. 'She was telling you just the kind of thing that you men ought to know, the kind of thing you get little chance of knowing about from men. Yet those wretched girls who die young of lead-poisoning, or live long enough to bring sickly babies into the world, those poor working women look to you working men for help. Are they wrong to look to you, or are they right? You working men represent the majority of the electorate. *You* can change things if you will. If you don't, don't think the woman will suffer alone. We shall all suffer together. More and more the masters are saying, "We'll get rid of these men — they're too many for us with their unions and their political pull. We'll get women. We'll get them for two-thirds of what we pay the men. Good business!" say the masters. But it's bad business ——'

'For all but the masters,' muttered the tramp.

'Bad for the masters, too,' said the girl, 'only they can't see it, or else they don't care what sort of world they leave to their children. If you men weren't so blind, you'd see the women will be in politics what they are in the home — your best friends.'

'Haw! haw! Listen at 'er!'

'*With* the women you would be strong. Without them you are — what you are!'

The ringing contempt in her tone was more than one gentleman could put up with.

'How do you think the world got on before you came to show it *how?*'

'It got on very badly. Not only in England — all over the world men have insisted on governing alone. What's the result? Misery and degradation to the masses, and to the few — the rich and high-placed — for them corruption and decline.'

'That's it, always 'ammering away at the men — pore devils!'

'Some people are so foolish as to think we are working against the men.'

'So you are!'

'It's just what the old-school politicians would like you to think. But it's nonsense. Nobody knows better than we that the best interests of men and women are identical — they *can't be separated.* It's trying to separate them that's made the whole trouble.'

'Oh, you know it all!'

'Well, you see' — she put on her most friendly and reasonable air — 'men have never been obliged to study women's point of view. But we've been obliged to study the men's point of view. It's natural we should understand you a great deal better than you understand us. And though you sometimes disappoint us, we don't lose hope of you.' .

'Thanks awfully.'

'We think that if we can only make you understand the meaning of this agitation, then you'll help us to get what we want. We believe the day will come when the old ideal of men standing by the women — when that ideal will be realized. For don't believe it ever *has* been realized. It never has! Now our last speaker for to-day will say a few words to you. Mrs. Thomas.'

'Haven't you had about enough?' said Borrodaile, impatiently.

'Don't wait for me,' was all her answer.

'Shall you stay, then, till the bitter end?'

'It will only be a few moments now. I may as well see it out.'

He glanced at his watch, detached it, and held it across the back of the seat.

She nodded, and repeated, 'Don't wait.'

His answer to that was to turn not only a bored but a slightly injured face towards the woman who had, not without difficulty, balanced her rotund form on the bench at the far end. She might have been the comfortable wife of a rural grocer. She spoke the good English you may not infrequently hear among that class, but it became clear, as she went on, that she was a person of a wider cultivation.

'You'd better go. She'll be stodgy and dull.' Vida spoke with a real sympathy for her friend's sufferings. 'Oh, portentous dull.'

'And no waist!' sighed Borrodaile, but he sank back in his corner.

Presently his wandering eye discovered something in his companion's aspect that told him subtly she was not listening to the mauve matron. Neither were some of the others. A number had moved away, and the little lane their going left was not yet closed, for the whole general attention was obviously slackened. This woman wasn't interesting enough even to boo at. The people who didn't go home began to talk to one another. But in Vida's face—what had brought to it that still intensity? Borrodaile moved so that he could follow the fixed look. One of the infrequently passing hansoms had stopped. Was she looking at that? Two laughing people leaning out, straining to catch what the mauve orator was saying. Suddenly Borrodaile pulled his slack figure together.

'Sophia!' he ejaculated softly, 'and Stonor!—by the beard of the prophet!' He half rose, whether more annoyed or amazed it would be hard to tell. 'We're discovered!' he said, in a laughing whisper. As he turned to add 'The murder's out,' he saw that Vida had quietly averted her face. She was leaning her head on her hand, so that it masked her features. Even if the woman who was speaking had not been the object of such interest as the people in the hansom had to bestow, even had either of them looked towards Vida's corner, only a hat and a gauze ruffle would have been seen.

Borrodaile took the hint. His waning sense of the humour of the situation revived.

'Perhaps, after all, if we lay low,' he said, smiling more broadly. 'It would be nuts for Stonor to catch us sitting at the feet of Mrs. Thomas.' He positively chuckled at the absurdity of the situation. He had slipped back into his corner, but he couldn't help craning his neck to watch those two leaning over the door of the hansom, while they discussed some point with animation. Several times the man raised his hand as if to give an order through the trap door. Each time Sophia laughingly arrested him. 'He wants to go on,' reported Borrodaile, sympathetically. 'She wants him to wait a minute. Now he's jumped out. What's he—looking for another hansom? No—now *she's* out. Bless me, she's shaking hands with him. He's back in the hansom!—driving away. Sophia's actually—— 'Pon my soul, I don't know what's come over the women! I'm rather relieved on the whole.' He turned round and spoke into Vida's ear. 'I've been a little sorry for Sophia. She's never had the smallest interest in any man but that cousin of hers — and, of course, it's quite hopeless.'

Vida sat perfectly motionless, back to the speaker, back to the disappearing hansom, staring at the parapet.

'You can turn round now — quite safe. Sophia's out of range. Poor Sophia!' After a little pause, 'Of course you know Stonor?'

'Why, of course.'

'Oh, well, my distinguished cousin used not to be so hard to get hold of — not in the old days when we were seeing so much of your father.'

'That must have been when I was in the schoolroom — wasn't it?'

He turned suddenly and looked at her. 'I'd forgotten. You know Geoffrey, and you don't like him. I saw that once before.'

'Once before?' she echoed.

He reminded her of the time she hurried away from Ulland House to Bishopsmead.

'*I* wasn't deceived,' he said, with his look of smiling malice. 'You didn't care two pins about your Cousin Mary and her influenza.'

Vida moved her expressionless face a little to the right. 'I can see Sophia. But she's listening to the speech;' and Vida herself, with something of an effort, seemed now to be following the sordid experiences of a girl that the speaker had befriended some years before. It was through this girl, the mauve matron said, that she herself had come into touch with the abject poor. She took a big barrack of a house in a poverty-stricken neighbourhood, and it became known that there she received and helped both men and women. 'I sympathized with the men, but it was the things the women told me that appalled me. They were too bad to be entirely believed, but I wrote them down. They haunted me. I investigated. I found I had no excuse for doubting those stories.'

'This woman's a find,' Vida whispered to the chairman.

Ernestine shook her head.

'Why, she's making a first-rate speech!' said Vida, astonished. 'There's nobody here who will care about it.'

'Why do you say that?'

'Oh, all she's saying is a commonplace to these people. Lead-poisoning was new, to *them*—something they could take hold of.'

'Well, I stick to it, you've got a good ally in this woman. Let her stand up in Somerset Hall, and tell the people——'

'It wouldn't do,' said the young Daniel, firmly.

'You don't believe her story?'

'Oh, I don't say the things aren't true. But'—she moved uneasily—'the subject's too prickly.'

'Too prickly for you!'

The girl nodded with an anxious eye on the speaker. 'We sometimes make a passing reference—just to set men thinking, and there leave it. But it always makes them furious, of course. It does no good. Either people know and just accept it, or else they won't believe, and it only gets them on the raw. I'll have to stop her if——' She leaned forward.

'It's odd your taking it like this. I suppose it's because you're so young,' said Vida, wondering. 'It must be because for you it isn't real.'

'No, it's because I see no decent woman can think much about it and keep sane. That's why I say this one won't be any good to us. She'll never be able to see anything clearly but that one thing. She'll always be forgetting the main issue.'

'What do you call the main issue?'

'Why, political power, of course.'

'Oh, wise young Daniel!' she murmured, as Miss Blunt touched the speaker's sleeve and interjected a word into the middle of a piece of depressing narrative.

Mrs. Thomas stopped, faltered, and pulled herself up with, 'Well, as I say, with my own verifications these experiences form a body of testimony that should stir the conscience of the community. I *myself* felt'—she glanced at Ernestine—'I felt it was too ghastly to publish, but it ought to be used. Those who doubted the evidence should examine it. I went to a lady who is well known to be concerned about public questions; her husband is a member of Parliament, and a person of influence. You don't know, perhaps, but she did, that there's a Parliamentary Commission going to sit here in London in a few weeks for the purpose of inquiring into certain police regulations which greatly concern women. Who do you think are invited to serve on that Commission? Men. All men. Not a woman in England is being consulted. The husband of the lady I went to see — he was one of the Commissioners. I said to her, "*You* ought to be serving on that board." She said, "Oh, no," but that women like her could influence the men who sat on the Commission.'

'This is better!' whispered the ever-watchful Ernestine, with a smile.

'So I told her about my ten years' work. I showed her some of my records — not the worst, the average, sifted and verified. She could hardly be persuaded to glance at what I had been at so much pains to collect. You see' — she spoke as though in apology for the lady — 'you see I had no official or recognized position.'

'Hear, hear,' said Ernestine.

'I was simply a woman whose standing in the community was all right, but I had nothing to recommend me to serious attention. I had nothing but the courage to look wrong in the face, and the conscience to report it honestly. When I told her certain things — things that are so stinging a disgrace that no decent person can hear them unmoved — when I told her of the degrading discomforts, the cruelties, that are practised against homeless women even in some of the rate-supported casual wards and the mixed lodging-houses, that lady said — sitting there in her pleasant drawing-room — she said it could not be true! My reports were exaggerated — women were sentimental — the authorities managed these places with great wisdom. They are so horrible, I said, they drive women to the streets. She assured me I was mistaken. I asked her if she had ever been inside a mixed lodging-house. She never had. But the casual wards she knew about. They were so well managed she herself wouldn't mind at all spending a night in one of these municipal provisions for the homeless. Then I said, "You are the woman I am looking for! Come with me one night and try it. What night shall it be?" She said she was engaged in writing a book. She could not interrupt her work. But I said, if those rate-supported places are so comfortable, it won't interfere with your work. She *turned the conversation.* She talked about the Commission. The Commission was going to make a thorough scientific investigation. Nothing amateur about the Commission. The lady was sincere' — Mrs. Thomas vouched for it — 'she had a comfortable faith in the Commission. But, I say' — the woman leaned forward in her earnestness — 'I say that Commission will waste its time! I don't deny it will investigate and discuss the position of the outcast women of this country. Their plight, which is the work of men, will once more be inquired into by men. I say there should be women on that Commission. If the middle and upper class women have the dignity and influence men pretend they have, why aren't they represented there? Nobody pretends the matter doesn't concern the mothers of the nation. It concerns them horribly. Nobody can think so ill of them as to suppose they don't care. It's monstrous that men should sit upon that committee alone. Women have had to think about these things. We believe this evil can be met — if men will let us try. It may be that only women comprehend it, since men through the ages have been helpless before it. Why, then, once again, this Commission of *men?* The mockery of it! Setting men to make their report upon this matter to men! I am not a public speaker, but I am a wife and a mother. Do you wonder that hearing about that Commission gave me courage to take the first opportunity to join these brave sisters of mine who are fighting for political liberty?'

She seemed for the first time to notice that a little group of sniggerers were becoming more obstreperous.

'We knew, of course, that whatever we say some of you will laugh and jeer; but, speaking for myself, no mockery that you are able to fling at us, can sting *me* like the thought of the hypocrisy of that Commission! Do you wonder that when we think of it — you men who have power and don't use it! — do you wonder that women come out of their homes — young, and old, and middle-aged — that we stand up here in the public places and give you scorn for scorn?'

As the unheroic figure trembling stepped off the bench, she found Vida Levering's hand held out to steady her.

'Take my seat,' said the younger woman.

She stood beside her, for once oblivious of Ernestine, who was calling for new members, and giving out notices.

Vida bent over the shapeless mauve bundle. 'You asked that woman to go with you. I wish you'd take me.'

'Ah, my dear, *I* don't need to go again. I thought to have that lady see it would do good. Her husband has influence, you see.'

'But you've just said the men are useless in this matter.'

She had no answer.

'But, I believe,' Vida went on, 'if more women were like you — if they looked into the thing ——'

'Very few could stand it.'

'But don't hundreds of poor women "stand" much worse?'

'No; they drink and they die. I was ill for three months after my first experience even of the tramp ward.'

'Was that the first thing you tried?'

'No. The first thing I tried was putting on a Salvation Army bonnet, and following the people I wanted to help into the public-houses, selling the *War Cry*.'

'May one wear the uniform who isn't a member of the Army?'

'It isn't usual,' she said slowly. And then, as though to give the *coup de grace* to the fine lady's curiosity, 'But that was child's play. Before I sampled the tramp ward, I covered myself with Keating's powder from head to foot. It wasn't a bit of good.'

'When may I come and talk to you?'

'Hello, Mrs. Thomas!' Vida turned and found the Lady Sophia at her side. 'Why, father! — Oh, I see, Miss Levering. Well' — she turned to the woman in the corner — 'how's the House of Help?'

'Do you know about Mrs. Thomas's work?' Vida asked.

'Well, rather! I collect rents in her district.'

'Oh, do you? You never told me.'

'Why should I tell you?'

Ernestine was dismissing the meeting.

'You are very tired,' said Lord Borrodaile, looking at Vida Levering's face.

'Yes,' she said. 'I'll go now. Come, Sophia!'

'We shall be here on Thursday,' Ernestine was saying, 'at the same hour, and we hope a great many of you will want to join us.'

'In a trip to 'Olloway? No, thank you!'

Upon that something indistinguishable to the three who were withdrawing was said in the group that had sniggered through

Mrs. Thomas's speech. Another one of that choice circle gave a great guffaw. There were still more who were amused, but less indiscreetly. Three men, looking like gentlemen, paused in the act of strolling by. They, too, were smiling.

'You laugh!' Ernestine's voice rang out.

'Wait a moment,' said Vida to her companions.

She looked back. It was plain, from Ernestine's face, she was not going to let the meeting break up on that note.

'Don't you think it a little strange, considering the well-known chivalry among men — don't you think it strange that against no reform the world has ever seen ——?'

'Reform! Wot rot!'

'If you don't admit it's reform, call it revolt!' She threw the red-hot word out among the people as if its fire scorched her. 'Against no revolt has there ever been such a torrent of ridicule let loose as against the Women's Movement. It almost seems as if — in spite of men's well-known protecting tenderness towards woman — it almost seems as if there's nothing in this world so funny to a man as a woman!'

'Haw! Haw! Got it right that time!'

Borrodaile was smiling, too.

'Do you know,' Vida asked, 'who those men are who have just stopped?'

'No.'

'I believe Ernestine does.'

'Oh, perhaps they're bold bad members of Parliament.'

'Some of us,' she was saying, 'have read a little history. We have read how every struggle towards freedom has met with opposition and abuse. We expected to have our share of those things. But we find that no movement before ours has ever had so much laughter to face.' Through the renewed merriment she went on: 'Yes, you wonder I admit that. We don't deny anything that's true. And I'll tell you another thing! We aren't made any prouder of our men-folk by the discovery that behind their old theory of woman as "half angel, half idiot," is a sneaking feeling that "woman is a huge joke."'

'Or just a little one for a penny like you!'

'Men have imagined — they imagine still, that we have never noticed how ridiculous *they* can be. You see' — she leaned over and spoke confidentially — 'we've never dared break it to them.'

'Haw! Haw!'

'We know they *couldn't bear it.*'

'Oh-h!'

'So we've done all our laughing in our sleeves. Yes — and some years our sleeves had to be made — like balloons!' She pulled out the loose alpaca of her own while the workmen chuckled with appreciation.

'I bet on Ernestine, any'ow,' said a young man, with an air of admitting himself a bold original fellow.

'Well, open laughter is less dangerous laughter. It's even a guide; it helps us to find out things some of us wouldn't know otherwise. Lots of women used to be taken in by that talk about feminine influence and about men's immense respect for them! But any number of women have come to see that underneath that old mask of chivalry was a broad grin. — We are reminded of that every time the House of Commons talks about us.' She flung it at the three supercilious strangers. 'The dullest gentleman there can raise a laugh if he speaks of the "fair sex." Such jokes! — even when they are clean such poor little feeble efforts that even a member of Parliament couldn't laugh at them, unless he had grown up with the idea that woman was somehow essentially funny — and that *he*, oh, no! there was nothing whatever to laugh at in man! Those members of Parliament don't have the enlightenment that you men have — of hearing what women *really* think when we hear men laugh as you did just now about our going to prison. They don't know that we find it just a little strange' — she bent over the scattering rabble and gathered it into a sudden fellowship — 'doesn't it strike you, too, as strange that when a strong man goes to prison for his convictions it is thought to be something rather fine (I don't say it is myself — though it's the general impression). But when a weak woman goes for *her* convictions, men find it very humorous indeed. Our prisoners have to bear not only the hardships of Holloway Gaol, but they have to bear the worse pains and penalties inflicted by the general public. You, too, you laugh! And yet I say' — she lifted her arms and spread them out above the people — 'I say it was not until women were found ready to go to prison —

not till then was the success of the cause assured.' Her bright eyes were shining brighter still with tears.

'If prison's so good fur the cause, why didn't *you* go?'

'Here's a gentleman who asks why I didn't go to prison. The answer to that is, I did go.'

She tossed the information down among the cheers and groans as lightly as though it had no more personal significance for her than a dropped leaflet setting forth some minor fact.

'That delicate little girl!' breathed Vida.

'You never told me that item in her history,' said Borrodaile.

'She never told *me* — never once spoke of it! They put her in prison!' It was as if she couldn't grasp it.

'Of course one person's going isn't of much consequence,' Ernestine was winding up with equal spirit and *sang-froid*. 'But the fact that dozens and scores — all sorts and conditions — are ready to go — *that* matters! And that's the place our reprehensible tactics have brought the movement to. The meeting is closed.'

* * * * * * *

They dropped Sophia at her own door, but Lord Borrodaile said he would take Vida home. They drove along in silence.

When they stopped before the tall house in Queen Anne's Gate, Vida held out her hand.

'It's late. I won't ask you in.'

'You are over-tired. Go to bed.'

'I wish I could. I'm dining out.'

He looked at her out of kind eyes. 'It begins to be dreadfully stuffy in town. I'm glad, after all, we're going on that absurd yachting trip.'

'I'm not going,' she said.

'Oh, nonsense! Sophia and I would break our hearts.'

'I'm sure about Sophia.'

'It will do you good to come and have a look at the Land of the Midnight Sun,' he said.

'I'm going to have a look at the Land of Midnight where there's no sun. And everybody but you and Sophia and my sister will think I'm in Norway.'

When she explained, he broke out:

'It's the very wildest nonsense that ever —— It would kill you.' The intensity of his opposition made him incoherent. 'You, of all women in the world! A creature who can't even stand people who say "serviette" instead of "table-napkin"!'

'Fancy the little Blunt having been in prison!'

'Oh, let the little Blunt go to ——' He checked himself. 'Be reasonable, child.' He turned and looked at her with an earnestness she had never seen in his eyes before. 'Why in heaven should *you* ——'

'Why? You heard what that woman said.'

'I heard *nothing* to account for ——'

'That's partly,' she interrupted, 'why I must make this experiment. When a man like you — as good a man as you' — she repeated with slow wonder — 'when you and all the other good men that the world is full of — when you all know everything that that woman knows — and more! and yet see nothing in it to account for what she feels, and what I — I too, am beginning to feel ——!' she broke off. 'Good-bye! If I go far on this new road, it's you I shall have to thank.'

'I?'

He shrugged drearily at the absurd charge, making no motion to take the offered hand, but sat there in the corner of the hansom looking rather old and shrunken.

'You and one other,' she said.

That roused him. 'Ah, he has come, then.'

'Who?'

'The other. The man who is going to count.'

Her eyelids drooped. 'The man who was to count most for me came a long while ago. And a long while ago — he went.'

Borrodaile looked at her. 'But this —— Who is the gentleman who shares with me the doubtful, I may without undue modesty say the undeserved, honour of urging you to disappear into the slums? Who is it?'

'The man who wrote this.'

It was the book he had seen in her hands before the meeting. He read on the green cover, 'In the Days of the Comet.'

'Oh, that fellow! Well, he's not my novelist, but it's the keenest intelligence we have applied to fiction.'

'He *is* my novelist. So I've a right to be sorry he knows nothing about women. See here! Even in his most rationalized vision of the New Time, he can't help betraying his old-fashioned prejudice in favour of the "dolly" view of women. His hero says, "I prayed that night, let me confess it, to an image I had set up in my heart, an image that still serves with me as a symbol for things inconceivable, to a Master Artificer, the unseen captain of all who go about the building of the world, the making of mankind ——"' Vida's finger skipped, lifting to fall on the heroine's name. '"Nettie . . . She never came into the temple of that worshipping with me."' Swiftly she turned the pages back. 'Where's that other place? Here! The man says to the heroine — to his ideal woman he says, "Behind you and above you rises the coming City of the World, and I am in that building. Dear heart! you are only happiness!" That's the whole view of man in a nutshell. Even the highest type of woman such an imagination as this can conjure up ——' She shook her head. '"You are only happiness, dear" — a minister of pleasure, negligible in all the nobler moods, all the times of wider vision or exalted effort! Tell me' — she bent her head and looked into her companion's face with a new passion dawning in her eyes — 'in the building of that City of the Future, in the making of it beautiful, shall women really have no share?'

'My dear, I only know that I shall have no share myself.'

'Ah, we don't speak of ourselves.' She opened the hansom doors and her companion got out. 'But this Comet man,' she said as she followed, '*he* might have a share if only he knew why all the great visions have never yet been more than dreams. That this man should think foundations can be well and truly laid when the best of one half the race are "only happiness, dear!"' She turned on the threshold. '*Whose* happiness?'

CHAPTER XIV

The fall of the Liberal Ministry was said by the simple-minded to have come as a bolt from the blue. Certainly into the subsequent General Election were entering elements but little foreseen.

Nevertheless, the last two bye-elections before the crash had resulted in the defeat of the Liberal candidate not by the Tory antagonist, but in one case by the nominee of the Labour party, in the other by an independent Socialist. Both these men had publicly thanked the Suffragettes for their notable share in piling up those triumphant and highly significant majorities. Now the country was facing an election where, for the first time in the history of any great nation, women were playing a part that even their political enemies could hardly with easy minds call subordinate.

Only faint echoes of the din penetrated the spacious quiet of Ulland House. Although the frequent week-end party was there, the great hall on this particular morning presented a deserted appearance as the tall clock by the staircase chimed the hour of noon. The insistence of the ancient timepiece seemed to have set up a rival in destruction of the Sunday peace, for no sooner had the twelfth stroke died than a bell began to ring. The little door in the wainscot beyond the clock was opened. An elderly butler put his head round the huge screen of Spanish leather that masked the very existence of the modest means of communication with the quarters of the Ulland domestics. So little was a ring at the front door expected at this hour that Sutton was still slowly getting into the left sleeve of his coat when his mistress appeared from the garden by way of the French window. The old butler withdrew a discreet instant behind the screen to put the last touches to his toilet, but Lady John had seen that he was there.

'Has Miss Levering gone for a walk?' she inquired of the servant.

'I don't know, m' lady.'

'She's not in the garden. Do you think she's not down yet?'

'I haven't seen her, m' lady,' said Sutton, emerging from his retirement and approaching the wide staircase on his way to answer the front-door bell.

'Never mind' — his mistress went briskly over to a wide-winged writing-table and seated herself before a litter of papers — 'I won't have her disturbed if she's resting,' Lady John said, adding half to herself, 'she certainly needs it.'

'Yes, m' lady,' said Sutton, adjusting the maroon collar of his livery which had insisted upon riding up at the back.

'But I want her to know' — Lady John spoke while glancing through a letter before consigning it to the wastepaper basket — 'the moment she comes down she must be told that the new plans arrived by the morning post.'

'Plans, m' la——'

'She'll understand. There they are.' The lady held up a packet about which she had just snapped an elastic band. 'I'll put them here. It's very important she should have them in time to look over before she goes.'

'Yes, m' lady.'

Sutton opened a door and disappeared. A footstep sounded on the marble floor of the lobby.

Over her shoulder Lady John called out, 'Is *that* Miss Levering?'

'*No,* m' lady. Mr. Farnborough.'

'I'm afraid I'm scandalously early.' In spite of his words the young man whipped off his dust coat and flung it to the servant with as much precipitation as though what he had meant to say was 'scandalously late.' 'I motored up from Dutfield. It didn't take me nearly so long as Lord John said.'

The lady had given the young man her hand without rising. 'I'm afraid my husband is no authority on motoring — and he's not home yet from church.'

'It's the greatest luck finding *you.*' Farnborough sat himself down in the easy-chair on the other side of the wide writing-table undaunted by its business-like air or the preoccupied look of the woman before it. 'I thought Miss Levering was the only person under this roof who was ever allowed to observe Sunday as a real day of rest.'

'If you've come to see Miss Levering ——' began Lady John.

'Is she here? I give you my word I didn't know it.'

'Oh?' said the lady, unconvinced.

'I thought she'd given up coming.'

'Well, she's begun again. She's helping me about something.'

'Oh, helping you, is she?' said Farnborough with absent eyes; and then suddenly 'all there,' 'Lady John, I've come to ask you to help *me*.'

'With Miss Levering?' said Hermione Heriot's aunt. 'I can't do it.'

'No, no — all that's no good. She only laughs.'

'Oh,' breathed the lady, relieved, 'she looks upon you as a boy.'

'Such nonsense,' he burst out suddenly. 'What do you think she said to me the day before she went off yachting?'

'That she was four years older than you?'

'Oh, I knew that. No. She said *she* knew she was all the charming things I'd been saying, but there was only one way to prove it, and that was to marry some one young enough to be her son. She'd noticed, she said, that was what the *most* attractive women did — and she named names.'

Lady John laughed. '*You* were too old!'

He nodded. 'Her future husband, she said, was probably just entering Eton.'

'Exactly like her.'

'No, no.' Dick Farnborough waived the subject away. 'I wanted to see you about the secretaryship.'

'You didn't get it then?'

'No. It's the grief of my life.'

'Oh, if you don't get one you'll get another.'

'But there *is* only one,' he said desperately.

'Only one vacancy?'

'Only one man I'd give my ears to work for.'

Lady John smiled. 'I remember.'

He turned his sanguine head with a quick look. 'Do I *always* talk about Stonor? Well, it's a habit people have got into.'

'I forget, do you know Mr. Stonor personally, or' — she smiled her good-humoured tolerant smile — 'or are you just dazzled from afar?'

'Oh, I know him! The trouble is he doesn't know me. If

he did he'd realize he can't be sure of winning his election without my valuable services.'

'Geoffrey Stonor's re-election is always a foregone conclusion.'

Farnborough banged his hand on the arm of the chair. 'That the great man shares that opinion is precisely his weak point' — then breaking into a pleasant smile as he made a clean breast of his hero-worship — 'his *only* weak point!'

'Oh, you think,' inquired Lady John, lightly, 'just because the Liberals swept the country the last time, there's danger of their ——'

'How can we be sure *any* Conservative seat is safe, after ——' as Lady John smiled and turned to her papers again. 'Forgive me,' said the young man, with a tolerant air, 'I know you're not interested in politics *qua* politics. But this concerns Geoffrey Stonor.'

'And you count on my being interested in him like all the rest?'

He leaned forward. 'Lady John, I've heard the news.'

'What news?'

'That your little niece, the Scotch heiress, is going to marry him.'

'Who told you that?'

She dropped the paper she had picked up and stared. No doubt about his having won her whole attention at last.

'Please don't mind my knowing.'

But Lady John was visibly perturbed. 'Jean had set her heart on having a few days with just her family in the secret, before the flood of congratulation broke loose.'

'Oh, *that's* all right,' he said soothingly. 'I always hear things before other people.'

'Well, I must ask you to be good enough to be very circumspect.' Lady John spoke gravely. 'I wouldn't have my niece or Mr. Stonor think that any of us ——'

'Oh, of course not.'

'She'll suspect something if you so much as mention Stonor; and you can't help mentioning Stonor!'

'Yes, I can. Besides I shan't see her!'

'But you will' — Lady John glanced at the clock. 'She'll be here in an hour.'

He jumped up delighted. 'What? To-day. The future Mrs. Stonor!'

'Yes,' said his hostess, with a harassed air. 'Unfortunately we had one or two people already asked for the week and ——'

'And I go and invite myself to luncheon! Lady John.' He pushed back the armchair like one who clears the field for action. He stood before her with his legs wide apart, and a look of enterprise on his face. 'You can buy me off! I'll promise to remove myself in five minutes if you'll put in a word for me.'

'Ah!' Lady John shook her head. 'Mr. Stonor inspires a similar enthusiasm in so many young ——'

'They haven't studied the situation as I have.' He sat down to explain his own excellence. 'They don't know what's at stake. They don't go to that hole Dutfield, as I did, just to hear his Friday speech.'

'But you were rewarded. My niece, Jean, wrote me it was "glorious."'

'Well, you know, I was disappointed,' he said judicially. 'Stonor's too content just to criticize, just to make his delicate pungent fun of the men who are grappling — very inadequately of course — still *grappling* with the big questions. There's a carrying power' — he jumped to his feet again and faced an imaginary audience — 'some of Stonor's friends ought to point it out — there's a driving power in the poorest constructive policy that makes the most brilliant criticism look barren.'

She regarded the budding politician with good-humoured malice.

'Who told you that?'

'You think there's nothing in it because *I* say it. But now that he's coming into the family, Lord John or somebody really ought to point out — Stonor's overdoing his rôle of magnificent security.'

The lady sat very straight. 'I don't see even Lord John offering to instruct Mr. Stonor,' she said, with dignity.

'Believe me, that's just Stonor's danger! Nobody saying a word, everybody hoping he's on the point of adopting some definite line, something strong and original, that's going to fire the public imagination and bring the Tories back into power ——'

'So he will.'

'Not if he disappoints meetings,' said Farnborough, hotly; 'not if he goes calmly up to town, and leaves the field to the Liberals.'

'When did he do anything like that?'

'Yesterday!' Farnborough flung out the accusation as he strode up and down before the divan. 'And now he's got this other preoccupation——'

'You mean—— ?'

'Yes, your niece — the spoilt child of fortune.' Farnborough stopped suddenly and smacked his forehead. 'Of *course!*' — he wheeled round upon Lady John with accusing face — 'I understand it now. *She* kept him from the meeting last night! *Well!*' — he collapsed in the nearest chair — 'if that's the effect she's going to have, it's pretty serious!'

'You are,' said his hostess.

'I can assure you the election agent's more so. He's simply tearing his hair.'

She had risen. 'How do you know?' she asked more gravely.

'He told me so himself, yesterday. I scraped acquaintance with the agent, just to see if — if——'

'I see,' she smiled. 'It's not only here that you manœuvre for that secretaryship!'

As Lady John moved towards the staircase she looked at the clock. Farnborough jumped up and followed her, saying confidentially —

'You see, you can never tell when your chance might come. The election chap's promised to keep me posted. Why, I've even taken the trouble to arrange with the people at the station to receive any message that might come over from Dutfield.'

'For you?' She smiled at his self-importance.

Breathlessly he hurried on: 'Immense unexpected pressure of work, you know — now that we've forced the Liberals to appeal to the country——'

He stopped as the sound of light steps came flying through the lobby, and a young girl rushed into the hall calling out gaily —

'Aunt Ellen! Here I—— '

She stopped precipitately, and her outstretched arms fell to her sides. A radiant, gracious figure, she stood poised an instant, the light of gladness in her eyes only partially dimmed by the horrid spectacle of an interloper in the person of a strange young man.

'My darling Jean!'

Lady John went forward and kissed her at the moment that the master of the house came hurrying in from the garden with a cheerful —

'I *thought* that was you running up the avenue!'

'Uncle, dear!'

The pretty vision greeted him with the air of a privileged child of the house, interrupting only for an instant the babel of cross-purpose explanation about carriages and trains.

Lord John had shaken hands with Dick Farnborough and walked him towards the window, saying through the torrent —

'Now they'll tell each other for the next ten minutes that she's an hour earlier than we expected.'

Although young Farnborough had looked upon the blooming addition to the party with an undisguised interest, he readily fell in with Lord John's diplomatic move to get him out of the way. He even helped towards his own effacement, looking out through the window with —

'The Freddy Tunbridges said they were coming to you this week.'

'Yes, they're dawdling through the park with the Church Brigade.'

'Oh, I'll go and meet them;' and Farnborough disappeared.

As Lord John turned back to his two ladies he offered it as his opinion —

'That discreet young man will get on.'

'But *how* did you get here?' Lady John was still wondering.

Breathless, the girl answered, 'He motored me down.'

'Geoffrey Stonor?'

She nodded, beaming.

'Why, where is he then?'

'He dropped me at the end of the avenue, and went on to see a supporter about something.'

'You let him go off like that!' Lord John reproached her.

'Without ever ——' Lady John interrupted herself to take Jean's two hands in hers. 'Just tell me, my child, is it all right?'

'My engagement? Absolutely.'

Such radiant security shone in the soft face that the older woman, drawing the girl down beside her on the divan, dared to say —

'Geoffrey Stonor isn't going to be — a little too old for you.'

Jean chimed out the gayest laugh in the world. 'Bless me! am I such a chicken?'

'Twenty-four used not to be so young, but it's become so.'

'Yes, we don't grow up so quick,' she agreed merrily. 'But, on the other hand, we *stay* up longer.'

'You've got what's vulgarly called "looks," my dear,' said her uncle, 'and that will help to *keep* you up.'

'I know what Uncle John's thinking,' she turned on him with a pretty air of challenge. 'But I'm not the only girl who's been left "what's vulgarly called" money.'

'You're the only one of our immediate circle who's been left so beautifully much.'

'Ah! but remember, Geoffrey could — everybody *knows* he could have married any one in England.'

'I am afraid everybody does know it,' said her ladyship, faintly ironic, 'not excepting Mr. Stonor.'

'Well, how spoilt is the great man?' inquired Lord John, mischievously.

'Not the least little bit in the world. You'll see! He so wants to know my best-beloved relations better.' She stopped to bestow another embrace on Lady John. 'An orphan has so few belongings, she has to make the most of them.'

'Let us hope he'll approve of us on further acquaintance.'

'Oh, he will! He's an angel. Why, he gets on with my grandfather!'

'Does he?' said her aunt, unable to forbear teasing her a little. 'You mean to say Mr. Geoffrey Stonor isn't just a tiny bit "superior" about Dissenters.'

'Not half as much so as Uncle John, and all the rest of you! My grandfather's been ill again, you know, and rather difficult — bless him! but Geoffrey ——' she clasped her hands to fill out her wordless content with him.

'Geoffrey *must* have powers of persuasion, to get that old Covenanter to let you come in an abhorred motor-car, on Sunday, too!'

Jean pursed her red lips and put up a cautionary finger with a droll little air of alarm.

'Grandfather didn't know!' she half whispered.

'Didn't know?'

'I honestly meant to come by train,' she hastened to exculpate herself. 'Geoffrey met me on my way to the station. We had the most glorious run! Oh, Aunt Ellen, we're so happy!' She pressed her cheek against Lady John's shoulder. 'I've so looked forward to having you to myself the whole day just to talk to you about ——'

Lord John turned away with affected displeasure. 'Oh, very well ——'

She jumped up and caught him affectionately by the arm. '*You'd* find it dreffly dull to hear me talk about Geoffrey the whole blessed day!'

'Well, till luncheon, my dear ——' Lady John had risen with a glance at the clock. 'You mustn't mind if I ——' She broke off and went to the writing-table, saying aside to her husband, 'I'm beginning to feel a little anxious; Miss Levering wasn't only tired last night, she was ill.'

'I thought she looked very white,' said Lord John.

'Oh, dear! Have you got other people?' demanded the happy egoist.

'One or two. Your uncle's responsible for asking that old cynic, St. John Greatorex, and I'm responsible for ——'

Jean stopped in the act of taking off her long gloves. 'Mr. Greatorex! He's a Liberal, isn't he?' she said with sudden gravity.

'Little Jean!' Lord John chuckled, 'beginning to "think in parties!"'

'It's very natural now that she should ——'

'I only meant it was odd he should be *here*. Of course I'm not so silly ——'

'It's all right, my child,' said her uncle, kindly. 'We naturally expect now that you'll begin to think like Geoffrey Stonor, and to feel like Geoffrey Stonor, and to talk like Geoffrey Stonor. And quite proper, too!'

'Well,' — Jean quickly recovered her smiles — 'if I *do* think with my husband, and feel with him — as of course I shall — it will surprise me if I ever find myself talking a tenth as well!' In her enthusiasm she followed her uncle to the French window. 'You should have heard him at Dutfield.' She stopped short. 'The Freddy Tunbridges!' she exclaimed, looking out into the garden. A moment later her gay look fell. 'What? Not Aunt Lydia! Oh—h!' She glanced back reproachfully at Lady John, to find her making a discreet motion of 'I couldn't help it!' as the party from the garden came in.

The greetings of the Freddys were cut short by Mrs. Heriot, who embraced her niece with a significant warmth.

'*I* wasn't surprised,' she said *sotto voce.* 'I always prophesied ——'

'Sh — *Please* ——' the girl escaped.

'We haven't met since you were in short skirts,' said the young man who had been watching his opportunity. 'I'm Dick Farnborough.'

'Oh, I remember.' Jean gave him her hand.

Mrs. Freddy was looking round and asking where was the Elusive One?

'Who is the Elusive One?' Jean demanded.

'Lady John's new ally in good works!' said Mrs. Freddy. 'Why, you met her one day at my house before you went back to Scotland.'

'Oh, you mean Miss Levering.'

'Yes; nice creature, isn't she?' said Lord John, benevolently.

'I used rather to love her,' said Mrs. Freddy, brightly, 'but she doesn't come to us any more. She seems to be giving up going anywhere, except here, so far as I can make out.'

'She knows she can rest here,' said Lady John.

'What does she do to tire her?' demanded Mr. Freddy. 'Hasn't she been amusing herself in Norway?'

'Since she came back she's been helping my sister and me with a scheme of ours,' said Lady John.

'She certainly knows how to juggle money out of the men!' admitted Mrs. Heriot.

'It would sound less equivocal, Lydia, if you added that the money is to build baths in our Shelter for Homeless Women.'

'Homeless women?' echoed Mr. Freddy.

'Yes; in the most insanitary part of Soho.'

'Oh — a — really.' Mr. Freddy stroked his smart little moustache.

'It doesn't sound quite in Miss Levering's line,' Farnborough hazarded.

'My dear boy,' said his hostess, 'you know as little about what's in a woman's line as most men.'

'Oh, I say!' Mr. Freddy looked round with a laugh.

Lord John threw out his chest and dangled his eyeglass with an indulgent air.

'Philanthropy,' he said, 'in a woman like Miss Levering, is a form of restlessness. But she's a *nice* creature. All she needs is to get some "nice" fella to marry her!'

Mrs. Freddy laughingly hooked herself on her husband's arm.

'Yes; a woman needs a balance wheel, if only to keep her from flying back to town on a hot day like this.'

'Who,' demanded the host, 'is proposing anything so ——'

'The Elusive One,' said Mrs. Freddy.

'Not Miss ——'

'Yes; before luncheon.'

Dick Farnborough glanced quickly at the clock, and then his eyes went questing up the great staircase. Lady John had met the chorus of disapproval with —

'She must be in London by three, she says.'

Lord John stared. '*To-day?* Why she only came late last night! What must she go back for, in the name of ——'

'Well, *that* I didn't ask her. But it must be something important, or she would stay and talk over the plans for the new Shelter.'

Farnborough had pulled out his cigarette case and stepped out through the window into the garden. But he went not as one who means to take a stroll and enjoy a smoke, rather as a man on a mission.

A few minutes after, the desultory conversation in the hall was arrested by the sound of voices near the windows.

They were in full view now — Vida Levering, hatless, a cool figure in pearl-grey with a red umbrella; St. John Greatorex, wearing a Panama hat, talking and gesticulating with a small book, in which his fingers still kept the place; Farnborough, a little supercilious, looking on.

'I protest! Good Lord! what are the women of this country coming to? I *protest* against Miss Levering being carried indoors to discuss anything so revolting.'

As Lord John moved towards the window the vermilion disk of the umbrella closed and dropped like a poppy before it blooms.

As the owner of it entered the hall, Greatorex followed in her wake, calling out —

'Bless my soul! what can a woman like you *know* about such a thing?'

'Little enough,' said Miss Levering, smiling and scattering good-mornings.

'I should think so indeed!' He breathed a sigh of relief and recovered his waggishness. 'It's all this fellow Farnborough's wicked jealousy — routing us out of the summer-house where we were sitting, *perfectly* happy — weren't we?'

'Ideally,' said the lady.

'There. You hear!'

He interrupted Lord John's inquiry as to the seriousness of Miss Levering's unpopular and mysterious programme for the afternoon. But the lady quietly confirmed it, and looked over her hostess's shoulder at the plan-sheet that Lady John was silently holding out between two extended hands.

'Haled indoors on a day like this' — Greatorex affected a mighty scorn of the document — 'to talk about — Public Sanitation, forsooth! Why, God bless my soul, do you realize that's *drains!*'

'I'm dreadfully afraid it is,' said Miss Levering, smiling down at the architectural drawing.

'And we in the act of discussing Italian literature!' Greatorex held out the little book with an air of comic despair. 'Perhaps you'll tell me that isn't a more savoury topic for a lady.'

'But for the tramp population less conducive to savouriness — don't you think — than baths?' She took the book from him, shutting her handkerchief in the place where his finger had been.

'No, no' — Greatorex, Panama in hand, was shaking his piebald head — 'I can't understand this morbid interest in vagrants. You're too — much too —— Leave it to others!'

'What others?'

'Oh, the sort of woman who smells of india-rubber,' he said, with smiling impertinence. 'The typical English spinster. You've seen her. Italy's full of her. She never goes anywhere without a mackintosh and a collapsible bath — *rubber*. When you look at her it's borne in upon you that she doesn't only smell of rubber. She is rubber, too.'

They all laughed.

'Now you frivolous people go away,' Lady John said. 'We've only got a few minutes to talk over the terms of the late Mr. Barlow's munificence before the carriage comes for Miss Levering.'

In the midst of the general movement to the garden, Mrs. Freddy asked Farnborough did he know she'd got that old horror to give Lady John £8000 for her charity before he died?

'Who got him to?' demanded Greatorex.

'Miss Levering,' answered Lady John. 'He wouldn't do it for me, but she brought him round.'

'Bah-ee Jove!' said Freddy. 'I expect so.'

'Yes.' Mrs. Freddy beamed in turn at her lord and at Farnborough as she strolled with them through the window. '*Isn't* she wonderful?'

'Too wonderful,' said Greatorex to the lady in question, lowering his voice, 'to waste your time on the wrong people.'

'I shall waste less of my time after this.' Miss Levering spoke thoughtfully.

'I'm relieved to hear it. I can't see you wheedling money for shelters and rot of that sort out of retired grocers.'

'You see, you call it rot. We couldn't have got £8000 out of *you*.'

Speaking still lower, 'I'm not sure,' he said slyly.

She looked at him.

'If I gave you that much — for your little projects — what would you give me?' he demanded.

'Barlow didn't ask that.' She spoke quietly.

'Barlow!' he echoed, with a truly horrified look. 'I should think not!'

'Barlow!' Lord John caught up the name on his way out with Jean. 'You two still talking Barlow? How flattered the old beggar'd be! Did you hear' — he turned back and linked his arm in Greatorex's — 'did you hear what Mrs. Heriot said about him? "So kind, so munificent — so *vulgar*, poor soul, we couldn't know him in London — but we shall meet him in heaven!"'

The two men went out chuckling.

Jean stood hesitating a moment, glancing through the window at the laughing men, and back at the group of women, Mrs. Heriot seated magisterially at the head of the writing-table, looking with inimical eyes at Miss Levering, who stood in the middle of the hall with head bent over the plan.

'Sit here, my dear,' Lady John called to her. Then with a glance at her niece, 'You needn't stay, Jean; this won't interest you.'

Miss Levering glanced over her shoulder as she moved to the chair opposite Lady John, and in the tone of one agreeing with the dictum just uttered, 'It's only an effort to meet the greatest evil in the world,' she said, and sat down with her back to the girl.

'What do you call the greatest evil in the world?' Jean asked.

A quick look passed between Mrs. Heriot and Lady John.

Miss Levering answered without emphasis, 'The helplessness of women.'

The girl still stood where the phrase had arrested her.

After a moment's hesitation, Lady John went over to her and put an arm about her shoulder.

'I know, darling, you can think of nothing but "him," so just go ——'

'Indeed, indeed,' interrupted the girl, brightly, 'I can think of everything better than I ever did before. He has lit up everything for me — made everything vivider, more — more significant.'

'Who has?' Miss Levering asked, turning round.

As though she had not heard, Jean went on, 'Oh, yes, I don't care about other things less but a thousand times more.'

'You *are* in love,' said Lady John.

'Oh, that's it. I congratulate you.' Over her shoulder Miss Levering smiled at the girl.

'Well, now' — Lady John returned to the outspread plan — '*this*, you see, obviates the difficulty you raised.'

'Yes, it's a great improvement,' Miss Levering agreed.

Mrs. Heriot, joining in for the first time, spoke with emphasis —

'But it's going to cost a great deal more.'

'It's worth it,' said Miss Levering.

'But we'll have nothing left for the organ at St. Pilgrim's.'

'My dear Lydia,' said Lady John, 'we're putting the organ aside.'

'We can't afford to "put aside" the elevating influence of music.' Mrs. Heriot spoke with some asperity.

'What we must make for, first, is the cheap and humanely conducted lodging-house.'

'There are several of those already; but poor St. Pilgrim's ——'

'There are none for the poorest women,' said Miss Levering.

'No; even the excellent Barlow was for multiplying Rowton Houses. You can never get men to realize — you can't always get women ——'

'It's the work least able to wait,' said Miss Levering.

'I don't agree with you,' Mrs. Heriot bridled, 'and I happen to have spent a great deal of my life in works of charity.'

'Ah, then,' — Miss Levering lifted her eyes from the map to Mrs. Heriot's face — 'you'll be interested in the girl I saw dying in a tramp ward a little while ago. *Glad* her cough was worse, only she mustn't die before her father. Two reasons. Nobody but her to keep the old man out of the workhouse, and "father is so proud." If she died first, he would starve — worst of all, he might hear what had happened up in London to his girl.'

With an air of profound suspicion, Mrs. Heriot interrupted —

'She didn't say, I suppose, how she happened to fall so low?'

'Yes, she did. She had been in service. She lost the train back one Sunday night, and was too terrified of her employer to dare to ring him up after hours. The wrong person found her crying on the platform.'

'She should have gone to one of the Friendly Societies.'

'At eleven at night?'

'And there are the Rescue Leagues. I myself have been connected with one for twenty years ——'

'Twenty years!' echoed Miss Levering. 'Always arriving "after the train's gone," — after the girl and the wrong person have got to the journey's end.'

Mrs. Heriot's eyes flashed, but before she could speak Jean asked —

'Where is she now?'

'Never mind.' Lady John turned again to the plan.

'Two nights ago she was waiting at a street corner in the rain.

'Near a public-house, I suppose?' Mrs. Heriot threw in.

'Yes; a sort of public-house. She was plainly dying. She

was told she shouldn't be out in the rain. "I mustn't go in yet," she said. "*This* is what he gave me," and she began to cry. In her hand were two pennies silvered over to look like half-crowns.'

'I don't believe that story!' Mrs. Heriot announced. 'It's just the sort of thing some sensation-monger trumps up. Now, who tells you these —— ?'

'Several credible people. I didn't believe them till —— '

'Till?' Jean came nearer.

'Till I saw for myself.'

'*Saw?*' exclaimed Mrs. Heriot. 'Where —— ?'

'In a low lodging-house not a hundred yards from the church you want a new organ for.'

'How did *you* happen to be there?'

'I was on a pilgrimage.'

'A pilgrimage?' echoed Jean.

Miss Levering nodded. 'Into the Underworld.'

'*You* went!' Even Lady John was aghast.

'How could you?' Jean whispered.

'I put on an old gown and a tawdry hat ——' She turned suddenly to her hostess. 'You'll never know how many things are hidden from a woman in good clothes. The bold free look of a man at a woman he believes to be destitute — you must *feel* that look on you before you can understand — a good half of history.'

Mrs. Heriot rose as her niece sat down on the footstool just below the writing-table.

'Where did you go — dressed like that?' the girl asked.

'Down among the homeless women, on a wet night, looking for shelter.'

'Jean!' called Mrs. Heriot.

'No wonder you've been ill,' Lady John interposed hastily.

'And it's like *that?*' Jean spoke under her breath.

'No,' came the answer, in the same hushed tone.

'No?'

'It's so much worse I dare not tell about it, even if you weren't here I couldn't.'

But Mrs. Heriot's anger was unappeased. 'You needn't suppose, darling, that those wretched creatures feel it as we would.'

Miss Levering raised grave eyes. 'The girls who need shelter and work aren't *all* serving-maids.'

'We know,' said Mrs. Heriot, with an involuntary flash, 'that all the women who make mistakes aren't.'

'That is why *every* woman ought to take an interest in this,' said Miss Levering, steadily; 'every girl, too.'

'Yes. Oh, yes!' Jean agreed.

'No.' Lady John was very decisive. 'This is a matter for us older ——'

'Or for a person who has some special knowledge,' Mrs. Heriot amended, with an air of sly challenge. '*We* can't pretend to have access to such sources of information as Miss Levering.'

'Yes, you can' — she met Mrs. Heriot's eye — 'for I can give you access. As you suggest, I have some personal knowledge about homeless girls.'

'Well, my dear' — with a manufactured cheerfulness Lady John turned it aside — 'it will all come in convenient.' She tapped the plan.

Miss Levering took no notice. 'It once happened to me to take offence at an ugly thing that was going on under my father's roof. Oh, *years* ago! I was an impulsive girl. I turned my back on my father's house.'

'That was ill-advised.' Lady John glanced at her niece.

'So all my relations said' — Miss Levering, too, looked at Jean — 'and I couldn't explain.'

'Not to your mother?' the girl asked.

'My mother was dead. I went to London to a small hotel, and tried to find employment. I wandered about all day and every day from agency to agency. I was supposed to be educated. I'd been brought up partly in Paris, I could play several instruments and sing little songs in four different tongues.'

In the pause Jean asked, 'Did nobody want you to teach French or sing the little songs?'

'The heads of schools thought me too young. There were people ready to listen to my singing. But the terms, they were too hard. Soon my money was gone. I began to pawn my trinkets. *They* went.'

'And still no work?'

'No; but by that time I had some real education — an unpaid

hotel bill, and not a shilling in the world. Some girls think it hardship to have to earn their living. The horror is not to be allowed to.'

Jean bent forward. 'What happened?'

Lady John stood up. 'My dear,' she asked her visitor, 'have your things been sent down?'

'Yes. I am quite ready, all but my hat.'

'Well?' insisted Jean.

'Well, by chance I met a friend of my family.'

'That was lucky.'

'I thought so. He was nearly ten years older than I. He said he wanted to help me.' Again she paused.

'And didn't he?' Jean asked.

Lady John laid her hand on Miss Levering's shoulder.

'Perhaps, after all, he did,' she said. 'Why do I waste time over myself? I belonged to the little class of armed women. My body wasn't born weak, and my spirit wasn't broken by the *habit* of slavery. But, as Mrs. Heriot was kind enough to hint, I do know something about the possible fate of homeless girls. What was true a dozen years ago is true to-day. There are pleasant parks, museums, free libraries in our great rich London, and not one single place where destitute women can be sure of work that isn't killing, or food that isn't worse than prison fare. That's why women ought not to sleep o' nights till this Shelter stands spreading out wide arms.'

'No, no,' said the girl, jumping up.

'Even when it's built,' — Mrs. Heriot was angrily gathering up her gloves, her fan and her Prayer-book — 'you'll see! Many of those creatures will prefer the life they lead. They *like* it. A woman told me — one of the sort that knows — told me many of them like it so much that they are indifferent to the risk of being sent to prison. "*It gives them a rest,*" ' she said.

'A rest!' breathed Lady John, horror-struck.

Miss Levering glanced at the clock as she rose to go upstairs, while Lady John and Mrs. Heriot bent their heads over the plan covertly talking.

Jean ran forward and caught the tall grey figure on the lower step.

'I want to begin to understand something of ——,' she began in a beseeching tone. 'I'm horribly ignorant.'

Miss Levering looked down upon her searchingly. 'I'm a rather busy person,' she said.

'I have a quite special reason for wanting *not* to be ignorant. I'll go to town to-morrow,' said Jean, impulsively, 'if you'll come and lunch with me — or let me come to you.'

'Jean!' It was Aunt Lydia's voice.

'I must go and put my hat on,' said Miss Levering, hurrying up the stair.

Mrs. Heriot bent towards her sister and half whispered, 'How little she minds talking about horrors!'

'They turn me cold. Ugh! I wonder if she's signed the visitor's book.' Lady John rose with harassed look. 'Such foolishness John's new plan of keeping it in the lobby. It's twice as likely to be forgotten.'

'For all her Shelter schemes, she's a hard woman,' said Aunt Lydia.

'Miss Levering is!' exclaimed Jean.

'Oh, of course *you* won't think so. She has angled very adroitly for your sympathy.'

'She doesn't look ——' protested the girl.

Lady John, glancing at her niece, seemed in some intangible way to take alarm.

'I'm not sure but what she does. Her mouth — always like this — as if she were holding back something by main force.'

'Well, so she is,' slipped out from between Aunt Lydia's thin lips as Lady John disappeared into the lobby.

'Why haven't I seen Miss Levering before this summer?' Jean asked.

'Oh, she's lived abroad.' The lady was debating with herself. 'You don't know about her, I suppose?'

'I don't know how Aunt Ellen came across her, if that's what you mean.'

'Her father was a person everybody knew. One of his daughters made a very good marriage. But this one — I didn't bargain for you and Hermione getting mixed up with her.'

'I don't see that we're either of us —— But Miss Levering seems to go everywhere. Why shouldn't she?'

With sudden emphasis, 'You mustn't ask her to Eaton Square,' said Aunt Lydia.

'I have.'

Mrs. Heriot half rose from her seat. 'Then you'll have to get out of it!'

'Why?'

'I am sure your grandfather would agree with me. I warn you I won't stand by and see that woman getting you into her clutches.'

'Clutches? Why should you think she wants me in her clutches?'

'Just for the pleasure of clutching! She's the kind that's never satisfied till she has everybody in the pitiful state your Aunt Ellen's in about her. Richard Farnborough, too, just on the very verge of asking Hermione to marry him!'

'Oh, is that it?' the girl smiled wisely.

'No!' Too late Mrs. Heriot saw her misstep. 'That's *not* it! And I am sure, if Mr. Stonor knew what I do, he would agree with me that you must not ask her to the house.'

'Of course I'd do anything he asked me to. But he would give me a reason. And a very good reason, too!' The pretty face was very stubborn.

Aunt Lydia's wore the inflamed look not so much of one who is angry as of a person who has a cold in the head.

'I'll give you the reason!' she said. 'It's not a thing I should have preferred to tell you, but I know how difficult you are to guide — so I suppose you'll have to know.' She looked round and lowered her voice. 'It was ten or twelve years ago. I found her horribly ill in a lonely Welsh farmhouse.'

'Miss Levering?'

Mrs. Heriot nodded. 'We had taken the Manor for that August. The farmer's wife was frightened, and begged me to go and see what I thought. I soon saw how it was — I thought she was dying.'

'*Dying?* What was the ——'

'I got no more out of her than the farmer's wife did. She had no letters. There had been no one to see her except a man down from London, a shady-looking doctor — nameless, of course. And then this result. The farmer and his wife, highly respectable people, were incensed. They were for turning the girl out.'

'*Oh!* but ——'

'Yes. Pitiless some of these people are! Although she had

forfeited all claim — still she was a daughter of Sir Hervey Levering. I insisted they should treat the girl humanely, and we became friends — that is, "sort of." In spite of all I did for her ——'

'What did you do?'

'I — I've told you, and I lent her money. No small sum either ——'

'Has she never paid it back?'

'Oh, yes; after a time. But I *always* kept her secret — as much as I knew.'

'But you've been telling me ——'

'That was my duty — and I never had her full confidence.'

'Wasn't it natural she ——'

'Well, all things considered, she might have wanted to tell me who was responsible.'

'Oh, Aunt Lydia.'

'All she ever said was that she was ashamed' — Mrs. Heriot was fast losing her temper and her fine feeling for the innocence of her auditor — 'ashamed that she "hadn't had the courage to resist" — not the original temptation, but the pressure brought to bear on her "not to go through with it," as she said.'

With a shrinking look the girl wrinkled her brows. 'You are being so delicate — I'm not sure I understand.'

'The only thing you need understand,' said her aunt, irritably, 'is that she's not a desirable companion for a young girl.'

There was a pause.

'When did you see her after — after ——'

Mrs. Heriot made a slight grimace. 'I met her last winter at — of all places — the Bishop's!'

'They're relations of hers.'

'Yes. It was while you were in Scotland. They'd got her to help with some of their work. Now she's taken hold of ours. Your aunt and uncle are quite foolish about her, and I'm debarred from taking any steps, at least till the Shelter is out of hand.'

The girl's face was shadowed — even a little frightened. It was evident she was struggling not to give way altogether to alarm and repulsion.

'I do rather wonder that after that, she can bring herself to talk about — the unfortunate women of the world.'

'The effrontery of it!' said her aunt.

'Or — the courage!' The girl put her hand up to her throat as if the sentence had caught there.

'Even presumes to set *me* right! Of course I don't *mind* in the least, poor soul — but I feel I owe it to your dead mother to tell you about her, especially as you're old enough now to know something about life.'

'And since a girl needn't be very old to suffer for her ignorance' — she spoke slowly, moving a little away. But she stopped on the final sentence: 'I *felt* she was rather wonderful!'

'*Wonderful!*'

'To have lived through *that*, when she was — how old?'

Mrs. Heriot rose with an increased irritation. 'Nineteen or thereabouts.'

'Five years younger than I!' Jean sat down on the divan and stared at the floor. 'To be abandoned, and to come out of it like this!'

Mrs. Heriot went to her and laid her hand on the girl's shoulder.

'It was too bad to have to tell you such a sordid story to-day of all days.'

'It *is* a terrible story, but this wasn't a bad time. I feel very sorry to-day for women who aren't happy.' She started as a motor-horn was faintly heard. 'That's Geoffrey!' She jumped to her feet.

'Mr. Stonor. What makes you think ——?'

'Yes, yes. I'm sure. I'm sure!' Every shadow fled out of her face in the sudden burst of sunshine.

Lord John hurried in from the garden as the motor-horn sounded louder.

'Who do you think is coming round the drive?'

Jean caught hold of him. 'Oh, dear! are those other people all about? How am I ever going to be able to behave like a girl who — who isn't engaged to the only man in the world worth marrying!'

'You were expecting Mr. Stonor all the time!' exclaimed Aunt Lydia.

'He promised he'd come to luncheon if it was humanly possible. I was afraid to tell you for fear he'd be prevented.'

Lord John was laughing as he went towards the lobby. 'You felt we couldn't have borne the disappointment!'

'I felt I couldn't,' said the girl, standing there with a rapt look.

CHAPTER XV

SHE did not look round when Dick Farnborough ran in from the garden, saying: '*Is* it — is it really?' For just then on the opposite side of the great hall, the centre of a little buzz of welcome, Stonor's tall figure appeared between host and hostess.

'What luck!' Farnborough said under his breath.

He hurried back and faced the rest of the party who were clustered outside the window trying to look unconcerned.

'Yes, by Jove!' he set their incredulity at rest. 'It *is!*'

Discreetly they glanced and craned and then elaborately turned their backs, pretending to be talking among themselves. But, as though the girl standing there expectant in the middle of the hall were well aware of the enormous sensation the new arrival had created, she herself contributed nothing to it. Stonor came forward, and she met him with a soft, happy look, and the low words: 'What a good thing you managed it!' Then she made way for Mrs. Heriot's far more impressive greeting, innocent of the smallest reminder of the last encounter!

It was Lord John who cut these amenities short by chaffing Stonor for being so enterprising all of a sudden. 'Fancy your motoring out of town to see a supporter on Sunday!'

'I don't know how we ever covered the ground in the old days,' he answered. 'It's no use to stand for your borough any more. The American, you know, he "runs" for Congress. By-and-by we shall all be flying after the thing we want.' He smiled at Jean.

'Sh!' She glanced over her shoulder and spoke low. 'All sorts of irrelevant people here.'

One of them, unable any longer to resist the temptation, was making a second foray into the hall.

'How do you do, Mr. Stonor?' Farnborough stood there holding out his hand.

The great man seemed not to see it, but he murmured, 'How do you do?' and proceeded to share with Lady John his dislike of any means of locomotion except his own legs or those of a horse.

It took a great deal to disconcert Farnborough. 'Some of us were arguing in the smoking-room last night,' he said, 'whether it didn't hurt a candidate's chances going about in a motor.'

As Mr. Stonor, not deigning to reply to this, paused the merest instant in what he was saying to his hostess, Lord John came to the rescue of the audacious young gentleman.

'Yes, we've been hearing a great many stories about the unpopularity of motor-cars — among the class that hasn't got 'em, of course.'

'I'm sure,' Lady John put in, 'you gain more votes by being able to reach so many more of your constituents than we used ——'

'Well, I don't know,' said Stonor. 'I've sometimes wondered whether the charm of our presence wasn't counterbalanced by the way we tear about smothering our fellow-beings in dust and running down their pigs and chickens, — not to speak of their children.'

'What on the whole are the prospects?' Lord John asked.

'We shall have to work harder than we realized,' Stonor answered gravely.

Farnborough let slip an 'Ah, I said so!' meant for Lady John, and then before Stonor's raised eyes, the over-zealous young politician retreated towards the window — but with hands in his pockets and head held high, like one who has made his mark. And so in truth he had. For Lady John let drop one or two good-natured phrases — what he had done, his hero-worship, his mother had been a Betham — Yes, he was one of the Farnboroughs of Moore Abbey. Though Stonor made no comment beyond a dry, 'The staple product of this country, young men like that!' — it appeared later that Lady John's good offices in favour of a probable nephew-in-law had not been invoked in vain.

Despite the menace of 'the irrelevant' dotting the lawn immediately outside the windows, the little group on the farther side of the hall still stood there talking in low tones with the sense of intimacy which belongs to a family party.

Jean had slipped her arm in her uncle's, and was smiling at Stonor —

'He says he believes I'll be able to make a real difference to his chances,' she said, half aside. 'Isn't it angelic of him?'

'Angelic?' laughed the great man. 'Macchiavellian. I pin all my hopes on your being able to counteract the pernicious influence of my opponent's glib wife.'

'You want me to have a real share in it all, don't you, Geoffrey?'

'Of course I do.' He smiled into her eyes.

That moth Farnborough, whirling in the political effulgence, was again hovering on the outskirts. He even made conversation to Mrs. Heriot, as an excuse to remain inside the window.

'But you don't mean seriously,' Lord John asked his guest, 'you don't mean, do you, that there's any possible complication about *your* seat?'

'Oh, I dare say it's all right' — Stonor drew a Sunday paper out of his pocket. 'There's this agitation about the Woman Question. Oddly enough, it seems as if it might — there's just the off-chance — it *might* affect the issue.'

'Affect it? How? God bless my soul!' Lord John's transparent skin flushed up to his white hair. 'Don't tell me any responsible person is going even to consider the lunacy of tampering with the British Constitution ——'

'We *have* heard that suggested, though for better reasons,' Stonor laughed, but not Lord John.

'Turn over the destinies of the Empire,' he said hotly, 'to a lot of ignorant women just because a few of 'em have odious manners and violent tongues!' The sight of Stonor's cool impassivity calmed him somewhat. He went on more temperately. 'Every sane person sees that the only trouble with England to-day is that too many ignorant people have votes already.'

'The penalty we pay for being more republican than the Republics.'

Lord John had picked up the Sunday paper and glanced down a column.

'If the worst came to the worst, you can do what the other four hundred have done.'

'Easily! But the mere fact that four hundred and twenty members have been worried into promising support — and then, once in the House, have let the matter severely alone ——'

'Let it alone?' Lord John burst out again. 'I should think so indeed!'

'Yes,' laughed Stonor, 'only it's a device that's somewhat worn.'

'Still,' Lord John put on a Macchiavellian air that sat rather incongruously on his honest English face, 'Still, if they think they're getting a future Cabinet Minister on their side ——'

'It will be sufficiently embarrassing for the Cabinet Minister.'

Stonor caught sight of Farnborough approaching and lowered his voice. He leaned his elbow on the end of the wide mantelpiece and gave his attention exclusively to Lord John, seeming to ignore even the pretty girl who still stood by her uncle with a hand slipped through his arm.

'Nobody says much about it,' Stonor went on, 'but it's realized that the last Labour member, and that Colne Valley Socialist — those men got in largely through the tireless activity of the women.'

'The Suffragettes!' exclaimed the girl, '*they* were able to do that?'

'They're always saying they don't favour *any* party,' said a voice.

Stonor looked up, and, to Jean's obvious relief, refrained from snubbing the irrepressible Farnborough.

'I don't know what they *say* ——' began Stonor.

'Oh, *I* do!' Farnborough interrupted. 'They're not *for* anybody. They're simply agin the Government.'

'Whatever they say, they're all Socialists.' Lord John gave a snort.

'No,' said Farnborough, with cool audacity. 'It only looks like that.'

Jean turned quite pink with anxiety. She, and all who knew him well, had seen Stonor crush the cocksure and the unwary with an awful effectualness. But Farnborough, with the courage of enthusiasm — enthusiasm for himself and his own future — went stoutly on.

'There are Liberals and even Unionists among 'em. And they do manage to hold the balance pretty even. I go and hear them, you see!'

'And speaking from the height of your advantage,' although Stonor was slightly satirical, he was exercising an exceptional forbearance, 'do you mean to tell me they are not more in sympathy with the Labour party than with any other?'

'If they are, it's not because the Suffragists are all for Socialism. But because the Labour party is the only one that puts Women's Suffrage in the forefront of its programme.'

Stonor took his elbow off the mantel. 'Whatever the reason,' he said airily, 'the result is momentarily inconvenient. Though I am one of those who think it would be easy to overestimate the importance ——'

He broke off with an effect of dismissing both the matter and the man. As he turned away, he found himself without the smallest warning face to face with Vida Levering. She had come down the great staircase unobserved and unobserving; her head bent, and she in the act of forcing a recalcitrant hatpin through her hat — doing it under certain disadvantages, as she held her gloves and her veil in one hand.

As she paused there, confronting the tall figure of the new-comer, although it was obvious that her unpreparedness was not less than his own, there was to the most acute eye nothing in the remotest degree dramatic about the encounter — hardly more than a cool surprise, and yet there was that which made Jean say, smiling —

'Oh, you know one another already?'

'Everybody in this part of the world knows Mr. Stonor,' the lady said, 'but he doesn't know me.'

'This is Miss Levering. You knew her father, didn't you?'

Even before Lady John had introduced them, the people in the garden seemed not to be able to support the prospect of Miss Levering's threatened monopoly of the lion. They swarmed in — Hermione Heriot and Paul Filey appearing for the first time since church — they overflowed into the Hall, while Jean Dunbarton, with artless enthusiasm, was demanding of Miss Levering if the reason she knew Mr. Stonor was that she had been hearing him speak.

'Yes,' the lady met his eyes, 'I was visiting some relations near Dutfield. They took me to hear you.'

'Oh — the night the Suffragettes made their customary row ——'

'They didn't attack *you*,' she reminded him.

'They will if we win the election!' he said, with a cynical anticipation.

It was a mark of how far the Women's Cause had travelled that, although there was no man there (except the ineffectual Farnborough) — no one to speak of it even with tolerance, there was also no one, not even Greatorex, who any longer felt the matter to be much of a joke. Here again in this gathering was happening what the unprejudiced observer was seeing in similar circumstances all over England. The mere mention of Women's Suffrage in general society (rarest of happenings now) — that topic which had been the prolific mother of so much merriment, bred in these days but silence and constraint. The quickest-witted changed the topic amid a general sense of grateful relief. The thing couldn't be laughed at any longer, but it could still be pretended it wasn't there.

'You've come just in time to rescue me!' Mrs. Freddy said, sparkling at Stonor.

'You don't appear to be in any serious danger,' he said.

'But I am, or I *was!* They were just insisting I should go upstairs and change my frock.'

'Is there anybody here so difficult as not to like that one?'

She made him a smart little curtsey. 'Although we're going to have luncheon in less than an hour, somebody was going to insist (out of pure mistaken philanthropy) in taking me for a walk. I've told Freddy that when I've departed for realms of bliss, he is to put on my tombstone, "Died of changing her clothes." I know the end will come some Sunday. We appear at breakfast dressed for church. That's a long skirt. We are usually shooed upstairs directly we get back, to put on a short one, so that we can go and look at the kennels or the prize bull. We come back muddy and smelling of stables. We get into something fresh for luncheon. After luncheon some one says, "Walk!" Another short skirt. We come back draggled and dreadful. We change. Something sweetly feminine for tea! The gong. We rush and dress for dinner! You've saved me one change, anyhow. You are my benefactor. Why don't you ask after my babies?'

'Well, how are the young barbarians?' He rubbed his hand over the lower part of his face. 'Your concern for personal appearance reminds me that a little soap and water after my dusty drive ——'

Little as had fallen from him since his entrance, as he followed Lord John upstairs, he left behind that sense of blankness so curiously independent of either words or deeds. Greatorex, in his patent leather shoes and immaculate white gaiters, pattered over to Miss Levering, but she unkindly presented her back, and sat down at the writing-table to make a note on the abhorred

Shelter plan. He showed his disapproval by marching off with Mr. Freddy, and there was a general trickling back into the garden in that aimless, before-luncheon mood.

But Mrs. Heriot and Lady John sat with their heads close together on the sofa, discussing in undertones the absorbing subject of the prospective new member of the family.

Mrs. Freddy perched on the edge of the writing-table between Miss Levering, who sat in front of it, and Jean, whose chair was on the other side. She was nearest Jean, but it was to her children's sworn friend that she turned to say enthusiastically —

'Delightful his coming in like that!' And no one needed to be told whose coming brought delight. 'We must tell Sara and Cecil.'

As Miss Levering seemed to be still absorbed in making notes on that boring plan, the lively Mrs. Freddy turned to her other neighbour.

'Penny for your thoughts,' she demanded with such suddenness that Jean Dunbarton started and reddened. 'Something very weighty, to judge from ——'

'I believe I was thinking it was rather odd to hear two men like my uncle and Mr. Stonor talking about the influence of the Suffrage women really quite seriously. *Oh!'* — she clutched Mrs. Freddy's arm, laughing apologetically — 'I beg your pardon. I forgot. Besides, I wasn't thinking of your kind; I was thinking of the Suffragettes.'

'As the only conceivable ones to be exercising any influence. Thank you.'

'Oh, no, no. Indeed, I didn't mean ——'

'Yes, you did. You're like the rest. You don't realize how we prepared the ground. All the same,' she went on, with her unfailing good humour, 'it's frightfully exciting seeing the Question come into practical politics at last. I only hope those women won't go and upset the apple-cart again.'

'How?'

'Oh, by doing something that will alienate all our good friends in both parties. It's queer they can't see our only chance to get what we want is by winning over the men.'

There was a low sound of impatience from the person at the writing-table, and a rustle of paper as the plan was thrown down.

'What's the matter?' said Mrs. Freddy.

'"Winning over the men" has been the woman's way since the Creation. Do you think the result should make us proud of our policy? Yes? Then go and walk in Piccadilly at midnight.'

Lady John and Mrs. Heriot rose as one, while Miss Levering was adding —

'No, I forgot ——'

'Yes,' interposed Mrs. Heriot, with majesty, 'it is not the first time you've forgotten.'

'What I forgot was the magistrate's ruling. He said no decent woman had any business to be in London's main thoroughfares at night "*unless she has a man with her.*" You can hear that in Soho, too. "You're obliged to take up with a chap!" is what the women say.'

In a highly significant silence, Mrs. Heriot withdrew with her niece and Mrs. Freddy to where Hermione sat contentedly between two young men on the window-step. Lady John, naturally somewhat ruffled, but still quite kind, bent over her indiscreet guest to say —

'What an odd mood you are in to-day, my dear. I think Lydia Heriot's right. We oughtn't to do anything, or *say* anything to encourage this ferment of feminism — and I'll tell you why: it's likely to bring a very terrible thing in its train.'

'What terrible thing?'

'Sex-Antagonism.'

'It's here.'

'Don't say that!' Lady John spoke very gravely.

'You're so conscious it's here, you're afraid to have it mentioned.'

Lady John perceived that Jean had quietly slipped away from the others, and was standing behind her.

If Mrs. Heriot had not been too absorbed in Dick Farnborough and Hermione she would have had a moment's pleasure in her handiwork — that half-shamed scrutiny in Jean Dunbarton's face. But as the young girl studied the quiet figure, looked into the tender eyes that gazed so steadily into some grey country far away, the effect of Mrs. Heriot's revelation was either weakened or transmuted subtly to something stronger than the thing that it replaced.

As the woman sat there leaning her head a little wearily on her hand, there was about the whole *Wesen* an indefinable nobility that answered questions before they were asked.

But Lady John, upon perceiving her niece, had said hurriedly —

'If what you say is so, it's the fault of those women agitators.'

'Sex-Antagonism wasn't their invention,' Miss Levering answered. 'No woman begins that way. Every woman is in a state of natural subjection' — she looked up, and seeing Jean's face, smiled — 'no, I'd rather say "allegiance" to her idea of romance and her hope of motherhood; they're embodied for her in man. They're the strongest things in life till man kills them. Let's be fair. If that allegiance dies, each woman knows why.'

Lady John, always keenly alive to any change in the social atmosphere, looked up and saw her husband coming downstairs with their guest. As she went to meet them, Stonor stopped halfway down to say something. The two men halted there deep in discussion. But scarcely deeper than those other two Lady John had left by the writing-table.

'Who is it you are going to marry?' Miss Levering had asked.

'It isn't going to be announced for a few days yet.' And then Jean relented enough to say in an undertone, almost confidentially, 'I should think you'd guess.'

'Guess what?' said the other, absent-mindedly, but again lifting her eyes.

'Who I'm going to marry.'

'Oh, I know him, then?' she said, surprised.

'Well, you've seen him.'

Miss Levering shook her head. 'There are so very many young men in the world.' But she looked with a moment's wondering towards the window, seeming to consider first Filey and then Farnborough.

'What made you think of going on that terrible pilgrimage?' asked the girl.

'Something I heard at a Suffrage meeting.'

'Well, do you know, ever since that Sunday at the Freddys', when you told us about the Suffragettes, I — I've been curious about them.'

'You said nothing would ever induce you to listen to such people.'

'I know, and it's rather silly, but one says a thing like that on the spur of the moment, and then one is bound by it.'

'You mean one imagines one is bound.'

'Then, too, I've been in Scotland ever since; but I've often thought about you and what you said that day at the Freddys'!'

'And yet you've been a good deal absorbed ——'

'You see,' the girl put on a pretty little air of superiority, 'it isn't as if the man I'm going to marry wasn't very broad-minded. He wants me to be intelligent about politics. Are those women holding meetings in London now as well as in the constituencies?'

They both became aware at the same moment that Lord John was coming slowly down the last steps, with Stonor still more slowly following, talking Land Tenure. As Miss Levering rose and hurriedly turned over the things on the table to look for her veil, the handkerchief she had shut in her little Italian book dropped out. A further shifting of plans and papers sent it unobserved to the floor. Jean put once more the question that had remained unanswered.

'They collect too great crowds,' Miss Levering answered her. 'The authorities won't let them meet in Trafalgar Square after to-day. They have their last meeting there at three o'clock.'

'To-day! That's no use to people out of town — unless I could invent some excuse ——'

'Wait till you can go without inventions and excuses.'

'You think all that wrong!'

'I think it rather undignified.'

'So do I — but if I'm ever to go ——'

Lord John came forward, leaving Stonor to his hostess. 'Still talking over your Shelter plan?' he asked benevolently.

'No,' answered Miss Levering, 'we left the Shelter some time ago.'

He pinched his niece's ear with affectionate playfulness.

'Then what's all this chatterment about?'

The girl, a little confused, looked at her fellow-conspirator.

'The latest things in veils,' said Miss Levering, smiling, as she caught up hers.

'The invincible frivolity of women!' said Lord John, with immense geniality.

'Oh, they're coming for you,' Jean said. 'Don't forget your book. When shall I see you again, I wonder?'

But instead of announcing the carriage the servant held out a salver. On it lay a telegraph form scribbled over in pencil.

'A telephone message, miss.'

'For me?' said Jean, in surprise.

'Yes, miss. I didn't know you was here, miss. They asked me to write it down, and let you have it as soon as possible.'

'I knew how it would be if I gave in about that telephone!' Lord John arraigned his wife. Even Mr. Stonor had to sympathize. 'They won't leave people in peace even one day in the week.'

'I've got your book,' Jean said, looking at Miss Levering over the top of the telegraph form, and then glancing at the title as she restored the volume to its owner. 'Dante! Whereabouts are you?' She opened it without waiting to hear. 'Oh, the Inferno.'

'No, I'm in a worse place,' said the other, smiling vaguely as she drew on her gloves.

'I didn't know there was a worse.'

'Yes, it's worse with the Vigliacchi.'

'I forget, were they Guelf or Ghibelline?'

'They weren't either, and that was why Dante couldn't stand them. He said there was no place in Heaven nor in Purgatory — not even a corner in Hell, for the souls who had stood aloof from strife.' The smile faded as she stood there looking steadily into the girl's eyes. 'He called them "wretches who never lived," Dante did, because they'd never felt the pangs of partisanship. And so they wander homeless on the skirts of limbo, among the abortions and off-scourings of Creation.'

The girl drew a fluttering breath. Miss Levering glanced at the clock, and turned away to make her leisurely adieux among the group at the window.

Mrs. Heriot left it at once. 'What was that about a telephone message, Jean darling?'

The girl glanced at the paper, and then quite suddenly said to Lady John —

'Aunt Ellen, I've got to go to London!'

'Not to-day!'

'My dear child!'

'Nonsense!'

'Is your grandfather worse?'

'N — no. I don't think my grandfather is any worse. But I must go, all the same.'

'You *can't* go away,' whispered Mrs. Heriot, 'when Mr. Stonor ——'

'Back me up!' Jean whispered to Lady John. 'He said he'd have to leave directly after luncheon. And anyhow — all these people — please have us another time.'

'I'll just see Miss Levering off,' said Lady John, 'and then I'll come back and talk about it.'

In the midst of the good-byeing that was going on over by the window, Jean suddenly exclaimed —

'There mayn't be another train! Miss Levering!'

But Stonor was standing in front of the girl barring the way. 'What if there isn't? I'll take you back in my motor,' he said aside.

'*Will* you?' In her rapture at the thought Jean clasped her hands, and the paper fluttered to the floor. 'But I must be there by three,' she said.

He had picked up the telegraph form as well as the handkerchief lying near.

'Why, it's only an invitation to dine — Wednesday!'

'Sh!' She took the paper.

'Oh! I see!' He smiled and lowered his voice. 'It's rather dear of you to arrange our going off like that. You *are* a clever little girl!'

'It's not exactly that I was arranging. I want to hear those women in Trafalgar Square — the Suffragettes.'

He stared at her more than half incredulous, but smiling still.

'How perfectly absurd! Besides,' — he looked across the room at Lady John — 'besides, I expect she wouldn't like my carrying you off like that.'

'Then she'll have to make an excuse, and come too.'

'Ah, it wouldn't be quite the same if she did that.'

But Jean had thought it out. 'Aunt Ellen and I could get back quite well in time for dinner.'

The group that had closed about the departing guest dissolved.

'Why are you saying good-bye as if you were never coming back?' Lord John demanded.

'One never knows,' Miss Levering laughed. 'Maybe I shan't come back.'

'Don't talk as if you meant never!' said Mrs. Freddy.

'Perhaps I do mean never.' She nodded to Stonor.

He bowed ceremoniously.

'Never come back! What nonsense are you talking?' said Lady John.

'Is it premonition of death, or don't you like us any more?' laughed her husband.

The little group trailed across the great room, escorting the guest to the front door, Lady John leading the way. As they passed, Geoffrey Stonor was obviously not listening very attentively to Jean's enthusiastic explanation of her plan for the afternoon. He kept his eyes lowered. They rested on the handkerchief he had picked up, but hardly as if, after all, they saw it, though he turned the filmy square from corner to corner with an air partly of nervousness, partly of abstraction.

'Is it mine?' asked Jean.

He paused an instant. 'No. Yours,' he said, mechanically, and held out the handkerchief to Miss Levering.

She seemed not to hear. Lord John had blocked the door a moment, insisting on a date for the next visit. Jean caught up the handkerchief and went running forward with it. Suddenly she stopped, glancing down at the embroidered corner.

'But that's not an L! It's V—i——'

Stonor turned his back, and took up a magazine.

Lady John's voice sounded clear from the lobby. 'You must let Vida go, John, or she'll miss her train.'

Miss Levering vanished.

'I didn't know her name was Vida; how did you?' said Jean.

Stonor bent his head silently over the book. Perhaps he hadn't heard. That deafening old gong was sounding for luncheon.

CHAPTER XVI

THE last of the Trafalgar Square meetings was half over when the great chocolate-coloured motor, containing three persons besides the chauffeur, slowed up on the west side of the square. Neither of the two ladies in their all-enveloping veils was easily recognizable, still less the be-goggled countenance of the Hon. Geoffrey Stonor. When he took off his motor glasses, he did not turn down his dust collar. He even pulled farther over his eyes the peak of his linen cap.

By coming at all on this expedition, he had given Jean a signal proof of his desire to please her — but it was plain that he had no mind to see in the papers that he had been assisting at such a spectacle. While he gave instructions as to where the car should wait, Jean was staring at the vast crowd massed on the north side of the column. It extended back among the fountains, and even escaped on each side beyond the vigilance of the guardian lions. There were scores listening there who could not see the speakers even as well as could the occupants of the car. In front of the little row of women on the plinth a gaunt figure in brown serge was waving her arms. What she was saying was blurred in the general uproar.

'Oh, that's one!' Jean called out excitedly. 'Oh, let's hurry.'

But even after they left the car and reached the crowd, to hurry was a thing no man could do. For some minutes the motor-party had only occasional glimpses of the speakers, and heard little more than fragments.

'Who is that, Geoffrey?'

'The tall young fellow with the stoop? That appears to be the chairman.' Stonor himself stooped — to the eager girl who had clutched his sleeve from behind, and was following him closely through the press. 'The artless chairman, I take it, is scolding the people for not giving the woman a hearing!' They laughed together at the young man's foolishness.

Even had an open-air meeting been more of a commonplace to Stonor, it would have had for him that effect of newness that an old thing wears when seen by an act of sympathy through new eyes.

'You must be sure and explain *everything* to me, Geoffrey,' said the girl. 'This is to be an important chapter in my education.' Merrily and without a shadow of misgiving she spoke in jest a truer word than she dreamed. He fell in with her mood.

'Well, I rather gather that he's been criticizing the late Government, and Liberals have made it hot for him.'

'I shall never be able to hear unless we get nearer,' said Jean, anxiously.

'There's a very rough element in front there ——'

'Oh, don't let us mind!'

'Most certainly I mind!'

'Oh, but I should be miserable if I didn't hear.'

She pleaded so bewitchingly for a front seat at the Show that unwillingly he wormed his way on. Suddenly he stood still and stared about.

'What's the matter?' said Lady John.

'I can't have you ladies pushed about in this crowd,' he said under his breath. 'I must get hold of a policeman. You wait just here. I'll find one.'

The adoring eyes of the girl watched the tall figure disappear.

'Look at her face!' Lady John, with her eyeglass up, was staring in the opposite direction. 'She's like an inspired charwoman!'

Jean turned, and in her eagerness pressed on, Lady John following.

The agreeable presence of the young chairman was withdrawn from the fighting-line, and the figure of the working woman stood alone. With her lean brown finger pointing straight at the more outrageous of the young hooligans, and her voice raised shrill above their impertinence —

'I've got boys of me own,' she said, 'and we laugh at all sorts o' things, but I should be ashymed, and so would they, if ever they wus to be'yve as you're doin' to-d'y.'

When they had duly hooted that sentiment, they were quieter for a moment.

'People 'ave been sayin' this is a Middle-Class Woman's Movement. It's a libel. I'm a workin' woman m'self, the wife of a workin' man ——'

'Pore devil!'

'Don't envy 'im, m'self!'

As one giving her credentials, she went on, 'I'm a Pore Law Guardian ——'

'Think o' that, now! Gracious me!'

A friendly person in the crowd turned upon the scoffer.

'Shut up, cawn't yer.'

'Not fur you!'

Further statements on the part of the orator were drowned by —

'Go 'ome and darn your ol' man's stockin's.'

'Just clean yer *own* doorstep.'

She glowered her contempt upon the interrupters. 'It's a pore sort of 'ousekeeper that leaves 'er doorstep till Sunday afternoon. Maybe that's when you would do your doorstep. I do mine in the mornin', before you men are awake!' They relished that and gave her credit for a bull's eye.

'You think,' she went on quietly, seeing she had 'got them' — 'you think we women 'ave no business servin' on Boards and thinking about politics.' In a tone of exquisite contempt, 'But wot's politics!' she demanded. 'It's just 'ousekeepin' on a big scyle.' Somebody applauded. 'Oo among you workin' men 'as the most comfortable 'omes? Those of you that gives yer wives yer wyges.'

'That's it! That's it!' they roared with passion.

'Wantin' our money.'

'That's all this agitation's about.'

'Listen to me!' She came close to the edge of the plinth. 'If it wus only to use fur *our* comfort, d'ye think many o' you workin' men would be found turnin' over their wyges to their wives? No! Wot's the reason thousands do — and the best and the soberest? Because the workin' man knows that wot's a pound to '*im* is twenty shillins to 'is wife, and she'll myke every penny in every one o' them shillins *tell*. She gets more fur 'im out of 'is wyges than wot 'e can. Some o' you know wot the 'omes is like w'ere the men *don't* let the women manage. Well, the Poor Laws and the 'ole Government is just in the syme muddle because the men 'ave tried to do the national 'ousekeepin' without the women!'

They hooted, but they listened, too.

'Like I said to you before, it's a libel to say it's only the well-off women wot's wantin' the vote. I can tell you wot plenty o' the poor women think about it. I'm one o' them! And I can tell you we see there's reforms needed. *We ought to 'ave the vote;* and we know 'ow to appreciate the other women 'oo go to prison for tryin' to get it for us!'

With a little final bob of emphasis, and a glance over her shoulder at the old woman and the young one behind her, she was about to retire. But she paused as the murmur in the crowd grew into distinct phrases.

''Inderin' policemen!' — 'Mykin' rows in the street;' and a voice called out so near Jean that the girl jumped, 'It's the w'y yer goes on as mykes 'em keep ye from gettin' votes. They see ye ain't fit to 'ave ——'

And then all the varied charges were swallowed in a general uproar.

'Where's Geoffrey? Oh, *isn't* she too funny for words?'

The agitated chairman had come forward. 'You evidently don't know,' he said, 'what had to be done by *men* before the extension of suffrage in '67. If it hadn't been for demonstrations ——' But the rest was drowned.

The brown-serge woman stood there waiting, wavering a moment; and suddenly her shrill note rose clear over the indistinguishable Babel.

'You s'y woman's plyce is 'ome! Don't you know there's a third of the women in this country can't afford the luxury of stayin' in their 'omes? They *got* to go out and 'elp make money to p'y the rent and keep the 'ome from bein' sold up. Then there's all the women that 'aven't got even miserable 'omes. They 'aven't got any 'omes *at all*.'

'You said *you* got one. W'y don't you stop in it?'

'Yes, that's like a man. If one o' you is all right he thinks the rest don't matter. We women ——'

But they overwhelmed her. She stood there with her gaunt arms folded — waiting. You felt that she had met other crises of her life with just that same smouldering patience. When the wave of noise subsided again, she was discovered to be speaking.

'P'raps *your* 'omes are all right! P'raps your children never goes 'ungry. P'raps you aren't livin', old and young, married and single, in one room.'

'I suppose life is like that for a good many people,' Jean Dunbarton turned round to say.

'Oh, yes,' said her aunt.

'I come from a plyce where many fam'lies, if they're to go on livin' *at all*, 'ave to live like that. If you don't believe me, come and let me show you!' She spread out her lean arms. 'Come with me to Canning Town — come with me to Bromley — come to Poplar and to Bow. No, you won't even think about the overworked women and the underfed children, and the 'ovels they live in. And you want that *we* shouldn't think neither ——'

'We'll do the thinkin'. You go 'ome and nuss the byby.'

'I do nurse my byby; I've nursed seven. What have you done for yours?' She waited in vain for the answer. 'P'raps,' her voice quivered, 'p'raps your children never goes 'ungry, and maybe you're satisfied — though I must say I wouldn't a thought it from the look o' yer.'

'Oh, I s'y!'

'But we women are not satisfied. We don't only want better things for our own children; we want better things for all. *Every* child is our child. We know in our 'earts we oughtn't to rest till we've mothered 'em every one.'

'Wot about the men? Are *they* all 'appy?'

There was derisive laughter at that, and 'No! No!' 'Not precisely!' ''*Appy?* Lord!'

'No, there's lots o' you men I'm sorry for,' she said.

'Thanks, awfully!'

'And we'll 'elp you if you let us,' she said.

''Elp us? You tyke the bread out of our mouths.'

'Now you're goin' to begin about us blackleggin' the men! *W'y* does any woman tyke less wyges than a man for the same work? Only because we can't get anything better. That's part the reason w'y we're yere to-d'y. Do you reely think,' she reasoned with them as man to man; 'do you think, now, we tyke those low wyges because we got a likin' fur low wyges? No. We're just like you. We want as much as ever we can get.'

''Ear! 'ear!'

'We got a gryte deal to do with our wgyes, we women has. We

got the children to think about. And w'en we get our rights, a woman's flesh and blood won't be so much cheaper than a man's that employers can get rich on keepin' you out o' work and sweatin' us. If you men only could see it, we got the syme cause, and if you 'elped us you'd be 'elpin' yerselves.'

'Rot!'

'True as gospel!' some one said.

'Drivel!'

As she retired against the banner with the others, there was some applause.

'Well, now,' said a man patronizingly, 'that wusn't so bad — fur a woman.'

'N — naw. Not fur a woman.'

Jean had been standing on tip-toe making signals. Ah, at last Geoffrey saw her! But why was he looking so grave?

'No policeman?' Lady John asked.

'Not on that side. They seem to have surrounded the storm centre, which is just in front of the place you've rather unwisely chosen.' Indeed it was possible to see, further on, half a dozen helmets among the hats.

What was happening on the plinth seemed to have a lessened interest for Jean Dunbarton. She kept glancing sideways up under the cap brim at the eyes of the man at her side.

Lady John on the other hand was losing nothing. 'Is *she* one of them? That little thing?'

'I — I suppose so,' answered Stonor, doubtfully, though the chairman, with a cheerful air of relief, had introduced Miss Ernestine Blunt to the accompaniment of cheers and a general moving closer to the monument.

Lady John, after studying Ernestine an instant through her glass, turned to a dingy person next her, who was smoking a short pipe.

'Among those women up there,' said Lady John, 'can you tell me, my man, which are the ones that a — that make the disturbances?'

The man removed his pipe and spat carefully between his feet. Then with deliberation he said —

'The one that's doing the talking now — she's the disturbingest o' the lot.'

'Not that nice little——'

'Don't you be took in, mum;' and he resumed the consolatory pipe.

'What is it, Geoffrey? Have I done anything?' Jean said very low.

'Why didn't you stay where I left you?" he answered, without looking at her.

'I couldn't hear. I couldn't even see. Please don't look like that. Forgive me,' she pleaded, covertly seeking his hand.

His set face softened. 'It frightened me when I didn't see you where I left you.'

She smiled, with recovered spirits. She could attend now to the thing she had come to see.

'I'm sorry you missed the inspired charwoman. It's rather upsetting to think—do you suppose any of our servants have—views?'

Stonor laughed. 'Oh, no! Our servants are all too superior.' He moved forward and touched a policeman on the shoulder. What was said was not audible—the policeman at first shook his head, then suddenly he turned round, looked sharply into the gentleman's face, and his whole manner changed. Obliging, genial, almost obsequious. 'Oh, he's recognized Geoffrey!' Jean said to her aunt. 'They *have* to do what a member tells them! They'll stop the traffic any time to let Geoffrey go by!' she exulted.

Stonor beckoned to his ladies. The policeman was forging a way in which they followed.

'This will do,' Stonor said at last, and he whispered again to the policeman. The man replied, grinning. 'Oh, really,' Stonor smiled, too. 'This is the redoubtable Miss Ernestine Blunt,' he explained over his shoulder, and he drew back so that Jean could pass, and standing so, directly in front of him, she could be protected right and left, if need were, by a barrier made of his arms.

'Now can you see?' he asked.

She looked round and nodded. Her face was without cloud again. She leaned lightly against his arm.

Miss Ernestine had meanwhile been catapulting into election issues with all the fervour of a hot-gospeller.

'What outrageous things she says about important people—

people she ought to respect and be rather afraid of,' objected Jean, rather scandalized.

'Impudent little baggage!' said Stonor.

Reasons, a plenty, the baggage had why the Party which had so recently refused to enfranchise women should not be returned to power.

'You're in too big a hurry,' some one shouted. 'All the Liberals want is a little time.'

'Time! You seem not to know that the first petition in favour of giving us the Franchise was signed in 1866.'

'How do *you* know?'

She paused a moment, taken off her guard by the suddenness of the attack.

'*You* wasn't there!'

'That was the trouble. Haw! Haw!'

'That petition,' she said, 'was presented forty years ago.'

'Give 'er a 'reain' now she *'as* got out of 'er crydle.'

'It was presented to the House of Commons by John Stuart Mill. Give the Liberals time!' she echoed. 'Thirty-three years ago memorials in favour of the suffrage were presented to Mr. Gladstone and Mr. Disraeli. In 1896, 257,000 women of these British Isles signed an appeal to the members of Parliament. Bills or Resolutions have been before the House, on and off, for the last thirty-six years. All that "time" thrown away! At the opening of this year we found ourselves with no assurance that if we went on in the same way, any girl born into the world in our time would ever be able to exercise the rights of citizenship though she lived to be a hundred. That was why we said all this has been in vain. We must try some other way. How did you working men get the suffrage, we asked ourselves. Well, we turned up the records — and we *saw*. We don't want to follow such a violent example. We would much rather not — but if that's the only way we can make the country see we're in earnest — we are prepared to show them!'

'An' they'll show *you!*'

'Give ye another month 'ard!'

In the midst of the laughter and interruptions, a dirty, beery fellow of fifty or so, from whom Stonor's arm was shielding Jean, turned to the pal behind him with —

'Ow'd yer like to be *that* one's 'usband? Think o' comin' 'ome to *that!*'

'I'd soon learn 'er!' answered the other, with a meaning look.

'Don't think that going to prison again has any fears for us. We'd go for life if by doing that we got freedom for the rest of the women.'

'Hear! Hear!'

'Rot!'

'W'y don't the men 'elp ye to get yer rights?'

'Here's some one asking why the men don't help. It's partly they don't understand yet — they *will* before we've done!' She wagged her head in a sort of comical menace, and the crowd screamed with laughter — 'partly, they don't understand yet what's at stake ——'

'Lord!' said an old fellow, with a rich chuckle. 'She's a educatin' of us!

'— and partly that the bravest man is afraid of ridicule. Oh, yes, we've heard a great deal all our lives about the timidity and the sensitiveness of women. And it's true — we *are* sensitive. But I tell you, ridicule crumples a man up. It steels a woman. We've come to know the value of ridicule. We've educated ourselves so that we welcome ridicule. We owe our sincerest thanks to the comic writers. The cartoonist is our unconscious friend. Who cartoons people who are of no importance? What advertisement is so sure of being remembered? If we didn't know it by any other sign, the comic papers would tell us — *we've arrived!*'

She stood there for one triumphant moment in an attitude of such audacious self-confidence, that Jean turned excitedly to her lover with —

'I know what she's like! The girl in Ibsen's "Master Builder"!'

'I don't think I know the young lady.'

'Oh, there was a knock at the door that set the Master Builder's nerves quivering. He felt in his bones it was the Younger Generation coming to upset things. He *thought* it was a young man ——'

'And it was really Miss Ernestine Blunt? He has my sympathies.'

The Younger Generation was declaring from the monument —

'Our greatest debt of gratitude we owe to the man who called us female hooligans!'

That tickled the crowd, too; she was such a charming little pink-cheeked specimen of a hooligan.

'I'm being frightfully amused, Geoffrey,' said Jean.

He looked down at her with a large indulgence. 'That's right,' he said.

'We aren't hooligans, but we hope the fact will be overlooked. If everybody said we were nice, well-behaved women, who'd come to hear us? *Not the men.*'

The people dissolved in laughter, but she was grave enough.

'Men tell us it isn't womanly for us to care about politics. How do they know what's womanly? It's for women to decide that. Let them attend to being manly. It will take them all their time.'

'Pore benighted man!'

'Some of you have heard it would be dreadful if we got the vote, because then we'd be pitted against men in the economic struggle. But it's too late to guard against that. It's fact. But facts, we've discovered, are just what men find it so hard to recognize. Men are so dreadfully sentimental.' She smiled with the crowd at that, but she proceeded to hammer in her pet nail. 'They won't recognize those eighty-two women out of every hundred who are wage-earners. We used to believe men when they told us that it was unfeminine — hardly respectable — for women to be students and to aspire to the arts that bring fame and fortune. But men have never told us it was unfeminine for women to do the heavy drudgery that's badly paid. That kind of work had to be done by somebody, and men didn't hanker after it. *Oh*, no! Let the women scrub and cook and wash, or teach without diplomas on half pay. That's all right. But if they want to try their hand at the better-rewarded work of the liberal professions — oh, very unfeminine indeed.'

As Ernestine proceeded to show how all this obsolete unfairness had its roots in political inequality, Lady John dropped her glass with a sigh.

'You are right,' she said to Jean. 'This is Hilda, harnessed to a purpose. A portent to shake middle-aged nerves.'

With Jean blooming there before him, Stonor had no wish to prove his own nerves middle-aged.

'I think she's rather fun, myself. Though she ought to be taken home and well smacked.'

Somebody had interrupted to ask, 'If the House of Commons won't give you justice, why don't you go to the House of Lords?'

'What?' She hadn't heard, but the question was answered by some one who had.

'She'd 'ave to 'urry up. Case of early closin'!'

'You'll be allowed to ask any question you like,' she said, 'at the end of the meeting.'

'Wot's that? Oh, is it question time? I s'y, miss, 'oo killed Cock Robin?'

'I've got a question, too,' a boy called through his hollowed hands. 'Are — you — married?'

''Ere's your chance. 'E's a bachelor.'

'Here's a man,' says Ernestine, 'asking, "If the women get full citizenship, and a war is declared, will the women fight?"'

'Haw! haw!'

'Yes.'

'Yes. Just tell us *that!*'

'Well' — she smiled — 'you know some say the whole trouble about us is that we *do* fight. But it's only hard necessity makes us do that. We don't want to fight — as men seem to — just for fighting's sake. Women are for peace.'

'Hear! hear!'

'And when we have a share in public affairs there'll be less likelihood of war. Wasn't it a woman, the Baroness von Suttner, whose book about peace was the corner-stone of the Peace Congress? Wasn't it that book that converted the millionaire maker of armaments of war? Wasn't it the Baroness von Suttner's book that made Nobel offer those great international prizes for the Arts of Peace? I'm not saying women can't fight. But we women know all war is evil, and we're for peace. Our part — we're proud to remember it — our part has been to go about after you men in war time and *pick up the pieces!*'

A great shout went up as the truth of that rolled in upon the people.

'Yes; seems funny, doesn't it? You men blow people to

bits, and then we come along and put them together again. If you know anything about military nursing, you know a good deal of our work has been done in the face of danger; *but it's always been done.*'

'That's so. That's so.'

'Well, what of it?' said a voice. 'Women must do something for their keep.'

'You complain that more and more we're taking away from you men the work that's always been yours. You can't any longer keep woman out of the industries. The only question is, on what terms shall she continue to be in? As long as she's in on bad terms, she's not only hurting herself, she's hurting you. But if you're feeling discouraged about our competing with you, we're willing to leave you your trade in war. Let the men take life! We *give* life!' Her voice was once more moved and proud. 'No one will pretend ours isn't one of the dangerous trades either. I won't say any more to you now, because we've got others to speak to you, and a new woman helper that I want you to hear.'

With an accompaniment of clapping she retired to hold a hurried consultation with the chairman.

Jean turned to see how Geoffrey had taken it. 'Well?'

He smiled down at her, echoing, 'Well?'

'Nothing so *very* reprehensible in what she said, was there?'

'Oh, "reprehensible"!'

'It makes one rather miserable all the same.'

He pressed his guardian arm the closer. 'You mustn't take it as much to heart as all that.'

'I can't help it. I can't indeed, Geoffrey. I shall *never* be able to make a speech like that.'

He stared, considerably taken aback. 'I hope not indeed.'

'Why? I thought you said you wanted me to——'

'To make nice little speeches with composure? So I did. So I do——' as he looked down upon the upturned face he seemed to lose his thread.

She was for helping him to recover it. 'Don't you remember how you said——'

'That you have very pink cheeks? Well, I stick to it.'

She smiled. 'Sh! Don't tell everybody.'

'And you're the only female creature——'

'That's a most proper sentiment.'

'The only one I ever saw who didn't look a fright in motor things.'

'I'm glad you don't think me a fright. Oh!'—she turned at the sound of applause—'we're forgetting all about——'

A big sandy man, not hitherto seen, was rolling his loose-knit body up and down the platform, smiling at the people and mopping a great bony skull, on which, low down, a few scanty wisps of colourless hair were growing.

'If you can't afford a bottle of Tatcho,' a boy called out, 'w'y don't you get yer 'air cut?'

He just shot out one hand and wagged it in grotesque greeting, not in the least discomposed.

'I've been addressin' a big meetin' at 'Ammersmith this morning, and w'en I told 'em I wus comin' 'ere this awfternoon to speak fur the women—well—then the usual thing began.'

An appreciative roar rose from the crowd.

'Yes,' he grinned, 'if you want peace and quiet at a public meetin', better not go mentionin' the lydies these times!'

He stopped, and the crowd filled in the hiatus with laughter.

'There wus a man at 'Ammersmith, too, talkin' about Woman's sphere bein' 'Ome. 'Ome do you call it? *'Ome!'* and at the word his *bonhomie* suffered a singular eclipse. ''Ome!' he bellowed, as if some one had struck him in a vital spot, and the word was merely a roar of pain. *''Ome!* You've got a kennel w'ere you can munch your tommy. You got a corner w'ere you can curl up fur a few hours till you go out to work again. But 'omes! No, my men, there's too many of you ain't able to *give* the women 'omes fit to live in; too many of you in that fix fur you to go on jawin' at those o' the women 'oo want to myke the 'omes a little more deservin' o' the name.'

'If the vote ain't done us any good,' a man bawled up at him, ''ow'll it do the women any good?'

'Look 'ere! See 'ere!' he rolled his shapeless body up and down the stone platform, taking in great draughts of cheer from some invisible fountain. 'Any men here belongin' to the Labour Party?' he inquired.

To an accompaniment of shouts and applause he went on, smiling and rubbing his hands in a state of bubbling Brotherliness.

'Well, I don't need tell those men the vote 'as done us *some* good. They *know* it. And it'll do us a lot more good w'en you know 'ow to use the power you got in your 'and.'

'Power!' grumbled an old fellow. 'It's those fellows at the bottom of the street' — he hitched his head toward St. Stephen's — 'it's them that's got the power.'

The speaker pounced on him. 'It's you and men like you that give it to them. Wot did you do last election? You carried the Liberals into Parliament Street on your own shoulders. You believed all their fine words. You never asked yerselves, "Wot's a Liberal, anyway?"'

In the chorus of cheers and booing some one sang out, 'He's a jolly good fellow!'

'No 'e ain't,' said the Labour man, with another wheel about and a pounce. 'No 'e ain't, or, if 'e's jolly, it's only because 'e thinks you're such a cod-fish you'll go swellin' 'is majority again.'

Stonor joined in that laugh. He rather liked the man.

'Yes, it's enough to make any Liberal "jolly" to see a sheep like you lookin' on, proud and 'appy, while you see Liberal leaders desertin' Liberal principles.'

Through the roar of protest and argument, he held out those grotesque great hands of his with the suggestion —

'You show me a Liberal, and I'll show you a Mr. Facing-both-ways. Yuss. The Liberal, 'e sheds the light of his warm and 'andsome smile on the workin' man, and round on the other side 'e's tippin' the wink to the great landowners. Yuss. That's to let 'em know 'e's standin' between them and Socialists. Ha! the Socialists!' Puffing and flushed and perspiring he hurled it out again and again over the heads of the people. 'The Socialists! Yuss. *Socialists!* Ha! ha!' When he and the audience had a little calmed down, 'The Liberal,' he said, with that look of sly humour, ''e's the judicial sort o' chap that sits in the middle.'

'On the fence.'

He nodded. 'Tories one side, Socialists the other. Well, it ain't always so comfortable in the middle. No. Yer like to get squeezed. Now, I says to the women, wot I says is, the Conservatives don't promise you much, but wot they promise they *do*.' He whacked one fist into the other with tremendous effect.

'This fellow isn't half bad,' Stonor said to Lady John.

'But the Liberals, they'll promise you the earth and give you the whole o' nothin'.'

There were roars of approval. Liberal stock had sunk rather low in Trafalgar Square.

'Isn't it fun?' said Jean. 'Now aren't you glad I brought you?'

'Oh, this chap's all right!'

'We men 'ave seen it 'appen over and over. But the women can tyke an 'int quicker 'n what we can. They won't stand the nonsense men do. Only they 'aven't got a fair chawnce even to agitate fur their rights. As I wus comin' up ere, I 'eard a man sayin', "Look at this big crowd. W'y, we're all *men!* If the women want the vote, w'y ain't they here to s'y so? Well, I'll tell you w'y. It's because they've 'ad to get the dinner fur you and me, and now they're washin' up dishes.'

'D'you think we ought to st'y at 'ome and wash the dishes?'

He laughed with good-natured shrewdness. 'Well, if they'd leave it to us once or twice per'aps we'd understand a little more about the Woman Question. I know w'y *my* wife isn't here. It's because she *knows* I can't cook, and she's 'opin' I can talk to some purpose. Yuss,' — he acknowledged another possible view, — 'yuss, maybe she's mistaken. Any'ow, here I am to vote for her and all the other women, and to ——'

They nearly drowned him with '*Oh-h!*' and 'Hear! hear!'

'And to tell you men what improvements you can expect to see w'en women 'as the share in public affairs they ought to 'ave!'

Out of the babel came the question, 'What do you know about it? You can't even talk grammar.'

His broad smile faltered a little.

'Oh, what shame!' said Jean, full of sympathy. 'He's a dear — that funny cockney.'

But he had been dashed for the merest moment.

'I'm not 'ere to talk grammar, but to talk Reform. I ain't defendin' my grammar,' he said, on second thoughts, 'but I'll say in pawssing that if my mother 'ad 'ad 'er rights, maybe my grammar would 'ave been better.'

It was a thrust that seemed to go home. But, all the same, it was clear that many of his friends couldn't stomach the sight of him up there demeaning himself by espousing the cause of the

Suffragettes. He kept on about woman and justice, but his performance was little more than vigorous pantomime. The boyish chairman looked harassed and anxious, Miss Ernestine Blunt alert, watchful.

Stonor bent his head to whisper something in Jean Dunbarton's ear. She listened with lowered eyes and happy face. The discreet little interchange went on for several minutes, while the crowd booed at the bald-headed Labourite for his mistaken enthusiasm. Geoffrey Stonor and his bride-to-be were more alone now in the midst of this shouting mob than they had been since the Ulland House luncheon-gong had broken in upon and banished momentary wonderment about the name — that name beginning with V. Plain to see in the flushed and happy face that Jean Dunbarton was not 'asking questions.' She was listening absorbed to the oldest of all the stories.

And now the champion of the Suffragettes had come to the surface again with his —

'Wait a bit — 'arf a minute, my man.'

'Oo you talkin' to? I ain't your man!'

'Oh, that's lucky for me. There seems to be an individual here who doesn't think women ought to 'ave the vote.'

'One? Oh-h!'

They all but wiped him out again in laughter; but he climbed on the top of the great wave of sound with —

'P'raps the gentleman who thinks they oughtn't to 'ave a vote, p'raps 'e don't know much about women. Wot? Oh, the gentleman says 'e's married. Well, then, fur the syke of 'is wife we mustn't be too sorry 'e's 'ere. No doubt she's s'ying, "'Eaven be prysed those women are mykin' a demonstrytion in Trafalgar Square, and I'll 'ave a little peace and quiet at 'ome for one Sunday in me life."'

The crowd liked that, and found themselves jeering at the interrupter as well as at the speaker.

'Why, you' — he pointed at some one in the crowd — '*you*'re like the man at 'Ammersmith this morning. 'E wus awskin' me, "'Ow would you like men to st'y at 'ome and do the fam'ly washin'?" I told 'im I wouldn't advise it. I 'ave too much respect fur' — they waited while slyly he brought out — 'me clo'es.'

'It's their place,' said some one in a rage; 'the women *ought* to do the washin'.'

'I'm not sure you aren't right. For a good many o' you fellas from the look o' you, you cawn't even wash yourselves.'

This was outrageous. It was resented in an incipient riot. The helmets of the police bobbed about. An angry voice had called out —

'Oo are you talkin' to?'

The anxiety of the inexperienced chairman was almost touching.

The Socialist revelled in the disturbance he'd created. He walked up and down with that funny rolling gait, poking out his head at intervals in a turtle-esque fashion highty provocative, holding his huge paws kangaroo fashion, only with fingers stiffly pointed, and shooting them out at intervals towards the crowd in a very ecstasy of good-natured contempt.

'Better go 'ome and awsk yer wife to wash yer fice,' he advised. '*You* cawn't even do *that* bit o' fam'ly washin'. Go and awsk *some* woman.'

There was a scuffle in the crowd. A section of it surged up towards the monument.

'Which of us d'you mean?' demanded a threatening voice.

'Well,' said the Socialist, coolly looking down, 'it takes about ten of your sort to make a man, so you may take it I mean the lot of you.' Again the hands shot out and scattered scorn amongst his critics.

There were angry, indistinguishable retorts, and the crowd swayed. Miss Ernestine Blunt, who had been watching the fray with serious face, turned suddenly, catching sight of some one just arrived at the end of the platform. She jumped up, saying audibly to the speaker as she passed him, 'Here she is,' and proceeded to offer her hand to help some one to get up the improvised steps behind the lion.

The Socialist had seized with fervour upon his last chance, and was flinging out showers of caustic advice among his foes, stirring them up to frenzy.

Stonor, with contracted brows, had stared one dazed instant as the head of the new-comer came up behind the lion on the left.

Jean, her eyes wide, incredulous, as though unable to accept their testimony, pressed a shade nearer the monument. Stonor made a sharp move forward, and took her by the arm.

'We're going now,' he said.

'Not yet — oh, *please* not just yet,' she pleaded as he drew her round. 'Geoffrey, I do believe ——'

She looked back, with an air almost bewildered, over her shoulder, like one struggling to wake from a dream.

Stonor was saying with decision to Lady John, 'I'm going to take Jean out of this mob. Will you come?'

'What? Oh, yes, if you think' — she had disengaged the chain of her eyeglass at last. 'But isn't that, surely it's ——'

'Geoffrey ——!' Jean began.

'Lady John's tired,' he interrupted. 'We've had enough of this idiotic ——'

'But you don't see who it is, Geoffrey. That last one is ——' Suddenly Jean bent forward as he was trying to extricate her from the crowd, and she looked in his face. Something that she found there made her tighten her hold on his arm.

'We can't run away and leave Aunt Ellen,' was all she said; but her voice sounded scared. Stonor repressed a gesture of anger, and came to a standstill just behind two big policemen.

The last-comer to that strange platform, after standing for some seconds with her back to the people and talking to Ernestine Blunt, the tall figure in a long sage-green dust coat and familiar hat, had turned and glanced apprehensively at the crowd.

It was Vida Levering.

The girl down in the crowd locked her hands together and stood motionless.

The Socialist had left the platform with the threat that he was 'coming down now to attend to that microbe that's vitiating the air on my right, while a lady will say a few words to you — if she can myke 'erself 'eard.'

He retired to a chorus of cheers and booing, while the chairman, more harassed than ever, it would seem, but determined to create a diversion, was saying that some one had suggested — 'and it's such a good idea I'd like you to listen to it — that a clause shall be inserted in the next Suffrage Bill that shall expressly give to each Cabinet Minister, and to any respectable man, the power to prevent a vote being given to the female members of his family, on his public declaration of their lack of sufficient intelligence to entitle them to one.'

'Oh! oh!'

'Now, I ask you to listen as quietly as you can to a lady who is not accustomed to speaking — a — in Trafalgar Square, or — a — as a matter of fact, at all.'

'A dumb lady!'

'Hooray!'

'Three cheers for the dumb lady!'

The chairman was dreadfully flustered at the unfortunate turn his speech had taken.

'A lady who, as I've said, will tell you, if you'll behave yourselves ——'

'Oh! oh!'

'Will tell you something of her impression of police-court justice in this country.'

Jean stole a wondering look at Stonor's sphinx-like face as Vida Levering came forward.

There she stood, obviously very much frightened, with the unaccustomed colour coming and going in her white face — farther back than any of the practised speakers — there she stood like one who too much values the space between her and the mob voluntarily to lessen it by half an inch. The voice was steady enough, though low, as she began.

'Mr. Chairman, men, and women ——'

'Speak up.'

She flushed, came nearer to the edge of the platform, and raised the key a little.

'I just wanted to tell you that I was — I was present in the police court when the women were charged for creating a disturbance.'

'You oughtn't to get mix'd up in wot didn't concern you!'

'I — I ——' She stumbled and stopped.

'Give the lady a hearing,' said a shabby art-student, magisterially. He seemed not ill-pleased when he had drawn a certain number of eyes to his long hair, picturesque hat, and flowing Byronic tie.

'Wot's the lydy's nyme?'

'I ain't seen this one before.'

'Is she Mrs. or Miss?'

'She's dumb, anyway, like 'e said.'

'Haw! haw!'

The anxious chairman was fidgeting in an agony of apprehension. He whispered some kind prompting word after he had flung out —

'Now, see here, men; fair play, you know.'

'I think I ought ——' Vida began.

'No wonder she can't find a word to say for 'em. They're a disgryce, miss — them women behind you. It's the w'y they goes on as mykes the Govermint keep ye from gettin' yer rights.'

The chairman had lost his temper. 'It's the way *you* go on,' he screamed; but the din was now so great, not even he could be heard. He stood there waving his arms and moving his lips while his dark eyes glittered.

Miss Levering turned and pantomimed to Ernestine, 'You see it's no use!'

Thus appealed to, the girl came forward, and said something in the ear of the frantic chairman. When he stopped gyrating, and nodded, Miss Blunt came to the edge of the platform, and held up her hand as if determined to stem this tide of unfavourable comment upon the dreadful women who were complicating the Election difficulties of both parties.

'Listen,' says Ernestine; 'I've got something to propose.' They waited an instant to hear what this precious proposal might be. 'If the Government withholds the vote because they don't like the way some of us ask for it, let them give it to the quiet ones. Do they want to punish all women because they don't like the manners of a handful? Perhaps that's men's notion of justice. It isn't ours.'

'Haw! haw!'

'Yes' — Miss Levering plucked up courage, seeing her friend sailing along so safely. 'This is the first time I've ever "gone on," as you call it, but they never gave me a vote.'

'*No*,' says Miss Ernestine, with energy — 'and there are' — she turned briskly, with forefinger uplifted punctuating her count — 'there are two, three, four women on this platform. Now, we all want the vote, as you know.'

'Lord, yes, we know *that*.'

'Well, we'd agree to be disfranchised all our lives if they'd give the vote to all the other women.'

'Look here! You made one speech — give the lady a chance.'

Miss Blunt made a smiling little bob of triumph. 'That's just what I wanted you to say!' And she retired.

Miss Levering came forward again. But the call to 'go on' had come a little suddenly.

'Perhaps you — you don't know — you don't know ——'

'*How*'re we going to know if you can't tell us?' demanded a sarcastic voice.

It steadied her. 'Thank you for that,' she said, smiling. 'We couldn't have a better motto. How *are* you to know if we can't somehow manage to tell you?' With a visible effort she went on, 'Well, *I* certainly didn't know before that the sergeants and policemen are instructed to deceive the people as to the time such cases are heard.'

'It's just as hard,' said a bystander to his companion, '*just* as hard for learned counsel in the august quiet of the Chancery Division to find out when their cases are really coming on.'

'You ask, and you're sent to Marlborough Police Court,' said Miss Levering, 'instead of to Marylebone.'

'They oughter send yer to 'Olloway — do y' good.'

'You go on, miss. Nobody minds 'im.'

'Wot can you expect from a pig but a grunt?'

'You are told the case will be at two o'clock, and it's really called for eleven. Well, I took a great deal of trouble, and I didn't believe what I was told.' She was warming a little to her task. 'Yes, that's almost the first thing we have to learn — to get over our touching faith that because a man tells us something, it's true. I got to the right court, and I was so anxious not to be late, I was too early.'

'Like a woman!'

'The case before the Suffragists' was just coming on. I heard a noise. I saw the helmets of two policemen.'

'No, you didn't. They don't wear their helmets in court.'

'They were coming in from the corridor. As I saw them, I said to myself, "What sort of crime shall I have to sit and hear about? Is this a burglar being brought along between the two big policemen, or will it be a murderer? What sort of felon is to stand in the dock before the people, whose crime is, they ask for the vote?' But try as I would, I couldn't see the prisoner. My heart misgave me. Is it some poor woman, I wondered?'

A tipsy tramp, with his battered bowler over one eye, wheezed out, 'Drunk again!' with an accent of weary philosophy. 'Syme old tyle.'

'Then the policemen got nearer, and I saw'—she waited an instant—'a little thin, half-starved boy. What do you think he was charged with?'

'Travellin' first with a third-class ticket.' A boy offered a page out of personal history.

'Stealing. What had he been stealing, that small criminal? *Milk*. It seemed to me, as I sat there looking on, that the men who had had the affairs of the world in their hands from the beginning, and who've made so poor a business of it——'

'Oh, pore devils! give 'em a rest!'

'Who've made so bad a business of it as to have the poor and the unemployed in the condition they're in to-day, whose only remedy for a starving child is to hale him off to the police court, because he had managed to get a little milk, well, I did wonder that the men refuse to be helped with a problem they've so notoriously failed at. I began to say to myself, "Isn't it time the women lent a hand?"'

'Doin' pretty well fur a dumb lady!'

'Would you have women magistrates?'

She was stumped by the suddenness of the query.

'Haw! haw! Magistrates and judges! *Women!*'

'Let 'em prove first they're able to——'

It was more than the shabby art-student could stand.

'The schools are full of them!' he shouted. 'Where's their Michael Angelo? They study music by thousands: where's their Beethoven? Where's their Plato? Where's the woman Shakespeare?'

'Where's their Harry Lauder?'

At last a name that stirred the general enthusiasm.

'Who is Harry Lauder?' Jean asked her aunt.

Lady John shook her head.

'Yes, wot 'ave women ever *done?*'

The speaker had clenched her hands, but she was not going

to lose her presence of mind again. By the time the chairman could make himself heard with, 'Now, men, it's one of our British characteristics that we're always ready to give the people we differ from a hearing,' Miss Levering, making the slightest of gestures, waved him aside with a low —

'It's all right.'

'These questions are quite proper,' she said, raising her voice. 'They are often asked elsewhere; and I would like to ask in return: Since when was human society held to exist for its handful of geniuses? How many Platos are there here in this crowd?'

'Divil a wan!' And a roar of laughter followed that free confession.

'Not one,' she repeated. 'Yet that doesn't keep you men off the register. How many Shakespeares are there in all England to-day? Not one. Yet the State doesn't tumble to pieces. Railroads and ships are built, homes are kept going, and babies are born. The world goes on' — she bent over the crowd with lit eyes — 'the world goes on *by virtue of its common people.*'

There was a subdued 'Hear! hear!'

'I am not concerned that you should think we women could paint great pictures, or compose immortal music, or write good books. I am content' — and it was strange to see the pride with which she said it, a pride that might have humbled Vere de Vere — 'I am content that we should be classed with the common people, who keep the world going. But' — her face grew softer, there was even a kind of camaraderie where before there had been shrinking — 'I'd like the world to go a great deal better. We were talking about justice. I have been inquiring into the kind of lodging the poorest class of homeless women can get in this town of London. I find that only the men of that class are provided for. Some measure to establish Rowton Houses for Women has been before the London County Council. They looked into the question very carefully — so their apologists say. And what did they decide? They decided that they could do nothing.

'Why could that great, all-powerful body do nothing? Because, they said, if these cheap and decent houses were opened, the homeless women in the streets would make use of them. You'll think I'm not in earnest, but that was actually the decision, and the reason given for it. Women that the bitter struggle for existence had forced into a life of horror might take advantage of the shelter these decent, cheap places offered. But the *men*, I said! Are the men who avail themselves of Lord Rowton's hostels, are *they* all angels? Or does wrong-doing in a man not matter? Yet women are recommended to depend on the chivalry of men!'

The two tall policemen who had been standing for some minutes in front of Mr. Stonor in readiness to serve him, seeming to feel there was no further need of them in this quarter, shouldered their way to the left, leaving exposed the hitherto masked figure of the tall gentleman in the motor cap. He moved uneasily, and, looking round, he met Jean's eyes fixed on him. As each looked away again, each saw that for the first time Vida Levering had become aware of his presence. A change passed over her face, and her figure swayed as if some species of mountain-sickness had assailed her, looking down from that perilous high perch of hers upon the things of the plain. While the people were asking one another, 'What is it? Is she going to faint?' she lifted one hand to her eyes, and her fingers trembled an instant against the lowered lids. But as suddenly as she had faltered, she was forging on again, repeating like an echo of a thing heard in a dream —

'Justice and chivalry! Justice and chivalry remind me of the story that those of you who read the police-court news — I have begun only lately to do that — but *you*'ve seen the accounts of the girl who's been tried in Manchester lately for the murder of her child.'

People here and there in the crowd regaled one another with choice details of the horror.

'Not pleasant reading. Even if we'd noticed it, we wouldn't speak of it in my world. A few months ago I should have turned away my eyes and forgotten even the headline as quickly as I could.'

'My opinion,' said a shrewd-looking young man, 'is that she's forgot what she meant to say, and just clutched at this to keep her from drying up.'

'Since that morning in the police-court I read these things. This, as you know, was the story of a working girl — an orphan of seventeen — who crawled with the dead body of her new-born child to her master's back door and left the baby there. She dragged herself a little way off and fainted. A few days later she found herself in court being tried for the murder of her child. Her master, a married man, had of course reported the "find" at his back door to the police, and he had been summoned to give evidence. The girl cried out to him in the open court, "You are the father!" He couldn't deny it. The coroner, at the jury's request, censured the man, and regretted that the law didn't make him responsible. But'—she leaned down from the plinth with eyes blazing—'he went scot free. And that girl is at this moment serving her sentence in Strangeways Gaol.'

Through the moved and murmuring crowd, Jean forced her way, coming in between Lady John and Stonor, who stood there immovable. The girl strained to bring her lips near his ear.

'Why do you dislike her so?'

'I?' he said. 'Why should you think——'

'I never saw you look as you did;' with a vaguely frightened air she added, 'as you do.'

'Men make boast'—the voice came clear from the monument—'that an English citizen is tried by his peers. What woman is tried by hers?'

'She mistakes the sense in which the word was employed,' said a man who looked like an Oxford Don.

But there was evidently a sense, larger than that one purely academic, in which her use of the word could claim its pertinence. The strong feeling that had seized her as she put the question was sweeping the crowd along with her.

'A woman is arrested by a man, brought before a man judge, tried by a jury of men, condemned by men, taken to prison by a man, and by a man she's hanged! Where in all this were *her* "peers"? Why did men, when British justice was born—why did they so long ago insist on trial by "a jury of their peers"? So that justice shouldn't miscarry—wasn't it? A man's peers would best understand his circumstances, his temptation, the degree of his guilt. Yet there's no such unlikeness between different classes of men as exists between man and woman. What man has the knowledge that makes him a fit judge of woman's deeds at that time of anguish—that hour that some woman struggled through to put each man here into the world. I noticed when a previous speaker quoted the Labour Party, you applauded. Some of you here, I gather, call yourselves Labour men. Every woman who has borne a child is a Labour woman. No man among you can judge what she goes through in her hour of darkness.'

Jean's eyes had dropped from her lover's set white face early in the recital. But she whispered his name.

He seemed not to hear.

The speaker up there had caught her fluttering breath, and went on so low that people strained to follow.

'In that great agony, even under the best conditions that money and devotion can buy, many a woman falls into temporary mania, and not a few go down to death. In the case of this poor little abandoned working girl, what man can be the fit judge of her deeds in that awful moment of half-crazed temptation? Women know of these things as those know burning who have walked through fire.'

Stonor looked down at the girl at his side. He saw her hands go up to her throat as though she were suffocating. The young face, where some harsh knowledge was struggling for birth, was in pity turned away from the man she loved.

The woman leaned down from the platform, and spoke her last words with a low and thrilling earnestness.

'I would say in conclusion to the women here, it's not enough to be sorry for these, our unfortunate sisters. We must get the conditions of life made fairer. We women must organize. We must learn to work together. We have all (rich and poor, happy and unhappy) worked so long and so exclusively for men, we hardly know how to work for one another. But we must learn. Those who can, may give money. Those who haven't pennies to give, even those people are not so poor but what they can give some part of their labour — some share of their sympathy and support. I know of a woman — she isn't of our country — but a woman who, to help the women strikers of an oppressed industry to hold out, gave a thousand pounds a week for thirteen weeks to get them and their children bread, and help them to stand firm. The masters were amazed. Week after week went by, and still the people weren't starved into submission. Where did this mysterious stream of help come from? The employers couldn't discover, and they gave in. The women got back their old wages, and I am glad to say many of them began to put by pennies to help a little to pay back the great sum that had been advanced to them.'

'She took their pennies — a rich woman like that?'

'Yes — to use again, as well as to let the working women feel they were helping others. I hope you'll all join the Union. Come up after the meeting is over and give us your names.'

As she turned away, 'You won't get any men!' a taunting voice called after her.

The truth in the gibe seemed to sting. Forestalling the chairman, quickly she confronted the people again, a new fire in her eyes.

'Then,' she said, holding out her hands — 'then *it is to the women I appeal!*' She stood so an instant, stilling the murmur, and holding the people by that sudden concentration of passion in her face. 'I don't mean to say it wouldn't be better if men and women did this work together, shoulder to shoulder. But the mass of men won't have it so. I only hope they'll realize in time the good they've renounced and the spirit they've aroused. For I know as well as any man could tell me, it would be a bad day for England if all women felt about all men *as I do*.'

She retired in a tumult. The others on the platform closed about her. The chairman tried in vain to get a hearing from the swaying and dissolving crowd.

Jean made a blind forward movement towards the monument. Stonor called out, in a toneless voice —

'Here! follow me!'

'No — no — I ——' The girl pressed on.

'You're going the wrong way.'

'*This* is the way ——'

'We can get out quicker on this side.'

'I don't *want* to get out.'

'What?'

He had left Lady John, and was following Jean through the press.

'Where are you going?' he asked sharply.

'To ask that woman to let me have the honour of working with her.'

The crowd surged round the girl.

'Jean!' he called upon so stern a note that people stared and stopped.

Others — not Jean.

CHAPTER XVII

A LITTLE before six o'clock on that same Sunday, Jean Dunbarton opened the communicating door between her own little sitting-room and the big bare drawing-room of her grandfather's house in Eaton Square. She stood a moment on the threshold, looking back over her shoulder, and then crossed the drawing-room, treading softly on the parquet spaces between the rugs. She went straight to the window, and was in the act of parting the lace curtains to look out, when she heard the folding doors open. With raised finger she turned to say 'Sh!' The servant stood silently waiting, while she went back to the door she had left open and with an air of caution closed it.

When she turned round again the butler had stepped aside to admit Mr. Stonor. He came in with a quick impatient step; but before he had time to get a word out — 'Speak low, please,' the girl said. He was obviously too much annoyed to pay much heed to her request, which if he thought about it at all, he must have interpreted as consideration for the ailing grandfather.

'I waited a full half-hour for you to come back,' he said in a tone no lower than usual.

The girl had led the way to the side of the room furthest from the communicating door. 'I am sorry,' she said dully.

'If you didn't mind leaving me like that,' he followed her up with his arraignment, 'you might at least have considered Lady John.'

'Is she here with you?' Jean stopped by the sofa near the window.

'No,' he said curtly. 'My place was nearer than this and she was tired. I left her to get some tea. We couldn't tell whether you'd be here, or *what* had become of you!'

'Mr. Trent got us a hansom.'

'Trent?'

'The chairman of the meeting.'

'Got us ——?'

'Miss Levering and me.'

Stonor's incensed face turned almost brick colour as he repeated, '*Miss Lev* ——!'

Before he got the name out, the folding doors had opened again, and the butler was saying, 'Mr. Farnborough.'

That young gentleman was far too anxious and flurried himself, to have sufficient detachment of mind to consider the moods of other people. 'At last!' he said, stopping short as soon as he caught sight of Stonor.

'Don't speak loud, please,' said Miss Dunbarton; 'some one is resting in the next room.'

'Oh, did you find your grandfather worse?'—but he never waited to learn. 'You'll forgive the incursion when you hear'—he turned abruptly to Stonor again. 'They've been telegraphing you all over London,' he said, putting his hat down in the nearest chair. 'In sheer despair they set me on your track.'

'Who did?'

Farnborough was fumbling agitatedly in his breast-pocket. 'There was the devil to pay at Dutfield last night. The Liberal chap tore down from London, and took over your meeting.'

'Oh? Nothing about it in the Sunday paper I saw.'

'Wait till you see the press to-morrow! There was a great rally, and the beggar made a rousing speech.'

'What about?'

'Abolition of the Upper House.'

'They were at that when I was at Eton.' Stonor turned on his heel.

'Yes, but this man has got a way of putting things — the people went mad.'

It was all very well for a mere girl to be staring indifferently out of the window, while a great historic party was steering straight for shipwreck; but it really was too much to see this man who ought to be taking the situation with the seriousness it deserved, strolling about the room with that abstracted air, looking superciliously at Mr. Dunbarton's examples of the Glasgow school. Farnborough balanced himself on wide-apart legs and thrust one hand in his trousers' pocket. The other hand held a telegram. 'The Liberal platform as defined at Dutfield is going to make a big difference,' he pronounced.

'You think so,' said Stonor, dryly.

'Well, your agent says as much.' He pulled off the orange-brown envelope, threw it and the reply-paid form on the table, and held the message under the eyes of the obviously surprised gentleman in front of him.

'My agent!' Stonor had echoed with faint incredulity.

He took the telegram. '"Try find Stonor,"' he read. 'H'm! H'm!' His eyes ran on.

Farnborough looked first at the expressionless face, and then at the message.

'You see!' — he glanced over Stonor's shoulder — '"tremendous effect of last night's Liberal manifesto ought to be counteracted in to-morrow's papers."' Then withdrawing a couple of paces, he said very earnestly, 'You see, Mr. Stonor, it's a battle-cry we want.'

'Clap-trap,' said the great man, throwing the telegram down on the table.

'Well,' said Farnborough, distinctly dashed, 'they've been saying we have nothing to offer but personal popularity. No practical reform, no ——'

'No truckling to the masses, I suppose.'

Poor Farnborough bit his lip. 'Well, in these democratic days, you're obliged (I should *think*), to consider ——' In his baulked and snubbed condition he turned to Miss Dunbarton for countenance. 'I hope you'll forgive my bursting in like this, but' — he gathered courage as he caught a glimpse of her averted face — 'I can see you realize the gravity of the situation.' He found her in the embrasure of the window, and went on with an air of speaking for her ear alone. 'My excuse for being so officious — you see it isn't as if he were going to be a mere private member. Everybody knows he'll be in the Cabinet.'

'It may be a Liberal Cabinet,' came from Stonor at his dryest.

Farnborough leapt back into the fray. 'Nobody thought so up to last night. Why, even your brother ——' he brought up short. 'But I'm afraid I'm really seeming rather *too* ——' He took up his hat.

'What about my brother?'

'Oh, only that I went from your house to the club, you know — and I met Lord Windlesham as I rushed up the Carlton steps.'

'Well?'

'I told him the Dutfield news.'

Stonor turned sharply round. His face was much more interested than any of his words had been.

As though in the silence, Stonor had asked a question, Farnborough produced the answer.

'Your brother said it only confirmed his fears.'

'Said that, did he?' Stonor spoke half under his breath.

'Yes. Defeat is inevitable, he thinks, unless ——' Farnborough waited, intently watching the big figure that had begun pacing back and forth. It paused, but no word came, even the eyes were not raised.

'Unless,' Farnborough went on, 'you can manufacture some political dynamite within the next few hours. Those were his words.'

As Stonor resumed his walk he raised his head and caught sight of Jean's face. He stopped short directly in front of her.

'You are very tired,' he said.

'No, no.' She turned again to the window.

'I'm obliged to you for troubling about this,' he said, offering Farnborough his hand with the air of civilly dismissing him. 'I'll see what can be done.'

Farnborough caught up the reply-paid form from the table. 'If you'd like to wire I'll take it.'

Faintly amused at this summary view of large complexities, 'You don't understand, my young friend,' he said, not unkindly. 'Moves of this sort are not rushed at by responsible politicians. I must have time for consideration.'

Farnborough's face fell. 'Oh. Well, I only hope some one else won't jump into the breach before you.' With his watch in one hand, he held out the other to Miss Dunbarton. 'Good-bye. I'll just go and find out what time the newspapers go to press on Sunday. I'll be at the Club,' he threw over his shoulder, 'just in case I can be of any use.'

'No; don't do that. If I should have anything new to say ——'

'B-b-but with our party, as your brother said, "heading straight for a vast electoral disaster," and the Liberals ——'

'If I decide on a counter-blast, I shall simply telegraph to headquarters. Good-bye.'

'Oh! A — a — good-bye.'

With a gesture of 'the country's going to the dogs,' Farnborough opened the doors and closed them behind him.

Jean had rung the bell. She came back with her eyes on the ground, and paused near the table where the crumpled envelope made a dash of yellow-brown on the polished satinwood. Stonor stood studying the carpet, more concern in his face now that there was only Jean to see it.

'"Political dynamite," eh?' he repeated, walking a few paces away. He returned with, 'After all, women are much more Conservative *naturally* than men, aren't they?'

Jean's lowered eyes showed no spark of interest in the issue. Her only motion, an occasional locking and unlocking of her fingers. But no words came. He glanced at her, as if for the first time conscious of her silence.

'You see now' — he threw himself into a chair — 'one reason why I've encouraged you to take an interest in public questions. Because people like us don't go screaming about it, is no sign we don't — some of us — see what's on the way. However little they may want to, women of our class will have to come into line. All the best things in the world, everything civilization has won, will be in danger if — when this change comes — the only women who have practical political training are the women of the lower classes. Women of the lower classes,' he repeated, '*and*' — the line between his eyebrows deepening — 'women inoculated by the Socialist virus.'

'Geoffrey!'

He was in no mood to discuss a concrete type. To so intelligent a girl, a hint should be enough. He drew the telegraph-form that still lay on the table towards him.

'Let us see how it would sound, shall we?'

He detached a gold pencil from one end of his watch-chain, and, with face more and more intent, bent over the paper, writing.

The girl opened her lips more than once to speak, and each time fell back again on her silent, half-incredulous misery.

When Stonor finished writing, he held the paper off, smiling a little, with the craftsman's satisfaction in his work, and more than a touch of shrewd malice —

'Enough dynamite in that,' he commented. 'Rather too much, isn't there, little girl?'

'Geoffrey, I know her story.'

He looked at her for the first time since Farnborough left the room.

'Whose story?'

'Miss Levering's.'

'*Whose?*' He crushed the rough note of his manifesto into his pocket.

'Vida Levering's.'

He stared at the girl, till across the moment's silence a cry of misery went out —

'Why did you desert her?'

'I?' he said, like one staggered by the sheer wildness of the charge. '*I?*'

But no comfort of doubting seemed to cross the darkness of Jean's backward look into the past.

'Oh, why did you do it?'

'What, in the name of ——? What has she been saying to you?'

'Some one else told me part. Then the way you looked when you saw her at Aunt Ellen's — Miss Levering's saying you didn't know her — then your letting out that you knew even the curious name on the handkerchief — oh, I pieced it together.'

While she poured out the disjointed sentences, he had recovered his self-possession.

'Your ingenuity is undeniable,' he said coldly, rising to his feet. But he paused as the girl went on —

'And then when she said that at the meeting about "the dark hour," and I looked at her face, it flashed over me —— Oh, why did you desert her?'

It was as if the iteration of that charge stung him out of his chill anger.

'I *didn't* desert her,' he said.

'Ah-h!' Her hands went fluttering up to her eyes, and hid the quivering face. Something in the action touched him, his face changed, and he made a sudden passionate movement toward the trembling figure standing there with hidden eyes. In another moment his arms would have been round her. Her muffled voice saying, 'I'm glad. I'm glad,' checked him. He stood bewildered, making with noiseless lips the word '*Glad?*' She was 'glad' he hadn't tired of her rival? The girl brushed the tears from her eyes, and steadied herself against the table.

'She went away from you, then?'

The momentary softening had vanished out of Geoffrey Stonor's face. In its stead the look of aloofness that few dared brave, the warning 'thus far and no farther' stamped on every feature, he answered —

'You can hardly expect me to enter into ——'

She broke through the barrier without ruth — such strength, such courage has honest pain.

'You mean she went away from you?'

'Yes!' The sharp monosyllable fell out like a thing metallic.

'Was that because you wouldn't marry her?'

'I couldn't marry her — and she knew it.' He turned on his heel.

'Did you want to?'

He paused nearly at the window, and looked back at her. She deserved to have the bare 'yes,' but she was a child. He would soften a little the truth's harsh impact upon the young creature's shrinking jealousy.

'I thought I wanted to marry her then. It's a long time ago.'

'And why couldn't you?'

He controlled a movement of strong irritation. 'Why are you catechizing me? It's a matter that concerns another woman.'

'If you say it doesn't concern me, you're saying' — her lip trembled — 'saying that you don't concern me.'

With more difficulty than the girl dreamed, he compelled himself to answer quietly —

'In those days — I — I was absolutely dependent on my father.'

'Why, you must have been thirty, Geoffrey.'

'What? Oh — thereabouts.'

'And everybody says you're so clever.'

'Well, everybody's mistaken.'

She left the table, and drew nearer to him. 'It must have been terribly hard ——'

Sounding the depth of sympathy in the gentle voice, he turned towards her to meet a check in the phrase —

'—— terribly hard for you both.'

He stood there stonily, but looking rather handsome in his big, sulky way. The sort of person who dictates terms rather than one to accept meekly the thing that might befall.

Something of that overbearing look of his must have penetrated the clouded consciousness of the girl, for she was saying —

'You! a man like *you* not to have had the freedom, that even the lowest seem to have ——'

'Freedom?'

'To marry the woman they choose.'

'She didn't break off our relations because I couldn't marry her.'

'Why was it, then?'

'You're too young to discuss such a story.' He turned away.

'I'm not so young,' said the shaking voice, 'as she was when ——'

'Very well, then, if you will have it!' His look was ill to meet, for any one who loved him. 'The truth is, it didn't weigh upon her as it seems to on you, that I wasn't able to marry her.'

'Why are you so sure of that?'

'Because she didn't so much as hint at it when she wrote that she meant to break off the — the ——'

'What made her write like that?'

'Why *will* you go on talking of what's so long over and ended?'

'What reason did she give?'

'If your curiosity has so got the upper hand, *ask her*.'

Her eyes were upon him. In a whisper, 'You're afraid to tell me,' she said.

He went over to the window, seeming to wait there for something that did not come. He turned round at last.

'I still hoped, at *that* time, to win my father over. She blamed me because' — again he faced the window and looked blindly out — 'if the child had lived it wouldn't have been possible to get my father to — to overlook it.'

'You — wanted — it *overlooked?*' the girl said faintly. 'I don't underst ——'

He came back to her on a wave of passion. 'Of course you

don't understand. If you did you wouldn't be the beautiful, tender, innocent child you are.' He took her hand, and tried to draw her to him.

She withdrew her hand, and shrank from him with a movement, slight as it was, so tragically eloquent, that fear for the first time caught hold of him.

'I am glad you didn't mean to desert her, Geoffrey. It wasn't your fault, after all — only some misunderstanding that can be cleared up.'

'*Cleared up?*'

'Yes, cleared up.'

'You aren't thinking that this miserable old affair I'd as good as forgotten ——'

He did not see the horror-struck glance at the door, but he heard the whisper —

'*Forgotten!*'

'No, no' — he caught himself up — 'I don't mean exactly forgotten. But you're torturing me so that I don't know what I'm saying.' He went closer. 'You aren't going to let this old thing come between you and me?'

She pressed her handkerchief to her lips, and then took it away.

'I can't make or unmake the past,' she said steadily. 'But I'm glad, at least, that you didn't mean to desert her in her trouble. You'll remind her of that first of all, won't you?'

She was moving across the room as she spoke, and, when she had ended, the handkerchief went quickly to her lips again as if to shut the door on sobbing.

'Where are you going?' He raised his voice. 'Why should I remind *any*body of what I want only to forget?'

'Hush! Oh, hush!' A moment she looked back, holding up praying hands.

His eyes had flown to the door. 'You don't mean *she's* ——'

'Yes. I left her to get a little rest.'

He recoiled in an access of uncontrollable anger. She followed him. Speechless, he eluded her, and went for his hat.

'Geoffrey,' she cried, 'don't go before you hear me. I don't know if what I think matters to you now, but I hope it does. You can still' — her voice was faint with tears — 'still make me think of you without shrinking — if you will.'

He fixed her for a moment with eyes more stern than she had ever seen.

'What is it you are asking of me?' he said.

'To make amends, Geoffrey.'

His anger went out on a wave of pity. 'You poor little innocent!'

'I'm poor enough. But' — she locked her hands together like one who summons all her resolution — 'I'm not so innocent but what I know you must right that old wrong now, if you're ever to right it.'

'You aren't insane enough to think I would turn round in these few hours and go back to something that ten years ago was ended forever!' As he saw how unmoved her face was, 'Why,' he burst out, 'it's stark, staring madness!'

'No!' She caught his arm. 'What you did ten years ago — that was mad. This is paying a debt.'

Any man looking on, or hearing of Stonor's dilemma, would have said, 'Leave the girl alone to come to her senses.' But only a stupid man would himself have done it. Stonor caught her two hands in his, and drew her into his arms.

'Look, here, Jeannie, you're dreadfully wrought up and excited — tired, too.'

'No!' She freed herself, and averted the tear-stained face. 'Not tired, though I've travelled far to-day. I know you smile at sudden conversions. You think they're hysterical — worse — vulgar. But people must get their revelation how they can. And, Geoffrey, if I can't make you see this one of mine, I shall know your love could never mean strength to me — only weakness. And I shall be afraid,' she whispered. Her dilated eyes might have seen a ghost lurking there in the commonplace room. 'So afraid I should never dare give you the chance of making me loathe myself.' There was a pause, and out of the silence fell words that were like the taking of a vow. 'I would never see you again.'

'How right I was to be afraid of that vein of fanaticism in you!'

'Certainly you couldn't make a greater mistake than to go away now and think it any good ever to come back. Even if I came to feel different, I couldn't *do* anything different. I should *know* all this couldn't be forgotten. I should know that it would poison my life in the end — yours too.'

'She has made good use of her time!' he said bitterly. Then, upon a sudden thought, 'What has changed *her?* Has she been seeing visions too?'

'What do you mean?'

'Why is she intriguing to get hold of a man that ten years ago she flatly refused to see or hold any communication with?'

'Intriguing to get hold of? She hasn't mentioned you!'

'What! Then how, in the name of Heaven, do you know — she wants — what you ask?'

'There can't be any doubt about that,' said the girl, firmly.

With all his tenderness for her, so little still did he understand what she was going through, that he plainly thought all her pain had come of knowing that this other page was in his life — he had no glimpse of the girl's passionate need to think of that same long-turned-over page as unmarred by the darker blot.

'You absurd, ridiculous child!' With immense relief he dropped into the nearest chair. 'Then all this is just your own unaided invention. Well, I could thank God!' He passed his handkerchief over his face.

'For what are you thanking God?'

He sat there obviously thinking out his plan of action.

'Suppose — I'm not going to risk it — but *suppose* ——' He looked up, and at the sight of Jean's face he rose with an expression strangely gentle. The rather hard eyes were softened in a sudden mist. 'Whether *I* deserve to suffer or not, it's quite certain *you* don't. Don't cry, dear one. It never was the real thing. I had to wait till I knew you before I understood.'

Her own eyes were brimming as she lifted them in a passion of gratitude to his face.

'Oh! is that true? Loving you has made things clear to me I didn't dream of before. If I could think that because of me you were able to do this ——'

'You go back to that?' He seized her by the shoulders, and said hoarsely, 'Look here! Do you seriously ask me to give up the girl I love — to go and offer to marry a woman that even to think of ——'

'You cared for her once!' she cried. 'You'll care about her again. She is beautiful and brilliant — *every*thing. I've heard she could win any man ——'

He pushed the girl from him. 'She's bewitched you!' He was halfway to the door.

'Geoffrey, Geoffrey, you aren't going away like that? This isn't *the end?*'

The face he turned back upon her was dark and hesitating. 'I suppose if she refused me, you'd ——'

'She won't refuse you.'

'She did once.'

'She didn't refuse to marry you.'

As she passed him on the way to her sitting-room he caught her by the arm.

'Stop!' he said, glancing about like one hunting desperately for a means of gaining a few minutes. 'Lady John is waiting all this time at my house for the car to go back with a message.'

'*That's* not a matter of life and death!' she said, with all the impatience of the young at that tyranny of little things which seems to hold its unrelenting sway, though the battlements of righteousness are rocking, and the tall towers of love are shaken to the nethermost foundation-stones.

'No, it's not a matter of life and death,' Stonor said quietly. 'All the same, I'll go down and give the order.'

'Very well.' Of her own accord this time she stopped on her way to that other door, behind which was the Past and the Future incarnate in one woman. 'I'll wait,' said Jean. She went to the table. Sitting there with her face turned from him, she said, quite low, 'You'll come back, if you're the man I pray you are.'

Her self-control seemed all at once to fail. She leaned her elbows on the table and broke into a flood of silent tears, with face hidden in her hands.

He came swiftly back, and bent over her a moved, adoring face.

'Dearest of all the world,' he began, in that beautiful voice of his.

His arms were closing round her, when the door on the left was softly opened. Vida Levering stood on the threshold.

CHAPTER XVIII

She drew back as soon as she saw him, but Stonor had looked round. His face darkened as he stood there an instant, silently challenging her. Not a word spoken by either of them, no sound but the faint, muffled sobbing of the girl, who sat with hidden face. With a look of speechless anger, the man went out and shut the doors behind him. Not seeing, only hearing that he had gone, Jean threw her arms out across the table in an abandonment of grief. The other woman laid on a chair the hat and cloak that she was carrying. Then she went slowly across the room and stood silent a moment at Jean's side.

'What is the matter?'

The girl started. Impossible for her to speak in that first moment. But when she had dried her eyes, she said, with a pathetic childish air —

'I — I've been seeing Geoffrey.'

'Is this the effect "seeing Geoffrey" has?' said the other, with an attempt at lightness.

'You see, I know now,' Jean explained, with the brave directness that was characteristic.

The more sophisticated woman presented an aspect totally unenlightened.

'I know how he' — Jean dropped her eyes — 'how he spoiled some one else's life.'

'Who tells you that?' asked Miss Levering.

'Several people have told me.'

'Well, you should be very careful how you believe what you hear.'

'You know it's true!' said the girl, passionately.

'I know that it's possible to be mistaken.'

'I see! You're trying to shield him ——'

'Why should I? What is it to me?'

'Oh—h, how you must love him!' she said with tears.

'I? Listen to me,' said Vida, gravely. As she drew up a chair the girl rose to her feet.

'What's the use — what's the use of your going on denying it?' As she saw Vida was about to break in, she silenced her with two words, '*Geoffrey doesn't.*' And with that she fled away to the window.

Vida half rose, and then relinquished the idea of following the girl, seemed presently to forget her, and sat as one alone with sorrow. When Jean had mastered herself, she came slowly back. Not till she was close to the motionless figure did the girl lift her eyes.

'Oh, don't look like that,' the girl prayed. 'I shall bring him back to you.'

She was on her knees by Vida's chair. The fixed abstraction went out of the older face, but it was very cold as she began —

'You would be impertinent — if — you weren't a romantic child. You can't bring him back.'

'Yes, yes, he ——'

'No. But' — Vida looked deep into the candid eyes — 'there is something you *can* do ——'

'What?'

'Bring him to a point where he recognizes that he is in our debt.'

'In *our* debt?'

Vida nodded. 'In debt to Women. He can't repay the one he robbed.'

Jean winced at that. The young do not know that nothing but money can ever be paid back.

'Yes,' she insisted, out of the faith she still had in him, ready to be his surety. 'Yes, he can. He will.'

The other shook her head. 'No, he can't repay the dead. But there are the living. There are the thousands with hope still in their hearts and youth in their blood. Let him help *them*. Let him be a Friend to Women.'

'I understand!' Jean rose up, wide-eyed. 'Yes, *that* too.'

The door had opened, and Lady John was coming in with Stonor towering beside her. When he saw the girl rising from her knees, he turned to Lady John with a little gesture of, 'What did I tell you?'

The moment Jean caught sight of him, 'Thank you!' she said,

while her aunt was briskly advancing, filling all the room with a pleasant silken rustling, and a something nameless, that was like clear noonday after storm-cloud or haunted twilight.

'Well,' she said in a cheerful commonplace tone to Jean; 'you rather gave us the slip! Vida, I believe Mr. Stonor wants to see you for a few minutes, but' — she glanced at her watch — 'I'd like a word with you first, as I must get back. Do you think the car' — she turned to Stonor — 'your man said something about recharging ——'

'Oh, did he? I'll see about it.' As he went out he brushed past the butler.

'Mr. Trent has called, miss, to take the lady to the meeting,' said that functionary.

'Bring Mr. Trent into my sitting-room,' said Jean hastily, and then to Miss Levering, 'I'll tell him you can't go to-night.'

Lady John stood watching the girl with critical eyes till she had disappeared into the adjoining room and shut the door behind her. Then —

'I know, my dear' — she spoke almost apologetically — 'you're not aware of what that impulsive child wants to insist on. I feel it an embarrassment even to tell you.'

'I know.'

'You know?' Lady John waited for condemnation of Jean's idea. She waited in vain. 'It isn't with your sanction, surely, that she makes this extraordinary demand?'

'I didn't sanction it at first,' said the other slowly; 'but I've been thinking it over.'

Lady John's suavity stiffened perceptibly. 'Then all I can say is, I am greatly disappointed in you. You threw this man over years ago, for reasons, whatever they were, that seemed to you good and sufficient. And now you come in between him and a younger woman, just to play Nemesis, so far as I can make out.'

'Is that what he says?'

'He says nothing that isn't fair and considerate.'

'I can see he's changed.'

'And you're unchanged — is that it?'

'I'm changed even more than he.'

Lady John sat down, with pity and annoyance struggling for the mastery.

'You care about him still?'

'No.'

'No? And yet you — I see! There are obviously certain things he can give his wife, and you naturally want to marry somebody.'

'Oh, Lady John,' said Vida, wearily, 'there are no men listening.'

'No' — she looked round surprised — 'I didn't suppose there were.'

'Then why keep up that old pretence?'

'What pret ——'

'That to marry *at all costs* is every woman's dearest ambition till the grave closes over her. You and I *know* it isn't true.'

'Well, but ——' Her ladyship blinked, suddenly seeing daylight. 'Oh! It was just the unexpected sight of him bringing it all back! *That* was what fired you this afternoon. Of course' — she made an honest attempt at sympathetic understanding — 'the memory of a thing like that can never die — can never even be dimmed for the woman.'

'I mean her to think so.'

'Jean?'

Vida nodded.

'But it isn't so?'

Lady John was a little bewildered.

'You don't seriously believe,' said Vida, 'that a woman, with anything else to think about, comes to the end of ten years still absorbed in a memory of that sort?'

Lady John stared speechless a moment. 'You've got over it, then?'

'If it weren't for the papers, I shouldn't remember twice a year there was ever such a person as Geoffrey Stonor in the world.'

'Oh, I'm *so* glad!' said Lady John, with unconscious rapture.

Vida smiled grimly. 'Yes, I'm glad, too.'

'And if Geoffrey Stonor offered you — er — "reparation," you'd refuse it?'

'Geoffrey Stonor! For me he's simply one of the far back links in a chain of evidence. It's certain I think a hundred times of other women's present unhappiness to once that I remember that old unhappiness of mine that's past. I think of the nail and chain makers of Cradley Heath, the sweated girls of the slums; I think,' her voice fell, 'of the army of ill-used women, whose very existence I mustn't mention ——'

Lady John interrupted her hurriedly. 'Then why in heaven's name do you let poor Jean imagine ——'

Vida suddenly bent forward. 'Look — I'll trust you, Lady John. I don't suffer from that old wrong as Jean thinks I do, but I shall coin her sympathy into gold for a greater cause than mine.'

'I don't understand you.'

'Jean isn't old enough to be able to care as much about a principle as about a person. But if my old half-forgotten pain can turn her generosity into the common treasury ——'

'What do you propose she shall do, poor child?'

'Use her hold over Geoffrey Stonor to make him help us.'

'To help you?'

'The man who served one woman — God knows how many more — very ill, shall serve hundreds of thousands well. Geoffrey Stonor shall make it harder for his son, harder still for his grandson, to treat any woman as he treated me.'

'How will he do that?' said the lady coldly.

'By putting an end to the helplessness of women.'

'You must think he has a great deal of power,' said her ladyship, with some irony.

'Power? Yes,' answered the other, 'men have too much over penniless and frightened women.'

'What nonsense! You talk as though the women hadn't their share of human nature. *We* aren't made of ice any more than the men.'

'No, but we have more self-control.'

'Than men?'

Vida had risen. She looked down at her friend. 'You know we have,' she said.

'I know,' said Lady John shrewdly, 'we mustn't admit it.'

'For fear they'd call us fishes?'

Lady John had been frankly shocked at the previous plain speaking, but she found herself stimulated to show in this moment of privacy that even she had not travelled her sheltered way through the world altogether in blinkers.

'They talk of our lack of self-control, but,' she admitted, 'it's the last thing men *want* women to have.'

'Oh, we know what they want us to have! So we make shift to have it. If we don't, we go without hope — sometimes we go without bread.'

'Vida! Do you mean to say that you ——'

'I mean to say that men's vanity won't let them see it, but the thing's largely a question of economics.'

'You *never* loved him, then!'

'Yes, I loved him — once. It was my helplessness that turned the best thing life can bring into a curse for both of us.'

'I don't understand you ——'

'Oh, being "understood"! that's too much to expect. I make myself no illusions. When people come to know that I've joined the Women's Union ——'

'But you won't.'

'—— who is there who will resist the temptation to say "Poor Vida Levering! What a pity she hasn't got a husband and a baby to keep her quiet"? The few who know about me, they'll be equally sure that, not the larger view of life I've gained, but my own poor little story, is responsible for my new departure.' She leaned forward and looked into Lady John's face. 'My best friend, she will be surest of all, that it's a private sense of loss, or lower yet, a grudge, that's responsible for my attitude. I tell you the only difference between me and thousands of women with husbands and babies is that I am free to say what I think. *They aren't!*'

Lady John opened her lips and then closed them firmly. After all, why pursue the matter? She had got the information she had come for.

'I must hurry back;' she rose, murmuring, 'my poor ill-used guests ——'

Vida stood there quiet, a little cold. 'I won't ring,' she said. 'I think you'll find Mr. Stonor downstairs waiting for you.'

'Oh — a — he will have left word about the car in any case.'

Lady John's embarrassment was not so much at seeing that her friend had divined the gist of the arrangement that had been effected downstairs. It was that Vida should be at no pains to throw a decent veil over the fact of her realization that Lady John had come there in the character of scout. With an openness not wholly free from scorn, the younger woman had laid her own cards on the table. She made no scruple at turning her back on Lady John's somewhat incoherent evasion. Ignoring it she crossed the room and opened the door for her.

Jean was in the corridor saying good-bye to the chairman of the afternoon.

'Well, Mr. Trent,' said Miss Levering in even tones, 'I didn't expect to see you this evening.'

He came forward and stood in the doorway. 'Why not? Have I ever failed?'

'Lady John,' said Vida, turning, 'this is one of our allies. He is good enough to squire me through the rabble from time to time.'

'Well,' said Lady John, advancing quite graciously, 'I think it's very handsome of you after what she said to-day about men.'

'I've no great opinion of most men myself,' said the young gentleman. 'I might add, or of most women.'

'Oh!' Lady John laughed. 'At any rate I shall go away relieved to think that Miss Levering's plain speaking hasn't alienated *all* masculine regard.'

'Why should it?' he said.

'That's right.' Lady John metaphorically patted him on the back. 'Don't believe all she says in the heat of propaganda.'

'I *do* believe all she says. But I'm not cast down.'

'Not when she says ——'

'Was there never,' he made bold to interrupt, 'a misogynist of *my* sex who ended by deciding to make an exception?'

'Oh!' Lady John smiled significantly; 'if *that's* what you build on!'

'Why,' he demanded with an effort to convey 'pure logic,' 'why shouldn't a man-hater on your side prove equally open to reason?'

'That aspect of the question has become irrelevant so far as I'm personally concerned,' said Vida, exasperated by Lady John's look of pleased significance. 'I've got to a place where I realize that the first battles of this new campaign must be fought by women alone. The only effective help men could give — amendment of the law — they refuse. The rest is nothing.'

'Don't be ungrateful, Vida. Here is this gentleman ready to face criticism in publicly championing you ——'

'Yes, but it's an illusion that I, as an individual, need a champion. I am quite safe in the crowd. Please don't wait for me and don't come for me again.'

The sensitive dark face flushed. 'Of course if you'd rather ——'

'And that reminds me,' she went on, unfairly punishing poor Mr. Trent for Lady John's meaning looks, 'I was asked to thank you, and to tell you, too, that they won't need your chairmanship any more — though that, I beg you to believe, has nothing to do with any feeling of mine.'

He was hurt and he showed it. 'Of course I know there must be other men ready — better known men ——'

'It isn't that. It's simply that we find a man can't keep a rowdy meeting in order as well as a woman.'

He stared.

'You aren't serious?' said Lady John.

'Haven't you noticed,' Miss Levering put it to Trent, 'that all our worst disturbances come when men are in charge?'

'Ha! ha! Well — a — I hadn't connected the two ideas.'

Still laughing a little ruefully, he suffered himself to be taken downstairs by kind little Miss Dunbarton, who had stood without a word waiting there with absent face.

'That nice boy's in love with you,' said Lady John, *sotto voce.*

Vida looked at her without answering.

'Good-bye.' They shook hands. 'I *wish* you hadn't been so unkind to that nice boy.'

'Do you?'

'Yes; for then I would be more sure of your telling Geoffrey Stonor that intelligent women don't nurse their wrongs indefinitely, and lie in wait to punish them.'

'You are *not* sure?'

Lady John went up close and looked into her face with searching anxiety. 'Are *you?*' she asked.

Vida stood there mute, with eyes on the ground. Lady John glanced nervously at her watch, and, with a gesture of perturbation, hurriedly left the room. The other went slowly back to her place by the table.

*   *   *   *   *   *   *

The look she bent on Stonor as he came in seemed to take no acccount of those hurried glimpses at the Tunbridges' months before, and twice to-day when other eyes were watching. It was as if now, for the first time since they parted, he stood forth clearly. This man with the changed face, coming in at the door and carefully shutting it — he had once been Mystery's high priest and had held the keys of Joy. To-day, beyond a faint pallor, there was no trace of emotion in that face that was the same and yet so different. Not even anger there. Where a less complex man would have brought in, if not the menace of a storm, at least an intimation of masterfulness that should advertise the uselessness of opposition, Stonor brought a subtler ally in what, for lack of better words, must be called an air of heightened fastidiousness — mainly physical. Man has no shrewder weapon against the woman he has loved and wishes to exorcise from his path. For the simple, and even for those not so much simple as merely sensitive, there is something in that cool, sure assumption of unapproachableness on the part of one who once had been so near — something that lames advance and hypnotizes vision. Geoffrey Stonor's aloofness was not in the 'high look' alone; it was as much as anything in the very way he walked, as if the ground were hardly good enough, in the way he laid his shapely hand on the carved back of the sofa, the way his eyes rested on inanimate things in the room, reducing whoever was responsible for them to the need of justifying their presence and defending their value.

As the woman in the chair, leaning cheek on hand, sat silently watching him, it may have been that obscure things in those headlong hours of the past grew plainer.

However ludicrous the result may look in the last analysis, it is clear that a faculty such as Stonor's for overrating the value of the individual in the scheme of things, does seem more effectually than any mere patent of nobility to confer upon a man the 'divine right' to dictate to his fellows and to look down upon them. The thing is founded on illusion, but it is founded as firm as many another figment that has governed men and seen the generations come to heel and go crouching to their graves.

But the shining superiority of the man seemed to be a little dimmed for the woman sitting there. The old face and the new face, she saw them both through a cloud of long-past memories and a mist of present tears.

'Well, have they primed you?' she said very low. 'Have you got your lesson — by heart at last?'

He looked at her from immeasurable distance. 'I am not sure that I understand you,' he said. He waited an instant, then, seeing no explanation vouchsafed, 'However unpropitious your mood may be,' he went on with a satirical edge in his tone, 'I shall discharge my errand.'

Still she waited.

Her silence seemed to irritate him. 'I have promised,' he said, with a formality that smacked of insolence, 'to offer you what I believe is called "amends."'

The quick change in the brooding look should have warned him.

'You have come to realize, then — after all these years — that you owed me something?'

He checked himself on the brink of protest. 'I am not here to deny it.'

'Pay, then,' she said fiercely — 'pay.'

A moment's dread flickered in his eye and then was gone. 'I have said that, if you exact it, I will.'

'Ah! If I insist, you'll "make it all good"! Then, don't you know, you must pay me in kind?'

He looked down upon her — a long, long way. 'What do you mean?'

'Give me back what you took from me — my old faith,' she said, with shaking voice. 'Give me that.'

'Oh, if you mean to make phrases ——' He half turned away, but the swift words overtook him.

'Or, give me back mere kindness — or even tolerance! Oh, I don't mean *your* tolerance.' She was on her feet to meet his eyes as he faced her again. 'Give me back the power to think fairly of my brothers — not as mockers — thieves.'

'I have not mocked you. And I have asked you ——'

'Something you knew I should refuse. Or' — her eyes blazed — 'or did you dare to be afraid I wouldn't?'

'Oh, I suppose' — he buttressed his good faith with bitterness —'I suppose if we set our teeth we could ——'

'I couldn't — not even if I set my teeth. And you wouldn't dream of asking me if you thought there was the smallest chance.'

Ever so faintly he raised his heavy shoulders. 'I can do no more than make you an offer of such reparation as is in my power. If you don't accept it ——' He turned away with an air of '*that's* done.'

But her emotion had swept her out of her course. She found herself at his side.

'Accept it? No! Go away and live in debt. Pay and pay and pay — and find yourself still in debt — for a thing you'll never be able to give me back. And when you come to die' — her voice fell — 'say to yourself, "I paid all my creditors but one."'

He stopped on his way to the door and faced her again. 'I'm rather tired, you know, of this talk of debt. If I hear that you persist in it, I shall have to ——' Again he checked himself.

'What?'

'No. I'll keep to my resolution.'

He had nearly reached the threshold. She saw what she had lost by her momentary lack of that boasted self-control. She forestalled him at the door.

'What resolution?' she asked.

He looked down at her an instant, clothed from head to foot in that indefinable armour of unapproachableness. This was a man who asked other people questions, himself ill-accustomed to be catechised. If he replied it was a grace.

'I came here,' he said, 'under considerable pressure, to speak of the future. Not to reopen the past.'

'The future and the past are one,' said the woman at the door. 'You talk as if that old madness was mine alone; it is the woman's way.'

'I know,' she agreed, to his obvious surprise, 'and it's not fair. Men suffer as well as we by the woman's starting wrong. We are taught to think the man a sort of demi-god. If he tells her, "Go down into hell," down into hell she goes.'

He would not have been human had he not resented that harsh summary of those days that lay behind.

'Make no mistake,' he said. 'Not the woman alone. *They go down together.*'

'Yes, they go down together. But the man comes up alone. As a rule. It is more convenient so — *for him*. And even for the other woman.'

Both pairs of eyes went to Jean's door.

'My conscience is clear,' he said angrily. 'I know — and so do you — that most men in my position wouldn't have troubled themselves. I gave myself endless trouble.'

She looked at him with wondering eyes. 'So you've gone about all these years feeling that you'd discharged every obligation?'

'Not only that. I stood by you with a fidelity that was nothing short of Quixotic. If, woman-like, you *must* recall the past, I insist on your recalling it correctly.'

'You think I don't recall it correctly?' she said very low.

'Not when you make — other people believe that I deserted you!' The gathering volume of his righteous wrath swept the cool precision out of his voice. 'It's a curious enough charge,' he said, 'when you stop to consider ——' Again he checked himself, and, with a gesture of impatience, was for sweeping the whole thing out of his way, including that figure at the door.

But she stood there. 'Well, when we do just for five minutes out of ten years — when we do stop to consider ——'

'We remember it was *you* who did the deserting. And since you had to rake the story up, you might have had the fairness to tell the facts.'

'You think "the facts" would have excused you?'

It was a new view. She left the door, and sat down in the nearest chair.

'No doubt you've forgotten the facts, since Lady John tells me you wouldn't remember my existence once a year, if the papers didn't ——'

'Ah!' she interrupted, with a sorry little smile, 'you minded that!'

'I mind your giving false impressions,' he said with spirit. As she was about to speak he advanced upon her. 'Do you deny' — he bent over her, and told off those three words by striking one clenched fist into the palm of the other hand — 'do you deny that you returned my letters unopened?'

'No,' she said.

'Do you deny that you refused to see me, and that when I persisted you vanished?'

'I don't deny any of those things.'

'Why' — he stood up straight again, and his shoulders grew

more square with justification — 'why I had no trace of you for years.'

'I suppose not.'

'Very well, then.' He walked away. 'What could I do?'

'Nothing. It was too late to do anything.'

'It wasn't too late! You knew, since you "read the papers," that my father died that same year. There was no longer any barrier between us.'

'Oh, yes, there was a barrier.'

'Of your own making, then.'

'I had my guilty share in it, but the barrier' — her voice trembled on the word — 'the barrier was your invention.'

'The only barrier I knew of was no "invention." If you had ever known my father ——'

'Oh, the echoes! the echoes!' She lay back in the chair. 'How often you used to say, if I "knew your father." But you said, too' — her voice sank — 'you called the greatest "barrier" by another name.'

'What name?'

So low that even he could hardly hear she answered, 'The child that was to come.'

'That was before my father died,' Stonor returned hastily, 'while I still hoped to get his consent.'

She nodded, and her eyes were set like wide doors for memory to enter in.

'How the thought of that all-powerful personage used to terrorize me! What chance had a little unborn child against "the last of the great feudal lords," as you called him?'

'You *know* the child would have stood between you and me.'

'I know the child did stand between you and me.'

He stared at her. With vague uneasiness he repeated, '*Did* stand ——'

She seemed not to hear. The tears were running down her rigid face.

'Happy mothers teach their children. Mine had to teach me ——'

'You talk as if ——'

'—— teach me that a woman may do that for love's sake that shall kill love.'

Neither spoke for some seconds. Fearing and putting from him fuller comprehension, he broke the silence, saying with an air of finality —

'You certainly made it plain you had no love left for me.'

'I had need of it all for the child.' Her voice had a curious crooning note in it.

He came closer. He bent down to put the low question, 'Do you mean, then, that after all — it lived?'

'No. I mean that it was sacrificed. But it showed me no barrier is so impassable as the one a little child can raise.'

It was as if lightning had flashed across the old picture. He drew back from the fierce illumination.

'Was *that* why you ——' he began, in a voice that was almost a whisper. 'Was that why?'

She nodded, speechless a moment for tears. 'Day and night there it was between my thought of you and me.'

He sat down, staring at her.

'When I was most unhappy,' she went on, in that low voice, 'I would wake thinking I heard it cry. It was my own crying I heard, but I seemed to have it in my arms. I suppose I was mad. I used to lie there in that lonely farmhouse pretending to hush it. It was so I hushed myself.'

'I never knew ——'

'I didn't blame you. You couldn't risk being with me.'

'You agreed that, for both our sakes ——'

'Yes, you had to be very circumspect. You were so well known. Your autocratic father, your brilliant political future ——'

'Be fair. Our future — as I saw it then.'

'Yes, everything hung on concealment. It must have looked quite simple to you. You didn't know the ghost of a child that had never seen the light, the frail thing you meant to sweep aside and forget' — she was on her feet — '*have* swept aside and forgotten! — you didn't know it was strong enough to push you out of my life.' With an added intensity, 'It can do more!' she said. She leaned over his bowed figure and whispered, 'It can push that girl out!' As again she stood erect, half to herself she added, 'It can do more still.'

'Are you threatening me?' he said dully.

'No, I am preparing you.'

'For what?'

'For the work that must be done. Either with your help or that girl's.'

The man's eyes lifted a moment.

'One of two things,' she said — 'either her life, and all she has, given to this new Service; or a ransom if I give her up to you.'

'I see. A price. Well ——?'

She looked searchingly at him for an instant, and then slowly shook her head.

'Even if I could trust you to pay the price,' she said, 'I'm not sure but what a young and ardent soul as faithful and as pure as hers — I'm not sure but I should make a poor bargain for my sex to give that up for anything you could do.'

He found his feet like a man roused out of an evil dream to some reality darker than the dream. 'In spite of your assumption, she may not be your tool,' he said.

'You are horribly afraid she is! But you are wrong. She's an instrument in stronger hands than mine. Soon my little personal influence over her will be merged in something infinitely greater. Oh, don't think it's merely I that have got hold of Jean Dunbarton.'

'Who else?'

'The New Spirit that's abroad.'

With an exclamation he turned away. And though his look branded the idea for a wild absurdity, sentinel-like he began to pace up and down a few yards from Jean's door.

'How else,' said the woman, 'should that inexperienced girl have felt the new loyalty and responded as she did?'

'"New," indeed!' he said under his breath, 'however little "loyal."'

'Loyal, above all. But no newer than electricity was when it first lit up the world. It had been there since the world began — waiting to do away with the dark. *So has the thing you're fighting.*'

'The thing I'm fighting' — and the violence with which he spoke was only in his face and air; he held his voice down to its lowest register — 'the thing I'm fighting is nothing more than one person's hold upon a highly sensitive imagination. I consented to this interview with the hope' — he made a gesture of impotence.

'It only remains for me to show her that your true motive is revenge.'

'Once say that to her, and you are lost.'

He stole an uneasy look at the woman out of a face that had grown haggard.

'If you were fighting for that girl only against me, you'd win,' she said. 'It isn't so — and you will fail. The influence that has hold of her is in the very air. No soul knows where it comes from, except that it comes from the higher sources of civilization.'

'I see the origin of it before my eyes!'

'As little as you see the beginnings of life. This is like the other mysterious forces of Mother Earth. No warning given — no sign. A night wind passes over the brown land, and in the morning the fields are green.'

His look was the look of one who sees happiness slipping away. 'Or it passes over gardens like a frost,' he said, 'and the flowers die.'

'I know that is what men fear. It even seems as if it must be through fear that your enlightenment will come. The strangest things make you men afraid! That's why I see a value in Jean Dunbarton far beyond her fortune.'

He looked at her dully.

'More than any other girl I know — if I keep her from you, that gentle, inflexible creature could rouse in men the old half-superstitious fear ——'

'Fear! Are you mad?'

'Mad!' she echoed. 'Unsexed' — those are the words to-day. In the Middle Ages men cried out 'Witch!' and burnt her — the woman who served no man's bed or board.

'You want to make the poor child believe ——'

'She sees for herself we've come to a place where we find there's a value in women apart from the value men see in them. You teach us not to look to you for some of the things we need most. If women must be freed by women, we have need of such as ——' Her eyes went to the door that Stonor still had an air of guarding. 'Who knows — she may be the new Joan of Arc.'

He paused, and for that moment he semed as bankrupt in denunciation as he was in hope. This personal application of the new heresy found him merely aghast, with no words but 'That *she* should be the sacrifice!'

'You have taught us to look very calmly on the sacrifice of women,' was the ruthless answer. 'Men tell us in every tongue, it's "a necessary evil."'

He stood still a moment, staring at the ground.

'One girl's happiness — against a thing nobler than happiness for thousands — who can hesitate? *Not Jean.*'

'Good God! can't you see that this crazed campaign you'd start her on — even if it's successful, it can only be so through the help of men? What excuse shall you make your own soul for not going straight to the goal?'

'You think we wouldn't be glad,' she said, 'to go straight to the goal?'

'I do. I see you'd much rather punish me and see her revel in a morbid self-sacrifice.'

'You say I want to punish you only because, like other men, you won't take the trouble to understand what we do want — or how determined we are to have it. You can't kill this New Spirit among women.' She went nearer. 'And you couldn't make a greater mistake than to think it finds a home only in the exceptional or the unhappy. It is so strange to see a man like you as much deluded as the Hyde Park loafers, who say to Ernestine Blunt, "Who's hurt *your* feelings?" Why not realize' — she came still closer, if she had put out her hand she would have touched him — 'this is a thing that goes deeper than personal experience? And yet,' she said in a voice so hushed that it was full of a sense of the girl on the other side of the door, 'if you take only the narrowest personal view, a good deal depends on what you and I agree upon in the next five minutes.'

'You recommend my realizing the larger issues. But in your ambition to attach that poor girl to the chariot-wheels of Progress' — his voice put the drag of ironic pomposity upon the phrase — 'you quite ignore the fact that people fitter for such work, the men you look to enlist in the end, are ready waiting' — he pulled himself up in time for an anti-climax — 'to give the thing a chance.'

'Men are ready! What men?'

His eyes evaded hers. He picked his words. 'Women have themselves to blame that the question has grown so delicate that responsible people shrink for the moment from being implicated in it.'

'We have seen the shrinking.'

'Without quoting any one else, I might point out that the New Antagonism seems to have blinded you to the small fact that I for one am not an opponent.'

'The phrase has a familiar ring. We have heard it four hundred and twenty times.'

His eyes were shining with anger. 'I spoke, if I may say so, of some one who would count. Some one who can carry his party along with him — or risk a seat in the cabinet over the issue.'

'Did you mean you are "ready" to do that?' she exclaimed.

'An hour ago I was.'

'Ah! an hour ago!'

'Exactly! You don't understand men. They can be led; they can't be driven. Ten minutes before you came into the room I was ready to say I would throw in my political lot with this Reform.'

'And now?'

'Now you block my way by an attempt at coercion. By forcing my hand you give my adherence an air of bargain-driving for a personal end. Exactly the mistake of the ignorant agitators in Trafalgar Square. You have a great deal to learn. This movement will go forward, not because of the agitation outside, but in spite of it. There are men in Parliament who would have been actively serving the Reform to-day — as actively as so vast a constitutional change ——'

She smiled faintly. 'And they haven't done it because ——'

'Because it would have put a premium on breaches of decent behaviour and defiance of the law!'

She looked at him with an attempt to appear to accept this version. What did it matter what reasons were given for past failure, if only the future might be assured? He had taken a piece of crumpled paper from his pocket and smoothed it out.

'Look here!' He held the telegram before her.

She flushed with excitement as she read. 'This is very good. I see only one objection.'

'Objection!'

'You haven't sent it.'

'That is your fault.' And he looked as if he thought he spoke the truth.

'When did you write this?'

'Just before you came in — when she began to talk about ——'

'Ah, Jean!' Vida gave him back the paper. 'That must have pleased Jean.'

It was a master stroke, the casual giving back, and the invocation of a pleasure that had been strangled at the birth along with something greater. Did he see before him again the girl's tear-filled, hopeless eyes, that had not so much as read the wonderful message, too intent upon the death-warrant of their common happiness? He threw himself heavily into a chair, staring at the closed door. Behind it, in a prison of which this woman held the key, Jean waited for her life sentence. Stonor's look, his attitude, seemed to say that he too only waited now to hear it. He dropped his head in his hand.

When Vida spoke, it was without raising her eyes from the ground.

'I could drive a hard-and-fast bargain with you; but I think I won't. If love and ambition both urge you on, perhaps ——' She looked up a little defiantly, seeming to expect to meet triumph in his face. Instead, her eye took in the profound hopelessness of the bent head, the slackness of the big frame, that so suddenly had assumed a look of age. She went over to him silently, and stood by his side. 'After all,' she said, 'life hasn't been quite fair to you.' At the new thing in her voice he raised his heavy eyes. 'You fall out of one ardent woman's dreams into another's,' she said.

'Then you don't — after all, you don't mean to ——'

'To keep you and her apart? No.'

For the first time tears came into his eyes.

After a little silence he held out his hand. 'What can I do for you?'

She seemed not to see the hand he offered. Or did she only see that it was empty? She was looking at the other. Mere instinct made him close his left hand more firmly on the message.

It was as if something finer than her slim fingers, the woman's invisible antennæ, felt the force that would need be overcome if trial of strength should be precipitated then. Upon his 'What can I do?' she shook her head.

'For the real you,' he said. 'Not the Reformer, or the would-be politician — for the woman I so unwillingly hurt.' As she only turned away, he stood up, detaining her with a hold upon her arm. 'You may not believe it, but now that I understand, there is almost nothing I wouldn't do to right that old wrong.'

'There's nothing to be done,' she said; and then, shrinking under that look of almost cheerful benevolence, 'You can never give me back my child.'

More than at the words, at the anguish in her face, his own had changed.

'Will that ghost give you no rest?' he said.

'Yes, oh, yes.' She was calm again. 'I see life is nobler than I knew. There is work to do.'

On her way to the great folding doors, once again he stopped her.

'Why should you think that it's only you these ten years have taught something to? Why not give even a man credit for a willingness to learn something of life, and for being sorry — profoundly sorry — for the pain his instruction has cost others? You seem to think I've taken it all quite lightly. That's not fair. All my life, ever since you disappeared, the thought of you has hurt. I would give anything I possess to know you — were happy again.'

'Oh, happiness!'

'Why shouldn't you find it still?'

He said it with a significance that made her stare, and then —

'I see! she couldn't help telling you about Allen Trent — Lady John couldn't!'

He ignored the interpretation.

'You're one of the people the years have not taken from, but given more to. You are more than ever —— You haven't lost your beauty.'

'The gods saw it was so little effectual, it wasn't worth taking away.'

She stood staring out into the void. 'One woman's mishap — what is that? A thing as trivial to the great world as it's sordid in most eyes. But the time has come when a woman may look about her and say, What general significance has my secret pain? Does it "join on" to anything? And I find it *does*. I'm no longer simply a woman who has stumbled on the way.' With difficulty she controlled the shake in her voice. 'I'm one who has got up bruised and bleeding, wiped the dust from her hands and the tears from her face — and said to herself not merely: Here's one luckless woman! but — here is a stone of stumbling to many. Let's see if it can't be moved out of other women's way. And she calls people to come and help. No mortal man, let alone a woman, *by herself*, can move that rock of offence. But,' she ended with a sudden sombre flare of enthusiasm, 'if *many* help, Geoffrey, the thing can be done.'

He looked down on her from his height with a wondering pity.

'Lord! how you care!' he said, while the mist deepened before his eyes.

'Don't be so sad,' she said — not seeming to see his sadness was not for himself. It was as if she could not turn her back on him this last time without leaving him comforted. 'Shall I tell you a secret? Jean's ardent dreams needn't frighten you, if she has a child. *That* — from the beginning it was not the strong arm — it was the weakest, the little, little arms that subdued the fiercest of us.'

He held out a shaking hand, so uncertain, that it might have been begging pity, or it might have been bestowing it. Even then she did not take it, but a great gentleness was in her face as she said —

'You will have other children, Geoffrey; for me there was to be only one. Well, well,' she brushed the tears away, 'since men have tried, and failed to make a decent world for the little children to live in, it's as well some of us are childless. Yes,' she said quietly, taking up the hat and cloak, '*we* are the ones who have no excuse for standing aloof from the fight!'

Her hand was on the door.

'Vida!'

'What?'

'You forgot something.'

She looked back.

He was signing the message. '*This;*' he said.

She went out with the paper in her hand.

THE MACMILLAN STANDARD LIBRARY

This series has taken its place as one of the most important popular-priced editions. The "Library" includes only those books which have been put to the test of public opinion and have not been found wanting, — books, in other words, which have come to be regarded as standards in the fields of knowledge — literature, religion, biography, history, politics, art, economics, sports, sociology, and belles lettres. Together they make the most complete and authoritative works on the several subjects.

Each volume, cloth, 12mo, 50 cents net; postage, 10 cents extra

Addams — The Spirit of Youth and the City Streets

By Jane Addams

"Shows such sanity, such breadth and tolerance of mind, and such penetration into the inner meanings of outward phenomena as to make it a book which no one can afford to miss." — *New York Times.*

Bailey — The Country Life Movement in the United States

By L. H. Bailey

". . . clearly thought out, admirably written, and always stimulating in its generalization and in the perspectives it opens." — *Philadelphia Press.*

Bailey and Hunn — The Practical Garden Book

By L. H. Bailey and C. E. Hunn

"Presents only those facts that have been proved by experience, and which are most capable of application on the farm." — *Los Angeles Express.*

Campbell — The New Theology

By R. J. Campbell

"A fine contribution to the better thought of our times written in the spirit of the Master." — *St. Paul Dispatch.*

Clark — The Care of a House

By T. M. Clark

"If the average man knew one-ninth of what Mr. Clark tells him in this book, he would be able to save money every year on repairs, etc." — *Chicago Tribune.*

Conyngton — How to Help: A Manual of Practical Charity

By Mary Conyngton

"An exceedingly comprehensive work with chapters on the homeless man and woman, care of needy families, and the discussions of the problems of child labor."

Coolidge — The United States as a World Power

By Archibald Cary Coolidge

"A work of real distinction . . . which moves the reader to thought." — *The Nation.*

Croly — The Promise of American Life

By Herbert Croly

"The most profound and illuminating study of our national conditions which has appeared in many years." — Theodore Roosevelt.

Devine — Misery and Its Causes

By Edward T. Devine

"One rarely comes across a book so rich in every page, yet so sound, so logical, and thorough." — *Chicago Tribune.*

Earle — Home Life in Colonial Days

By Alice Morse Earle

"A book which throws new light on our early history."

Ely — Evolution of Industrial Society

By Richard T. Ely

"The benefit of competition and the improvement of the race, municipal ownership, and concentration of wealth are treated in a sane, helpful, and interesting manner." — *Philadelphia Telegraph.*

Ely — Monopolies and Trusts

By Richard T. Ely

"The evils of monopoly are plainly stated, and remedies are proposed. This book should be a help to every man in active business life." — *Baltimore Sun.*

French — How to Grow Vegetables

By Allen French

"Particularly valuable to a beginner in vegetable gardening, giving not only a convenient and reliable planting-table, but giving particular attention to the culture of the vegetables." — *Suburban Life.*

Goodyear — Renaissance and Modern Art

W. H. Goodyear

"A thorough and scholarly interpretation of artistic development."

Hapgood — Abraham Lincoln: The Man of the People

By Norman Hapgood

"A life of Lincoln that has never been surpassed in vividness, compactness, and homelike reality." — *Chicago Tribune.*

Haultain — The Mystery of Golf

By Arnold Haultain

"It is more than a golf book. These is interwoven with it a play of mild philosophy and of pointed wit." — *Boston Globe.*

Hearn — Japan: An Attempt at Interpretation

By Lafcadio Hearn

"A thousand books have been written about Japan, but this one is one of the rarely precious volumes which opens the door to an intimate acquaintance with the wonderful people who command the attention of the world to-day." — *Boston Herald.*

Hillis — The Quest of Happiness

By Rev. Newell Dwight Hillis

"Its whole tone and spirit is of a sane, healthy optimism." — *Philadelphia Telegraph.*

Hillquit — Socialism in Theory and Practice

By Morris Hillquit

"An interesting historical sketch of the movement." — *Newark Evening News.*

Hodges — Everyman's Religion

By George Hodges

"Religion to-day is preëminently ethical and social, and such is the religion so ably and attractively set forth in these pages." — *Boston Herald.*

Horne — David Livingstone

By Silvester C. Horne

The centenary edition of this popular work. A clear, simple, narrative biography of the great missionary, explorer, and scientist.

Hunter — Poverty

By Robert Hunter

"Mr. Hunter's book is at once sympathetic and scientific. He brings to the task a store of practical experience in settlement work gathered in many parts of the country." — *Boston Transcript.*

Hunter — Socialists at Work

By Robert Hunter

"A vivid, running characterization of the foremost personalities in the Socialist movement throughout the world." — *Review of Reviews.*

Jefferson — The Building of the Church

By Charles E. Jefferson

"A book that should be read by every minister."

King — The Ethics of Jesus

By Henry Churchill King

"I know no other study of the ethical teaching of Jesus so scholarly, so careful, clear and compact as this." — G. H. Palmer, Harvard University.

King — Rational Living

By Henry Churchill King

"An able conspectus of modern psychological investigation, viewed from the Christian standpoint." — *Philadelphia Public Ledger.*

London — The War of the Classes

By Jack London

"Mr. London's book is thoroughly interesting, and his point of view is very different from that of the closest theorist." — *Springfield Republican.*

London — Revolution and Other Essays

By Jack London

"Vigorous, socialistic essays, animating and insistent."

Lyon — How to Keep Bees for Profit

By Everett D. Lyon

"A book which gives an insight into the life history of the bee family, as well as telling the novice how to start an apiary and care for it." — *Country Life in America.*

McLennan — A Manual of Practical Farming

By John McLennan

"The author has placed before the reader in the simplest terms a means of assistance in the ordinary problems of farming." — *National Nurseryman.*

Mabie — William Shakespeare: Poet, Dramatist, and Man

By Hamilton W. Mabie

"It is rather an interpretation than a record." — *Chicago Standard.*

Mahaffy — Rambles and Studies in Greece

By J. P. Mahaffy

"To the intelligent traveler and lover of Greece this volume will prove a most sympathetic guide and companion."

Mathews — The Church and the Changing Order

By Shailer Mathews

"The book throughout is characterized by good sense and restraint. . . . A notable book and one that every Christian may read with profit." — *The Living Church.*

Mathews — The Gospel and the Modern Man

By Shailer Mathews

"A succinct statement of the essentials of the New Testament." — *Service.*

Patten — The Social Basis of Religion

By Simon N. Patten

"A work of substantial value" — *Continent.*

Peabody — The Approach to the Social Question

By Francis Greenwood Peabody

"This book is at once the most delightful, persuasive, and sagacious contribution to the subject." — *Louisville Courier-Journal.*

Pierce — The Tariff and the Trusts

By Franklin Pierce

"An excellent campaign document for a non-protectionist." — *Independent.*

Rauschenbusch — Christianity and the Social Crisis

By Walter Rauschenbusch

"It is a book to like, to learn from, and to be charmed with." — *New York Times.*

Riis — The Making of an American

By Jacob Riis

"Its romance and vivid incident make it as varied and delightful as any romance." — *Publisher's Weekly.*

Riis — Theodore Roosevelt, the Citizen

By Jacob Riis

"A refreshing and stimulating picture." — *New York Tribune.*

Ryan — A Living Wage; Its Ethical and Economic Aspects

By Rev. J. A. Ryan

"The most judicious and balanced discussion at the disposal of the general reader." — *World To-day.*

St. Maur — A Self-supporting Home

By Kate V. St. Maur

"Each chapter is the detailed account of all the work necessary for one month — in the vegetable garden, among the small fruits, with the fowls, guineas, rabbits, and in every branch of husbandry to be met with on the small farm." — *Louisville Courier-Journal.*

Sherman — What is Shakespeare?

By L. A. Sherman

"Emphatically a work without which the library of the Shakespeare student will be incomplete." — *Daily Telegram.*

Sidgwick — Home Life in Germany

By A. Sidgwick

"A vivid picture of social life and customs in Germany to-day."

Smith — The Spirit of American Government

By J. Allen Smith

"Not since Bryce's 'American Commonwealth' has a book been produced which deals so searchingly with American political institutions and their history." — *New York Evening Telegram.*

Spargo — Socialism

By John Spargo

"One of the ablest expositions of Socialism that has ever been written." — *New York Evening Call.*

Tarbell — History of Greek Art

By T. B. Tarbell

"A sympathetic and understanding conception of the golden age of art."

Valentine — How to Keep Hens for Profit

By C. S. Valentine

"Beginners and seasoned poultrymen will find in it much of value." — *Chicago Tribune.*

Van Dyke — The Gospel for a World of Sin

By Henry Van Dyke

"One of the basic books of true Christian thought of to-day and of all times." — *Boston Courier.*

Van Dyke — The Spirit of America

By Henry Van Dyke

"Undoubtedly the most notable interpretation in years of the real America. It compares favorably with Bryce's 'American Commonwealth.'" — *Philadelphia Press.*

Veblen — The Theory of the Leisure Class

By Thorstein B. Veblen

"The most valuable recent contribution to the elucidation of this subject." — *London Times.*

Wells — New Worlds for Old

By H. G. Wells

"As a presentation of Socialistic thought as it is working to-day, this is the most judicious and balanced discussion at the disposal of the general reader." — *World To-day.*

White — The Old Order Changeth

By William Allen White

"The present status of society in America. An excellent antidote to the pessimism of modern writers on our social system." — *Baltimore Sun.*

THE MACMILLAN FICTION LIBRARY

A new and important series of some of the best popular novels which have been published in recent years.

These successful books are now made available at a popular price in response to the insistent demand for cheaper editions.

Each volume, cloth, 12mo, 50 cents net; postage, 10 cents extra

Allen — A Kentucky Cardinal

By James Lane Allen

"A narrative, told with naïve simplicity, of how a man who was devoted to his fruits and flowers and birds came to fall in love with a fair neighbor." —*New York Tribune.*

Allen — The Reign of Law *A Tale of the Kentucky Hempfields*

By James Lane Allen

"Mr. Allen has style as original and almost as perfectly finished as Hawthorne's. . . . And rich in the qualities that are lacking in so many novels of the period." —*San Francisco Chronicle.*

Atherton — Patience Sparhawk

By Gertrude Atherton

"One of the most interesting works of the foremost American novelist."

Child — Jim Hands

By Richard Washburn Child

"A big, simple, leisurely moving chronicle of life. Commands the profoundest respect and admiration. Jim is a real man, sound and fine." —*Daily News.*

Crawford — The Heart of Rome

By Marion Crawford

"A story of underground mysterie."

Crawford — Fair Margaret: A Portrait

By Marion Crawford

"A story of modern life in Italy, visualizing the country and its people, and warm with the red blood of romance and melodrama." — *Boston Transcript.*

Davis — A Friend of Cæsar

By William Stearns Davis

"There are many incidents so vivid, so brilliant, that they fix themselves in the memory." — Nancy Huston Banks in *The Bookman.*

Drummond — The Justice of the King

By Hamilton Drummond

"Read the story for the sake of the living, breathing people, the adventures, but most for the sake of the boy who served love and the King." — *Chicago Record-Herald.*

Elizabeth and Her German Garden

"It is full of nature in many phases — of breeze and sunshine, of the glory of the land, and the sheer joy of living." — *New York Times.*

Gale — Loves of Pelleas and Etarre

By Zona Gale

" . . . full of fresh feeling and grace of style, a draught from the fountain of youth." — *Outlook.*

Herrick — The Common Lot

By Robert Herrick

"A story of present-day life, intensely real in its picture of a young architect whose ideals in the beginning were, at their highest, æsthetic rather than spiritual. It is an unusual novel of great interest."

London — Adventure

By Jack London

"No reader of Jack London's stories need be told that this abounds with romantic and dramatic incident." — *Los Angeles Tribune.*

London — Burning Daylight

By Jack London

"Jack London has outdone himself in 'Burning Daylight.'" — *The Springfield Union.*

Loti — Disenchanted

By Pierre Loti

"It gives a more graphic picture of the life of the rich Turkish women of to-day than anything that has ever been written." — *Brooklyn Daily Eagle.*

Lucas — Mr. Ingleside

By E. V. Lucas

"He displays himself as an intellectual and amusing observer of life's foibles with a hero characterized by inimitable kindness and humor." — *The Independent.*

Mason — The Four Feathers

By A. E. W. Mason

"'The Four Feathers' is a first-rate story, with more legitimate thrills than any novel we have read in a long time." — *New York Press.*

Norris — Mother

By Kathleen Norris

"Worth its weight in gold." — *Catholic Columbian.*

Oxenham — The Long Road

By John Oxenham

"'The Long Road' is a tragic, heart-gripping story of Russian political and social conditions." — *The Craftsman.*

Pryor — The Colonel's Story

By Mrs. Roger A. Pryor

"The story is one in which the spirit of the Old South figures largely; adventure and romance have their play and carry the plot to a satisfying end."

Remington — Ermine of the Yellowstone

By John Remington

"A very original and remarkable novel wonderful in its vigor and freshness."

Roberts — Kings in Exile

By Charles G. D. Roberts

"The author catches the spirit of forest and sea life, and the reader comes to have a personal love and knowledge of our animal friends." — *Boston Globe.*

Robins — The Convert

By Elizabeth Robins

"'The Convert' devotes itself to the exploitation of the recent suffragist movement in England. It is a book not easily forgotten, by any thoughtful reader." — *Chicago Evening Post.*

Robins — A Dark Lantern

By Elizabeth Robins

A powerful and striking novel, English in scene, which takes an essentially modern view of society and of certain dramatic situations.

Ward — David Grieve

By Mrs. Humphrey Ward

"A perfect picture of life, remarkable for its humor and extraordinary success at character analysis."

Wells — The Wheels of Chance

By H. G. Wells

"Mr. Wells is beyond question the most plausible romancer of the time." — *The New York Tribune.*

THE MACMILLAN JUVENILE LIBRARY

This collection of juvenile books contains works of standard quality, on a variety of subjects — history, biography, fiction, science, and poetry — carefully chosen to meet the needs and interests of both boys and girls.

Each volume, cloth, 12mo, 50 cents net; postage, 10 cents extra

Altsheler — The Horsemen of the Plains

By Joseph A. Altsheler

"A story of the West, of Indians, of scouts, trappers, fur traders, and, in short, of everything that is dear to the imagination of a healthy American boy." — *New York Sun.*

Bacon — While Caroline Was Growing

By Josephine Daskam Bacon

"Only a genuine lover of children, and a keenly sympathetic observer of human nature, could have given us a book as this." — *Boston Herald.*

Carroll — Alice's Adventures, and Through the Looking Glass

By Lewis Carroll

"One of the immortal books for children."

Dix — A Little Captive Lad

By Marie Beulah Dix

"The human interest is strong, and children are sure to like it." — *Washington Times.*

Greene — Pickett's Gap

By Homer Greene

"The story presents a picture of truth and honor that cannot fail to have a vivid impression upon the reader." — *Toledo Blade.*

Lucas — Slowcoach

By E. V. Lucas

"The record of an English family's coaching tour in a great old-fashioned wagon. A charming narrative, as quaint and original as its name." — *Booknews Monthly.*

Mabie — Book of Christmas

By H. W. Mabie

"A beautiful collection of Christmas verse and prose in which all the old favorites will be found in an artistic setting." — *The St. Louis Mirror.*

Major — The Bears of Blue River

By Charles Major

"An exciting story with all the thrills the title implies."

Major — Uncle Tom Andy Bill

By Charles Major

"A stirring story full of bears, Indians, and hidden treasures." — *Cleveland Leader.*

Nesbit — The Railway Children

By E. Nesbit

"A delightful story revealing the author's intimate knowledge of juvenile ways." — *The Nation.*

Whyte — The Story Book Girls

By Christina G. Whyte

"A book that all girls will read with delight — a sweet, wholesome story of girl life."

Wright — Dream Fox Story Book

By Mabel Osgood Wright

"The whole book is delicious with its wise and kindly humor, its just perspective of the true value of things."

Wright — Aunt Jimmy's Will

By Mabel Osgood Wright

"Barbara has written no more delightful book than this."

Lightning Source UK Ltd.
Milton Keynes UK
UKOW051807280912

199828UK00011B/123/P

9 781290 331463